Turn of the Dice

Turn of the Dice

Janet Edmonds

St. Martin's Press
New York

Library of Congress Cataloging-in-Publication Data

Edmonds, Janet.
    Turn of the dice / Janet Edmonds.
        p.   cm.
    ISBN 0-312-03970-0
    I. Title.
    PR6055.D62T8   1990
    823'.914—dc20   89-48528
                                          CIP

First published in Great Britain by Judy Piatkus Ltd.

First U.S. Edition

10 9 8 7 6 5 4 3 2 1

Historical Note

Williamsburg really existed – and exists today, restored to its colonial appearance, thanks to the generosity of John D. Rockefeller. With the exception of the Cuddesdon, Haworth and Vatsetter houses, all the buildings mentioned were there. The Haworth and Vatsetter houses are on the sites of actual Williamsburg buildings but are otherwise entirely fictional. The Cuddesdon house, also on the site of a real mansion, is based very precisely on one of the great glories of American Georgian architecture, Carter's Grove, which actually stands some five miles southeast of Williamsburg. If you visit Carter's Grove today you will find that the dependencies are now joined to the main block, providing a beautifully proportioned house some 250 feet long. The garden, however, is entirely my own creation, as is Kingswood.

The town was much more bustling than the size of its permanent population would suggest. It was the colony's social and administrative centre and the taverns were usually overflowing with representatives to the legislature and the courts, as well as with merchants and businessmen of all sorts, from all over the colony.

Mid-eighteenth-century Williamsburg was very much an English society. Only in its slaves, its climate and therefore its plants and architecture, did it differ from Bath or Harrogate, though it thought of itself as more akin to London. The people, the laws, the currency were all English and the citizens thought of themselves as Englishmen and women, not as Americans. Already, however, certain social mores that are essentially American were becoming evident, in particular the use of money as a criterion of merit.

Turn of the Dice is set in the second half of the eighteenth century and only four of the characters really existed: Mrs Hunter, the milliner, Mrs Wythe, Mrs Bracken-Carter and the 'madcap widow', Lucy Ludwell-Paradise. (Double-barrelled names of some clumsiness seem to have been a feature of American life at the time!) Houses appear always to have been named after their owners and were still usually referred to as, say, 'the Cuddesdon house' rather than the later 'Cuddesdon House.'

Unbelievable as it may seem to us, it was possible in the eighteenth century for a debtor to become a bond-slave or to put his child in that unenviable situation. This was not an expedient normally resorted to by the aristocracy and I know of no case such as our heroine's, but it was an entirely possible situation, given the law of the time. Nevertheless, it was relatively rare, unlike indentured servitude which was often the only way in which a pauper could get to the New World and was perhaps the commonest means by which eighteenth-century English emigrants made their way across the Atlantic.

Janet Edmonds

Prelude

Abigail knelt on the floor in the dark patch of shadow at the top of the stairs and peered between the ornately carved banisters into the candle-lit hall below. The last of the guests had gone, their brightly-coloured brocades and velvets covered against the night air by darker, heavier cloaks. She shouldn't be here, of course, and if Maidstone caught her, she would be unceremoniously despatched back to the nursery by means of that useful, if painful, handle – her ear.

She loved the parties her parents gave. Merefield seemed to come alive when the house was full of guests and candles shone forth from every sconce as if the price of beeswax was immaterial. On evenings such as this, when any good six year old, once put to bed, would stay there, even her parents looked different. Lady Broughton, her fair hair powdered to white, always wore blue because it brought out the colour of her eyes, further enhanced by the sapphire and diamond necklace that had been her father's wedding-present to her. Abigail always pictured her mother as she appeared on these occasions, because she looked so young and pretty and not at all cross or careworn.

Sir Thomas was only a few years older than his wife but his stocky figure with its tendency to stoutness and his ruddy complexion made the difference in their ages seem greater than it was. His bluff and superficially genial manner disguised a fundamental weakness of character coupled with the obstinacy so often exhibited by those of limited intellect. Abigail was too young to analyse the difference in her feelings towards each parent. Everyone loved their parents – that was a duty expected of every child. She was only aware that the love she felt for her mother was a very different commodity from that she owed her father.

A manservant closed the door behind the last departing guest and discreetly melted away in the direction of the kitchens. The door of the large saloon was still open and the sound of voices, initially only

1

murmurs, floated up to Abigail. One did not listen to conversations to which one was not party, she had been taught that quite unequivocally. It did not alter the fact that such conversations were invariably far more interesting than those in which one was included and, just so long as she was unobserved, she had no compunction about staying where she was and straining her ears.

' – for very much longer,' were the first words she heard clearly. The voice was her mother's.

'Indeed, madam?' Abigail could imagine her father drawing himself up to his full height, his chest self-importantly to the fore. 'It should not be necessary to remind you that you will "put up", as you so vulgarly phrase it, with precisely what I demand of you. Had I married a substantial heiress, I might have conceded you some control over the purse-strings. As it is, the financial affairs of this family are best left in my hands.'

Lady Broughton snorted in a most unladylike manner. 'There are precious few purse-strings left to control,' she snapped, 'and I should infinitely prefer you to have a greater regard for the truth. I brought a very respectable dowry with me – or so you thought at the time – and, in addition, my father set money aside to provide for any children we might have. You will not, for example, be obliged to find a dowry for little Abigail when the time comes, and will even be relieved of the responsibility of giving her an allowance when she is of an age to need one. You have worked your way through my dowry and your own income. Merefield is mortgaged, yet *still* you gamble and, not content with that, spend money we can ill afford on evenings like this one, which only result in even greater losses. You would have been better advised to put the costs incurred by this evening into the improvement of the estate. God knows, it needs it.'

To Abigail, crouched at the top of the stairs clutching the banisters, the words conveyed little but the tone conveyed as much as a six year old could comprehend, and when her mother's comment was followed by the sound of a heavy slap – a sound with which she was all too familiar – the shock and vicarious pain brought tears to her eyes. She drew back from the edge of the stairs as if she herself had been slapped and when a second, heavier, blow followed the first, and was itself followed by a cry from Lady Broughton, the child fled to her room.

The tallow candle was long dead and no one was foolish enough to have left a tinder-box within a child's reach. Only Sir Thomas still enjoyed the luxury of a fire in his bedroom, so there was neither light nor warmth in the former nursery. Abigail scrambled into bed and pulled the bedclothes over her head. A nursemaid had once told her this was the quickest way of getting warm and she was shivering from head to foot. Angry voices at Merefield were not unusual, especially when children were thought not to be about, and usually they had something to do with money. That seemed to be a very important topic. Indoor servants came and went according to its abundance. Only Cook, who was essential, and Maidstone, her mother's old nurse and now her maid, remained constant; the one because she was indispensable, the other because she had no intention of leaving. Gardeners came and went, too, but Sir Thomas' horses were too important for economies to be made in that quarter. This was not quite as selfish as it appeared. Sir Thomas had few talents but one of them was undoubtedly the ability to buy top quality youngsters and bring them to such a level of perfection on the hunting-field that he was besieged with discreet offers of purchase. It was unthinkable for a gentleman to engage in anything resembling trade, but Sir Thomas Broughton's hunters had more than once stood between his family and destitution, while his wife's rigorous economies in the house made it possible from time to time for them to entertain with a degree of lavishness calculated to encourage their acquaintance to bet freely on both dice and cards. Unfortunately, the winner on these occasions – and on others, in other houses – was all too seldom Sir Thomas himself.

Abigial was dimly aware of all this and although angry words on the subject were distressing, they were too familiar to be shocking. The sound of the slap she had heard was another matter. Children were slapped, not grown-ups, and for one grown-up to strike another was unthinkable. Yet she had heard it happen, and it had happened despite the fact that a husband and wife had as much duty to love one another as a child and its parents. When Maidstone slapped her, she always told Abigial it was for her own good. 'One day you'll thank me,' she used to say, though Abigail remained unconvinced. Could that be what was in her father's mind? Surely not? After all, Lady Broughton was no child needing to be taught how to go on.

When Maidstone slapped her or Cook rapped her knucles to stop her picking at the pastry, it was invariably deserved and, though painful, left her deeper feelings unharmed. On the rare occasions when Lady Broughton found it necessary to slap her daughter, the physical pain was far less but the inner hurt was considerable. How much must her mother be suffering just now! Abigail wept in sympathy into the dark cave beneath the bedclothes.

Lady Broughton did not appear next day, nor the one after that, and Abigail's offer to visit her was politely but firmly declined by the maid.

3

'You leave your mama till she sees fit to send for you,' she said. 'All this partying has left her quite worn out and she needs a good long rest.'

When Lady Broughton reappeared two days after that, a liberal application of powder was not quite enough to efface the bruise lingering on her cheek-bone. Abigail recognised it for what it was and frowned, but her mother seemed far from in her best spirits so she said nothing. She found no comfort at all in the recollection that any slap she herself had received had left nothing more than a red imprint which was gone in a few hours. Could a slap, even a heavy one, result in such a bruise? She delayed asking Maidstone because she was not supposed to have been a witness of the scene that night, and it was difficult to see how she could make the enquiry without letting the maid realise she had not been fast asleep in bed but finally settled for a direct question and a surprise attack.

'What caused that bruise on Mama's face?' she asked suddenly as she ate her lunch in the kitchen under the supervision of Maidstone and Cook. The evening party must have been disastrous because the footmen hired only a week beforehand had all been dismissed.

Cook gave a startled glance at Maidstone but the elderly maid seemed unperturbed. 'You noticed that, did you? Her ladyship hoped you wouldn't – that's why she powdered it. Silly really. She turned in a hurry and her face struck the bedpost – there's a bulgy bit at just that height. Took her by surprise, it did, and made her feel quite unwell.'

The story was plausible enough but little Abigail was not convinced.

Neither Sir Thomas' temper nor his finances improved in the ensuing ten years and Abigail grew up inured both to the genteel penury in which they lived, and to repeated arguments about Sir Thomas' recurrent efforts to retrieve the situation. He continually urged retrenchment upon his family, which now included a younger Thomas, but the retrenchment seemed always to exclude himself and certainly did not preclude his continued recourse to dice and cards as a means of putting things to rights 'once and for all'.

The older Abigail was able to see more clearly behind the façade her mother managed painfully to maintain, and it hurt her to see the pretty, spirited woman she remembered become increasingly careworn and resigned. There were still arguments but they were less heated and, as far as Abigail could tell, never again provoked so savage a reaction.

During many nights immediately following the incident she had clandestinely witnessed, Abigail woke up suddenly, convinced she heard her mother cry out or that she had heard again the sharp, flat sound of a slap. But when she crept out of bed and opened the door to peer round, the house was in darkness and there was not so much as a line of light under the door to either of her parents' rooms. It was not until the same sound woke her up on a night when she knew Sir Thomas to be absent that she realised she must have been dreaming. Even so, she was not entirely convinced until she discovered that her father had not only failed to return that night but was not expected for several days, eventually fulfilling the household's expectations to the hour. Thereafter, that particular dream ceased to haunt her, to Abigail's great relief, but the memory of it and its cause stayed with her and she vowed that, once she was grown up, not father, brother, husband, or lover – would strike her. Or if they did, she corrected herself, for she was nothing if not practical, she'd see to it they never did so again. She gave no thought to how this should be achieved because the very fact of the situation arising was almost inconceivable.

On her sixteenth birthday Sir Thomas had been in a particularly benign mood. Abigail knew better than to attribute this to her anniversary but since Sir Thomas had just returned from London where he increasingly spent his time these days, she presumed he had enjoyed one of his rare but welcome runs of good luck.

He handed her a prettily wrapped little box which contained several ells of ribbon in various shades of blue. 'You're a clever little thing with your fingers. I've noticed it often, though I may not have remarked upon it,' he said. 'With a bit of help from Maidstone, I don't doubt but that you can transform some of your gowns and you're just like your mother, you know: blue will set off your eyes very becomingly.'

Abigail thanked him politely and forbore to point out that blue ribbon was hardly likely to be much use in transforming the thrice-turned dresses, their colours faded and dull, that she was now reduced to wearing. She had the small allowance her late grandfather had settled on her but it did not seem right to be making new clothes for herself when Mama was managing without, though once, when she had suggested to Lady Broughton that she, Abigail, should buy her mother the material for a new dress, Lady Broughton had been quite upset and most adamant that she should not.

Sir Thomas was still beaming. 'That is not the only present we have for you, my dear,' he continued.

Truly, Abigail thought, he must have had a very good run of luck. 'Yes, Papa?' was all she said aloud.

Sir Thomas stood by his wife's chair and puffed out his chest. 'In a few months, Abigail, you will have another little brother or sister. What do you think of that?'

Abigail looked at the thin, tired form of her mother, now smiling wanly in the approval her husband was temporarily exuding. 'I'm delighted, Papa, as everyone must be. Does Maidstone know yet? We shall have to look after you well, Mama, and make sure you're in the best of health.'

Sir Thomas was quick to sense an implied criticism and his face reddened. 'There's nothing wrong with your mother's health, my girl. She's like you: small-boned and looks delicate, but as tough as a Welsh Mountain Pony – you both are. It doesn't do to set too much store by appearances.'

Abigail bobbed a curtsey. 'As you say, sir. I meant to imply nothing.'

He snorted disbelievingly but made no further comment and Abigail quickly withdrew to her own room. She put the box of very pretty ribbons away and went in search of Maidstone.

When she found her, she came straight to the point. 'Did you know Mama was increasing?' she asked.

'Hm. Told him at last, has she? No doubt he's puffing himself out like a barnyard rooster.'

'Papa was certainly very pleased,' Abigail said, repressing a smile at the aptness of the description and refraining from drawing attention to the lack of respect it demonstrated.

'I don't think Mama looks at all well but Papa says, nonsense, she's tougher than she looks.'

'She's needed to be, hasn't she?' Maidstone retorted, and then her voice softened. 'Don't you worry about your mother. I've looked after her since she was a babe in arms and I'm not about to stop now. The best thing Sir Thomas can do is get back to London where he can't interfere, and leave me to it.'

It was extremely unlikely that even the outspoken Maidstone would have expressed these views to her master so it was to be assumed Sir Thomas had his own reasons for returning to the capital when he did, which was early the very next day.

In the ensuing weeks, Abigail watched her mother with some anxiety. No matter how optimistically she tried to convince herself that there was nothing amiss, she knew the truth was otherwise. Maidstone, who had the additional knowledge that neither of Lady Broughton's two previous pregnancies had been easy, looked after her mistress with ever increasing concern but took very good care to keep her worries from Abigail.

Sir Thomas had assured his daugher that he would return home in time for his wife's confinement, though Abigail suspected this was more because his acquaintance in London would expect it of him than out of any concern for Lady Broughton. When her mother went into labour a month before her time, Abigail had no hesitation in disregarding the expense and sending a letter to her father urging his immediate return, and when the midwife shook her head and tut-tutted, Abigail spoke briefly with Maidstone and then sent a groom to fetch Dr Wilcote.

The physician was a mild-mannered, kindly man. He came more quickly than she had expected him to and spent a long time with his patient. When he emerged, he was uncharacteristically curt and Abigail had the impression of a man who was very angry indeed and going to considerable lengths to conceal the fact.

'Sir Thomas has been sent for?'

'I wrote urgently as soon as Maidstone told me Mama's time had come.'

Dr Wilcote took a large watch from his pocket and studied it. 'We must hope he returns at once.'

'I'm sure he will,' Abigail said, alarmed, 'but with the best will in the world, he can hardly reach Merefield before tomorrow evening.'

'I suppose not.' The doctor's acceptance of this indisputable fact was grudging, a circumstance which served to increase Abigail's alarm.

'Mama will be all right, won't she?' she asked anxiously. 'And the baby, too, of course,' she added as an afterthought. Somehow a baby she had never seen seemed less important than the mother she loved.

Dr Wilcote was torn between a desire to reassure and the need to forewarn. He managed a perfuntory smile and patted her hand. 'Try not to worry, my dear. It's always better if babies go their full term, but they often live when they're early and I believe Maidstone used to be a very good nurse.'

'Indeed, she was,' Abigail assured him warmly, 'but what about Mama?'

'When a baby comes early like this it is invariably a great deal smaller than it would otherwise have been and that, of course, has the merit of making its actual birth somewhat easier.' Then why are you so obviously worried? Abigail wanted to ask him but it was not her place to do so, so she just smiled acknowledgement of his reassurance and let him return to his patient.

Dr Wilcote stayed at Merefield all that day and night and on into the next day, a circumstance sufficiently unusual in itself to warn Abigail that matters were far from normal. A glimpse of a harrassed, worried Maidstone did nothing to reassure her and she heaved a sigh of relief when the old maid came downstairs to tell her she had a little brother and that mama wished to see her.

'But she's very tired, Miss Abby, so don't you stay long or tire her any more.'

Abigail promised and ran upstairs, relieved that her worries were at last over.

She gave her new brother only a very cursory glance. He really was extremely small and not in the least attractive. She had half expected to see Lady Broughton looking fresh and revived now that the months of waiting and a full day's labour were over. She was shocked and distressed to see how utterly exhausted her mother looked. Lady Broughton was drawn and pale, with damp tendrils of fair hair clinging to her forehead and dark shadows beneath her eyes.

Abigail bent over her and kissed her. 'Oh, Mama, I'm so glad it's all over and you're all right,' she said, and then added anxiously, 'You *are* all right, aren't you?'

Lady Broughton smiled weakly and patted her hand. Then she looked past her daughter to Maidstone, who had followed Abigail into the room. 'Do you have it?' she asked.

Maidstone leant across and handed her mistress a blue leather box. Abigail knew that box. It housed her mother's cherished diamond and sapphire necklace. Lady Broughton pressed it into her daughter's hands.

'It's yours, Abby,' she whispered. 'Yours. Do you understand? It can only be disposed of with my written consent. Dr Wilcote has just drawn up such a consent. I have signed it, and Maidstone and the midwife have witnessed it. So it is entirely yours and no one can take it from you.' She paused, the effort of saying so much exhausting her. With a shake of her head she brushed away Abigail's protestation that she would rather continue to see her mother wear it. 'I should like to think you will eventually pass it on to your own daughter one day,' Lady Broughton went on when she had marshalled a little more strength. 'But that is up to you: if you really *need* to, then sell it — but don't let your father persuade you into doing so and don't let any husband get his hands on it. I know one shouldn't speak so of fathers and husbands but so often they turn out not to be the estimable characters one expects.'

Dr Wilcote moved forward then. 'Your mama needs rest now, my dear,' he said. 'I suggest you take your leave of her and let her sleep.'

Reluctantly, Abigail kissed her mother and returned to her own room. In any other circumstances she would have rushed to the looking-glass to try on her mother's magnificent gift, but she knew

Lady Broughton had given it to her because she did not expect to live and Abigail would gladly have thrown the necklace into the lake if by doing so she could have proved her mother mistaken. She put it in a drawer of the chest of her room, together with the letter. Then she had second thoughts and removed the letter. She slid it under the mattress. Not the perfect hiding-place but it would do for the time being. Later she would give more considered thought to a safe place for it.

She sat by the window looking out over the park and the lake from which the house took its name, but seeing nothing. Her mother was expected to die. That much was very evident, and there was nothing Abigail could do about it except pray that it would not happen. When she was small, she believed that if she prayed hard enough the desired outcome would come to pass. At sixteen, she knew it was not so simple. Her eyes swam with tears. Marriage was every girl's ambition but when she thought of the married life Lady Broughton had had, she could not help wondering what advantages it offered. Abigail had taken the state for granted until the night Sir Thomas had struck his wife. After that she became more acutely aware of the nuances of day-to-day life at Merefield and, in truth, could not recall a time when her mother had ever seemed to be truly happy. Was marriage really so estimable a condition, or was it simply a means of ensuring one didn't starve? As she grew older and became better acquainted with neighbours, she realised that not all men were like her father but even the most benign and considerate of husbands placed himself before his wife in importance, and did so with the full acquiescence of his spouse.

A world without Lady Broughton was unimaginable. She had guided Abigail in every phase of her growing-up. She had been both teacher and companion, mentor and friend, and there was no one to take her place. Abigail knew that her tears were as much for herself as for her mother. They were not for Sir Thomas.

The baronet arrived home late that night, having very clearly wasted no time in responding to Abigail's summons, a fact which his daughter privately conceded was to his credit. He was surprised to find Dr Wilcote waiting for him, especially since there was no immediate further need for his services. Sir Thomas looked in on his wife and lavished praise on her for having provided him with another son. Then he turned his attention and his enthusiasm on young Timothy who was, he declared, the very spit of his papa and would doubtless grow up to be a chip off the old block. If Dr Wilcote thought this was an infelicitous prophecy, he said nothing, only pursing his lips. When Sir Thomas' eulogies began to slow down, he quietly suggested that a few words with the proud father might be in order – and downstairs, didn't Sir Thomas think, so that Lady Broughton might return to the sleep she so badly needed?

Abigail followed them out of the room and closed the door gently behind them, leaving Maidstone to sit up with her mistress. The two men went downstairs and Abigail continued along the landing towards her room, pausing momentarily by the corner where she had so often crouched as a child. She saw her father and the physician go into the large saloon. She was about to continue on her way when a few words, uttered before the door of the room was quite closed, drifted up to her. The voice was Dr Wilcote's.

'I did warn you, Sir Thomas . . .' she caught, and then the voices were cut off.

Abigail hesitated briefly. Then she looked cautiously around and, having ascertained that she was indeed unobserved, ran quickly downstairs to place herself firmly before the keyhole of the saloon.

Sir Thomas was blustering, a sure sign that he knew himself to be in the wrong but would not admit it. '. . . presuming to tell me that I have no right to ensure the continuance of my family?'

'You already have a son, Sir Thomas. A perfectly healthy little boy. You had no need to endanger your wife's life by getting her with child again – and had the baby been another girl, your professed purpose would not have been achieved.'

'But it wasn't, was it?' There was an almost malicious triumph in his voice.

'No, it wasn't, but Lady Broughton will almost certainly die and the child is premature, small and sickly. You could yet lose both of them. And why? Let us not bandy words, Sir Thomas. You decided that the gratification of your physical needs was more important than your wife's life.'

Abigail felt her world reel and she clutched at the door-jamb for support. What she heard was beyond belief but she could not tear herself away.

'Your wife is no brood mare,' the doctor continued. 'She hasn't the build for it, nor the constitution. I told you when young Thomas was born that you were lucky to have had two healthy children from her and that it would be the height of refined cruelty to make her endure a third pregnancy. I thought that for once in your life you had listened to advice. I was appalled when I learnt that it had been only a temporary respite. Appalled and sickened at such unmitigated selfishness.'

There was a silence and Abigail could imagine her father's indignation at being thus spoken to by a country doctor. She was not mistaken.

'I will have you know, sir, that I see no reason to hold myself accountable to you. I conduct my affairs to my own satisfaction – always have and always will.'

'I don't doubt it,' Dr Wilcote said drily. 'It might be less blame-worthy if you managed to do so without putting others at risk.'

'If you imagine Lady Broughton objected to the continuance of her conjugal duties, I assure you you are much mistaken!'

'I doubt if you would even have noticed had she raised an objection,' the doctor said angrily. 'As it is, I believe you: Lady Broughton had a very strong, and, in my opinion, frequently misguided – sense of duty. You may bluster as you will, Sir Thomas, but the fact remains that, knowing your wife's compliant nature, the responsibility was entirely yours. I shall, of course, continue to attend her ladyship in the faint hope of a miraculous recovery. We must try to save the child: it would be particularly tragic if Lady Broughton were to die for no reason.' He paused, and when he continued it was with more restraint. 'In view of my bluntness, Sir Thomas, I shall entirely understand if you would prefer to replace me with another physician. However, I do request that I am not dismissed until he arrives.'

The doctor's willingness to be replaced succeeded in deflating Sir Thomas in a way that blunt accusation had not. 'Oh, well, I'm not sure ... No, that won't be necessary. You've taken good care of my family over the years and I'm prepared to overlook your impertinence on this occasion. You've been up all night, I gather, and are doubtless tired – and a little upset that things haven't been as straightforward as they have been in the past. A change of physician would only upset Lady Broughton at this stage. No, you may remain.'

Dr Wilcote sighed with exasperation. 'Sir Thomas, things were not straightforward in the past. Your wife has never had an easy confinement. That is my whole point, can't you see that?' He paused. 'No, I suppose you can't – or won't. Very well, I shall remain. As you rightly observe, a new physician at this stage would only upset her ladyship.'

They moved towards the door and Abigail fled upstairs to her room. She threw herself on to the bed and burst into tears. She had suspected her mother might die. It was no relief to have that suspicion confirmed. Confirmation removed hope. Only when she had cried herself out was she in any condition to ponder the implications of the rest of the exchange she had overheard. Her attempts to come to terms with it were hindered by the fact that she did not entirely understand all the issues involved. One thing was crystal clear, however: if her mother died, the blame, according to Dr Wilcote, lay squarely at her father's feet. He would be as responsibile for her death as if he had strangled her. Abigail did not pause to consider whether Dr Wilcote might have overstated the case. She had known him since before she was born, in a manner of speaking. She trusted him implicitly and knew he was not given to overstatement − rather the reverse, if anything.

She had always observed her duty to love her father, even though it wasn't always easy, but how could one continue to love someone who was responsible for the death of another, whom one loved even more deeply? She felt nothing but revulsion for her father, and that was wrong and must be overcome. Achieving this luadable aim was more difficult and she tossed and turned for most of the night, trying to equate her sense of duty with pure instinct. When finally she succumbed to sleep it was deep but troubled and she woke pale and heavy-eyed, a fact which Maidstone noticed but did not remark upon.

Lady Broughton lingered for two days and when her soul slipped quietly from her body, it surprised no one. It seemed to Abigail that, as her mother's strength waned, that of little Timothy, now in the care of a respectable wet-nurse, waxed. She knew this should be a matter for rejoicing but she could not entirely suppress a wish that it might be the child who faded and not the mother. Young Thomas was brought back from school to be with his mother during her last hours and upon his sister fell the unenviable task of comforting the child who, unlike the rest of the household, had had no chance of preparing himself for his loss.

The funeral in the little parish church was well attended for, while Sir Thomas was generally disliked or despised in the locality − and not infrequently both − his wife had been greatly loved and, though she had not been aware of it, much pitied.

The day after the funeral, Sir Thomas sent for his daughter. He was in Lady Broughton's bedroom which bore clear signs of a very thorough search of her possessions.

'Abby, Maidstone tells me you can help me. I'm trying to sort out your mother's things and one item seems to be missing. I can find no trace of the necklace her father gave her. You recall the one − a particularly fine collection of sapphires set in diamonds? I did think that perhaps Maidstone was looking after but she seemed to think you might know something about it.' He frowned. 'I had the feeling she wasn't being entirely open with me. I hope I'm not going to have to dismiss her.'

'There's nothing mysterious about it, Papa. Mama gave me the necklace just before she died.'

Sir Thomas beamed with relief. 'Then I've been worrying

12

needlessly. Run and fetch it, there's a good girl. You won't want the responsibility of keeping it safe.'

'No, Papa.'

Sir Thomas looked at her through imperceptibly narrowed eyes. '"No, Papa"?' he echoed. 'I take it that means you agree that you don't want the responsibility?'

Abigail's knees felt distinctly shaky. 'No, Papa,' she repeated. 'It means I shall not run and fetch it. Mama gave it to me. Her instructions were quite explicit.'

'And what − precisely − were her instructions?'

Abigail hesitated. Open defiance was not something her father was accustomed to receiving. 'She said it was mine and no one was to persuade me to sell it, and ... and I was not to give it to any husband.'

Sir Thomas relaxed a little and smiled indulgently. 'Very sensible advice, Abby, but I'm not suggesting you sell it. Just that you give it to me for safe keeping.'

Abigail took a deep breath. 'I think ... I am certain she did not intend you to have it. I'm sorry, Papa, but I know you had tried to persuade her to part with it in the past. Mama has bequeathed it to me. It is the only thing she had to leave me and I do not intend to part with it. Not to anyone,' she added vehemently.

Her father went pale and then he went very red and for a moment Abigail wondered whether he would strike her. Then a look of guile came into his eyes and he made a very obvious effort to hold his anger in check.

'I understand your feelings,' he said, 'but your mama was very ill and doubtless had forgotten that she simply hadn't the power to give it to you. The necklace came to her with quite specific instructions that it could only be disposed of by her written authority. Now, she can have been in no position to do that, which means, no matter what she may have *wished,* it must come to me on her death.'

'Does that mean that you don't intend to permit Mama's last wish to be fulfilled?' Abigail asked.

He reddened. 'Not at all, but that is a very valuable piece of jewellery and its best use is not necessarily sitting in some drawer.'

Abigail hesitated. Dare she tell her father that he was under a misapprehension? She supposed she must. 'I can set your qualms at rest, Papa. She got Dr Wilcote to write out her bequest and she signed it. When I looked at it, Maidstone and the midwife had both witnessed her signature. So you see, everything has been done as it should have been.'

Sir Thomas' mind did not appear to have been put at ease by the news. He reddened still further and blustered, 'You mean the doctor and the servants know all about this? What sort of picture does that leave them of me, I'd like to know?'

'You can't really have any doubts about the discretion of Dr Wilcote or Maidstone – or of the midwife, if it comes to that. As for the picture they have of you – well, really, Papa, they've all known you for longer than I have. I don't suppose they think any differently of you now, do you?'

Sir Thomas clenched his fists and stared at his daughter under lowered brows, unsure whether she was aware of the implications of what she had just said. Abigail was not normally impertinent, so perhaps she spoke in all innocence. Of course, she was not normally defiant, either. Perhaps he had been wrong to leave her so much with her mother. She was obviously upset at Lady Broughton's death. He would make allowances, at least for the time being.

'I'll speak to you about this later, when you're more youself,' he said at last. 'Don't imagine you're the only person to be upset by your mama's death. After all, I've lost my wife. Goodness knows what I shall do now.'

Thus dismissed, Abigail had no desire to linger. She found Maidstone waiting for her when she got back to her room.

The old maid listened to her story with pursed lips and then nodded. 'You did very well, Miss. Very well indeed. I wasn't at all sure you could stand up to Sir Thomas, but I'm proud of you – and so would her ladyship have been, and that's a fact.'

'You don't think Papa will hunt about until he finds the necklace, do you?' Abigail asked anxiously.

'He might, but I don't think he'll bother. It's a very well-known piece and I rather suspect that if your papa were to try to dispose of it, your mama's relatives would soon be informed by the jeweller.'

Abigail did not know enough about the world her father moved in to realise that there were certain basic flaws in Maidstone's reasoning so she accepted her assurances without comment. She was quiet for a long time and when she spoke again, it was hesitantly. 'Maidstone, may I ask you something?'

'You've never hesitated before.'

'This is different. Maidstone, I'm generally held to be very like Mama, aren't I?'

'Ye-es.' It was a cautious answer though the physical resemblance had been striking.

'Does that mean I can expect to have difficult confinements, as she did?' Abigail asked.

'Lord love you, why should you? You're small and fine-boned and fair, like her ladyship, but you've much broader hips, and that's important. What's more, you've not inherited her rather sickly constitution. You take after your papa in that respect – the constitution of an ox, for all you look as if a puff of wind would blow you down. It may not be generally held to be a ladylike characteristic, but don't ever under-estimate its importance.'

Abigail was not to know that Maidstone who, having come to Merefield with Lady Broughton, had never considered herself a Broughton servant, waited until Miss Broughton was asleep and then sought an interview with her employer.

'It's good of you to see me, Sir Thomas, especially since I don't doubt you'll wish you hadn't. It's about that necklace.' She saw Sir Thomas stiffen and knew that, by the time she had finished what she had come to say, she might very well be looking for another position. It still had to be said. 'I gather from something Miss Abigail said that you'd like to get your hands on it – and I can't say I blame you, since the finances of this household don't bear too much scrutiny.'

'Now, I know it's not my place to argue with you or to come between a man and his daughter, but I beg leave to tell you that you're in the wrong here, and you know it. That necklace has nothing to do with the Broughton side of the family and never has had and if you take it from Miss Abby, I'll tell you exactly what I'll do. I'll put on my bonnet and my cloak and I'll go straight to Miss Abby's uncles and tell them what you've done, and leave *them* to deal with it – which I've no doubt they will, seeing as how they've got strong feelings on the matter anyway. And before you dismiss me,' she added as he showed signs of recovering from his astonishment and anger, 'I beg leave to tell you that will only upset Miss Abby further, and I shall be obliged to tell her the reason why – for she doesn't know I've been to see you – and then I'll go straight to her uncles and warn them what you're up to, and that's a promise.'

Sir Thomas, who had never been spoken to like that in his life, had been speechless with an anger made all the more furious because he knew he was impotent to act. Maidstone, damn her eyes, was right. Laura's brothers – mealy-mouthed Puritans, the lot of them – could make themselves extremely unpleasant. So, not trusting himself to speak, he had turned his back on the old woman, who rightly judged this to be both victory and permission to leave the room.

Abigail fully expected another onslaught from her father on the subject of the necklace and was surprised and relieved that one was not forthcoming. He contented himself with strongly worded hints to his daughter about the usefulness of her inheritance to the welfare of her family and about the corrosive effects on character of pure selfishness, an argument which Abigail privately considered to be well

15

proven by his own example. The more veiled hints she appeared not to notice and the stronger ones she quite simply refused to consider, bearing with every outward sign of equanimity her father's consequent recriminations which were of a general nature and largely referred to the selfishness of the young.

Abigail's confidence in herself, and her ability to stand firm, increased. During the year of mourning – a formality upon which Sir Thomas insisted – it fell to her to take over the running of Merefield. She had a practical nature and a ruthless streak, both of which her mother had lacked, and carried out the task efficiently and well, prompting her father to comment more than once on his rare visits that she would make someone a useful wife some day. Abigail received these sallies with a dutiful smile while mentally resolving that she would choose her husband with a great deal more care than Lady Broughton had done.

On the anniversary of her mother's death, Abigail received a brief note from her father advising her of his intention to return to Merefield 'in a few days', accompanied by her maternal uncle and his wife, Earl and Countess Fawler, and instructing her to ensure that the house was fit to receive them.

This was going to be a difficult command to obey, since Abigail had a shrewd suspicion that the Earl and Countess might have expectations considerably in excess of Merefield's capacity to provide. She took the letter down to the kitchen to consult with Maidstone and Cook. Maidstone heard the news and stiffened.

'What's in the wind here, I wonder? They've not spoken to your father for well-nigh twenty years, Lady Fawler not having much opinion of him. Always used to be high sticklers and I doubt they've changed. They'll not be impressed with this place, and that's a fact. Still, the house is clean and the food is nourishing enough, though you'll need to provide more of it.'

'We'll get some girls in from the village to do the house from attic to cellar, and Cook will need a couple to give her a hand,' Abigail said, thinking aloud. 'We'll have to increase the dishes at each course but I really see no need to serve elaborate kickshaws – the household purse just won't run to them. As it is, I hope Papa realises he will have to let me have some more money if we are not to be utterly disgraced.'

'With respect, Miss Broughton,' Cook interpolated. 'Good plain cooking is what I've become accustomed to providing, and if it's all the same to you, I'd as lief not have to try something too elaborate.'

Abigail assured her that would not be necessary. 'I do wish Papa had given me a more precise idea when we can expect them, not to mention how long they may be staying. The uncertainty does not make it any easier.'

'Typical,' Maidstone remarked scornfully. 'Men think households run themselves. I wouldn't be at all surprised if they arrived on the doorstep tomorrow.'

Happily for Abigail, Maidstone was wrong. It was a week before the Fawler's elegant carriage rolled up to the door, closely followed by a more humble vehicle bearing the rest of their baggage and those of their staff who were indispensable to their comfort. The Earl was small and looked much older than he must have been, with the harrassed air of one accustomed constantly to deferring to another. Lady Fawler was the more decisive character, and she had spent an enjoyable journey missing no opportunity of putting Sir Thomas firmly in what she considered to be his place. One glance at her father's face was enough to tell Abigail that his mood was not benign.

The Countess cast a quick eye over her niece in a way that made Abigail very conscious of her shabbiness in contrast to her aunt's splendour. It was a relief that Lady Fawler's first words were nothing if not kind, despite a certain haughtiness in her tone.

'So you're Laura's Abigail. And very pretty, too. You take after your mama, thank goodness. I was half afraid you'd prove to be some ruddy-cheeked country-girl. I gather you've had the running of this place since Laura's death. Very laudable but your papa really should have engaged a housekeeper, as I've been telling him.'

'On the contrary, Aunt, I enjoy running Merefield and, besides, it has given me employment. How would I have filled my days if there had been a housekeeper?'

'Too much independence too young leads to a certain lack of deference, I've often noticed,' Lady Fawler remarked to the world at large. She crossed the hall to the saloon door, where Maidstone was standing, and paused. 'Maidstone, isn't it?'

The old servant bobbed affirmation.

Lady Fawler glanced at Abigail. 'Well, Maidstone, you and your mistress haven't done too bad a job, as far as I can see. Lady Broughton must have been glad to have you.'

'I'm sure I hope so, my lady,' Maidstone replied.

'It can't have been easy,' the Countess added, transferring her glance to Sir Thomas. She swept into the saloon, running a gloved finger over the top of a side-table just inside the door and inspecting the result. She glanced around the room and Abigail knew there wasn't one patch of worn carpet or faded curtain that escaped her keen eye. 'The place is going to rack and ruin,' the Countess announced. 'I'm surprised you've managed to keep it as well as you have. You'll make someone a *very* useful wife.'

It was not clear whether this remark required a response and before Abigail had decided whether it did, one of the girls from the village who had been enlisted into the kitchen arrived with a tray upon which were hot chocolate for the ladies and madeira for the gentlemen. Lady Fawler drank hers as quickly as politeness allowed and then announced that she and the Earl would like to go to their rooms so that they might rest before dinner. Abigail was amused to observe that her uncle accepted this disposal of his time without demur.

Cook was frantic with an apprehension made all the worse by the grandly disdainful manner of the visiting servants but Lady Fawler pronounced herself entirely satisfied with her meal. It was one of the most lavish Abigail had ever arranged and had stretched the kitchen's resources, both human and culinary, to the limit.

'How very wise of you, my dear, to eschew lavish display. A simple, basic meal like this is infinitely preferable. I do hope you won't feel obliged to over-extend your household's capacity in order to emulate the vulgar ostentation of some repasts.'

Abigail assured her there was no danger of that.

When the ladies withdrew to a small and shabby, but comfortable, sitting-room, Lady Fawler wasted little time coming to the purpose of her visit to Merefield.

'Your uncle and I have been very much concerned about you,' she said. 'Something positive has to be done about finding you a husband and while I have no desire to be disrespectful of your father, I don't think he has the least idea how to go about it.'

'I'm barely seventeen, Aunt. It can hardly be a matter of great urgency yet,' Abigail protested.

'So it may seem to you now,' her aunt said. 'Time passes very quickly, however, and you could very soon be at your last prayers. Furthermore, it is only to be expected that Sir Thomas will remarry and I can tell you this: if you've been running this household efficiently – as I can see you have – you will not enjoy having to defer to another woman. Much better to have acquired a household of your own.'

Abigail could find no fault with Lady Fawler's common-sense even if she found it hard to believe there could be many women who would be prepared to marry a compulsive gambler whose estates were known to be heavily mortgaged.

'Whom had you in mind, Aunt? There is an elderly bachelor curate at the church, and several families have sons a year or two younger than me but I can't see Papa considering any of them to be suitable. As for the curate, I think he'd die of shock if it were suggested!'

18

'Don't be flippant, Abigail,' Lady Fawler said sternly. 'Totally unsuitable, all of them. No, your uncle and I have discussed this with your father and we are agreed that the best thing to do would be for Lord Fawler and myself to take you under our wing and bring you out. Thanks to your Grandpapa's foresight, you have a modest dowry and a small annuity. Not enough to attract fortune-hunters but sufficient to encourage a respectable suitor, and if you come out under our aegis, it will inspire confidence in your suitability.'

'Which, as the daughter of Sir Thomas Broughton, might not otherwise be the case,' Abigail concluded drily.

'Open disrespect for one's elders is most unbecoming,' Lady Fawler remarked repressively. 'All the same, you have summed up the situation rather neatly. What do you say?'

Abigail turned the scheme over in her mind. It was all very well to have vowed to be selective in her choice of husband but before one could select, one needed to have some candidates from which to do so and there were certainly none in the immediate vicinity. It was a marvellous opportunity but she still had reservations.

'As you said, Aunt, my annuity is small. I have a little saved up but I'm far from confident it will be enough to buy the sort of clothes I shall need for such a visit, and I really don't believe Papa could find the sort of sums needed.'

'Consider your annuity to be pocket-money. As for Sir Thomas, we are already agreed that, if he will take a respectable house for the season − as he can very well afford to do if he sets his mind to it − your uncle will bear the full cost of bringing you out.'

'And Papa has agreed?' Abigail made no attempt to disguise her surprise.

'I think he holds the entirely reprehensible theory that, if he takes very good care not to let you down in any way, you may succeed in attracting a husband who will be wealthy enough to alleviate his recurrent financial crises. He's mistaken, of course, but I must confess, I chose not to disabuse him of the idea.'

'There is one other thing,' Abigail said hesitantly, afraid to appear ungrateful in the face of such unexpected generosity. 'You won't compel me − or allow Papa to compel me − to marry someone just because he's very wealthy?'

Lady Fawler smiled. 'I've no desire to hurt your feelings, Abigail, but the opportunity is unlikely to arise. The most we can hope for is a respectable offer from a gentleman who is sufficiently taken with you to overlook the shortcomings of your background.'

Her reservations thus dismissed, Abigail accepted her aunt's invitation with delight and found that the Earl and Countess had no intention of lingering at Merefield. Three days' rest for the horses would be sufficient, they were sure, for Abigail to get her things together. Maidstone was perfectly capable of running Merefield for the time being, and the Earl's man of business was already looking over the leases of houses sufficiently respectable to house a baronet yet within Sir Thomas' means. Lady Fawler had no intention of placing too much dependence upon her brother-in-law's ability to keep his promises unaided.

The next two days passed in a whirl of activity and excitement for Abigail, tempered only by regret that Maidstone was not accompanying her. The old servant herself took Lady Fawler's decision with equanimity.

'At least you know that when you come back, things will be just the way you like them,' she told her mistress.

Fawler House was large and imposing and furnished in the height of fashion – though not, Abigail decided regretfully, in a way which could be described as cosy. It was not easy to accustom oneself to a houseful of servants who waited on one hand and foot; to not lifting a finger to do anything more strenuous than turn a page or set a stitch. Not that Abigail was idle. On the contrary, every waking minute was filled with the bustle of visiting silk merchants, dress- and wig-makers and, when they had gone, there was the dancing-master and Lady Fawler's rigid instruction in the correct depth of curtsey for everyone from the sovereign to a dowager.

There was no need to discuss what Abigail should wear on her head for her presentation: a powdered wig – of modest proportions, in view of her age and unmarried status – topped by three ostrich plumes and backed by long lace lappets were *de rigueur* and a decision on them quickly arrived at by Lady Fawler and the wigmaker, without more than cursory reference to the wearer. The dress was quite another matter and Abigail found it no easy task to persuade Lady Fawler she was quite capable of making it herself, and indeed, would enjoy doing so.

There was no disagreement over colour. 'Blue,' Lady Fawler declared and Abigail found no fault with that decision, but there existed, of course, a multiplicity of blues. A heavy harebell-blue satin was finally settled upon, to be covered in silver-thread embroidery depicting country flowers and butterflies – 'An apposite reference to Merefield, I think,' the Countess commented. It was not unusual for the hoops of a petticoat to measure six feet across on a court dress, but Abigail jibbed at such an excess and her aunt grudgingly conceded that a young girl at her first Drawing Room would not incur criticism if her skirts were of more modest proportions. 'And then, of course, no one will think it strange if you wear it on another occasion – the Birthday Ball, for example,' Lady Fawler admitted. She was quite adamant that Abigail could not wear her necklace to a Drawing Room.

'Quite inappropriate for an unmarried girl – especially one of your age, being presented for the first time. I shall lend you some pearls – much more the thing, I assure you. I think, if your demeanour is seen to be modest, you might wear the sapphires on a later occasion – perhaps with your own hair. Yes, that would be unusual without being ostentatious.' In thus devising a situation in which Abigail might wear without incurring censure a necklace that was most unsuitable for a seventeen year old, Lady Fawler had two motives in mind. It would do Abigail's chances in the marriage market no harm to be seen to own such a piece, and the child was unlikely to make the sort of marriage which would give her an opportunity to wear it after the ceremony. She would make sure that the sticklers learnt that Abigail had insisted on wearing her inheritance – such affection to her mother's memory would do her no harm in the eyes of the world.

To Abigail, unaccustomed even to modest formal gatherings, the Drawing Room was an ordeal. It proved quite unnecessary for Lady Fawler to have warned her niece not to speak unless spoken to and not to initiate a topic of conversation when addressed by royalty. Abigail was far too overcome to do more than murmur a polite response to anyone. King George just smiled and nodded but Queen Caroline, said in some quarters to be the brains behind the throne, smiled kindly and expressed the hope that Abigail would enjoy the Season. There were no chairs, in case anyone committed the solecism of sitting in the presence of the monarch, and the little conversation offered was desultory and superficial. It all seemed, Abigail confided to her aunt when they had returned home and were more comfortably dressed, a great deal of expense and effort for very little.

The Countess threw up her hands in horror. 'Never let anyone hear you say so, child!' she exclaimed. 'I don't deny you have a point – several, in fact – but unless you've been presented, you are quite simply not received, and where would that leave you, I'd like to know? Obliged to persuade that elderly curate into considering matrimony. Most women would prefer the effort and tedium of a Drawing Room.'

Abigail could only agree.

In the weeks before the Queen's Birthday Ball, Abigail accompanied her aunt and uncle on visits, to concerts, exhibitions, evening parties, receptions and balls, and decided she must have a frivolous nature because, as her circle of acquaintance widened and she did not feel so isolated, she began to enjoy a life devoted entirely to pleasure.

Sir Thomas had kept his promise and had taken the house selected on his behalf by his relatives. He dined at Fawler House whenever the Earl and Countess were entertaining and Abigail frequently met him at other houses. This rather surprised her because she had come to think of her father as something of a boor but Sir Thomas was quite accustomed to moving in any circles, however exalted, where play was likely to be profitable and, since he was born a gentleman, he was accepted into those circles even if he was not a particularly popular member of them.

Abigail had dreaded the Drawing Room but she was sufficiently at home in society by now to look forward to the Birthday Ball, the grandest occasion on the Season's calendar. For this she was again to wear the harebell-blue gown, this time accompanied by her sapphires which Lady Fawler had insisted should make their debut on this occasion. She wore her own hair, heavily powdered, and when she looked at her reflection in the glass before they set out for St James' Palace, it was almost a shock to realise how like her mother she looked.

Not only was the ballroom crowded, but so were its adjacent anterooms, completely justifying the designation of 'a crush'. There were naturally no chairs and Abigail wondered how some of the older ladies present would sustain so many hours without being able to sit down.

Dancing at a Birthday Ball differed from more humble affairs in that the dancers took to the floor in strict order of precedence. Abigail was not sufficiently skilled at the intricate steps of the minuet to take part in that dance and was happy to follow her aunt's advice and restrict herself to the country dances.

It was after one of these, when she had returned to her aunt's side, that a gentleman approached them. He bowed briefly to Abigail and more deeply to the Earl and Countess, begging leave to be introduced to their companion.

Abigail had noticed him earlier, partly because she had never seen him before. He was tall, quite old – possibly as much as thirty-five, but it was always difficult to estimate when men wore powdered wigs – and, in an assembly where everyone else wore bright, light colours, his black velvet heavily embroidered with silver thread was startlingly prominent.

The Earl hesitated infinitesimally and glanced at his wife before turning to Abigail. 'My dear, allow me to present Lord Jasper Cuddesdon. Lord Jasper – my niece, Abigail Broughton, the daughter of Sir Thomas.'

Abigail dipped a curtsey and extended her hand to the newcomer who took it in long, pale fingers and brushed it with his lips. Then he looked at her with disconcertingly hooded eyes. 'The resemblance to your mother is quite remarkable, Miss Broughton,' he said.

'You knew Mama?'

'I was acquainted with her, yes. Tell me, Miss Broughton, do you have a dance for which you are not engaged?'

Abigail, who knew perfectly well there were no dances for which she was free save minuets, nevertheless consulted her card. 'No, my lord, I'm afraid I do not.'

He was unperturbed. 'A pity. On another occasion, perhaps?' He bowed again and withdrew.

Abigail shivered as if a cold draught had somehow found its way into these overheated rooms. Lord Jasper had been unexceptionably polite but she did not like him. It was quite wrong to make such a snap decision but there was something about him – perhaps his hooded eyes, or perhaps it was just that wearing black when no one else did gave him a sinister air – which she found a little frightening. Nevertheless, she found herself watching him for the rest of the evening, except when she was obliged to watch her steps instead, and was a little piqued that he made no attempt to approach the Fawler party again.

'Who was that man in black?' she asked her aunt next day. 'Lord Jasper Something,' she added by way of elucidation.

'Cuddesdon,' Lady Fawler said curtly. 'His father is the Duke of Cutteslowe. One of the highest sticklers you will find. I'm surprised the son has been allowed back. He seems just as unpleasant as ever.'

'Allowed back from where?' Abigail asked.

Lady Fawler hesitated and the Earl broke in.

'You may as well tell the girl. Certain women always found him devilish attractive, though I could never understand why.' He sounded a shade peevish, Abigail thought. 'If he's back in London, she'd better know about him.' And with this, the Earl left the room.

His wife lost no time in enlightening her charge. 'As I said, the Duke is a high stickler. The family pedigree is irreproachable and a succession of dynastic marriages has made it one of the most powerful, not to say one of the wealthiest, in the land. Lord Jasper has been a grave disappointment to them. I imagine the Duke must frequently have given thanks to the Almighty that he wasn't his first-born! He was at one time something of a crony of your father's. That should tell you something. A confirmed and compulsive gambler, though in general with more success than Sir Thomas, I'm bound to admit.

23

'Still, it didn't suit the Duke's notions to be continually having to settle his son's accounts when he had a run of bad luck, and then Lord Jasper killed – or was alleged to have killed – a card-sharp to whom he had lost a considerable sum of money. That was the last straw so far as his father was concerned, and Jasper was packed off to the family's Virginia estates. I think the idea was that it might turn him into something useful and if it didn't, well, at least it was out of sight. He would not have dared return without his father's permission, particularly with the possibility of a murder charge hanging over his head.'

'I shouldn't have thought he would *want* to return if that were the case, should you? He struck me as a rather unpleasant man, but not a stupid one,' Abigail commented.

'Oh, he's not stupid – far from it. Devious, underhand and ruthless, but not stupid.' The Countess looked anxiously at her niece. 'You don't find him attractive, do you? Your uncle's right – some women do.'

Abigail laughed. 'About as attractive as a snake, Aunt – and if he's a gambler, I have even less interest, I promise you. I saw what gambling did to Mama and it's not a lesson I'm likely to forget.'

'Of course,' Lady Fawler went on, determined to be fair, 'he may have reformed, though I don't think it's very likely.Gamblers don't, on the whole.'

Abigail agreed and the matter was dropped. She gave it no further thought beyond noting that Lord Jasper was not present at any function they attended in the next two or three weeks, and then she forgot about him. The Countess assumed he had left town.

Lady Fawler was becoming a trifle concerned that not one of the many eligible and respectable young men to whom she had introduced her niece had expressed an interest of any significance beyond that demanded by common courtesy. They were perfectly willing to exchange small-talk with Abigail, to take her into supper and to stand up with her for a country dance, but they took very good care – or so it seemed to Lady Fawler – not to do anything that might raise expectations. Lady Fawler laid the blame squarely on the Broughton name. She had made discreetly sure that it had become known that her charge had a respectable dowry and a small allowance, neither of which could be touched by her papa, but Sir Thomas was well-known and no family wished to see one of its sons condemned to a lifetime of towing the baronet out of the River Tick. Abigail's somewhat unconventional beauty and her socially complaisant manner ensured that she need never want for an escort, but that was as far as it went. She herself gave no indication that she was even aware of the situation, much less concerned by it, and her aunt kept her concern to herself apart from those increasingly frequent occasions when she unburdened herself to her husband in the privacy of their own rooms.

Both ladies' memories were jogged by the arrival of a gilt-edged card of invitation suggesting that Earl and Countess Fawler and Miss Broughton might enjoy a musical evening that His Grace the Duke of Cutteslowe was holding at his town house.

'Didn't know he liked music above half,' was the Earl's only comment, discounted by his wife as a total irrelevance. The Duke was a widower of long standing. His interest in the Season was minimal. An event at Cutteslowe House was An Occasion and on that ground alone Lady Fawler had no intention of being absent.

The problem of what Abigail should wear caused her aunt some anxiety. The dress she had worn to the Drawing Room and the Birthday Ball was eminently suitable for so glittering an event as an evening at Cutteslowe House was bound to be but, while it was perfectly acceptable to wear a gown twice, it was not at all the thing to wear it three times. On the other hand, to do so certainly indicated an ability to economise and, since there had never been any point in pretending Abigail was wealthy, it might be no bad thing for her to be seen in that gown again. Abigail loved the dress and raised no objections.

Cutteslowe House was a great deal more grand than St James' Palace and not very much less crowded. The Duke, together with his eldest son, the Marquess of Headington and his rather dull Marchioness, stood at the top of the huge, double-branched staircase to welcome guests. The Marquess bore a striking resemblance to his father but, apart from the aquiline nose, Abigail could detect little family likeness between these two elder members and her recollection of the younger son.

Lord Jasper was not present when the Fawler party arrived at a carefully gauged time which was neither too early nor sufficiently late to occasion comment, yet shortly after their arrival his tall figure could be seen making its way through the throng, a bow here, a pause to exchange words there, until he was in front of them. His clothes rendered him less conspicuous on this occasion though the heavy grey watered silk with its silver embroidery emphasised a general palor enhanced, as before, by his powdered wig. He bowed.

'Lady Fawler, Miss Broughton, how pleasant to see you again. Are you here because you like music or because it is Cutteslowe House?'

He must have known there was only one possible polite answer to that question and Abigail felt her aunt bristle with indignation that their host's son should have come so very close to the truth. Abigail, unlike her aunt, had found music to be one of the greater pleasures of her stay in London and it was she who answered, with undisguised enthusiasm.

'The music, my lord. We have been to two or three musical evenings this season and I have loved them. There is no such entertainment in the country, you know.'

'You find them entertaining?' There was something in his tone that made Abigail feel she had inadvertently said something *gauche*.

Her colour slightly heightened, she defended herself. 'Why, yes! Are such events not arranged to entertain? I find that, while the music is playing, this world is suspended and I'm transported – oh, to wherever I choose.'

He inclined his head. 'Then permit me to offer you those seats which will enable you to hear best. Anything that can suspend this world is to be encouraged.'

The Duke had invited so many guests that the huge ballroom had been taken over for the occasion by a forest of little gilt chairs and the accoustics were not equally good in every part of the room. This was of no matter for the majority of people who, like Lady Fawler, had come as much to see and be seen as to listen to the small orchestra. Abigail was not of their number and was very happy to be guided by Lord Jasper, while Lady Fawler was certainly not going to decline such particularity of attention, whatever her private opinion of the gentleman might be. The music was less superficial than any Abigail had heard before and required her full attention but she enjoyed it none the less and was particularly taken by a piece by an Italian of whom she had never before heard – a certain Signor Scarlatti. She was quite sorry when there was an interval during which the guests withdrew to another room where refreshments of a particularly lavish nature had been set out.

When the recital was resumed, the audience was noticeably thinner, many preferring to sustain their bodies rather than their minds. Lady Fawler might have been one of them, had her niece not been insistent on their return to the ballroom.

They did not see Lord Jasper again until they were almost ready to leave. They had been quite unaware of his presence until he materialised beside them. He accorded a cursory bow to the Earl and Countess and turned his attention to their companion.

'I hope the music met with your approval, Miss Broughton.'

Abigail's eyes shone. 'Indeed, it did, my lord. The music of Signor Scarlatti was new to me. I've never been to Italy, of course, but it was so bright, so sunny, that I could almost imagine myself there!'

A meagre smile crossed his thin lips. 'Then the evening has been worth while, he said. Then his attention was claimed by another guest and the Earl and his wife took leave of their host before collecting cloaks and carriage and returning home.

No comment on the evening was made until they were in the carriage. Then it was Lady Fawler who made it.

'A strange man, Lord Jasper. Very difficult to like.'

'And unregenerate, it would appear.' her husband added.

'Indeed? In what way?'

'I was invited – with others – to return later. Cards and dice are to be set up.'

'Did you accept, my lord?'

'I declined. I gather he plays as deep as ever.'

The Countess considered the matter. 'That was why the Duke sent him packing in the first place,' she remarked. 'I wonder why he has been allowed to return if he hasn't reformed?'

'That, my dear, is something you would have to ask either father or son.'

An unexpected visitor arrived the following afternoon, just in time to oblige the Countess and her niece to postpone their planned drive in the park. Sir Thomas was closeted for a long time with Lady Fawler before his daughter was sent for.

When Abigail entered her aunt's little sitting-room, that lady was sitting very upright with her lips pursed and her father was pacing up and down with the same air of suppressed excitement that usually followed his acquisition of the name of an absolute certainty at Newmarket.

Abigail kissed him dutifully and curtsied to Lady Fawler.

'You sent for me, Aunt?'

'Your Papa has something to say to you, Abigail.'

'Papa?'

'You know why you were sent here, Abby. Your aunt generously took upon herself all the expense of giving you a season in the hope that you might make a respectable marriage.'

Abigail blushed. 'I know that, Papa, only so far no one has expressed any interest beyond the purely social.'

'Now that's just where you're mistaken, my girl. I have this morning received a most flattering offer.' He paused to lend weight to the excitement he expected her to exhibit.

'Have you, Papa? Are you sure you haven't misunderstood? I assure you no one has given me the slightest reason to expect them to approach you.'

He smiled smugly. 'No, he said he thought it might be unexpected, but I told him, "The ladies have an instinct for this sort of thing. I

27

don't suppose it will surprise her one bit, my lord." That's what I told him.'

'"My lord"?' Only Sir Thomas's wishful thinking could have mistaken her genuinely bemused tone.

'Coming it too strong, Abby,' he chided her. 'Lord Jasper Cuddesdon's the man, you clever little puss, and it's better than I'd ever hoped for. Why, they say he's made a sizeable fortune in the Americas. And just think – you'll be Lady Jasper. All in all, you've done very well for yourself, though you'll not forget it was your aunt's generosity that made it possible. A son-in-law after my own heart, for all he's a bit high in the instep. I'm very pleased with you, my dear. Very pleased.'

'You make me sound like a gundog who's just retrieved a particularly difficult bird,' Abigail told him, with a sharpness that surprised her aunt. 'No, Papa. I shall not marry Lord Jasper and I hope you haven't told him I will, because if you have, you will be placed in the embarrassing position of telling him you were mistaken.'

Sir Thomas reddened and Abigail suspected that that was precisely what he had done. 'Stop and think, Abby,' he urged. 'Jewels, gowns, servants: all that would be yours. Far more than you could expect if you married some country squire, which is probably the only alternative. I can't conceive what you have against him.'

'I don't suppose you can, Papa. Let's just say we wouldn't suit.'

'How can you say anything so ridiculous. Why, you hardly know the man!'

'Exactly. I have met him just twice and both times in very formal circumstances. Papa, on those grounds alone I must decline the offer. Why, if he were a veritable saint – and by all accounts that is not the case – I wouldn't accept an offer without being better acquainted.'

'I told him very likely you'd expect him to fix his interest first. Seems to be all the thing these days. In my young days girls left important matters like finding a husband to their parents. I told him to let you sleep on the advantages and then pay you a visit. You can expect him tomorrow morning.'

'Papa, you would be better advised to tell him I won't see him,' Abigail insisted.

'Don't be ridiculous, girl. He's never shown you anything other than courtesy, has he? By your own account, he's not had a chance!'

'Your father's right,' Lady Fawler interrupted. 'There will be a certain awkwardness attached to the interview, I know, but Lord Jasper has paid you the compliment of offering for your hand. The very least you can do is receive him and give him your answer in person. I shall attend you, of course, but Lord Jasper was a born gentleman and will know how to behave.'

'You see him alone, my girl. Give the man a chance to show himself in a decent light. I know he seems a bit of a cold fish, but that's the result of being the Duke's son. All the Cuddesdons are like that. It don't mean a thing,' Sir Thomas urged.

'Your daughter will most assuredly *not* see him alone, Sir Thomas,' Lady Fawler declared. 'Not in my house, at all events! It would be scarcely forgivable if she *were* going to marry him. If she's going to decline, it becomes unthinkable.'

'I shouldn't be a bit surprised if you find she's changed her mind after a night to turn the matter over,' Sir Thomas said tetchily.

'I think I can promise you that, if Abigail does change her mind, you can depend upon me to judge when to withdraw discreetly. You have placed your daughter in my care, Sir Thomas. I insist you leave this to my judgement.'

Sir Thomas was not happy but he was astute enough to realise that he would get no further for the present.

'Very well,' he said grudgingly. 'You're a woman of the world, my lady. I depend upon you to spend this evening pointing out to my daughter how foolish she would be to reject this offer.'

'Your daughter's best interests will be at the forefront of my mind,' Lady Fawler assured him, and with that Sir Thomas was obliged to be content.

When he had gone, she turned to her niece. 'Your father's right, you know. There would be distinct advantages to this marriage.'

Abigail looked at her reproachfully. 'You promised I wouldn't be pressed into a marriage I didn't want,' she said.

'Nor shall you be, but I should be failing in my duty if I didn't point out the advantages.'

'Aunt, the man's a gamester!'

'A successful one, by all accounts.'

'Luck can change,' Abigail said bitterly. 'I have good reason to be well aware of that uncomfortable fact.'

'Very true, but I don't think the Duke will let his son − or his son's family − languish in a debtor's prison.'

'No − he will ship them out of the country, where they can no longer be an embarrassment to him. Besides, you told me there had been a suspicion Lord Jasper had killed someone. I've no desire to live with a murderer.'

'Few women would choose to do so, I imagine. However, we don't know how much truth can be placed upon that particular story.

29

Perhaps you should ask Lord Jasper.'

'There must be something in his character which makes the story plausible,' Abigail objected. 'Otherwise it would have been laughed out of court as soon as it was mooted.'

Since this was an extremely shrewd comment, Lady Fawler chose not to answer it. 'At least suggest to Lord Jasper that you would welcome an opportunity to become better acquainted with him,' the Countess suggested.

'But I wouldn't,' Abigail told her. 'I don't like him. There's something about him that's almost ...' she searched for the word '... sinister, and it makes me feel uncomfortable in his presence. I don't know how to explain it, and I admit he has given me no grounds for saying such a thing, but the fact remains that I'm more than a little frightened of him, and I don't think that's a very good omen for marriage, do you?'

Lady Fawler agreed that it was not and forbore to add that she knew exactly what her niece meant. Instead she said, 'You won't be quite that frank with him when he calls, I hope.'

Abigail smiled wryly. 'No, Aunt. I think I can avoid quite that degree of frankness.'

The Countess let the subject drop. Quite enough had been said to give Abigail plenty to mull over in the solitude of her room and nothing would be achieved by overstating the case. Indeed, Lady Fawler was not at all sure what she would do in Abigail's place: the advantages were obvious but there was no denying that Lord Jasper had never been a particularly pleasant man and a long absence seemed to have done little to improve him.

Sleep did not come easily to Abigail that night. She knew her duty. The Earl and Countess had taken her under their wing in order to help her find a suitable husband and no one had been beating a path to their door. It was all the more surprising that an offer should have come from such a quarter and from a man who had given no indication of any particular interest in her. Lord Jasper did not have the appearance of a man who was obliged to count his pennies but that, Abigail reflected, could be misleading. She recalled how her parents had always been able to summon up a lavish display when its purpose was to lure acquaintances into loosening their purse-strings. No, she would never marry a gambler. It was a decision made all the easier by her dislike of this particular one. She felt guilty for feeling such dislike, for Lord Jasper had given her no grounds for it − nor, she thought suddenly, had he made any effort to present himself in a favourable light. That might mean that his arrogance was such that he didn't care what she thought. It might also mean that he eschewed duplicity.

And if she turned him down, what then? There was no other likely husband in the offing and she certainly could not expect her uncle to sponsor her for a second season. Her father would undoubtedly be extremely angry. She supposed she would be sent back to Merefield where she would die an old maid unless the curate preceded her and his replacement was younger but equally eligible. Abigail sighed. It had not been difficult to learn to enjoy the frivolities of the fashionable life, and Lord Jasper moved in the very centre of that world. It would be hard to return to the humdrum world of Merefield. Perhaps Lord Jasper might give up his more reprehensible pastimes ... Her imagination dwelt happily on that picture before common-sense intervened. Her mother must have had some such idea when she married Sir Thomas. He had been a great deal younger when he married than Lord Jasper was now, and marriage had hardly reformed him. Lord Jasper was even less likely to change the habits of a lifetime. No, she would have to take him as he was or not at all. When Abigail finally fell asleep, she knew she faced a difficult interview on the morrow.

The footman who spent his entire working life sitting in a tall, hooded arm-chair in the hall ready to open the door to callers was instructed to deny Lady Fawler and Miss Broughton to everyone except Lord Jasper, an instruction which caused considerable surprise in the servants' quarters because it could only mean one thing and who'd have thought it? No sign of this intense speculation appeared on his well-schooled, expressionless face when Lord Jasper presented himself. His lordship was conducted to her ladyship's sitting-room where the object of his visit and her aunt were each setting stitches to pass the interminable time till he should appear.

He made a leg of almost equal depth to both ladies. 'Countess, Miss Broughton, you do me an honour to receive me.'

'Not at all, my lord. The honour is all ours.' Lady Fawler was nothing if not gracious.

Abigail was conscious of her heightened colour and lowered her eyes but not before she had observed that Lord Jasper was dressed with his customary extravagance of fabric and embroidery – gold thread this time, on a ground of rich brown velvet with breeches of heavy straw-coloured satin. She thought it made her own simple morning-dress of cream brocade sprigged with silk embroidered spring flowers look like something fit only for the schoolroom. Lady Fawler thought she looked charmingly. Lord Jasper's face gave no indication of his opinion.

'Miss Broughton,' he began. 'I will not waste your time. I come

31

with your aunt's permission and your father's blessing. As I believe you've been informed, the purpose of my visit is to ask you to do me the honour of becoming my wife.'

He was stiff, formal and, Abigail thought suddenly, ill-at-ease. The realisation gave her confidence.

'Why?' she asked.

Lady Fawler gasped and Lord Jasper was decidedly taken aback. '"Why?"' he repeated blankly. 'Why do men usually make such an offer?'

'I've no idea,' Abigail told him. 'This is the first I've ever had.'

He recovered his poise. 'Usually, madam, because they consider the lady in question will prove a compatible help-meet in life,' he suggested.

'Is that why you chose me?' Abigail asked.

'Of course!'

'But, my lord, you've only ever met me twice. How can you possibly have formed an opinion?'

Lord Jasper's formality became more pronounced and Lady Fawler was uncomfortably aware that he seemed to be suppressing considerable anger.

'I suppose it would be true to say that one can never be entirely certain, Miss Broughton. I am, however, prepared to take a chance. Will you?'

'My lord, I'm no better acquainted with you than you with me,' Abigail pointed out. 'I am by no means certain that we would be compatible.'

'I would that there were time for us to become better acquainted,' he replied. 'Alas, I return to Virginia in two days' time and would have your answer before I go. Come, Miss Broughton: will you take a chance?'

'You have put your finger on the very nub of it,' Abigail said. 'You are a gamester, my lord, and have no objection to "taking a chance". I am not, and a life-time with one who is has taken away any desire I might have had to leave things to chance. No, my lord. I am fully conscious of the honour you do me, but I am not prepared to "take a chance" on our mutual compatibility. I must therefore decline your very flattering offer.'

It seemed to Lady Fawler that their visitor went even paler under his powder and his eyes glittered in a way that she very much feared might betoken an outburst. None came. Lord Jasper bowed. 'Very well, Miss Broughton. I naturally regret your decision. You will not wish to suffer my continued presence. I bid you farewell. Lady Fawler, your servant.'

When the door closed behind him, a silence of several minutes fell upon the room to be broken at last by Lady Fawler.

'Abigail, how could you? To ask a man *why* he was offering for you.'

'It seemed a perfectly reasonable question to me,' Abigail said, surprised. 'After all, it's not as if we are old acquaintances, is it?'

'All the same, it was wrong of you – and very unwise, I fear, Lord Jasper was exceedingly angry.'

'Do you think so?' Abigail asked doubtfully. 'He didn't go red in the face and bluster like Papa does and, after all, if you propose to someone there must always be the chance they may turn you down.'

'I don't suppose Sir Thomas mentioned that possibility, do you?'

It was Abigail's turn to go pale. 'Papa will almost certainly have told him I would accept. Oh, Aunt, I never thought of that! Do you think I should write to Lord Jasper and explain?'

'Certainly not. Let sleeping dogs lie – fortunately this one will be out of the country in a couple of days which should at least preclude the awkwardness of meeting him again,' her aunt said and kept to herself the observation that sleeping dogs, if accidentally stumbled upon, were distressingly prone to bite.

If Lady Fawler had doubted her niece's description of an angry Sir Thomas, she was soon to learn its accuracy when that gentleman hastened round to Fawler House on receipt of a note from Lord Jasper. Sir Thomas was not in a benign frame of mind.

'Is this true?' he demanded. 'Have you turned down the chance to marry the Duke of Cutteslowe's son?'

Abigail wasted no energy in softening the blow. 'Yes,' she said baldly.

Her father's already heightened colour changed from red to a delicate shade of purple. 'Do you realise what you've done, my girl? You've brought your family to the brink of ruin, that's what you've done. You've removed any chance I might have had of redeeming the debts that will lose us Merefield and of providing for your young brothers – that's what you've done.'

Abigail blanched but held her ground. 'Nonsense, Papa. I've declined Lord Jasper's offer, that's all. It does mean I shall be a burden on you for a little longer but I'm a great deal cheaper than a good housekeeper, so I can't see how I can fairly be accused of bringing the family to the brink of ruin.'

'Because Lord Jasper was going to settle a large sum of money – a *very* large sum of money – on you in return for your hand.'

'On me? Then how would that help the family?'

Sir Thomas shifted uncomfortably. 'You have a very unattractive habit of picking one up on the least thing, Abby. I spoke loosely, of course.'

'He was, in fact, going to pay *you* handsomely for the privilege. Is that it?' Abigail asked shrewdly.

'An unnecessarily crude way of putting it, but I suppose that's what it amounted to. And you've thrown the chance away. You can't even indicate a change of mind because he's leaving the country tomorrow.'

'That's a blessing,' Abigail told him. 'At least it saves us all the arguments that would ensue when I told you I had no intention of changing my mind. Papa, I do not like Lord Jasper and I certainly don't like his way of life. He's far too old to change, and I really don't care what he was going to do for the family. I shall try not to marry to disoblige you, but that doesn't mean I'm prepared to be sacrificed on the altar of your debts. Perhaps you will bear that in mind if any other potential suitors make application to you.'

'Not an event I anticipate,' her father said tetchily. 'Your suitors have not exactly beaten a path to my door.'

'I know, Papa, and I'm truly sorry for that. It's just very unfortunate that the only man sufficiently interested to offer for me is one I dislike.'

Lady Fawler broke in. 'Since we are speaking frankly, Sir Thomas, it's only fair to Abigail to point out that she has done nothing to give any young man a dislike of her, but she is seriously handicapped by being the daughter of a man noted for his ruinous propensities.'

This comment, accurate as it might be, did nothing to assuage the baronet's anger. 'Very well, my lady. If my daughter labours under so great a handicap, the solution is simple: we cut our losses and she returns to housekeep for me. Now.'

Disappointment drained the colour from Abigail's cheeks. 'No, Papa. Let me finish the season,' she pleaded. 'Invitations have been accepted and gowns made. Oh, papa, you cannot be so unkind!'

'It seems a trifle severe,' Lady Fawler agreed. 'You have a perfect right to take Abigail back to Merefield, of course, but it will look very odd if you do so before the Season ends.'

'Not at all,' Sir Thomas insisted. 'She can come and keep house for me in town. That was a good house your man found for me and my luck has been much improved since I've been there. With Abigail instead of the present hired help, I shall be able to economise further – I fully intend to keep the house on.'

'Then you certainly can't insist that she accompanies you now,' Lady Fawler told him. 'It is imperative you send for her maid. Abigail cannot remain in a male household without a female companion.'

Sir Thomas was obliged grudgingly to agree with this. 'Very well,' he said. 'I shall send for Maidstone this afternoon. We can expect her the day after tomorrow. Abigail, unless you hear from me to the contrary, you will be ready to return with me then.'

'Do we go back to Merefield at the end of the season?' Abigail asked him doubtfully, Sir Thomas being seldom seen at home since the death of his wife.

'I don't think so. There's been such a marked change in my luck since I took this house that it would be foolish to risk upsetting it. No, we'll stay there as long as I can afford it.'

Thus it was that Abigail swallowed her disappointment and, for the next year, kept house for her father. Sir Thomas might insist that his luck had changed. If that was so − and one did not accuse one's father of being untruthful − it could only be marginally. It was true that the bailiffs were not at the door, but she was still expected to manage on the very barest minimum of money, yet, like her mama, to be able to put on a display when her father required it. The effort took a great deal of energy and, although it was disagreeable to have to economise, she found it an interesting challenge. She told herself she was no more unhappy than she would have been at Merefield and that she had better resign herself to it, because there was no likelihood of anything better presenting itself.

Chapter One

The atmosphere in the brightly lit room was suddenly tense. The assembled men, brilliant as exotic moths in their richly hued satins, were suddenly silent. Glasses waited, poised half-way to mouths. Conversation stopped. The only movement was the glitter of gold and silver embroidery in the flickering light of a myriad candles.

Two men, a study in contrast, sat at the table, the centre of attention.

Lord Jasper Cuddesdon, tall and pale, with lean, saturnine features, seemed the more at ease but perhaps that was merely because he was once more at home in his father's house. He leaned back slightly in his chair, his white, carefully manicured, long-fingered hands resting on the table before him, his eyelids half hiding his glittering eyes – a glitter that owed more to the brandy decanter beside him than to the candles. On the table between his outspread hands was a pile of gold almost submerged under notes of hand.

Opposite him, and infinitely ill-at-ease, sat a much older, florid man. Sir Thomas Broughton, too, had been drinking, but in his case it showed. His cheeks were flushed, his wig askew, and close observers noted that his hand on the dice-box was not entirely steady. In front of him were no guineas, but to one side stood a writing-stand on which rested a quill still wet with ink and grains of scattered sand, mute testimony to the source of the notes held by his opponent.

He shook the box. He raised it to his lips and kissed it. Then he shook it again. The ritual was familiar to the bystanders. It had accompanied every throw. More than one of them thought Sir Thomas' luck might change for the better if he discarded the ritual. It most assuredly could not change for the worse.

He threw. A one and a trey. Lord Jasper had thrown nine. Sir Thomas stared with unbelieving eyes. It could not be true. Not again. It was not possible for the luck to run against him so consistently. It must turn. If he could only go on for long enough, it would turn.

With an effort, he laughed. 'The luck is with you yet again, my lord,' he said, fighting hard not to let his desperation show. 'Let us throw once more. All or nothing.'

'Do you know, I had rather thought that to have been the stake before?' his opponent replied softly. 'Forgive me, Sir Thomas,' he went on, 'but are you aware of having anything further to stake? I appear to hold your guineas, your horses and your house.' One of his hands gestured gracefully at the pile in front of him.

This comment caused some head-shaking among those standing within earshot. It was true Sir Thomas was in deep – deeper, some thought, than he could afford to be – and it seemed certain that unless the luck changed, and soon, he would be ruined. Nevertheless, it was ungentlemanly of Lord Jasper to draw such public attention to the older man's plight. Had Sir Thomas been less drunk, he would not now be in his present unenviable predicament. The brandy had a lot to answer for.

'My lord,' he said, and his words were only slightly slurred, 'the dice have fallen against me for two hours. It must be time for them to change. You hold everything I own. You have it in your power to ruin me. Refuse me one last throw and ruined I shall be. Grant it, and one way or another I shall come through.'

Lord Jasper was silent awhile, watching Sir Thomas through hooded eyes. 'You intrigue me, Sir Thomas,' he said finally. 'I fully realise that if you win the next throw, you will be saved from ruin, but how can you gamble when you have nothing to stake?'

Sir Thomas shook his head as if to clear the fumes that clouded his judgment. He had spoken with a gambler's desperation and now, briefly, reality obtruded. 'I do not know . . . There must be something.'

Lord Jasper let the despair deepen on his opponent's face before speaking again, and when he did speak, his voice was silken-soft, so soft that the spectators at this memorable game had to strain to hear him.

'You have just one more article to stake,' he suggested.

The despair lifted for a moment and Sir Thomas stared at him in something close to disbelief. 'I have?' he asked.

'You have a daughter. If you win, all that I have won from you will be regained. If you lose, your daughter is substituted for your losses and I will add a further two thousand guineas.'

The onlookers gasped. There was not one among them who had not made a marriage of convenience or who would not encourage his daughter to marry to the family's advantage, but this was too crude, too obvious.

38

Sir Thomas stared at the younger man. 'So Abby's refusal rankled, did it? I knew you to be displeased but I had no idea your displeasure would fester so long. You know her feelings in the matter. You cannot imagine her mind to have changed in the last year or so. If you are determined to marry her in spite of that, you must realise she is not likely to make a very complaisant wife — nor a willing bride, for that matter — and I can't say I blame her. Nor, I suspect, will anyone else. Indeed, I'm not at all sure which of you I pity most.'

'With respect, Sir Thomas,' Lord Jasper said, that emotion noticeably absent in his tone, 'I care little for your pity. I would not, however, wish you to be under any misapprehensions. Let me make myself quite clear. I do not now propose marriage. Your daughter would go to my estates in Virginia and there she would work off your debt. In short, Sir Thomas, she would be a bond-slave.'

The bystanders were incredulous. They knew such things to be possible: among a certain class of person it was a not unusual way of escaping the debtors' prison. It was not, however, a measure to which gentlemen customarily had recourse, and to suggest that a gentleman's daughter be pledged on his behalf — well, it was no wonder the Duke of Cutteslowe had disowned his younger son and sent him off to the colonies. It seemed a pity he had relented sufficiently to allow him to return from time to time.

Lord Bishopstoke moved forward. 'Enough of this,' he said. 'The whole thing has gone far enough. Too far, some would say. For God's sake, Broughton, stop now. You may be ruined but you will remain a gentleman.'

Lord Jasper motioned him to back away. 'Be under no illusions as to what I offer, Sir Thomas. I am not proposing indentured servitude. An indentured servant repays with four years' free labour the cost of his passage out. Your daughter will be paying your debts as well as earning her passage. That is not an indentured servant. That is a bond-slave and I very much doubt whether she would live long enough to repay this vast debt.' He paused, sizing up the degree of his opponent's desperation and reflecting that, if Sir Thomas' luck continued to run to form, he would have another opportunity of acquiring any assets Miss Broughton might redeem over the years. 'But I am nothing if not a gamester and I am no Shylock, determined on the last ounce of flesh due me.' He pushed the pile of guineas and paper across the table. 'Let us say your daughter is bonded for fifteen years in lieu of these debts, together with the additional two thousand guineas. Give me your note to that effect and we will cast the dice again. All or nothing.'

There was total silence in the room while Sir Thomas wrote out the unprecedented stake, handed it to Lord Jasper and received back all he had lost that evening and an additional pile of guineas. The relief on his face was plain for all to see and many of the spectators felt a sense of rising disgust, yet such was the draw of this extraordinary wager that they could not pull themselves away from this, the final scene.

Lord Jasper shook the box and cast the dice. A two and a one. Sir Thomas smiled. He had known his luck would change. It had been a desperate last gamble, but he had won. He felt quite light-headed with relief as he took his turn. He shook the box. He raised it to his lips and kissed it. He shook it again and threw.

The dice rolled and settled. He stared at them in disbelief. A one and a one? No, it could not be. Fate could not have played so foul a trick on him. His eyes must be playing him false. He leaned over the table to stare. The evidence of his eyes, blurred by brandy though they were, was nonetheless unmistakable. He had thrown two.

Lord Jasper picked up his note of hand and rose from the table, smiling. 'Come, Sir Thomas,' he said. 'Let us settle our affairs now. I will accompany you home and receive payment from you.'

'Good God, man,' Lord Bishopstoke broke in. 'You cannot mean to go through with this!'

'But I do.' Lord Jasper smiled again. 'The stake was suggested. It was freely accepted and I won.'

The enormity of what he had done began to strike Sir Thomas Broughton and he made a tentative suggestion that they return to the table. He had regained his earlier stakes, he said. Why should they not continue to play for those?

Lord Jasper laughed. 'No, Sir Thomas. I am well pleased with my winnings and, besides, the hour grows late. We will call our chairs and repair to your house for settlement. Gentlemen, good morning.'

Together they left the room.

Abigail did not relish being woken up in the very early hours of the morning and being told by the weary footman who had been obliged to wait up pending Sir Thomas' return, that her father required her attendance forthwith in the drawing-room. The footman thoughtfully added that Sir Thomas was accompanied by a gentleman.

This information might have given any other well-brought up young lady pause. Most would, at the very least, have checked their appearance in the looking-glass. Abigail, however, was inured by long custom to her father's unreasonable demands when he was in his cups. She thought it very likely he wanted nothing more than his boots removed and had drunkenly decided that the footman's tired gloves were not to touch them. True, he had never returned with a friend before but, since the friend would almost certainly be as drunk as Sir Thomas, she felt he could be dismissed from consideration.

Abigail therefore paused only to throw a wrap around her shoulders and push her feet into satin slippers before making her way to the drawing-room.

On the threshold she paused. It wasn't his boots this time, she noticed, for her father's attire was not that of someone who had been travelling and, although Sir Thomas certainly looked drunk, his companion did not appear so.

This companion, elegant in pale lilac satin embellished with silver thread, the hilt of his small dress-sword glittering with diamonds, was leaning casually against the carved marble sphinxes of the mantelpiece. He looked Abigail up and down in a manner she found most distasteful. There was nothing of the lecher in his look. It was more the cold, calculating stare with which one assessed the value of a horse, yet no observer would have been able to determine from his face Lord Jasper's estimate of the value to be put upon the slightly built girl who stood in the doorway, her guinea-gold curls tumbling on her shoulders and her pale complexion brought to life by blue eyes of such unusual depth of colour that they had more than once been compared to sapphires.

Abigail was already annoyed at being woken up and her annoyance was in no degree diminished when she recognised her father's companion. Any embarrassment his insolent stare might have caused, had he been a stranger, was wiped out by her anger that this particular visitor had had so little delicacy of feeling as to remain in the house after her father had sent for her. She directed a scorching glance at the visitor (a glance which left him quite uncharred if his expression were any indication) and addressed herself to her father.

'I see you are home, Papa. How pleasant! Since you are not wearing boots, you cannot require me to remove them. Perhaps you would be kind enough to tell me just what you do want so that I may return to bed.'

'Come in, come in. Don't hover,' her father said tetchily, his vague but expansive gestures underlining the first of these instructions. Abigail came fully into the room obediently enough, though a closer observer would have noted the unusually firm set of her mouth and a pronounced rigidity to her jaw.

'Lord Jasper: my daughter Abigail, with whom you are acquainted,' Sir Thomas said. 'Abby, Lord Jasper was most anxious to renew his acquaintance with you, so I brought him home with me.'

Anxiety did not appear to figure very large on Lord Jasper's face or

41

in his bearing. He still lounged against the mantel and made no attempt to greet her as common politeness might have dictated. Abigail hastily suppressed her instinctive curtsey and instead lifted her chin slightly.

'I cannot imagine why, Papa. You know my views on Lord Jasper. I made it perfectly plain a year or so ago, when his lordship was last in England, that I had no intention of allying myself with a reprobate such as he.' She turned to her father's visitor. 'I do not apologise for my plain speaking, my lord. I said as much to you last year and I have had no cause to change my opinion. One would have thought, however, that even a dissolute younger son might have chosen a more conventional hour for this visit.'

'Lord, Abby, this ain't a social call,' her father ejaculated. 'Lord Jasper is here on a matter of business.'

'Then I am at a loss to understand why he should be so anxious — you did use the word "anxious", Papa, did you not? — to renew our acquaintance. He doesn't look in the least anxious. Indeed, "uninterested" would be a more accurate word.'

Lord Jasper's voice interrupted, silky and urbane. 'No, Miss Broughton. Not uninterested.'

Sir Thomas, in no condition to appreciate subtleties, broke in. 'The point is, Abby, you are the matter of business concerned.'

'I?' she exclaimed. 'How can that be? What do I know of business?'

'Nothing at all, if I may judge by the way you rattle through your allowance,' her father replied, nettled. 'The thing is, Abby,' and here he began to perceive, even through his brandy-befuddled brain, that explanations could become a shade difficult. 'The thing is, Abby, the dice were against me and it was lose Merefield or lose you — and Lord Jasper kindly accepted you.' A satisfied smile spread across Sir Thomas's florid features at his success in so succinctly explaining matters.

Abigail stared at him blankly. 'I do not think I fully understand, Papa. Do you mean you have arranged a marriage for me with this man, knowing full well the abhorrence in which I hold him, and all because of an unlucky throw?'

'Not precisely *an* unlucky throw, Abby. It was an evening of unlucky throws. Lord Jasper had won everything: my money, my horses — even Merefield — and then exchanged them all for you as a last stake. Only that went against me, too,' he added bitterly.

'So I'm to marry Lord Jasper, am I?' she asked angrily. 'I am sorry, my lord, and I have no wish to be impolite, but I have no intention of marrying you at all and I do not believe either you or my father can force me to do so.'

42

For the first time since he had entered the room, Lord Jasper eased himself away from the supporting sphinxes and bowed slightly in her direction.

'I'm relieved to hear you say so, Miss Broughton,' he said softly. 'It would have been distasteful for me to have to tell you that marriage is not at present in my mind, either.'

Abigail felt herself blushing furiously as what she assumed to be the implications of this remark burst upon her. She turned to her father.

'Papa, you cannot mean that you have agreed that this man should give me *carte blanche*!'

'Oh, no, my dear,' he hastened to assure her. 'Nothing of that sort, I promise you.'

'Your father is right,' his lordship interrupted, and Abigail noticed that he seemed to be enjoying himself. 'If I wished to set up a mistress in this country, I should not choose her from the ranks of the aristocracy.'

'I'm relieved to hear it, my lord. Perhaps one of you would be so very kind as to explain just what arrangement you have made for me?'

'It's like this, Abby,' her father began awkwardly. 'Lord Jasper has estates – very large estates, I understand – in Virginia. The Americas, you know.'

'Yes, Papa. I am aware that Virginia is in the Americas and I'm impressed that his lordship's estates are very large. They must be a source of great satisfaction to him. What is all this to the point, pray?'

'The point, Miss Broughton, is simple,' Lord Jasper broke in. 'You are bonded to me for fifteen years as payment for your father's gaming debts. You will go out to my Virginia estates and work for me for fifteen years, receiving bed and board but no more. After fifteen years you will be free. You may then choose whether to make a life for yourself in Virginia, a free woman, or work for wages with which to pay your passage home.'

Abigail stared at him open-mouthed before looking from one to the other of the two men. Then, since her father did not deny this extraordinary explanation, she sat down in the nearest chair to absorb Lord Jasper's information. Finally she looked at each man in turn.

'You can't possibly be serious,' she said. 'This has to be some kind of jest.'

'I assure you there is nothing remotely humorous about it,' Lord Jasper replied. 'Indeed, I had forgotten how slight was your build and how fair your colouring and I must confess I now think you may not be entirely suitable for such a purpose. However, it is done now and I must live with it.'

'How magnanimous!' Abigail snapped. 'But you must have realised I was under age or my father could not have made this commitment.'

He bowed.

'This is ridiculous,' Abigail went on. 'I cannot believe it is happening. Such an arrangement cannot possibly be legal!'

'I assure you it is entirely lawful,' Lord Jasper told her blandly.

'Oh, that my brothers were out of the schoolroom!' Abigail exclaimed. 'I could then at least appeal to them for help!'

'They could certainly make life uncomfortable for your father, had they attained their majorities, but they could do nothing more, since you are entirely in the control of Sir Thomas,' Lord Jasper pointed out.

'That is so,' Sir Thomas hastened to agree and added, to forestall a natural extension of his daughter's train of thought, 'nor would an appeal to your uncles serve any useful purpose, for the same reason. I've no doubt they would bluster and badger and be generally unpleasant, but I should remain firm.' He concluded with a flourish of unjustifiable self-righteousness.

Abigail looked from one to the other of the two men. A faint hope she might have entertained that this was some hare-brained scheme that would fade with the dawn's sobriety, waned rapidly as she noted the mulish set of her father's jaw and the coldly unsympathetic grey eyes of his visitor.

She turned to the latter. 'Is this how you revenge yourself for my refusal of your unacceptable offer of marriage?'

Lord Jasper inclined his head slightly and there was a grimness about the thin-lipped smile he permitted himself. 'If you choose to think so, Miss Broughton.'

She stared at him, her despair deepening. 'What work will I do? I am quite handy with a needle,' she added helpfully.

Lord Jasper laughed. Like his voice, his laugh was soft and it struck Abigail as not being particularly pleasant. 'That will be up to my overseer, Jem Steventon,' he said. 'It is a tobacco plantation and we have plenty of house-help already. Of course, with your fair skin you may be more trouble than you're worth in the fields. Still, you seem healthy enough.'

She looked at him with a fulminating eye. 'And do I go with you now, my lord?' she asked acidly.

'No, that would never do. My man of business will be round with the relevant papers tomorrow. I am returning to Virginia on tomorrow's tide. You will follow in steerage as soon as he can arrange it. I believe there is a suitable vessel leaving some time next week.' He paused as if assessing what her reaction to this might be. 'I should perhaps explain that once these papers are signed, any attempt to run away would be to put yourself outside the law. I do not precisely recollect the punishment – hanging or deportation, I rather fancy – and of course, your father would be ruined. At least you have the satisfaction of knowing you will have ensured there will be something left for your young brothers to inherit – unless, of course, Sir Thomas finds the luck continues to run against him. If your man has gone to bed, I will see myself out. Your servant, Sir Thomas, Miss Broughton.'

Lord Jasper bowed to his host and nodded in Abigail's direction. Then he left the room and the house.

Chapter Two

Any ideas Abigail might have had that the whole scheme was a drunken joke were dispelled next morning by the arrival at an unwontedly early hour of Lord Jasper Cuddesdon's man of business, and any hope she might have clung to that her father, sober, would remedy what he had undertaken, drunk, were soon dashed.

'For goodness' sake, Abby,' he said tetchily. 'Do try to be reasonable. This was a wager between gentlemen. Would you have me renege on such an agreement?'

'I am at a complete loss to understand how two *gentlemen* can enter into a wager which involves the life of a third party who isn't even consulted about it,' Abigail retorted. 'I'm sure you have only to point out to Lord Jasper − tactfully, of course − that perhaps you were both somewhat carried away by . . . by the excitement and . . . and the brandy − a heady mixture, I'm sure − and Lord Jasper will realise it wasn't at all the thing and accept a more conventional stake.'

'Tell the man he was drunk?' Sir Thomas was plainly appalled at the prospect. 'Lord, Abby, I can't do that! Besides, I haven't got anything else to stake: he's won it all.'

'I dare say Lord Jasper is himself realising the impossibility of it all and would be only too happy if you were to offer him a reasonable alternative,' Abigail persisted.

'If his lordship is regretting it, why has he sent his man of business round to arrange the final details?' her father pointed out reasonably.

This was not an easy argument to refute but Abigail had no intention of giving up quite so soon and insisted on accompanying her father to his interview with the soberly dressed, self-effacing individual who was waiting for Sir Thomas in the morning-room.

Mr Humber permitted a small frown of displeasure to cross his unremarkable features when his host entered accompanied by his daughter. It was not for the likes of Mr Humber to criticise his betters

46

but he had found this whole scheme distasteful when Lord Jasper had informed him of it earlier that morning and had not been able to think of any reason for changing his mind between then and now. Miss Broughton's presence merely added embarrassment to negotiating the arrangements.

Abigail wasted no time in coming to the point. 'Mr Humber, this scheme that your employer and my father have dreamed up between them is quite clearly impossible. You look like a reasonable man. What can we do about it?'

'The wager was entirely legal, Miss Broughton,' he said apologetically.

'Quite possibly, but it certainly wasn't reasonable. Lord Jasper has presumably authorised you to negotiate some alternative.'

Mr Humber seemed to efface himself still further. 'I'm afraid not, Miss Broughton. His lordship was quite clear on the subject. I was first to make arrangements for your passage and then to inform your father of the nature of those arrangements. That is precisely what I have done and why I am here.'

Abigail gave an exasperated sigh. 'Was his lordship still drunk, then? I suppose he must have been!'

'His lordship was entirely sober.'

This was not an encouraging answer but Abigail was not going to give up yet. 'Then we must assume he hasn't had the opportunity of considering an alternative,' she said.

Mr Humber coughed apologetically. 'I did venture to draw his lordship's attention to the ... the unconventionality of his action, and to suggest that he and Sir Thomas might make some sort of mutually acceptable accommodation in the matter. My suggestion was not sympathetically received,' he added, recalling Lord Jasper's withering reminder that his function was to execute, not instigate.

Abigail stared at him, something close to panic welling up inside her. 'Are you sure Lord Jasper was fully aware of ... of all the implications?' she asked.

'Quite sure, Miss Broughton. Of course, if Sir Thomas refuses to honour the wager ...'

'He won't,' Abigail said bitterly. 'You know his lordship better than I, do you think it would do any good if I were to call on him and ask him to reconsider?'

'Such an action is impossible, Miss Broughton: Lord Jasper set out for Plymouth at dawn. You will not see him until you're in Virginia.'

Abigail took a very deep breath and clutched the back of a chair to steady herself. 'Then there is no more to be done save to learn of the arrangements you've made for me. When do I leave?'

'The brig, the *Alice Nancy*, leaves Lyme next Wednesday. That gives you just over a week. She's a trim little craft and her master, Captain Yazor, is a Cornishman and one of the best. He's carrying a cargo of fine cloths and a dozen or so indentured servants and he'll not distinguish your status from theirs.'

'You've been able to arrange my passage very quickly,' Abigail said doubtfully.

'Much of the cloth is being carried on Lord Jasper's behalf — there was no space left for it on his own schooner, the *Raven*. Captain Yazor will find room for you.'

Mr Humber's tone left no room for hopeful doubt. 'So it seems it is all settled,' Abigail said, hopelessness emptying her voice of expression.

'I have only to give you the wherewithal to reach Lyme and my part in the business is finished,' Mr Humber told her, handing her a small pouch, the contents of which clinked encouragingly as it changed hands.

'The impudence of the man!' Sir Thomas interjected. 'As if I'm not perfectly capable of conveying my own daughter to Lyme!'

'I think Lord Jasper took the view that, since Miss Broughton is now his . . . responsibility, it was up to him to provide the means,' Mr Humber said, tactfully omitting to mention his lordship's warning to deliver the purse into Miss Broughton's hands because if it fell into her father's, it was likely to be diverted from its purpose. 'If you would prefer to make your own arrangements, Sir Thomas, I'm sure Miss Broughton can make use of Lord Jasper's money to equip herself with a suitable wardrobe. I imagine the *Alice Nancy* can accommodate a small trunk, though neither bond-slaves nor indentured servants customarily have a great deal of baggage.'

Abigail stared at him in dismay, his comments having raised points to which she had given no thought at all. 'A suitable wardrobe!' she exclaimed. 'Mr Humber, I've no idea what will be suitable for Virginia. Obviously, you don't think my usual wardrobe is appropriate, so I shall need guidance. What do you suggest?'

Mr Humber shifted a little uneasily. 'To tell the truth, Miss Broughton, I've never been to the colonies so I'm hardly in a position to advise you. I understand the climate to be both hot and humid in the summer, far more so than an English summer's day. As to style,' he went on doubtfully, eyeing the elegance of her profuse satin skirts with some misgivings, 'you would do well to remember that your position in Lord Jasper's household will be rather different from what you're accustomed to here. I suggest the sort of clothes you would expect your maid to wear will be rather more fitting.'

Sir Thomas snorted at this suggestion but Abigail thanked Mr Humber, acknowledging that his advice, while it might be unpalatable, was certainly eminently sensible. When he had obtained Sir Thomas' signature to certain papers, he took his leave and Abigail withdrew to her own room to summon Maidstone.

It was not easy to explain the situation with dignity and without appearing to criticise her father, and Abigail's attempts quite failed to bamboozle the old woman.

'So it's come to this, has it?' she demanded. 'I always knew his gambling would bring down the family one day. Didn't I warn your sainted mother about it before she married him? "Don't be silly, Maidstone," she said. "Sir Thomas has a tendency to be a little wild but he'll grow out of it. I know he will." That's what she said. Grow out of it, indeed! Grow into it, more like. And now look where it's led. Your dear mother, as never harmed a fly, will be turning in her grave, and that's a fact. And who's this Lord Jasper Cuddesdon? I've heard that name before.' She frowned, searching her mind. 'I know, it's that man who offered for you last year and you turned him down. Is this how he gets his revenge? A nice beginning this'll be, forced to work for him when you could have been mistress of all he owns, though by all accounts that might not be very much, seeing as how he was sent there in the first place to get him away from certain ruin in England!'

'If that was why he was sent to the colonies, it seems to have worked,' Abigail pointed out gently. 'By all acounts, he now has considerable estates.'

Maidstone sniffed. 'That's as may be but you'll never convince me that a bit of wilderness in the colonies can compare with English acres.' A glance at her mistress' face told her that such remarks, while they might relieve her own feelings, were doing nothing to make Abigail feel any happier and she abruptly changed her tack. 'Enough of that,' she said. 'If that's what's happening, it's no use us bemoaning the fact. We've got less than a week to get things ready. It's a good job you're handy with your needle, Miss Abby, for we'll have to work together to see you well equipped for such an adventure.' She paused and looked speculatively at her mistress. 'You don't suppose his lordship has a mind to marry you after all once you get there?' she asked.

'No, I don't,' Abigail said firmly. 'He made that perfectly clear. Besides, if I disliked him last year, this action is hardly calculated to change my view, is it? When I marry – perhaps I should amend that to "if" – I shall take very good care to choose a man with more sympathetic characteristics. Possibly,' she added wistfully, 'one who loves me.'

It occurred to Maidstone that marriage to almost anyone might be infinitely preferable to life in a strange country as a bond-slave, but since no useful purpose would be served by expressing this opinion she kept her views to herself and set about sorting through Abigail's wardrobe to see whether there was very much that was either suitable as it stood or capable of adaptation.

Despite the clothes that Lady Fawler had provided to equip Abigail for her abruptly curtailed Season the previous year, it was not an extensive wardrobe and neither those clothes nor the ones needed for the life of the daughter of a near-bankrupt baronet were remotely like those required by any woman in service so in the afternoon, Abigail and her maid took themselves off to a cloth warehouse to choose fabrics which were more appropriate than satins, taffetas, silks and velvets. Only some lawns and dimities were considered in any way appropriate and once lace and bows had been removed, Abigail conceded that the resulting simplicity was not without its charm.

Abigail insisted that a large trunk would not be necessary since, if she now belonged to Lord Jasper, it must follows that he would see to it that she was clothed when her present wardrobe wore out or if it should prove entirely unsuitable for Virginia.

She allowed herself one totally unnecessary luxury: the heavily embroidered harebell-blue dress with its vast panniers that she had worn at the Drawing Room and the Birthday Ball – and the Duke of Cutteslow's musical evening, an occasion of which, though enjoyable enough in itself, she had no great wish to be reminded. It was a dress she was unlikely ever to wear again, even if she stayed in England. In Virginia, it could serve no purpose at all. Its appeal lay in the fact that it was without question the most beautiful gown she had ever possessed – or was now ever likely to possess. She might never wear it, but she could look at it sometimes, and feel it, and recall times past and what might have been. She chose to ignore the jarring fact that this was the gown she had been wearing on those occasions when Lord Jasper had first seen her. She would remember only the pleasant associations.

The only other item she packed, wrapped in soft suede and encased in a pouch of the same before being hidden within the folds of her workaday clothes, was the necklace of diamonds and sapphires bequeathed her by her mother. Sir Thomas had several times tried to persuade her to part with them and had renewed his efforts in the past week but she had stood firm. She loved them dearly, not for their intrinsic value, of which she had only a hazy idea, but because they were the only thing her mother had been able to leave her, Sir Thomas' depredations having taken everything else. It had always been her intention to fulfil her mother's expressed wish and leave them to her own daughter some day. Now, however, it seemed more probable that she might need to realise the value they represented, if only to pay her passage home when her fifteen years were over.

As she lay in bed, tossing and turning and quite unable to get to sleep, Abigail found herself suddenly wondering whether Lord Jasper's offer would have been made at all, had he not seen that necklace. A gamester himself, he must have formed a far shrewder estimate of its value than Abigail could. It was hardly the sort of consideration on which most men would have based an offer of marriage but Abigail thought of her father and knew that, if he were in sufficiently dire straits, he would have deemed it worth the chance. She had declined his offer as much because Lord Jasper was a known gambler as because of her dislike, knowing that the latter was based on nothing more substantial than a first impression – though admittedly a first impression reinforced by the fact that Lord Jasper had apparently thought it totally unnecessary for them to become better acquainted before making his offer.

Abigail sighed. She had previously seen marriage as her only escape. Now another route had been given her and it was not a gift which inspired gratitude.

Compared with what lay before her, she had led a sheltered life surrounded by members of her family and servants who had known her since infancy. She was going to a new world where there would certainly be plenty of other people, but all of them strangers, where she would no longer automatically know what was expected of her or even what, in her new situation, she was or was not permitted to do.

Tears welled up beneath her eyelids. They were partly tears of self-pity – an entirely justified self-pity, she told herself fiercely – and partly fear of the unknown. There were slaves in the Americas, not just bond-slaves. Abigail could not quite imagine a society where all the work was done by slaves or where all the people who did the work were black. Several fashionable ladies had blackamoor pages and she had heard that some had black footmen but these were not slaves. They might have started life as such but the law decreed that no one living in England could be a slave so, despite their outlandish appearance, as long as they remained here they were as free as anyone else. Then there were the savages who had occupied the country before Europeans civilised it. In the school-room Abigail had heard blood-curdling tales of what they could do to settlers and the thought of living in what must amount to a fortified village, always on the alert for incursions by these savages was not an appealing one, even though it might well be exciting.

She sniffed. What she really wanted was a man on a white horse to gallop through the window and snatch her up with protestations of having loved her from afar for years, intent upon rescuing her from the fate to which her father had condemned her. She lingered over this alluring vision for fully two minutes before common-sense intervened to point out that, since her bedroom was on the second floor, the horse would encounter certain practical difficulties and that, even if it overcame these – which was highly improbable – it would be so cut about by the glass that it would almost certainly have to be shot, which would render it useless for a romantic flight to the Scottish border. The whole imagined scene was so ludicrous that Abigail found herself smiling in spite of her misery and, apart from a sigh for the fact that there was no one who loved her enough to risk his horse – or even her father's anger – in order to ensure for her a predictable, conventional and contented future, her tears abated and she finally fell asleep.

Sir Thomas Broughton was not a sensitive man but even he began to feel a certain tension in the atmosphere as his daughter's time became more taken up with preparations for her departure than with the smooth running of his household.

'I really do have quite a lot to see to, Papa,' she protested mildly when he complained that boiled mutton had been set upon the table two days running. 'It means that Cook is single-handed so I told her to send up whatever was easiest. When I am gone you will have to find her additional help, you know.'

'It's no good pretending you're indispensable,' her father replied tetchily. 'It's far too late for such a ploy to alter anything. I did what I thought best to secure the future for my sons and, while I concede that you will have to make one or two sacrifices for a while – well, it's no more than your duty. And, in any case, I don't doubt that within a few weeks of landing you'll have found yourself a prosperous farmer and married him, and I shall have done you a favour after all.'

'Then you must regard boiled mutton as your own sacrifice,' Abigail told him sharply, knowing there was no purpose to be served by pointing out that they obviously viewed her new situation from different perspectives.

'Watch your tone, my girl,' he advised her. 'Lord Jasper won't be spoken to like that.' But it seemed as if her sharpness had had some small effect because Sir Thomas noticeably absented himself during the ensuing days and raised not the whisper of a protest when cold mutton made its reappearance on the family table.

The truth was that the baronet was slowly becoming aware of the enormity of what he had done. It was not Abigail's occasional tart comment that caused enlightenment slowly to dawn, but the manner with which he was recieved – or, to be more precise *not* received – by his erstwhile cronies. There were initially a few embarrassed attempts at jocularity designed to find out whether the whole thing had been no more than a tasteless joke, but when it became clear that both parties had been in earnest, word spread rapidly and Sir Thomas found himself virtually ostracised and without the slight relief that might have been afforded had he been able to exchange commiserations with Lord Jasper. Sir Thomas might be able to convince himself that he had acted entirely in the interests of his two small sons back in the schoolroom at Merefield but no one else seemed to share that conviction, and even Sir Thomas felt a small qualm of pity for his daughter when it became evident that she would not have time to go to Merefield and take leave of her two small brothers to whom she was very attached.

In order to make amends for this unavoidable fact, Sir Thomas magnanimously decided that, not only should Abigail have the use of the carriage to take her to Lyme, but he would accompany her to see her settled comfortably on the *Alice Nancy*.

Maidstone went with them on the two-day journey and was in tears the whole time, thereby adding nothing to her employer's comfort, and when the carriage finally rolled down the narrow cobbled streets and came to a halt before the Cobb, he too felt quite sad to think that he might never see his daughter again.

'We must face up to the possibility, Abby,' he said. 'I'm not a young man and fifteen years is quite a long time. You'll be in your prime, of course: thirty-three is a very good age in a woman, especially if she's taken care of herself, but we have to accept that I may not be here to greet you.'

Abigail forbore to ask him whether he thought a bond-slave was very likely to have much opportunity to 'take care of herself', and instead enquired whether he thought that rather handsome two-masted vessel was the *Alice Nancy* and, if so, whether he would accompany her on board.

Sir Thomas was happy to agree. He was surprised to find himself fast becoming maudlin, a state which he could not entirely understand, having had nothing to drink except madeira with dinner the previous evening and ale with his breakfast. He helped his daughter down from the carriage, followed by Maidstone, still alternately sniffing and sobbing, and together they made their way along the sloping curve of the Cobb.

Chapter Three

The *Alice Nancy* seemed large enough as they approached along the Cobb. It was only when Abigail realised how many people she would be carrying and for how many weeks that she also realised just how very cramped a voyage it was going to be. There were some twenty indentured servants to be housed on the lower of the two decks and immediately above the hold. At one end of this deck were the cramped quarters of the crew, the passengers being accommodated amidships and all the more cramped because propriety demanded that the men be housed separately from the women. At the stern of this deck, under the poop, were Captain Yazor's cabin and another for the use of any other passenger who could afford to pay for it. Captain Yazor was unusual in not only undertaking to feed his passengers but in fulfilling that commitment to the best of his ability. The food served to such as these indentured servants was monotonous but filling and adequate. The crew ate marginally better. The Captain, his First Mate, and any privileged passenger ate relatively well. Lord Jasper's choice of ship had not been arbitrary.

The Captain was a short, stocky man with the leathery features to be expected of any individual who has spent two-thirds of his life at sea. He paid no attention at all to the slight, cloaked figure that came aboard: indentured servants were of little interest to him; bond-slaves of even less. For either category of passenger to arrive with a coachman to carry her trunk was marginally more interesting but that was largely on account of the trunk, which represented a considerable inconvenience.

Far more intrigued, because there was little else to occupy his mind, was the passenger standing on the poop deck idly watching the bustle of activity prior to setting sail. He had observed the Broughton carriage draw rein on the cobbles leading to the Cobb and had noticed the crest on the door, though at this distance it was not possible to identify it. He had watched the descent of the coachman and the emergence of three figures, all cloaked against the stiff sea breeze as, indeed, he was himself.

When it became apparent that they were coming along the Cobb and not entering one of the hostelries on the harbour, his interest sharpened. The only ship of any size in harbour at that time was the *Alice Nancy* and from this distance it looked as if a family of three would be travelling with them. Lance Haworth frowned. Their mode of arrival did not suggest a family accustomed to travelling in any degree of squalor and he had the only passenger cabin of any consequence; nor had Captain Yazor given any indication that passengers of this class, even if they were somewhat impoverished (as, upon reflection and despite the carriage, they must be to be travelling in the remaining passenger accommodation), were expected.

He moved to the side of the deck closest to the Cobb for a better view, his tall, cloaked figure quite unobserved by the objects of his attention.

Abigail looked at the wooden gangway with trepidation and a sinking feeling in her stomach. It was, in fact, quite wide because it was used to bring cargo aboard at smaller ports, and barrels of rum and bales of cotton or tobacco need space, but to Abigail it seemed not only unnecessarily narrow but it bridged a sheer drop into the sea between the Cobb and the deck, with nothing at all to hang on to. She bade her father a polite farewell and dutifully kissed him. She was shocked that she felt no particular dismay at the prospect of not seeing him again for fifteen years. One was obliged to love one's parents and, of course, she did. Nevertheless, it was difficult to inject much emotion into taking leave of a father who had, in effect, sold one to finance his gambling.

Saying goodbye to Maidstone was quite different. The old servant had looked after her mother and, when Lady Broughton died, had virtually filled her place in so far as it was possible for anyone to do so. In the absence of anyone else to whom she could turn, it had been only natural that Abigail should seek the advice of one who had been her mother's nurse and who had, unusually, moved on to become maid to the mother, nurse to the daughter, and then maid again. Maidstone's advice had not always been welcome nor had Abigail always followed it, but it had invariably been sound and given with Abigail's best interests at heart. Leaving her was a wrench indeed and Abigail threw her arms round the old woman's neck in genuine and deep-seated affection.

'Oh, Maidstone, I shall miss you,' she said. 'Where will I be without you to tell me how I should go on?'

'There'll be plenty of others to do so for me, I don't doubt,' the old woman replied grimly. 'Just you pay heed to what you're told and do the best you can. More than that is what no one can expect, not even his lordship, if he's got any sense. Which I take leave to doubt,' she added. Then her voice softened. 'Now you get on board that boat, miss. Long leavetakings don't do anyone any good. Just a quick hug and don't look back, that's what's best.'

Abigail smiled tremulously. 'I believe you're just relieved it's me and not you that has to cross that plank,' she said, instinctively trying to lighten the atmosphere.

Maidstone looked at the gangplank and sniffed. 'I can certainly think of things I'd be happier doing. Now be off with you – and don't forget to write home sometimes. It's not only me as'll want to be hearing from you. I dare say your brothers will want to know what it's like. Your father'll be glad for reassurance, too, no doubt,' she added tactfully, though she privately doubted whether Sir Thomas would give very much thought to a topic which could only make him feel uneasy, no matter how well he thought he could justify his actions.

Abigail knew that her maid was right. She gave her a last hug and a kiss and then turned to tackle the gangplank, gratefully thanking the seaman who extended a hand to help her across. She had no desire to stay on deck until they should sail, no desire to wave goodbye to the two figures on the Cobb, though she guessed that Maidstone would insist they remained until the ship was out of sight. Instead she asked the sailor to take her to her cabin.

She had had no very precise idea what to expect on board except a vague impression that she would have to learn to master a hammock. She was therefore undecided whether to be relieved or disappointed to discover that the acquisition of this skill would not be necessary. The passengers were to sleep on what she could only describe as a narrow shelf. Her trunk was stowed beneath this and she was advised to lash it securely lest it move in a storm and either crush some unfortunate or cause the vessel to become unbalanced. This, the sailor informed her, would cause the *Alice Nancy* to capsize. 'And you'll get precious little thanks if that happens,' he added cheerfully. She was sure he was right.

Her fellow-passengers looked at her with anxious curiosity to be expected from a group of strangers thrust together in close proximity for several weeks. The very fact of this newcomer having a trunk caused a certain amount of resentful hostility, her travelling companions having their meagre possessions tied up in blankets at best and in a threadbare cloak at worst. It was true she was dressed in

56

a simple brown stuff gown which, like her hooded cloak, might have been worn by any servant but probably cost as much as a shilling a yard. Nor were her hands the hands of a woman accustomed to hard work. Whom she might be and why she was travelling with indentured servants was something they would soon set about discovering. In the meantime, they were a little reassured by Abigail's diffident smile and they made such preparations as they could to ensure a modicum of comfort before the *Alice Nancy* set sail and they faced the unknown rigours of a sea voyage.

Abigail was no less interested in her fellow passengers than they in her. Some were poor but obviously respectable, hoping for a better life on their own account or unwilling to be left behind while their husbands worked out their indentures, so they, too, had come over on similar terms, unaware of the distances between plantations in the colony, and expecting to see something of their husbands while they each worked for the day when they would be free to make their own future together. Some had sought indentured servitude as being preferable to an existence 'on the parish' at a level marginally above destitution. Two of the ladies were, Abigail suspected, very far from respectable and she guessed it might be wiser not to ponder too deeply the precise nature of their indentures.

These two, together with a girl who could not have been more than thirteen, rushed up on deck to watch the actual departure but the others stayed below, any delight in the prospects the future might hold outweighed by fear of the unknown and the inevitable sadness of leaving behind that which was familiar. Abigail had a brief impulse to join them. She knew Maidstone and her father would still be there and the temptation of one last glimpse was almost overwhelming. Almost but not quite. She had said goodbye. They would soon be out of sight. A last wave would achieve nothing except to deepen her melancholy − and the sooner she cast that away from her, the better.

The increased motion of the ship told those below when they had left the sheltering arms of the Cobb, and the transition from the relative calm of Lyme Bay to the open waters of the Channel was, though gradual, equally unmistakable. Like most of her companions, Abigail took refuge on her piece of shelf. Only the girl, Betty, seemed unaffected by the ship's motion. She came bouncing down into the cabin.

'It doesn't seem half so bad up top in the fresh air,' she assured them. 'In fact, it's quite exciting. You ought to come up and try it. See if I'm not right.'

The other women groaned. 'Go away, you little tormentor,' one of them called out. 'Go up and get washed overboard if you want to, but don't expect us to follow you.'

'No, honestly, it's not like that at all. You don't feel it half so much up there. In fact, I'm going back on deck — I'm beginning to feel as if my stomach's going to part company with the rest of me down here.' And with these inspiring words, she danced out again.

Abigail had groaned with the rest of them. She certainly felt far from well and the whole topic was not one upon which she had any desire to dwell, but the fact remained that the only one of their number who was seemingly unaffected by the effect of sea on ship was the one who had not remained below. She forced herself to sit up and felt her stomach lurch in counterbalance to a sudden dip of the prow. She sat on the edge of her 'shelf' for a few moments, waiting to see what effect her change of position had upon her stomach, and when she was satisfied that that organ had settled back in its proper place, she gingerly got to her feet and stood, swaying slightly and clutching at one of the wooden bulkheads for support. She made her way cautiously and unsteadily to the cabin door and paused at the foot of the companionway. Had she really come down that? It ascended almost vertically to the open deck above! A sudden gust of fresh sea air swept down through the hatchway and, as her lungs filled, the sensation of impending nausea receded. Perhaps Betty was right after all!

Abigail took a deep, determined breath, gathered up her skirt in one hand and tackled the steps.

As the pale gold of her curls emerged and caught the sunlight and her eyes drew level with the deck, she found herself looking at two expensively made and highly polished boots. The boots of a gentleman standing, legs apart, at the top of the companionway. She expected them to step back as more of her emerged but instead a hand reached down to take hers and steady her on the last few steps. The hand was at odds with the boots. It was not the hand of a gentleman.

Her eyes had become adjusted to the gloom below decks and it took some moments for them to get used to the much brighter light up here. In those moments, Lance Haworth had plenty of time to appreciate the figure which emerged, cloakless, on to the deck. He was unashamedly curious. Her slight build told him that this was the last passenger to come aboard, the one who, incongruously for an indentured servant, had arrived in a crested carriage. He now saw that there was a tantalising maturity to her otherwise slight figure. The curve of her breasts beneath the brown stuff gown was modestly concealed under a gauze fichu round her shoulders and tucked carefully into the bosom of her dress. In this light her hair was so fair that, apart from the sudden glints as the sun caught and held it, it might almost have been white. Her skin, too, was of a fairness that

58

many women achieved only with powder. Smooth, unblemished and unpainted, it was heightened by two enormous deep sapphire-blue eyes set wide apart and shaped, he thought suddenly, like those of a deer. It was not the sort of beauty that convention currently admired, but she was no less a beauty for that. The voyage's prospects looked decidedly more promising.

Abigail shook her head slightly as if to shake away the last effects of her sudden emergence into the sunlight and smiled hesitantly up at him.

'Thank you, sir. Without your help I fancy I should have stumbled and fallen.'

He laughed. 'I fancy you might well have done,' he said. His voice was deep and caressing, with an accent Abigail could not quite place but which was reminiscent of the West Country. 'Had you done so,' he continued, 'it would have been unfortunate; fallen women can cause problems in a small community such as we have on board.'

Abigail blushed. She was not accustomed to such remarks and had no idea how to respond to them. She had already come to the conclusion that at least two of her fellow passengers were perhaps not of untarnished virtue and had no desire to be reckoned another such. She drew herself up with as much dignity as the motion of the ship allowed.

'Your action was a kind one,' she said, coldly haughty. 'It is unfortunate you chose to spoil it with so unwarranted an innuendo.'

He looked down at her, the laughter gone from his eyes, and as the ship once more dipped and rose, his hand under her elbow steadied her again.

'My apologies, ma'am,' he said. 'Forgive me, but I can't help feeling that between decks is not your rightful milieu.'

'It is now,' she replied ruefully. 'In fact, I am creditably informed that it's better than I deserve. I'm travelling with indentured servants, you see.'

'I realise that, but even this short acquaintance is enough to tell me that you're no indentured servant. Far from it. Why should travelling as one be more than you deserve?'

Abigail flushed. 'I'm a bond-slave. I go to Virginia in lieu of my father's gaming debts.'

The man whistled his surprise. 'What sort of man lets his daughter make such a sacrifice?'

'A desperate one, I think. Perhaps one should rather enquire into the nature of a man who would accept a man's daughter in place of a debt.'

'There is no puzzle there' he told her. 'Not when the daughter is as beautiful as you. To whom are you bonded?'

'Lord Jasper Cuddesdon.' The stranger raised his eyebrows in surprise but said nothing. 'Are you acquainted with him?' Abigail persisted.

'I know him. The colony is large in area but small in population. I doubt whether there are any plantation owners who are not acquainted with one another. And you? How well do you know Lord Jasper?'

'I have met him, sir. I confess I can't help hoping that he spends most of his time in England now that his father receives him once more.'

'So you know something of his history,' the man commented. 'You'll be disappointed. Lord Jasper is no absentee plantation owner. He spends most of his time in Virginia, either on the plantation or at his house in Williamsburg.'

Abigail could only regret that her strict upbringing precluded her returning the frank stare with which he regarded her. She had to be content with snatched glimpses when the sun was behind her.

She liked what she saw. Her first impression has been of a very tall man and, from the grip that had helped her through the hatchway, a very strong one. His hair was black and curly and all the more striking because fashion decreed powdered wigs that made all men and women of fashion grey-haired. The deep tan of his skin threw his surprisingly grey eyes into sharp relief and he had an unfashionable and piratical moustache that made him look positively barbaric.

'You seem to know Virginia well,' she suggested tentatively, hoping the comment would elicit information not only about her companion but also about her future home.

She was not disappointed.

'It's been my home for more years than I choose to calculate,' he replied. 'I went out as a boy, an indentured servant like your companions. When I had worked through my indentures, I stayed on for wages.'

Abigail looked at him doubtfully. 'You don't look like a man who works for others, Mr ...?' she began.

'Haworth. Lance Haworth. I'm not. Once I was earning money, I was able to do a little buying and selling on my own account. Now I have my own plantation, Kingswood − I named it after the part of Bristol where I was born − and my own house in Williamsburg. I've been successful by any standards but I freely admit you'll find Lord Jasper's house the grander.'

Abigail gave a tight little smile. 'I don't think the degree of grandeur is going to bother me very much.' She looked around her, taking note for the first time of her surroundings. Down below, the sensation had been of a ship dipping and rolling in a heavy sea. Up here there was sufficient motion to make her a little unsteady, but instead of heaving waves there were merely gently excited wavelets through which the *Alice Nancy* ran at a comfortable speed before the brisk breeze. 'Betty was quite right,' she exclaimed. 'It doesn't feel nearly as bad up here.'

Lance Haworth laughed. 'You'll soon get used to it and if you keep out of the seamen's way, Captain Yazor won't mind your being up here. In heavy seas you'll have to stay below, though, and then you'll really know what it can be like.'

Abigail's inclination was to stay where she was, and not only because her stomach stayed in its rightful place. But Abigail had been brought up by the rules of propriety and it would take make than a few miles of sea-water to wash them away. She had already spent longer in unchaperoned conversation with a man than was decorous and it made not one whit of difference that there was no one else on deck at the time to include in the conversation and thus lessen its particularity.

She turned back towards the companionway. 'My apologies, Mr Haworth, but I really must go below.'

He made no attempt to stop her but instead she felt his hand under her elbow, strong and supportive. Abigail suddenly felt herself to be small and infinitely fragile and it was not an unpleasant feeling though she knew that, whatever her appearance might suggest, fragility was not one of her characteristics. She smiled up at him.

'Thank you,' she said and turned to step backwards on to the top step.

'You're supposed to go down a companionway facing forwards, not backwards,' he commented, a smile in his voice.

Abigail looked over her shoulder into the darkness of the deck below. 'Indeed? When I want to break my neck, I may very well try it that way. In the meantime, if you've no objection, sir, I'll use the method that feels safest.'

'I'll raise no objection but I'll ask one favour,' he said.

Abigail paused in her descent and stared at him, her sapphire eyes wide. 'A favour? What favour can you possibly seek from me?'

'The favour of knowing who you are. After all, I made no secret of my identity.'

'And there's none attached to mine,' Abigail laughed. 'I'm Abigail Broughton. Good day, Mr Haworth.'

Lance watched her disappear cautiously between decks. He had boarded in anticipation of a tedious voyage. It began to look as if that might be far from the case.

Abigail's return below was greeted with an urgent inquiry from Betty to know whether she had been correct about the advantages of fresh air.

'You were quite right,' Abigail assured her. 'I felt better the instant I was up there – and slightly worse as soon as the deck closed over my head again.'

'You see?' Betty exclaimed triumphantly. 'I told you so, and now, Miss . . .' She looked questioningly at Abigail. 'We don't know your name,' she said.

Abigail was on the brink of telling her she was Miss Broughton when it struck her that there was something ridiculous about a bond-slave expecting to be addressed by a title, even one so insignificant as 'Miss'. 'Abigail,' she said. 'Abigail Broughton.'

'Now Abigail's discovered I'm right after all,' Betty concluded triumphantly, but the other women remained unconvinced and greeted her assurances with more groans.

Abigail did not have a restful night. She found it impossible to fall into her customary deep sleep and had to be content with dozing for a few minutes at a time. There was no doubt in her mind as to the cause of her sleeplessess: the motion of the ship and the very fact of having to share her sleeping quarters was enough to account for it. Her common-sense told her it was a temporary inconvenience that sheer exhaustion would soon put right.

The motion of the *Alice Nancy* seemed stronger at night but Abigail, recalling how calm the sea had actually been the previous day, thought that might be due to the fact that she was lying down. This thought did nothing to allay her queasiness which was not helped by the illness of those around her.

A pail of sea-water was left at the cabin door so that the passengers could wash but Abigail was the only one to take advantage of it, Betty being disinclined to waste time on what she regarded as an entirely unnecessary function. Abigail decided it was a mixed blessing: the sea-water drew her skin taught, dry and uncomfortable and the prospect of several weeks with only salt water to wash in was not an encouraging one.

Her stomach decided against any breakfast, even so plain a one as Captain Yazor provided. Instead, Abigail made her way up the companionway and into the fresh air where she knew she would feel better. Knowing nothing of the sea, she had been unaware how quickly its mood can change. She had expected the breeze-ruffled wavelets and bright sunshine of the previous day. Instead, she found a grey, louring sky and a decidedly choppy sea that mirrored the sky's greyness. The *Alice Nancy* was running before what one of the seamen called 'a stiff breeze' but which Abigail felt would have been more accurately designated 'a strong wind.' As a consequence, the motion of the ship had, indeed, become stronger, and Abigail – who had still to find her sea-legs – was obliged to hang on to ropes, rails and on one occasion a sailor, in order to progress from one part of the deck to another.

There was no other passenger on deck and Abigail was conscious of considerable disappointment that Mr Haworth was not in evidence. She had not realised how much she had been looking forward to seeing him again until he wasn't there. She stayed on deck for some time, partly because it was more pleasant than the cabin full of seasick women and partly in the hope that he would eventually appear. Instead, it was Captain Yazor she found at her side.

'Lord Jasper's passenger, I think,' he said.

Abigail coloured, very conscious of the precise reason she was 'Lord Jasper's passenger', but unsure how much his lordship – or, more likely, his lordship's man of business – had told the Captain. She nodded.

'Then if you'll take my advice, miss, you'll go below and stay there for the time being. This weather can only worsen, and in bad weather you'll be a liability on deck. Not meaning to be unkind, miss, but as a simple matter of straight fact.'

'How bad will it be?' Abigail asked.

He shrugged. 'Bad enough to make you wish you'd stayed at home but, God willing, nothing the *Alice Nancy* can't take in her stride.'

'Then I must take your advice,' Abigail commented, 'though the cabin won't be very pleasant.'

Captain Yazor permitted himself the faintest of appreciative smiles.

'I'd not worry too much about that, if I were you: you'll be in no condition to notice.'

With these encouraging words, he moved away, leaving Abigail to contemplate with a sharpened eye the rolling clouds ahead. She shivered, wishing she had thought to bring her cloak with her and considered returning for it. There seemed little point. There was still no sign of the stranger and she realised the soundness of the Captain's advice. Abigail smiled to herself. It had been worded as advice and most tactfully put, but it had none the less been an order rather than a suggestion. She returned to the cabin.

Captain Yazor's forecast proved entirely accurate. The weather worsened rapidly and by evening the brig was pitching and tossing to a degree that Abigail would not have believed possible. Sleep was out of the question and so was food. They were advised of every meal as it was ready and could only groan. In a lucid moment Meg, one of the two women Abigail had privately judged to be of somewhat easier virtue than was generally recommended, expressed her opinion with some feeling.

'No wonder he can afford to include three meals a day in the price,' she said bitterly. 'He must know we'll none of us be in a position to eat any of it and if we try, he'll get it back with interest.'

The picture this remark conjured up was enough to call forth a communal groan and a plea from someone to button her lip if she didn't want to end up overboard in the next calm spell. Abigail was beginning to wonder if there ever would be another calm spell, and the only consolation she could find in her present wretched condition was that at least it was unobserved by Mr Haworth.

The advent of calmer weather was announced by a seaman who threw open their door and put two pails of water and some brooms inside the cabin.

'Come on, ladies,' he shouted cheerfully. 'Time to be up and doing. Swill the place down with this lot unless you want to travel in this stench for the rest of the voyage. There's plenty more water where this came from.'

It wasn't a pleasant chore and Abigail, who had never wielded a broom in her life, earned some curious stares but no overt comments. When the job was finished, the women washed themselves and did what they could to tidy themselves up. Those with husbands in the men's cabin made their way there to find out how their menfolk were coping. Their spirits were raised considerably by the ineptness of the male sex whose general incompetence was being guided by one Len Deeping, an ostler and the only one among them who could use a broom as naturally as he could breathe.

Abigail wrapped herself in her cloak and went on deck. It was bliss to be able to fill her lungs with great gulps of clean, salt air. The day was bright and clear and the sea, though very far from calm, was so much better than it had been that Abigail found herself using comparisons such as 'flat calm' and 'millpond' even though she knew perfectly well they were inaccurate. It was chilly, though, and she was glad she had thought to bring her cloak. She shivered slightly and drew it round her.

'Cold, Miss Broughton?' said a deep voice behind her. She turned and smiled up at Lance Haworth, unaware that so obviously genuine a smile added radiance to a face that had been merely beautiful.

'A little,' she confirmed. 'It's a small price to pay for being out of that noxious cabin.'

'I imagine it must be.' He smiled, too, and Abigail noticed how

64

white and even were his teeth in his tanned skin. When his hand under her elbow guided her to the side of the ship, it seemed the most natural thing in the world. It was only afterwards that she reflected that her acquaintances back in England would have condemned such a willingness to be led apart as fast.

'You survived the storms, then?' he inquired.

She laughed. 'So it would appear. An unpleasant experience, though, and one I hope not to have to repeat though, if I may be permitted a small, immodest boast ...'

'You intrigue me. Permission granted, of course.'

'I seem to have been a great deal *less* ill than any of the other women. That isn't saying very much, I suppose, but I must confess to a certain small pride in the fact.'

He bowed. 'Clearly one of Nature's good sailors.'

'Coming it rather too strong, Mr Haworth. Flattery should always be credible.'

He raised one eyebrow, conscious of surprise and a very slight feeling of unease. She looked demure enough. Malleable, even. Yet that riposte betrayed an unexpected worldliness, almost cynicism, that made him wonder whether he should revise his initial estimate of her. 'All the same, you would be well advised to take advantage of the better weather while you can,' he said. 'There's no telling how long it may last.' He guided her in a gentle promenade round the deck for all the world, Abigail thought, as if they had been in Bath, though she had a strong suspicion that Mr Haworth would not have recognised the aptness of the allusion should she make it aloud.

In the interminable hours of enforced incarceration during the storm, she had had time to ponder her future. It was not her immediate future that occupied her thoughts, for that seemed settled and it was unlikely she could alter in any way what Lord Jasper might decide to do with her. It was the future that would remain when her fifteen years were up that her mind had been dwelling on. This man lived in Virginia; he had gone there in a capacity not too far removed from her own; he said he had been successful and, while he did not flaunt such wealth as he might have acquired, he had the assurance that only money or birth could provide – and he made no claims to high birth. Who would better know what choices lay before her at the end of her servitude? She ventured to ask him.

He looked down at her quizzically. 'What would you be advised to do in fifteen years' time?' he asked. 'My dear, you will be an old woman.'

Abigail was indignant. 'I shall be thirty-three,' she retorted, 'and, while that is scarcely the first flush of youth, I assure you society is full of ladies of that age – and more – who would be most offended by such a description.'

'But they have not served fifteen years as a bond-slave,' he pointed out. There was no smile in his eyes or his voice, a fact which caused Abigail to feel an involuntary shiver down her spine.

'Then what do I do? What do indentured servants and bond-slaves do when their time is up? Do they return home?'

'Rarely, since they are in no financial position to buy their passage. Most take over a piece of wilderness, settle it, scratch a living and live worse than plantation slaves – much worse. If hunger and exhaustion don't kill them, fever does. They seldom make old bones.' He paused. 'A few make something of themselves. I did. But I am an exception.'

'What was there about your circumstances that created the exception?' she asked.

He hesitated, seeming reluctant to expand on the subject, almost as if he were weighing up the pro's and con's of telling her too much about himself.

'I was running wild on the streets of Bristol,' he said at last. 'I was pressed into indentured servitude from there. Did you know that happened – children just taken off the streets and shipped out as cheap labour?'

Abigail shook her head. 'I knew the Navy used such methods but I had no idea it extended further. What about your parents? Why did they not keep a closer eye on you?'

'I never knew my father and my mother had died a couple of years before,' he said shortly. 'I knew there was always a risk I'd be pressed – it's been a hazard in sea-ports for years. I counted myself lucky to have avoided it so long. I was ten when I was taken, and only fourteen when my time was up. Younger than you are before you begin,' he added as if to emphasise a difference in their circumstances. 'I've never been afraid of hard work and luck, on the whole, tends to run in my favour. That was the combination that made my fortune. I worked initially for a shrewd master and by watching and listening I learnt how best to turn pence into shillings and shillings into pounds. He never knew how close was the attention I paid him. By the time I was twenty-five I was in a position to buy him out so that he could retire. I'll never forget his face when I arrived with an offer. "I knew you'd been doing quite nicely, young Lance," he said, "but I never guessed it was this nicely." From then on, I never looked back and finally I was able to join the ranks of plantation owners.'

The justifiable pride in his voice told Abigail that plantation ownership, despite its inevitable associations with trade, must confer a similar standing in the colony to the ownership of English acres in English society.

She considered his story carefully, searching for any application it might have for herself. She looked doubtful. 'I suppose thirty-three would be rather late to attempt to set up on my own like that,' she said. 'Perhaps I might start a ... a rooming-house or something.'

He laughed. 'With what? First you must acquire capital, though in your case I suppose that might not be so difficult. After all, what is it they say? That every woman is sitting on a fortune − though after fifteen years in the tobacco fields even that might not be such a sure source as it would be if you could begin as soon as you land.'

Abigail frowned. She had absolutely no idea what he meant. 'I'm sorry, I don't follow you,' she said doubtfully. 'What exactly do you mean?'

For a brief moment she thought he was going to shrug and change the subject but then, without warning, he pulled her roughly to him and his mouth, hard and demanding, sought hers, a hand in her hair forcing her head back while the other slid caressingly down her back until it could force the lower part of her body into such close contact with his that she could feel his disturbing hardness pressing against her. The kiss itself was a very different thing from the careless pecks bestowed upon her in the past by father or uncles. Its strength was such that her own mouth was forced open and his tongue sought hers and toyed with it.

Abigail found herself prey to wildly conflicting emotions. She was outraged both at the action itself and the force employed; she was insulted at the illumination this crushing embrace cast upon his words; at the same time she suddenly knew that the sensations he had induced struck a chord within her, a chord of which she had been totally unaware until now and which urged her to respond, to soften in his arms and to let her mouth and body answer his.

Upbringing prevailed over instinct. She fought against him, though the strength in those arms was such that she knew she could not escape until he thought fit to release her. When that time came, she rounded on him furiously, her anger stoked by the consciousness that they were being watched by grinning and nudging fellow-passengers.

'How dare you!' she exclaimed. 'How dare you treat me like a common maidservant! I will have you know you are no gentleman, sir.'

'Indeed, I'm not − nor ever have been,' he replied good-humouredly. 'You, on the other hand, *are* now a common maidservant and you'd be well advised to remember it. Besides, you didn't find it altogether unpleasant, now did you?'

67

Abigail was not prepared to answer that question, even to herself. Blushing angrily, she turned her back on him and made her way as fast as the motion of the ship permitted to the companionway and thence to the shared cabin. A resounding and unrepentant burst of laughter followed her and she knew she would have to suffer the further humiliation of fending off the jibes of her fellow-passengers. She could only feel grateful that, once they landed, she need never meet any of them — or the odious Mr Haworth — again.

But Virginia was still a long way off and, as the days passed, Abigail could not escape the thought that, ungentlemanly as his behaviour might be, Lance Haworth was an infinitely more congenial companion than anyone else on board. Perhaps, with so little to occupy passengers, it was inevitable that he should almost invariably be on deck when she was and, though she knew she should avoid him, she told herself it was ridiculous to do so on so small a vessel. She could not quite admit to herself the fact that she did not want to avoid him, that there was something about him, be it his good humour, his piratically handsome face or simply the fact that she felt strangely at home in his company, that drew her irresistibly towards him.

For his part, Lance Haworth acknowledged the fascination of her beauty, her unaccustomed fairness and the potential promise offered by the unconsciously inviting curves of her unawakened body. He found, too, an added spice in the contrast between what she had been and what she had become. He was by no means loath to pursue the acquaintance.

Nor was Lance Haworth the only one. Only a few of the passengers were travelling with their spouses. Of the seven women, three were with their husbands, while Abigail, the child Betty and the two women, Jane and Meg, whose behaviour gave Abigail no reason to revise her first opinion of them, were all single. Of the thirteen men, only three had their wives with them. Of the remainder, some were unmarried and most of the others were hoping to be able to make some sort of a life for themselves when their indentures were completed, at which time they would send for their wives. Word of Lance Haworth's history soon found its way among them and they looked at him with a certain surreptitious admiration, a palpable example of what was possible in the colonies. In the meantime, they were without the home comforts a man had the right to expect and, while Jane and Meg could be coaxed without too much difficulty into relieving some of the tedium of the voyage — though not, as more than one of them found out, if Captain Yazor saw either woman slipping into the men's cabin — there was no denying that Abigail Broughton was a far tastier dish, with an appeal that was all the stronger because it was hitherto unsampled.

They began to lay bets on who should be the first to succeed and Len Deeping, the former ostler, got no thanks for his contribution to the discussion.

'She's a lady, no matter why she's travelling with the likes of us, and she'd not take a shine to the likes of any of you even if that Haworth man wasn't on board. As it is, it's my belief he's got his sights set in that direction and, if I'm right, you're all wasting your time.'

Privately, they acknowledged that he had a point and, that being so, the only solution was to achieve the desired goal first; to take rather than coax.

Abigail was oblivious to the interest and speculation she aroused. With the exception of Lance Haworth, she had taken about as much notice of the other men on board as she would have taken of the grooms and indoor servants at Merefield. That is to say, she was aware of their presence and always courteously bade them 'Good day' but it never crossed her mind to engage them in any conversation beyond an exchange of remarks about the weather. She certainly gave them no opportunity to pursue such an exchange and thus push their interest. The cards were stacked in Mr Haworth's favour, that was undeniable.

To be fair, most of the men had laid bets for no other reason than that is was yet another device for relieving the monotony of the voyage. They had no expectation of winning themselves — and no real intention of trying — but a more than passing curiosity to see who did.

Eden Paisley did not come into this category. A gamekeeper turned poacher who had fled to the West Country a few days ahead of his former employer's warrant and got himself indentured in Dorchester to the first advertisement he had seen and under an assumed name, he was accustomed to thinking of himself as quite a ladies' man. The basis for this high opinion of himself was largely his success among the girls in the small Norfolk village where he grew up. He was well-built, robust and ruddy-faced, and made up in vigour what he lacked in finesse. At all events, the village girls had never hinted at any lack of satisfaction, and he could think of no good reason why this Abigail Broughton should complain. He rated his chances of success pretty high and if he could beat Haworth to it, she'd probably be drooling over him for the rest of the voyage like any village wench.

It remained to beat Lance Haworth to it, and to that end Eden Paisley watched his prey with as much care as any successful poacher. Ships are places run on routine and people travelling on them soon establish a routine of their own to fit in with that of the more important one which runs the vessel so efficiently. Abigail always strolled on deck in the evening if the weather permitted it, deferring as long as possible the moment when she must go below to an airless cabin lit only by a rank-smelling lamp. Very often, though not invariably, she was joined by Lance, and Eden had decided to make his move on the first evening that gentleman was not in evidence, taking full advantage of the deeper shadows and uncertain outlines of dusk. It would have been better if he could have been sure of getting her on her own down below but there were plenty of discreet corners on deck and only Captain Yazor to worry about. Word of the bets had filtered through to the crew who had laid a few of their own. None of them would give the game away.

When he judged the circumstances were right, Eden slipped out of the shadows and stood beside her at the rail.

'Pleasant evening,' he remarked.

'It is, isn't it?' Abigail replied affably.

He moved imperceptibly closer. 'Almost makes the voyage seem worth while.'

'Do you think so?' Abigail made no attempt to hide her surprise. 'I'd say it makes it barely tolerable, though I suppose it may prove preferable to whatever awaits us in Virginia.'

'I didn't know you felt like that,' Eden said, moving closer still. Abigail moved very slightly away from him. She had no desire to seem rude and perhaps he saw nothing indecorous in standing so close. She was prepared to give him the benefit of the doubt but she did not feel easy in quite such close proximity.

'Don't you feel anxious about what's in store for you?'

He shrugged. 'It can't be worse than what I've left behind. Different for you, I suppose. What you need is a strong arm to lean on.' And, presumably to illustrate his point, he slid his arm under her cloak and round her waist.

When Abigail tried to slide discreetly out of his hold and found it tightened as she did so, she was prepared to concede that he certainly possessed a strong arm. It was not one she had the slightest desire to lean on. She made another futile attempt to extricate herself and finally said, 'I'd be obliged if you'd let go of me. I've no need of support at this precise moment.'

'Maybe not, but a bit of comfort wouldn't come amiss, now would it? I can show you plenty of that.' His voice was little more than a whisper now. It was intended to coax her but to Abigail's ears it contained a hint of menace. She made a more determined effort to get away from him and this time found his free hand had grasped her wrist. He pulled her the few feet into the shadows cast by the superstructure at the prow. No one was likely to interrupt them here, save perhaps the occasional seaman paying a quick visit to the heads. Deep in the shadows, he pushed her back against the timbers and, as his mouth descended on hers and his hand fumbled briefly at her breast before reaching for her skirts, Abigail suddenly realised the precise nature of his intentions.

'No!' she cried out. She twisted as sharply and suddenly as she could but it was no use. Eden Paisley was no weakling. She opened her mouth and screamed. Surely in so confined a space as the *Alice Nancy* someone must hear her? She was able to scream once more before her assailant's hand closed over her mouth. Frantically, she tried to escape his clutches but he had chosen his spot well and she was crushed into a corner. Her only advantage was that the necessity of keeping one hand over her mouth left the former gamekeeper with only one hand to fumble with her skirts and his own breeches. He could have ripped the skirt off, of course, but then he would have had some difficulty convincing anyone that she had been a willing partner, whatever claims she might choose to make to the contrary. He had an idea that the punishment Captain Yazor might hand out for such an assault would be at least as bad as the one he was fleeing from. There must be no torn clothing.

Abigail was not prepared to give up her struggle and finally, after what seemed an age but was actually only a few minutes, she had an opportunity of sorts when the hand over her mouth fractionally slipped. She still could not open it sufficiently far to call out to any effect, but it was enough to be able to grab the edge of his hand with her teeth. She sunk her teeth into the flesh and, as he cried out in surprise and pain, she screamed as well and was rewarded with the sound of boots running along the deck.

The next moment, Eden Paisley was sprawled among the yards nursing that side of his head which Lance Haworth's blow had struck. Haworth, his tall silhouette, a block of denser dark against the still starless night, loomed over her.

'Are you all right?'

'A little shaken. More than a little,' she added candidly, suddenly aware that her teeth were beginning to chatter.

Other curious faces were peering down at the little group in the prow and Lance seemed to sense her embarrassment at the array of witnesses, all of whom were perfectly capable of putting two and two together and correctly interpreting the scene before them. He drew from her corner and arranged her cloak so that it enveloped her completely and any disarray was completely hidden.

'Come with me,' he said, leading her through the small crowd of onlookers. 'I know what you need.'

'What about him?' Abigail asked, nodding her head towards Eden Paisley who was still sprawled where he had fallen. 'Is he hurt?'

'I sincerely hope so. Don't you?'

'I suppose so. Yes, of course.' She shivered involuntarily and felt his arm round her shoulders tighten its hold infinitesimally, offering reassurance, even comfort.

As they made their way aft, they encountered Captain Yazor who had been alerted to the kerfuffle and had come to investigate. He quickly took in the situation.

'What's happened? Are you all right, Miss Broughton? Who else was involved?'

'One of the male passengers,' Lance told him. 'Inevitable, I suppose, but he's now wishing he hadn't. Miss Broughton seems to have coped but she's a little shaken. I've some rum in my cabin that will steady her.'

The Captain nodded. 'Best thing for it. I'll deal with the other party. Thank God it wasn't one of my crew.'

Abigail had never tasted rum and she was not at all sure she liked it but there was no denying the soothing effect as its warmth crept through her veins. The second glass she accepted with reluctance.

'Sip it slowly,' Lance told her. 'You won't need any more. You'll have had enough to send you to sleep in a warm glow, and by morning you'll feel more yourself. You'd better sleep here. You won't want to go back among those grinning, gawping women.'

Abigail coloured. 'No,' she said. 'It's out of the question. It would be most indecorous.' But she looked longingly at the luxuriously appointed cabin and acknowledged privately that she would much rather not have to face her companions just yet.

'I wasn't proposing to sleep here as well, if that's what's bothering you,' he said. 'I'll have a word with the Master. No doubt he'll find me a spare berth somewhere.'

Abigail was still doubtful, though the reasons for her doubts had changed. It seemed an unbelievably generous offer – and an unexpected gentlemanly one, too. She looked at the box bed with its down mattress, and was lost. She smiled diffidently. 'If you're really *sure* ...' she began and then smiled more confidently. 'To be truthful, I don't think I could bring myself to decline.'

'Then that's settled. I'll wish you sweet dreams that will consign this evening's events into a well-deserved oblivion. Good night, Abby.'

Abigail coloured self-consciously at his apparently unconscious use of the diminutive that she had never before heard on any lips save those of her family. 'Good night, Mr Haworth – and thank you.'

Lance Haworth closed the cabin door behind him with a smile of satisfaction. That young blackguard Paisley had behaved abominably and thoroughly deserved to have his plans thwarted but it looked as if he had inadvertently done Abby's saviour a favour. There was no doubt in his mind that the present situation was one which he could turn very much to his own advantage.

Abigail undressed down to her chemise and climbed gratefully into the box bed. It was harder than she was accustomed to at Merefield but an incalculable improvement of the shared 'shelf' in the communal cabin. She could stretch out or curl up with equal comfort though she supposed, as she luxuriated in the comfort, that Lance Haworth found it quite cramped. She snuggled between the sheets, the warmth induced by the rum now enhanced by the warmth of the bed. The combined glow permeated her mind as well as her body. Her father – and undoubtedly the cold Lord Jasper – might have respected Lane Haworth's wealth and business acumen but neither would have considered him a fit person with whom to associate socially. Abigail herself found it difficult to overcome the reservations her upbringing had instilled on the subject. Nevertheless, the fact remained that it had been a gentleman – her own father – who had 'sold' her, and another one – Lord Jasper – who had, to all intents and purposes, 'bought' her. The only man who was not a gentleman was the one who had behaved as a gentleman should. Not invariably, as she was obliged to admit, but when it had really mattered, Lance Haworth had behaved as he ought. If that was how colonial men behaved – even those engaged in trade – life in the colony might not be so bad after all. For some reason, possibly associated with two glasses of rum, it failed to occur to her that Lord Jasper, too, was a resident of the colony.

She turned, smiling drowsily to herself. An image of Lance Haworth's piratical features, his white teeth gleaming beneath his black moustache, floated into her head. She remembered the security of his grip when he had helped her through the hatchway the day they met, the comfort of his arm around her shoulders that very evening. She recalled, too, the feel of his body against hers on that inexcusable occasion when he had not behaved with complete propriety. What was it he had said at the time? That she had not found it unpleasant? Something like that, and the chastening thing was, he was right. She had been indignant at the time, though she hadn't said so, but if she was quite honest with herself – and Abigail always tried to be quite honest with herself – she would not be entirely averse to a repetition of the incident, though perhaps without an audience.

Why was it, then, that she felt so very differently about Eden Pasiley's advances which had been of a not dissimilar nature? She had not had the slightest desire to respond in any degree to his embrace and it had been just as unexpected and just as violent as Lance Haworth's. Perhaps it was the fact that Lance Haworth had taken advantage of her in broad daylight and before several spectators; there had been nothing underhand or secretive about it – and he most assuredly could not have carried it to its logical conclusion. Eden Paisley's assault on her person had been a very different matter and all the more frightening because she had never said more than 'Good morning' to him or done anything at all which might lead him to think such an approach would be welcome. Despite the warmth, she shivered. She would take good care to avoid him in future. Perhaps it would be wise to stay in the women's cabin. That way there could be no room for misunderstanding with any of the other men on board.

No, she couldn't do that. If she did, she wouldn't see Lance Haworth again. It was hard to see how she could be more circumspect than she already was, but she would try. She was unlikely to see much of Lance once they arrived in Virginia. She was not going to throw away opportunities to do so on the voyage. It was the memory of his face, still smiling, that accompanied her into a deep sleep.

She need not have worried about encountering the Norfolk gamekeeping poacher again. The circumstance of the man's being indentured to someone in the colony, who might reasonably be annoyed to find his investment had been hanged from the main yard-arm, was the only one which inhibited Captain Yazor's natural instinct to exact that punishment. Instead, the ship's carpenter was instructed to make a temporary brig down in the hold and there Eden Paisley languished for the rest of the voyage.

Abigail slept long into the next morning, not stirring until a succession of sharp raps at the cabin door woke her up. In answer to her call, the door was opened by the cabin's normal occupant who then stood aside to let in a seaman with a loaded tray.

'Breakfast, Abby?' Lance asked.

Abigail sat up in bed and then, realising that she was wearing only her chemise and had no wrap, clutched the sheet to her throat.

'Thank you,' she said. 'I shall enjoy that.'

She noticed that there was wine instead of beer, slices of ham and a little golden pile of scrambled egg, both delicacies not covered in the passage-money of indentured servants, though they knew the chicken coops on deck provided eggs for someone. The coarse bread to which she had become accustomed on board was here accompanied by the luxury of butter.

Lance picked the high-sided tray up from the table where it had been placed and brought it over to her. 'You can let go of that sheet, you know. You're perfectly decently covered.'

'I know, but it's not quite ... I mean, I shouldn't ... you shouldn't ...' Her voice tailed off. It seemed so churlish to protest.

'I shouldn't be here and you shouldn't be receiving me in your night clothes. Very true. The point is, who's to know?'

'It isn't the point at all!' Abigail protested. 'In any case, we both know, and that's enough.'

Lance looked down at her and smiled. 'Well, you're obviously not going to tell anyone and if I undertake not to do so, either, no one will be any the wiser. Forget convention, my dear. Just enjoy your breakfast before it gets cold.'

Abigail was disinclined to make an issue of it, though she felt guilty because she knew she ought. She fell to, suddenly ravenous but not so entirely oblivious of propriety as to fail to appreciate the fact that her host turned his back on her and stared out of the great stern windows in silence while she demolished the meal.

Not till he heard her knife and fork come to rest on the plate did he turn round. 'I thought it was considered indelicate for a lady to clear her plate,' he commented.

'It is. Very − but I'm not going to tell anyone and I hope you will undertake not to do so, either,' she replied pointedly.

'Agreed. I'm glad to see you can throw off the standards you were brought up with. It's a talent you'll need to make much use of in Virginia.'

'Really? Do the colonists pay so little regard to the standards of their homeland?'

'The upper reaches of Virginian society can be even greater sticklers than in London. They dread being thought of as provincial, you see, though sometimes their standards slip through ignorance or false assumptions which men such as your new master must be aware of but choose to accept. You, however, will not be moving in the upper reaches, will you? I promise you that lower down the ladder things are very different. You will need to adapt. I rather fancy you will succeed.'

Abigail was undecided whether his comments ranked as bald statements of fact or as threats, nor was she quite sure whether his final remark was altogether complimentary. Before she had made up her mind whether to ask him to elucidate, there was another tap on the door.

Without referring to her, Lance stepped over and opened it, admitting a seaman and Abigail's trunk.

'Tuck it away over there,' he said. He turned to her. 'I took the liberty of sending for it. You'll be more comfortable here than in that cramped cabin below and I don't think it would be a good idea to leave the trunk there while its owner is elsewhere.'

That was unarguable but Abigail coloured at the inference of his words.

'That's very thoughtful, Mr Haworth, but I can hardly share this cabin. I may well have to adapt to survive in Virginia but we're not there yet. In any case, that would not be the sort of adaptation I envisage.'

He smiled and seemed neither surprised nor discomposed. 'I've made other arrangements for myself,' he told her. 'You may rest assured I've no intention of forcing myself upon you or, indeed, of compromising you in any way without your consent.'

Since Abigail could not immediately conceive of a situation in which he could do either *with* her consent, she was a little nonplussed by this. The offer of this cabin for the rest of the voyage was one she would have great difficulty rejecting but she couldn't offer to pay for it and she felt very guilty at the thought that Lance Haworth would have to travel in the men's crowded cabin.

'It doesn't seem right that you should have to travel as an indentured servant again while a mere bond-slave travels in luxury,' she said doubtfully.

'Don't worry, I shan't. I've arranged to share a cabin with the Mate.' He hesitated as if he had something more to say but was uncertain how it would be received. 'I'd be grateful for one small favour, though,' he said.

'One I will gladly grant if I can,' Abigail told him, feeling that the qualification sounded churlish in the light of such generosity.

'I'd like to be able to share the use of this cabin in the daytime when I need to get away from our fellows.'

Abigail hesitated. It was a reasonable request in the circumstances even if it was somewhat outside the bounds of strict propriety. Still, she supposed she could always go on deck whenever he needed to make use of it. 'Of course,' she smiled. 'Whenever you like.'

Lance thanked her, then bowed and took his leave. 'I'll get them to send you some water,' he said as he departed, leaving Abigail to consider this change in her fortunes.

She washed and dressed at her leisure, enjoying the unwonted luxury of time and privacy. She still felt guilty that her presence here kept Lance Haworth from his own cabin, and was ashamed to realise that the guilt diminished as her pleasure in being here increased. She told herself that he had given up his quarters entirely of his own volition, a fact which spoke well of his basic good nature. It crossed her mind uneasily — but very briefly — that a man who started with nothing and became as rich as Mr Haworth seemed to have done was unlikely to be noted for sudden kindnesses to those who could be of no possible use to him, but she rejected the thought. It was unworthy and, besides, he would be continuing to use the cabin during the day-time, thus reducing his inconvenience to the minimum. She resolved not to let him think any awkwardness attended his continued use of the cabin: when he came in, she would take up her cloak and leave. If the weather was fine, she would go on deck. If not, she was sure the other women would be prepared to let her rejoin them until evening.

For the rest of that day, however, she had the cabin to herself. A light luncheon was brought her on a tray — the unusual privilege due to the unfortunate experience she had had, the seaman who brought it told her — and it was accompanied by an invitation to join Captain Yazor for supper. Abigail correctly interpreted this as being a polite way of indicating that no further meals would be served on a tray and told the seaman she would be happy to do so.

On a brig the size of the *Alice Nancy,* the only officers were the Captain and his Mate and, since one of them must be on deck at any given time, this meant that only the Captain himself, Lance Haworth and Abigail were assembled at the table in the Ward Robe for the evening meal. In earlier times, when all merchantmen had been armed, this cabin, situated just under the Great Cabins of the Captain and his adjacent passenger, had been used to store valuables taken as prizes from rival merchantmen. Nowadays it was increasingly used as a mess and, as Captain Yazor explained to Abigail, in the Naval fleet almost exclusively so.

Conversation was general and only became particular when Captain Yazor referred to the arrangements he was making to accommodate Eden Paisley.

'So you see, my dear, you needn't be afraid you will have to meet him if you choose to go about the ship,' he assured her.

'That will be a comfort, I must admit,' Abigail replied. 'I don't envy him his incarceration.'

'It's no more than he deserves,' the Captain said severely. 'Had it been one of the crew, I'd have hanged him.'

Abigail shuddered and the conversation turned to happier subjects.

When the meal was over and the Captain had left to relieve his Mate, Lance accompanied Abigail on deck and they made a few leisurely turns in a companionable silence which neither of them saw

77

any need to break. When their gentle stroll brought them back to the short companionway leading down to the cabin, Abigail paused.

'I'll bid you good-night, Mr Haworth.' She looked up at him. 'I really am exceedingly grateful to you for your generosity. I only wish I knew how to thank you more adequately.'

He smiled, his teeth under that piratical moustache gleaming in the moonlight.

'Don't give it a thought,' he said. 'It's my pleasure to be able to be of service — especially to so beautiful a woman.'

Abigail coloured. 'Don't spoil a kind gesture with flattery,' she remonstrated. 'I don't think flattery comes easily to you and it somehow manages to sound ... not insincere, precisely, but ... ulterior. As if you had some underlying purpose in using it.'

'And one which is not altogether laudable, is that what you mean?'

Put as bluntly as that it sounded far from grateful but he had summed up precisely what had been in Abigail's mind, and she said so.

He seemed to find this amusing, for he laughed. 'It will serve me right for trying to ape my betters,' he said. 'I thought women of your stamp expected flattery but I'll freely admit it's not something that comes easily to me. Lord Jasper would no doubt be more adept at it.'

Abigail frowned. The introduction of Lord Jasper's name was not welcome. She was trying to put him out of her mind for these last few weeks before she would be obliged to think about him. 'I don't know that he uses it at all,' she said consideringly. 'I don't know him very well, of course, but my observation is that he says very little and that little is very much to the point. I can't imagine him paying a compliment, but if he did, I rather fancy it would be sincere.'

'Quite a character reference,' Lance commented drily.

'Is it? Then it must be the only one he's ever had,' she said with some asperity. 'Good night, Mr Haworth.'

'Good night, Abby. Rest assured I'll not try my hand at flattery again.'

Abigail laughed as she turned from him and was still smiling when she closed the door. It had really been a very pleasant evening.

Lance Haworth was smiling, too, as he returned to the Mate's cabin. For him it had been a very successful evening, one way and another.

The weather continued fine for the next few days, though windy, and Abigail was able to adhere to her plan of enabling Lance to have unhindered use of his cabin. They only met in the Ward Robe. Invariably after supper they strolled together on the deck, sometimes in silence, sometimes talking of nothing in particular, and Abigail found herself looking forward to these evening interludes.

Then the weather changed. The First Mate warned her at breakfast that when she went on deck she would find a very different sort of day from that to which she had become accustomed. 'There's squalls ahead, and like as not worse,' he said. 'If it's fresh air you're after, you'd better take advantage of it while you can. I doubt it'll last much longer.'

Abigail took good care to wrap her cloak about her before going on deck and thought she was well protected but, as her head emerged above the companionway, a strong wind took her breath away and blew her hood from her head. The sky was overcast and leaden and was reflected in the leaden, sullen sea. Gone were the wind-whippéd, white-capped wavelets she had become accustomed to. In their place was a surly, heaving ocean. To Abigail's inexperienced eye, the *Alice Nancy* rode the swell effortlessly but she noticed that she was the only passenger on deck and that there were far more crewmen about than was customary. She took care to keep out of their way.

Despite the threatening sky and unpromising sea, Abigail found it exhilarating to be on deck in so strong a wind, even though she was forced from time to time to cling on to mast or rail in order to remain erect. It was very different from anything she had known before but in some strange way it represented a challenge. Abigail found it exciting.

The squall hit them suddenly and, so far as Abigail was concerned, unexpectedly. A wall of rain descended on them and enveloped them, battering eyelids shut and destroying visibility so that, even when Abigail forced her eyes open, there was nothing to see beyond a foot or two. She had barely time to catch her breath before she was drenched and she knew that she had no business on deck while the storm lasted — and that the crew were far too busy to assist her back to the cabin.

Fortunately, neither wind nor deluge had disorientated her and she was at least at the right end of the ship. The few steps aft into the storm which had followed and overtaken the *Alice Nancy* were the most difficult steps she had even taken and she crouched over the entrance to the companionway in some relief. She had taught herself to descend companionways in the correct manner but in this wind she needed the added security of clinging on to the sides and she had no hesitation in returning to the landsman's scorned technique. At the bottom of the steps, she paused in the sudden calm. The ship was pitching and tossing, of course, but the gale was absent and, although common-sense told her it must be so, it nevertheless came as a surprise, so all-pervading had the winds seemed on deck. She opened the cabin door and went in.

Lance Haworth stood up as she entered. 'The Mate's forecast was correct, I see.'

'Forgive me for interrupting you, Mr Haworth,' Abigail said apologetically, noticing that he had obviously been writing at the small table. 'I wouldn't have believed it possible to get so wet so quickly and am come to take my cloak off.' She fumbled with the cords that tied it at her throat but they were too wet and her fingers too numbed to be effective.

'Here, let me,' Lance said. He towered over her, dwarfing both Abigail and a cabin built for men of less than average height. Abigail tilted her chin to enable him to get at the knot, in much the same way as a child stands for parent or nurse in a similar situation.

The task accomplished, he tossed the wet cloak onto the floor. Then he put out his hand and touched her damp, fair curls. 'There's something remarkably appealing about a woman with her hair still wet,' he said. 'It makes her look so vulnerable.'

It was said in the tones of one who simply thinks aloud and Abigail coloured self-consciously. 'I don't think you should say such things, Mr Haworth. If you draw attention to a woman's vulnerability, you draw attention also to her helplessness.'

'I make no apologies for drawing attention to that aspect of womanhood which I find the most attractive. I promise you, it awakens the protective instincts in me rather than the aggressive ones.'

'I'm relieved to hear it,' Abigail said with some asperity. 'The fact of your having mentioned it, however, makes me very conscious that I am to a great extent at your mercy as well as in your debt.'

He laughed. 'You've no need to depend on my mercy and you're not in my debt — at all events, I don't see it like that. There's one promise I can make, if it will make you easier: nothing will ever happen between us that you don't desire as much as I.'

There was a tenderness in his laughing tones that made Abigail's heart give a little jump and she looked up at him questioningly.

He looked down her, the smile lingering in his brown eyes, and then gently, very gently, he drew her to him. Gently, very gently, his strong arms enfolded her regardless of the gown that was as wet as her recently discarded cloak. He kissed her, gently, yet with a lingering strength in his gentleness that erased any last remnants of resistance to his embrace that she might have felt obliged to put up.

Abigail gave herself to his arms and his kisses without reserve, and knew suddenly that the anger his earlier embrace had induced was in

80

truth more at the manner of it than at the fact. She knew, too, that this was what she had longed for: the strength and tenderness of this man's arms around her, as if he would protect her from all the storms into which life might toss her.

It seemed to her suddenly that this voyage was simply the calm eye of one of those storms. She might be free to love Lance Haworth — for she did not doubt that love was what she felt — but she was not free to allow that love to reach its final conclusion. She was bound to Lord Jasper Cuddesdon, that cold, sardonic gamester, and it would be fifteen years before she was free of him.

This realisation made her pull infinitesimally away from Lance and he glanced down at her, perturbed at the expression he saw.

'What troubles you, Abby, my dear,' he said gently.

She gave a brief, unhappy smile. 'Nothing,' she lied. 'Nothing I can do anything about, at all events,' she amended more truthfully.

'Perhaps I can,' he suggested.

'I was remembering that I'm no longer free,' she told him. 'For the next fifteen years I belong to Lord Jasper.'

'A depressing thought indeed. Contemplate this instead: Lord Jasper may own you; by the same token, he can sell you. Is that not an infinitely more optimistic thought?'

Abigail considered it. 'I suppose so,' she said at last. 'It would depend very much upon the nature of the person to whom he sold me, wouldn't it?'

'That's certainly unarguable. Let's consider more pleasant matters. Are you going to continue keeping out of my way all day long, as you have been doing?'

Abigail smiled up at him. 'I don't think I'll be able to. Indeed, I fancy my problem will be to greet you with the proper decorum. Will you mind?'

'I think I'll be able to bear it with equanimity. Of course, having clasped so wet a female to me for so long, I may well develop a chill and need nursing rather than converse.'

'Then you'll be nursed by one of the crew for if *you* stand in danger of a chill, how much greater must *my* danger be!'

'Very true. Such selfishness in staying here when you should be getting into something warm and dry is inexcusable.' He raised her fingers to his lips like the courtier he was not, and kissed them lightly, the smile in his eyes belying the formality of the gesture. He opened the cabin door. 'Till supper-time,' he said.

Abigail's heart was singing as she stepped out of her wet gown and chemise and rubbed herself down with a towel before taking a fresh chemise from her trunk and putting on another of her plain maidservant dresses. For the first time since that awful night when her father told her what he had done, she felt happy. As she dwelt upon her present joyful state of mind it struck her that she had never felt like this before. This was happiness undreamed of. It was true the recollection that she was the property of Lord Jasper Cuddesdon was hovering like an ominous, if elegant, black cloud over her future, but even that could not completely mar her present happiness. Had not Lance himself indicated a means by which that cloud might be dispelled? The fact that he had done so, Abigail took as an indication that he intended to remove the obstacle to their continued happiness by buying her from her present owner. She did not entirely relish the thought of being bought and sold like a hunter at Tattersall's but if such marketing was necessary to ensure her freedom in Lance's arms, it was a small consideration.

Then she remembered the huge price Lord Jasper had paid for her: her father's entire estate plus two thousand guineas. It would take a very rich man to find that sort of money and, while it was clear that Lance Haworth was no pauper, she had no way of knowing whether he had so huge a sum at his immediate disposal. She contented herself with the thought that he would not have raised the possibility if he were not in a position to execute it, and found her happiness could continue undiminished.

Far from diminishing, it seemed it could only increase. Abigail did not go down to supper that evening – the storm destroyed any desire to eat. Instead, she took to her bunk and stayed there. By morning it had abated sufficiently to enable her to contemplate breakfast and when she arrived at the breakfast-table, neither of the men present expressed surprise at her absence the previous evening.

'The storm seems to have eased,' she commented.

'It's better than it was,' Captain Yazor agreed. 'I don't think you'll want to spend much time on deck, though. It's still bitterly cold and there's a heavy sea running. Still, we're making very good time. I don't recall a voyage when we've had a following wind so consistently and for so long a period as we've experienced on this one. If it keeps up, we'll see land in a week.'

'And if not?' Abigail asked.

'That I'd not like to say – it's a brave seaman who risks predicting what the Fates have in store. After all, we've only to capsize and we don't make landfall at all.'

'But barring a disaster like that?' Abigail persisted.

He shook his head. 'I'll not tempt Providence,' he said. 'Just pray for the following wind.' He rose from the table to relieve his Mate.

Abigail stared across at Lance. 'Only another week,' she said.

'Unless the wind shifts,' he reminded her.

'I thought we had weeks and weeks left,' she went on. She turned to look at him and her eyes were desolate with yearning. 'If I could control the Fates, this voyage would never cease,' she said.

Lance smiled indulgently. 'We'd run out of food,' he reminded her gently and was rewarded with a reluctant laugh. He rose from the table. 'Come, Abby will you take the air with me?'

'I'd rather just sit and chat,' she told him. 'So little time! I don't want . . . ' She looked down at her hands in her lap. A lady should not allow her emotions to be so plainly seen. Perhaps bond-slaves were not under the same obligation. She looked up again. 'I don't want to share your company with anyone,' she said defiantly.

'Then let me escort you back to your cabin.' The words were prosaic enough and his expression gave her no indication at all of whether he approved or disapproved of her forthrightness.

He opened the cabin door and stood aside to let her enter and then, ducking under the lintle, he followed her and closed the door behind them. They stood looking at each other in silence for a few moments and Abigail was aware of emotions she could neither control nor explain welling up inside her. Then his arms were round her once more and it seemed her whole body reached hungrily for the kisses he showered on her, her eagerness exciting his own still further.

He removed the lawn kerchief and gently undid the front-lacing of her demure grey dress and Abigail felt her heart's increased beating as his lips nestled in her bosom's cleft. She had not known such joys existed and how glad she was at the revelation! As her heart beat faster, her nipples hardened with a desire that was well-nigh unbearable.

'Not yet,' he whispered. 'Not just yet.' He picked her up in his arms, feeling his own desire rising as her naked breasts thrust themselves forward towards him. He carried her the few short paces to the narrow box bed and laid her down, his lips caressing her nipples before he divested himself of his coat and boots.

He lay beside her then, his lips continuing their voyages of exploration while his questing fingers showed her how much of her body could participate in the delights she was learning for the first time.

'Come,' he murmured at last, 'we don't need this encumbrance,' and his deft and practised hands removed her gown and then her shift.

Abigail wanted nothing more than to be as close to him as nakedness made possible but her upbringing still had the power to embarrass her. 'I shouldn't,' she whispered. 'Not like this.'

Lance was unperturbed. Swiftly he removed his shirt and then his breeches and drew her to him. 'This is as it should be,' he said. 'We lie on level footing now.' And Abigail knew he was right. His kisses changed then and Abigail knew that this time they were more intent, more demanding, more insistent. Her lips, her neck, a lingering pleasuring of her breasts that roused her fires anew and then down, across her belly to the soft, fair curls that surmounted the Mound of Venus, and all the time his fingers coaxed and caressed her legs, her thighs, until it seemed fingers and lips would meet.

Abigail writhed in ecstacy, her thighs wide, inviting the hardness she had felt against her, and when he entered her it was slowly and strongly as if to let them both savour the full sensual delight of the welcome her body offered his. She cried out at the first shock of his manhood but it was not a cry of fear or pain, and as he plunged deeper and ever deeper, penetrating her whole being, Abigail thrust herself closer and closer to him as if by doing so he could plunge still deeper. The pace increased as he brought her to a climax of unrestrained ecstacy and then there came the release, the blessed calm of utter contentment. Now she found a fulfilment beyond her deepest imaginings in the joy of two bodies united as one in mutual delight; and an unexpected satisfaction in that quiet time, wrapped in the strong, protective comfort of his arms, oblivious to all but the overwhelming happiness she felt.

She reached up and stroked his sun-tanned cheek. 'I love you – oh, so much!' she breathed.

His answer was a kiss of infinitely lingering tenderness that told her, or so she thought, more than mere words could ever do.

The favourable winds continued but little was seen on deck of either Mr Lance Haworth or Lord Jasper's bond-slave.

Chapter Four

When word swept round the ship that Virginia had been sighted, the passengers flocked to the *Alice Nancy's* rail, anxious to catch a glimpse of their new home and apprehensive as to what it would be like. If staying in her cabin could have delayed their arrival, Abigail would have stayed there but, since nothing she could do could alter their course, she found herself drawn as if by an awful fascination to join the others at the rail. Her heart sank as Norfolk, the largest town in the colony, hove into sight. To be sure, one did not expect to see the finest buildings on the waterfront of any port, but this . . . She heard a step on the deck beside her and looked up to see Lance standing there.

He had no difficulty reading her expression. 'Disappointed?' he asked.

'It makes me wonder what Williamsburg can be like if this is indeed the largest town in Virginia,' she replied.

'Half the size and three times as handsome,' he told her. 'This is a commercial port. Tobacco comes down-river to be shipped to England. Ships and the sea are Norfolk's business. Plantation owners may have business premises here but this is not where they live.'

There was nothing about Norfolk to make Abigail regret that her destination lay further afield, but she still had no idea whether Lord Jasper intended her to serve out her bondage at his house in the capital or on his plantation further up the tidewater. Of more immediate concern to her was the fact that, wherever she was destined to live, it would be away from Lance Haworth. This was not a reflection that brought any comfort.

As if to touch him might keep him there, she reached out and laid her hand upon his arm and was comforted when he slipped it protectively round her waist. She leant against him, savouring these last minutes of his company, for she had no idea when she might be with him again once they had docked. Abigail had promised herself that nothing in her bearing would reveal the despair she knew she would feel as the inevitable parting grew closer, but it was a promise she now knew could not be kept.

'We must be parted soon,' she whispered as the seamen secured the cables that held the *Alice Nancy* close against the wharf.

'Very soon,' he said, and his calm acceptance of the fact seemed to Abigail to border on the callous. 'If Williamsburg proves to be your destination. I'm sure we shall meet again.'

'And if it isn't?'

'Then it will be more difficult. You'll have to content yourself for a while with your memories.'

'Will memories content you?'

Lance shrugged. 'Perhaps they must − for a time, at least,' he said, his tone off-hand, prompting Abigail to look up at him, puzzled. His eyes surveyed the other craft at wharves or lying at anchor in the Roads. 'There is my *Sparrowhawk*,' he said, pointing to one of them. 'And if I'm not mistaken, that's Lord Jasper's *Raven* over there.'

Abigail's eyes followed his pointing hand and was at a loss to understand how he could identify any ship with certainty at such a distance. 'Does that mean Lord Jasper has come to meet me?' she asked.

He laughed. 'To meet a bond-slave? I very much doubt it! No, there will have been a cargo to discharge and they'll be awaiting the *Alice Nancy's* arrival. I seem to recall Captain Yazor telling me she was carrying other goods for Lord Jasper besides his bond-slave.' His attention was caught by a burly man of middle height on the dockside. 'Vatsetter!' he called.

No sooner had the gang-plank been run out than the individual thus hailed ran aboard. 'My overseer,' Lance explained briefly to Abigail before striding forward to greet him.

Left standing at the rail, Abigail felt doubly bereft. There was the desolation of being a stranger in a foreign land and, on top of that, the desolation of seeing the one rock upon which she felt she could depend disappear from her side as if she were no longer there. She watched the broad shoulders and dark hair towering over the bustling deck as he talked with his overseer and she succeeded in persuading herself that, after so long away from the colony, it was only natural that business must supersede all else, though there was a twinge of unhappiness at the discovery that he did not seem to have quite so strong a need as she to stay together until the last possible moment.

She was able to push the thought to the back of her mind, however, when he returned to her side, closely followed by his overseer.

'This is Miss Broughton,' Lance told him. 'She's a bond-slave to Lord Jasper Cuddesdon and I see the *Raven* at anchor off-shore. Has Cuddesdon sent a man ashore yet, d'you know?'

Vatsetter looked Abigail over in a way she found repellant, as if he were mentally removing every stitch of her clothing with his pale eyes. There was nothing surreptitious in his gaze and she more than half expected his master to take him to task for such open insolence but Lance appeared to be oblivious.

'Aye,' the overseer said at last. 'I saw Cuddesdon's Jabez hanging around the dock-side. He can't be far off.' He looked across at the wharf and then pointed. 'There he is. Torn himself away from the tavern, I reckon.'

Hurrying towards the *Alice Nancy* was a huge black man at least as tall and as broad as Lance Haworth, and better and more neatly dressed than most people on the dock-side. Abigail had known the colony's work-force to be largely composed of black slaves but that had not prepared her for the preponderance of black faces she saw milling about on the dock, intermingled with the occasional white one. Only on the *Alice Nancy* were there no black ones to be seen.

Such of the black population of Norfolk as were gathered below were a far cry from the occasional liveried and pampered black page-boy or footman who graced the more fashionable households in London. These seemed to belong to the lowest ranks of society, on a par, so far as appearance went, with London's beggars rather than servants. All these people must be slaves. That was something to which Abigail had given very little thought. She wasn't at all sure what she had expected a society based on slavery to look like, but it wasn't like this. She supposed she hadn't expected them to be free to come and go, as these apparently were. On the other hand, she *had* expected their masters to see to it that they were neatly and tidily dressed, and that was very far from the case in general. So far slavery had had no significance as a specific condition, not even when she learnt it was to be her lot. Suddenly, it had acquired meaning for her.

She shuddered at the thought that in all too short a time she, too, might look as dirty, dishevelled and unsavoury as some of those jostling to help off-load cargo.

The man identified as Cuddesdon's Jabez shouldered his way unceremoniously along the gang-plank, his eyes ranging across the faces of those on deck.

'Abigail Broughton?' he called out. 'Abigail Broughton for Lord Jasper Cuddesdon?'

Vatsetter leant over the rail. 'Cuddesdon's Abigail's here, with us!' he shouted.

The black man frowned. 'You remember she's Lord Jasper's property, Ezra Vatsetter, and naught to do with you.'

'Rest easy, Jabez,' Lance interrupted. 'Ezra's only been on board these five minutes. She's come to no harm at his hands in that short time. I've supervised her safe transit and now she's yours. She's a trunk in the cabin, I believe.'

'She would have,' Jabez grumbled, 'and it'll probably not be got out until we've missed the tide. Hey, you!' and he grabbed a crewman, pressed something into his hand and told him to take him to where he could find Abigail's trunk.

The hurt she felt at Lance's summary disposal of her as if she were, indeed, no more than a piece of merchandise, must have been reflected in her eyes, for he took her by the elbow and led her just out of his overseer's hearing.

'You're upset – and it's hardly surprising,' he said. 'I don't think it's a good idea to let observers – and certainly not Lord Jasper's man – guess how things stand between us. Discretion must be our watchword. Agreed?'

She nodded, though she hated the necessity of it. She looked up at him, appeal in her eyes. 'When will we meet again?' she asked.

'Who knows? If you're to stay in Williamsburg, it's inevitable that we shall do so sometimes, however.' His finger lightly touched her cheek. 'Don't worry – you'll find things will work themselves out for the best, believe me.'

'Do you really think so?' Abigail pleaded for reassurance.

'I'm sure of it. Now come, or we shall give rise to the very comments we wish to avoid.'

Abigail's trunk, filled as it was with some of the clothes from her old life and such as could be made in a short time more suitable to her new, was not huge but neither was it light, yet Jabez carried it upon his shoulder as if it were no greater encumbrance than a feather mattress. He paused as he drew level with her. 'Follow me,' he said shortly and went on without waiting to see whether she had heard him.

Any faint hope Abigail might still have had of a lingering lovers' farewell being thus briskly disposed of, she had no choice but to take her leave immediately and follow the tall figure down the gang-plank. So tall was Jabez that she thought she would have little difficulty making him out across the crowds so, once safely on dry land, she glanced back up at the brig, expecting to see Lance's eyes following her progress and hoping that they might at least exchange a parting wave, but he had gone and there was no sign of either him or of his overseer. Nursing her disappointment, Abigail turned back to her present task of following Jabez.

This did not prove quite as easy as she had anticipated for she had not taken into account the effect on her balance of several weeks at sea. Now that the ground no longer rose to meet her or fell away from her at every step, she found herself stumbling and tripping in a way not unlike that which had characterised her father when he was in his cups.

Jabez was waiting for her in a skiff tied at the bottom of a wooden ladder that went perpendicularly down from the wooden jetty to the sea. Peering down, she could see her trunk already safely stowed in the bottom of the skiff.

'Must I climb down this ladder?' she asked, hoping there was an alternative.

'Not if you don't want to,' Jabez told her. 'You can always jump. I don't recommend it, though. Not till you've found your land legs again.'

There being nothing else for it, Abigail turned her back on the sea and ventured one cautious foot on the top-most rung. There was no hand-rail but once she was safely on the third rung, she found she could hold on to the rungs above. From then on her descent was relatively simple. It occurred to her that it would be much more difficult to go up such a ladder in her long skirts than it was to come down.

When she reached the bottom, Jabez put out a hand to steady her descent into the skiff and, pointing silently to the bow, indicated that she should sit there. He cast off and then settled himself amidships, sculling expertly into the Roads and across to the *Raven.*

Although Abigail realised that the *Raven* was much smaller than the *Alice Nancy,* it nevertheless loomed above her in a quite over-powering way with no apparent means of boarding until one of the crew dropped a ladder over the side. But this was no rigid wooden ladder. True, the rungs were of wood, but they were held together — or held apart, Abigail was not sure which — by ropes. She had already reflected on how difficult it would have been to ascend that earlier ladder. This was clearly impossible. She looked at Jabez.

'It can't be done,' she said.

He sniffed. 'Easier in breeches, I don't doubt. Can't say as it's a problem we've had to face before. Still, it's got to be done.' He lifted his head to the grinning crewmen staring down at them. 'I'll hold on to her from down here. You be sure to reach over and grab her as soon as you can. Those skirts are going to be the very devil.'

That proved to be an understatement. Abigail cursed the full brown kersey at every step. She dared not use one hand to lift her skirts clear of her feet, for she needed both hands to steady her on the unstable ladder so, with each step up, first one foot and then the other had to kick away her skirt before it could find a place on the rung and even then, more often than not, she found a fold of the material trapped under her shoe and had to kick it clear again.

However, Jabez was true to his word and held her as steady as two moving boats and a rope ladder permitted and, by the time he had nothing left to hold on to but her ankles, black arms had reached down to catch her wrists and she was unceremoniously hauled the rest of the way aboard. Her trunk remained in the skiff which Jabez rowed swiftly to the stern of the *Raven* and made fast, scrambling aboard by the anchor-line with a nimbleness unexpected from so large a man. He was barely board before they weighed anchor and set sail. The tide was on the turn and it was the tide that would carry them up the James River some forty miles to Jamestown.

Abigail looked at Jabez. 'Do I have to descend that thing when we get there?' she asked.

'You'll have it easy enough then,' he told her. 'There's a decent quayside left — about all there is to speak of. It'll be like walking off the *Alice Nancy*.'

She looked about her, at the sweat glistening on Jabez' brow as it glistened on the sailors', and she could feel her own dress sticking to her in the heat. 'Is it always as hot as this?' she asked.

'Hotter, generally. Hot and fever-ridden. Not a good climate for people but just right for tobacco.' He looked at her with the professional eye of one well-accustomed to assessing a labour force. 'I don't reckon you'll last long,' he said and Abigail, her spirits already dampened by the humidity, hoped she was mistaken in thinking she heard satisfaction in his voice.

It was hard to believe that Jamestown had once been the capital of this vast colony. The church still stood and some small wooden houses whose inhabitants tended the jetty and eked a living helping load and off-load cargoes, but the ivies and vines native to the landscape had run rampant in the hot, moist climate and covered such of the burnt remains as still stood.

Two waggons waited on the quayside to greet the *Raven* and take her cargo. Abigail rode high on one of them for the slow journey to Williamsburg.

Neither the squalor of Norfolk nor the ruins of Jamestown had prepared Abigail for the pleasantly laid out town that she eventually found herself entering. It was soon obvious that there had been nothing hapahazard about its development: someone had sat down and planned with great care this grid-iron of pleasant streets with houses, some of brick and some of wood — set along them, each in a substantial plot and each, at least along the main thoroughfares, with its own neat wall or fence.

Abigail was not surprised that Lord Jasper's house was one of the more impressive. Built of brick, the broad expanse of the main block of the house was flanked on either side by a lower building, one of which held the kitchens and dairy while the other was an office. Servants' bedrooms lay above these 'dependencies', as they were known. The gravelled drive led from a broad flight of steps below the door, between closely scythed lawns to magnificent wrought-iron gates set in an imposingly high brick wall. The gates gave on to the Palace Green, the tree-lined avenue of lawn that set off the steepled magnificance of the Governor's Palace to perfection.

The effect was impressive. To Abigail, convinced as she had been that she was coming to a wilderness, it was also reassuring.

Houses in Williamsburg were invariably referred to by their owner's name and Abigail's entry into the Cuddesdon house was naturally not through the front door. Instead she was taken initially round to the kitchen, where her appearance aroused undisguised curiosity but no comment. Jabez, after greeting a small girl of some eight years old named Nazarene, told Abigail to follow him and he would show her her quarters.

She found she had been assigned a bedroom over the kitchen which, both to her surprise and — had she but known it — to that of the rest of the staff, she did not have to share. It was a room neither large nor elegant, containing a simple wooden bed, a wash-stand, and a chair. There was neither closet nor coffer, so she would have to continue to keep her clothes in the trunk. This Jabez now deposited neatly at the foot of the bed. It would do prefectly well so the absence of a larger chest was no very great matter. Abigail surveyed her little room and peered out of the dormer window across the sweep of lawn. All in all, she supposed she must consider herself remarkably lucky. She had no idea what work would be expected of her but it seemed Lord Jasper intended her to stay in Williamsburg and in a degree of comfort she had not expected. If only she knew where Lance was and whether she was really likely to meet him again, she might even learn to be content.

Without exception, the other servants were black. Slaves, Abigail presumed. They were not unfriendly but treated her with a distance and a patronising manner that she found hard to accept. She swallowed her pride, reminding herself that she, too, was a slave and one who knew neither the customs of the district nor the routine of the household. She guessed that household gossip would have ensured that they were all aware of the nature of her bondage, and thought that perhaps the fact that hers had a term to it might account for their distancing themselves in this way. It also occurred to her that they might well mistrust a white slave amongst their number, thinking that perhaps she would seek to ingratiate herself with the master. If that were the case, their distrust would soon be dispelled when they realised how much she disliked and despised him.

Any new member of an English household would have been expected to take up their duties as soon as their belongings were put away. None of Lord Jasper's household seemed either to know or care what her duties might be. This was dispiriting, as if her presence could make little difference but, since she was thoroughly exhausted, she turned it to her own advantage and rested until Nazarene opened her door without bothering to knock and told her to come into the kitchen for her supper.

When Abigail actually met Lord Jasper next day, she had difficulty recognising him. At all their previous encounters he had been dressed in the satin and silver lace obligatory for any man of fashion in London society. More importantly, perhaps, his hair had then been so heavily powdered that she had assumed it to be a wig. Now that she saw him in the less exotic raiment of a wealthy land-owner, with his hair unpowdered and simply caught behind in a broad black ribbon, he looked both younger and more approachable.

It was not an impression that lasted long. The rather pale, sardonic face with its hooded eyes and the deeply etched lines of dissipation at either side of its thin-lipped mouth was not one which invited approach by any save the most foolhardy and since Jabez, who had brought Abigail through the house to the office where they now stood, did not think fit to break in upon Lord Jasper's attention, Abigail was certainly disinclined to do so.

Eventually Lord Jasper looked up from his papers. With an elegantly abrupt wave of the hand, he dismissed both Jabez and his secretary. As the door closed behind the two men, Lord Jasper leant back in his chair and surveyed his latest acquisition. Abigail, irritated by the frank yet impersonal stare, supposed she should be grateful he did not submit her to the impertinence of scrutinising her through a quizzing-glass as some fashionable young blades were said to do.

'So you arrived safely,' he said at last in a voice which held no hint of previous anxiety on the subject or of present relief.

'Obviously.' Abigail made no attempt at bland politeness.

'Jabez has expressed the opinion that you won't survive for long.'

'He told me as much. I trust he will prove mistaken.'

'I'm sure you do. However, seeing you now against a Virginian backdrop, I'm inclined to think he may be right.'

Abigail stiffened. 'Indeed? Why shouldn't I? After all, you appear to have survived remarkably well.'

She had the satisfaction of knowing that she had startled him, though he quickly wiped any trace of surprise from his face and his voice remained as impersonal as ever. 'Forgive me, Miss Broughton, but I fail to see the connection.'

'We both come from a similar background, don't we? I imagine that when you came here you were no more accustomed to work than I – rather less, if anything,' she added, remembering the extent to which she had been obliged to turn her hand to domestic duties when her father's gambling precluded the paying of servants' wages and they left.

'I fancy the similarity ends with our backgrounds. For one thing, I was neither bond-slave nor servant and was obliged to do nothing that I did not choose. For another, I wasn't five feet nothing and slightly built, nor did I have the colouring that accompanies such fair hair as yours and which fares ill in the Virginia summer.'

'You underestimate my height, my lord, and though I can't deny being slightly built, it doesn't mean I'm necessarily delicate, you know.'

Lord Jasper inclined his head. 'My apologies, Miss Broughton. You're doubtless as tough as an old boiling-fowl. Nevertheless, you will find the climate a problem.'

'I take it sun-bonnets are known in the colony?' Abigail maintained the icy tone that she felt the comparison with an old boiling-fowl merited.

'Naturally.' In the slight pause that ensued, Abigail had the uncomfortable feeling that Lord Jasper was laughing at her. 'It's not just the sun that will be a problem, however,' he went on. 'The damp heat of this colony is most debilitating and induces fevers to which many Europeans succumb. You'll find field-work particularly hard.'

Remembering the oven-like heat of the journey up-river and the even greater intensity on the waggon-ride that followed it, Abigail had no difficulty believing him.

'Am I to work in the fields, then?' she asked apprehensively.

'Who knows what the next fifteen years may not bring?' The question was purely rhetorical and entirely casual. Lord Jasper Cuddesdon would have no hesitation in setting his bond-slave to do precisely what suited him at any given time. It was a realisation that did nothing to relieve Abigail's apprehensions, but she was determined not to let him see that she was anything other than entirely satisfied.

'How very true,' she remarked. 'I'm sure no one could have foreseen my present situation! However, I presume you have some plans for my immediate employment. May I know what they are?'

Ignoring her question, Lord Jasper returned to her journey over. 'I gather from Jabez that you made the acquaintance on the *Alice Nancy* of a gentleman who came to the colony in circumstances not too dissimilar to your own,' he said.

'You mean Lance Haworth?' Abigail could not keep the warmth from her voice and Lord Jasper looked at her sharply. 'He was an indentured servant, I believe. He certainly seems to have prospered.'

'No one would deny it. Many do prosper, of course, but it would be unwise to forget that many more do not.'

Abigail looked at him curiously. 'What would you say such a person needs to prosper here?' she asked.

'Determination, I suppose – and ruthlessness. A readiness to put one's own interests first and to serve them regardless of anything – and anyone – else. I'd say those are the characteristics of successful men here.'

Abigail looked about the room. 'You've not precisely failed yourself, have you?' she said.

'Quite so. I advise you not to forget that fact. Am I to infer that Mr Haworth confided his life story to you?' he went on.

'Not in great detail. He told me in what capacity he came to Virginia and, since he has a plantation – an exceedingly large plantation, by all accounts – and his own ships, and since he travelled in some style, it wasn't difficult to deduce that he had managed to turn his unenviable circumstances to his own advantage.'

'You were in a position to gauge what you call his "style"? You surprise me. I shouldn't have thought a servant-girl travelling steerage would have been give much opportunity to form any opinion on the matter.'

Abigail flushed. 'Mr Haworth was . . . most kind. There was an . . . an unfortunate incident and he was generous enough to put his cabin at my disposal for the rest of the voyage.'

'Generous indeed,' Lord Jasper commented. 'You must have counted yourself most fortunate that his mood was so magnanimous. To give up his cabin to a complete stranger was philanthropy indeed.'

Abigail's colour deepend. 'Not a *complete* stranger,' she told him. 'We had fallen into conversation on several occasions, but I'm certain he would have done the same for any other of the female passengers.'

'I'm sure you're right.' Lord Jasper's voice was grave but once again Abigail had the disconcerting feeling that he was laughing at her. 'How fortunate for Mr Haworth,' Lord Jasper continued, 'that the woman with whom he had "fallen into conversation" was one of some considerable beauty.'

Abigail's cheeks flamed with a mixture of anger and indignation at his patronising and disbelieving tone. 'Am I supposed to simper and thank you for the compliment?' she asked. 'If that's what you want, you'll be disappointed. It was sheer chance that he was at hand to help me when I was still unaccustomed to managing the companionway. That was how we came to be acquainted.' She was angry with herself for feeling obliged to explain everything to this patently disbelieving man.

'I'm sure his presence was entirely coincidental,' Lord Jasper said smoothly. 'One simply wonders whether, had you been old and ugly, Mr Haworth would have sprung to your aid with any degree of alacrity.'

Abigail stared at him in disgust. 'Of all the odious and uncharitable remarks! You weren't there and you can't possibly know how it all came about!'

'Very true but you must remember that, while I was not privileged to witness the incident — which sounds most touching — I am rather well acquainted with Mr Haworth.'

'That's quite the most abominable remark you've yet made!' Abigail exclaimed.

'I'm sure you'll find me capable of excelling myself in that respect over the next fifteen years,' Lord Jasper told her, unperturbed by her censure. 'I trust you were suitably grateful for Mr Haworth's generosity?'

Abigail frowned, uncertain of his drift. 'What do you mean?' she asked suspiciously.

'Oh, come, Miss Broughton: a beautiful woman in a vulnerable position; a handsome man — and I can't deny that Mr Haworth is an excessively handsome man — with a private cabin in his gift and a willingness to put it at a lady's disposal. Add to those ingredients proximity, sea air and a lack of occupation, and what do you think I mean?'

Abigail stared at him open-mouthed. How dared he even think such a thing, let alone say it! The fact that the inference he had drawn was entirely accurate only served to increase her indignation. He made it sound so ... so ... squalid, and it had not been like that at all. For a fleeting moment she came close to telling this obnoxious man how things really stood, how much she loved Lance Haworth and how, for Lance Haworth — and only for Lance Haworth — she would walk barefoot over broken glass if it were necessary. But something held her back. Whether it was the sardonic cynicism of the face before her or an instinctive feeling that some things were best left unsaid, she was never sure. Whatever her reasons, she held her tongue, pursed her lips and drew herself up to her full height — which, she thought defiantly, was definitely *not* five feet.

'This conversation is getting us nowhere, my lord. Perhaps you would tell me what my duties are so that I may set about them without delay.'

Lord Jasper looked at her appreciatively, by no means disappointed to discover that his acquisition had lost none of the spirit that had attracted him sufficently in London to seduce him into laying himself open to the humiliation that had ensued. Had Abigail Broughton been the gambler her father was, doubtless she would have learnt to prevent emotions flitting across her face as revealingly as they did. Lord Jasper was tolerably certain he had made an accurate guess as to what had occurred between his bond-slave and Lance Haworth, and he found no gratification in the discovery. It now appeared that that gentleman had aroused a depth of feeling in Abigail that was new to her, and Lord Jasper was by no means pleased. This was a complication to his scheme that he had not bargained for and he did not knew whether to be glad or sorry that her face was so accurate a reflection of her emotions. He was impressed by the innate dignity that led her to change the subject with such finality. A gentleman would allow the subject to remain permanently changed. Lord Jasper did not feel at all inclined to behave like a gentleman.

'I'm sure the housekeeper will have her own ideas as to that,' he said. 'Do you find your room comfortable?'

'More so than I had expected,' Abigail told him, surprised he should express an interest. 'Certainly more so than my status justifies.'

Lord Jasper smiled blandly. 'Not at all. After all, what your status justifies will depend upon your duties, won't it?'

Abigail bit back the question that hovered on her tongue. She did not like Lord Jasper's habit of finding a deliberately disconcerting answer to the most natural questions and was loath to hand him another opportunity. Instead she turned to the door.

'Then it behoves me to speak to her without delay,' she said as she turned. 'I would wish her to find me duties commensurate with the privilege of a room to myself.'

Lord Jasper rose from his seat and was at the door before she could open it. He put a finger lightly under her chin and tipped her head back so that he looked down into her face. 'It's really a question of which of us keeps the other's bed warm, isn't it?' he said softly. 'At

96

least I need expect no missish protestations of innocence. Good day, Miss Broughton − and sweet dreams!'

Abigail stood on the path outside the closed door, fuming and grateful only for the complete absence of servants, so that her heightened colour could not be remarked upon. Her initial reaction was that Lord Jasper's ungentlemanly comment had been made for no purpose but to disconcert her. If that were so, he had certainly succeeded. She had a childish impulse to drum her heels on the ground and her fists on the door-panels in her impotent rage. It was an impulse she curbed. Wisely recalling that there is nothing quite like hard work for assuaging a temper, she found her way across to the kitchen and thence to the servants' hall to locate the housekeeper.

Jubilation was well past middle age but seemed to have lost none of the energy that must surely have characterised her all her life. Her greying hair seemed to Abigail, as yet unaccustomed to a largely black society, an odd accompaniment to her black skin. She carried herself with the assurance her place in the household warranted and Abigail soon learned that she ran that household with the proverbial rod of iron.

She also learned that Lord Jasper could do no wrong in Jubilation's eyes. Or almost no wrong: Jubilation made no secret of the fact that she felt he had been guilty of a bad error of judgement in buying Abigail and bringing her to Virginia.

She did not blame Abigail for this − after all, a slave had no control over who bought her − nor was there anything grudging in her behaviour towards this new arrival, but every time she glanced in Abigail's direction, she shook her head and tut-tutted, and she confided to Jabez that her work would be cut out trying to lick her into any shape worth having. Since Abigail seemed quite sure that the one thing she could do really well was ply a needle, Jubilation set her to repairing some sheets and was so agreeably surprised with the results that she told Abigail that, for the present at least, she could regard that as her work.

'But don't you get too set upon it,' she warned her. 'For 'tis my bounden duty to make sure you can turn your hand to anything around the place − and don't you forget it.'

Abigail promised she would not, grateful for having been given something of which she knew herself to be capable while she found her feet in this very different world.

Chapter Five

The day progressed a great deal better than Abigail might have expected. Jubilation, after checking two or three times on the quality of her work, left her to carry on at her own pace, satisfied that she knew what she was about. As the afternoon wore on, however, Abigail found a depression descending on her spirits for which she was at first unable to account. She told herself it was a delayed homesickness brought on by the end of novelty and the commencement of her new life of drudgery. Her arguments were unconvincing, not least because it was not to her home and family that her thoughts kept returning.

It was to Lance Haworth. Her needle slowed as she permitted herself the luxury of conjuring his face and figure before her. An intense longing engulfed her, a longing not only to see him and speak with him, but to feel his arms about her and to luxuriate in the protective strength of his love. It was some consolation that at least she wasn't being packed off to Lord Jasper's plantation: in Williamsburg she stood some chance of seeing him from time to time, though she had no very clear idea just how such chance meetings might come about if she were to spend all her time in the linen-room.

The recollection that Lance Haworth was in the same town as she might have served to lift her depression to some degree, but it had the opposite effect, for her spirits sank still further and when she eventually bade the other servants good-night and sought her room, the reason hit her with the force of a blow.

What was it Lord Jasper had said? "'It is really a question of which of us keeps the other's bed warm'" She had been furious but not because she had thought the inference was seriously meant; rather because she guessed it to have been made to discompose and embarrass her. Now that she slipped between the sheets of her solitary bed, she had doubts. It was most unusual for any servant other than the housekeeper and butler to have a room to themselves, and what more likely reason could there be than to enable her master — her owner, in this instance — to exercise his *droit de seigneur?*

She did not for one moment allow herself to be misled by any thoughts that Lord Jasper, son of an English duke, would not behave is such an ungentlemanly manner. Considerations of gentlemanly behaviour had not prevented his winning her in a game of chance and they certainly had not inhibited the indelicacy of his converse that morning. If there was one thing of which she was quite certain, it was that Lord Jasper would do precisely what suited him at any given time.

So Abigail lay there, rigid with fearful expectation. The thought of her cold, cynical master taking what she wished to give only to Lance Haworth was a dreadful one, and every fibre revolted against the very idea of his touch. Several times she heard steps on the wooden stairs outside her room and stiffened in anticipation of the expected turning of her door-knob, but each time the steps turned off and she knew they belonged to other servants going to their shared rooms.

As might have been expected, a deep silence fell upon the house when the last servant had gone to bed but to Abigail that silence seemed even more threatening: what more probable than that Lord Jasper was only waiting for the household to be asleep before making his way to her room? Her ears strained to catch the sound that might announce his arrival. They heard naught. Gradually, insidiously, sheer fatigue began to creep over her and she caught herself dozing until some slight sound — a mouse in the wainscot, a branch brushing a window — brought her sharply awake. The process repeated itself endlessly through the night until Abigail finally fell into a fitful and dream-laden sleep. Of Lord Jasper there was no sign.

When Jubilation hammered on her door at an hour Abigail had been scarcely aware existed, she awoke heavy-eyed and unrefreshed. A glance in the little glass by her wash-stand told her she looked as bad as she felt.

It was Jabez' duty to wait upon Lord Jasper at breakfast and Abigail was detailed to lay out the side dishes and generally assist him.

Lord Jasper seemed barely aware of her existence, for which Abigail counted herself grateful. She made sure she followed Jabez' directions as unobtrusively as possible. It struck her as exceedingly odd that the kitchens should be in a separate building, thus necessitating the transportation of food across a short stretch of drive, to enter the dining-room by way of a door at the top of a short flight of steps, but she was soon to learn that this arrangement was well established in the colony, springing from the plantation houses where slaves could start their early morning clatter without disturbing a sleeping household. That it did nothing to improve the quality of food seemed not to bother anyone. She learnt, too, that it was rare for any slaves to live in the house and that it was only in towns that the custom was encountered, plantations offering plenty of space for the erection of separate quarters.

She was returning from the kitchens when she encountered Lord Jasper. He was on his way to the stables, a route which passed between the main block of the house and the lesser one of the kitchens. He stopped short in front of her and she had no choice but to stop and bob a curtsy.

'You don't have the appearance of one who slept well,' he remarked. From anyone else the comment might have been sympathetic but there was no sympathy in Lord Jasper's voice.

'I found it difficult to sleep, my lord,' Abigail admitted. 'I've not yet accustomed myself to a bed that doesn't rise and fall with the waves.'

'Ah, was that the reason? I wondered whether you had been lying awake in anticipation.'

Abigail felt her colour rising. How could so insensitive a man read her mind so accurately? She kept her voice level – and haughty – but it was an effort to do so.

'I assure you, my lord, I anticipated nothing but sleep.'

'I'm relieved. I wouldn't like to have disappointed you.'

That he should so accurately have pin-pointed the reason for her lack of sleep and, at the same time, chosen so wilfully to misinterpret her feelings on the subject was beyond bearing and Abigail's hand came up in an unpremeditated attempt to strike him. But Lord Jasper saw it coming and saw, too, the naked fury on her face. Swiftly, he caught her upraised hand in an unexpectedly strong grasp and deflected the intended blow.

'Have a care, Miss Broughton,' he said softly. 'The punishment for a slave who strikes her master is death.'

Abigail paled. She had given no thought to possible consequences. She tossed her head in a gesture of defiance. 'And the master's punishment for striking a slave?' she inquired.

'None, Miss Broughton. None at all.'

In the days that followed, Abigail settled into her new life. She found herself gradually being allocated all the household's sewing, interspersed with much of the marketing and – appparently at Lord Jasper's insistence – some waiting at table. Only in the last capacity did she encounter her owner and nothing remotely resembling conversation passed between them. She had hoped that, on her occasional marketing expeditions, she might bump into Lance Haworth whom she knew, from kitchen gossip, to be still in Williamsburg. Lord Jasper's staff did not seem to have a very high opinion of Mr Haworth though it seemed to Abigail that this was due more to the snobbery attached to serving the son of a duke than to any inherent flaws in Mr Haworth. If their opinion of the master was poor, their opinion of his slaves was slanderous.

''tis a household of thieves and robbers,' the cook declared, pressing another piece of shoo-fly pie on Abigail who, she said, was as thin as two bean-sticks.

'That can't be so,' Abigail protested. 'No master would take the risk of having such people about him.'

Mama Lou winked and tapped one forefinger against the side of her nose. 'Maybe he's happier amongst his own kind. All I do know, girl, is this: you should thank the good Lord you're not bound to him!'

The others nodded knowingly and some instinct warned Abigail not to push her own very different view of Lance Haworth.

Jabez finished off the sickly-sweet pie crumbs before adding his mite to the conversation. 'You met his overseer, Ezra Vatsetter,' he reminded her. 'What did you make of him?'

Abigail wrinkled her nose in distaste. 'It was a short enough encounter, but I thought him unpleasant.'

'No one'll disagree with that,' Jabez nodded. 'Now you've not met his lordship's man, Jem Steventon, but you'll find him a very different sort. And for why? Because Vatsetter came out a convicted felon and Haworth took him on. Mr Steventon came out with his lordship — son of his lordship's father's bailiff, they do say — to manage the estates here. Two more different men you'll not meet — barring their respective masters, maybe — and no one who knows them both would have any doubts which one they'd rather take orders from.'

'Perhaps it's to Mr Haworth's credit that he gave a felon a chance,' Abigail suggested diffidently and was not altogether surprised that the suggestion should be greeted with shrieks of laughter.

'Girl, you must sure have seen the good side of him on that boat! Why, even Blanche Quenington ain't that gullible!' Mama Lou said, wiping the tears of laughter from her streaming eyes. 'There's felons and there's felons, and there ain't *nobody* would give one like Vatsetter a chance, no ma'am!'

'Yet Mr Haworth did,' Abigail pointed out.

'It's no good talking to her,' Jubilation butted in, not unkindly.

'When she's been here a while longer, she'll know what we mean.'

Such dispiriting conversations were the closest Abigail got to Lance Haworth. She had found out where he lived, of course. He had built himself a substantial brick house on Duke of Gloucester Street, not far from Chownings Tavern. The Haworth house was large without being particularly imposing; indeed, it had a provincial look about it that Abigail found a great deal more attractive than Lord Jasper's mansion. Its position right on the bustling main street was not one she would have chosen, but doubtless it was a situation which Lance found convenient for business.

When Jabez confided to his master that Abigail was shaping up quite nicely, all things considered, Lord Jasper decided that perhaps it was about time he celebrated his return to the colony with an evening party. The order was conveyed to the household and a veritable orgy of cleaning and polishing an already spotless house ensued.

Only one eccentricity was planned. Abigail was to wait at table and to attend the guests at any subsequent entertainments.

Jubilation protested. Abigail's help was needed in the kitchen, she said.

Jabez protested. There were men enough to do a manservant's work.

Lord Jasper was adamant. 'I have a fancy to set a fashion,' he said, his voice epitomising languid boredom. 'What could be more striking than a woman of Miss Broughton's beauty to serve at table?'

'No household of any standing has a woman to do such work,' Jabez protested indignantly.

His master stared at him. 'Are you suggesting my credit won't survive such a deviation from the accepted custom?' he demanded.

'Your credit'll survive more than that,' Jabez told him, 'and you know it, my lord. The thing is, it'll look decidedly odd and there's those invited as might count it an insult.'

'Nonsense. They'll write it off as another of my eccentricities. The men will envy me so beautiful a creature and their wives will determine never to let them follow suit.'

'In which case, you'll not be setting a fashion at all, my lord, will you? So why bother?'

Lord Jasper looked at him with an enigmatic smile. 'Humour me, Jabez. Humour me.'

Lord Jasper seemed in no hurry to startle his fellow citizens, for he made no immediate further plans to hold any kind of reception or evening-party at which to produce his new acquisition. Jabez and Jubilation argued over the possible reasons for this.

'It's my belief he's seen the sense of what I said. He ain't going to do no such daft thing.' Jabez was complacently sure, but Jubilation would have none of it.

'You've got a mighty opinion of yourself, I must say. He ain't changed his mind, If he had, you wouldn't still be training the girl, now would you? No, he's still set on it. Just waiting till she knows the work as if she was born to it, that's my guess.'

Abigail was privately of the opinion that Jubilation's judgement was the more likely to prove correct but she did not enter the discussion. The earlier mention of a Blanche Quenington in connection with Lance Haworth had aroused her curiosity, and her peace of mind was by no means eased when she learned that Williamsburg gossip was divided between a certainty that the wealthy heiress would settle for the handsome, buccaneering Mr Haworth or the equal certainty that she would prefer to become Lady Jasper Cuddesdon. So far as Abigail could gather, the balance was generally held to be in favour of the title and she fervently hoped they were right!

She reminded herself that any interest Lance might have exhibited in Miss Quenington had occured before the voyage in the *Alice Nancy*. At the end of that journey, Lance had given her as open a hint of his intentions as he could and such had been the intensity of their relationship that Abigail could not believe she had subsequently slipped from his mind. Nevertheless it was unsettling neither to have seen him nor heard from him since her arrival here, and there was no denying that a woman who was sole heir to a plantation adjacent to one's own would be regarded by most men as a better 'catch' than a bond-slave. Her thoughts were only distracted from their preoccupation when Lord Jasper finally announced, through Jabez, that he was inviting Williamsburg society to an assembly in ten days' time. The increased volume of work in the house, the kitchens and the linen-room was such that, at the end of each day, Abigail fell into bed and asleep with no energy for anything else but sleep.

Lord Jasper's staff found no surprises in the guest list but one name – already the subject of gossip – caused a great deal of natural speculation. Blanche Quenington was the daughter of William Beauregard Quenington, owner of the profitable Beauregard Plantation that marched with Lord Jasper's lands and faced those of Lance Haworth across the James. Since the widowed William Quenington had no other children and showed no interest in remarrying, his daughter was considered to be the greatest 'catch' in the colony. It was generaly believed that there was not an available man in Virginia who had not weighed up his chances with the heiress, and Lord Jasper's servants were united in thinking that the acquisition of a title would be a lure neither the lady nor her father could resist. Miss Quenington, therefore, as their possible future mistress, became an object of much interest to Lord Jasper's household.

Abigail's interest was no less than that of her fellows. It was not only because she wanted to see the woman whose name was also being linked to Lance's. Having herself rejected Lord Jasper's proposal, she was intrigued to see what sort of a woman he now considered appropriate as his consort. Since her master was insistent that his plan to have a female footman should be adhered to, it seemed she would have plenty of opportunity to form an opinion of the lady in question.

Lord Jasper was not a man to do things by halves. Abigail, in common with the rest of the household, had assumed that she would perform her duties in the clothes normally worn by housemaids: that is to say, in a simple, neat dress of a sombre colour with a crisply starched apron and cap. Lord Jasper had other ideas. On formal occasions his menservants wore white breeches and stockings, black shoes with silver buckles and cutaway coats of midnight blue velvet, the facings and cuffs decorated with silver thread in the military style. When Jubilation was ordered to furnish him with Abigail's measurements, both women assumed it was so she might be provided with a new dress for the occasion. They were right, but not in the way they had imagined.

The garment that was finally sent round to the servant's quarters was quite extraordinary, resembling a riding habit in hunt livery more than a servant's dress. Of the same midnight blue velvet as the men's livery, it had a full gathered skirt and a closely fitting military-style jacket with wide cuffs and facings decorated with silver in the same military style. At the neck she was to wear a very mannish starched stock. Her hair was to be pinned up and she was to wear no cap.

When Abigail looked at herself in the glass she was uncertain what to think. The effect was certainly striking and not unattractive, but if this was what she was to wear, she could forget any ideas she might have about remaining an unobtrusive figure hovering in the background.

Jabez sniffed when he saw her. 'Well, if that's what his lordship wants . . .' he said at last. 'Better come with me and get confirmation, I reckon.'

She followed him to the drawing-room and he stood aside to let her enter first, then coughed discreetly behind his gloved hand. Lord Jasper stood at the window opposite, looking out across the terrace. He turned at the sound of Jabez's cough.

'Abigail Broughton, my lord. Thought you'd better see her.'

'Thank you, Jabez. You may go.'

With the light behind him, it was impossible for Abigail to tell whether or not he was pleased with what he saw. She was no wiser when he moved away from the window. Lord Jasper's face was well schooled. It gave nothing away.

'Come here.' The voice was peremptory. 'Turn round.' She did so. 'I think that will serve the purpose quite well,' he said finally.

Abigail looked at him curiously. 'What purpose is that, my lord?'

He raised one elegant eyebrow. 'That, Miss Broughton, is my affair. I trust, however, you do not dislike your livery?'

'Would it make any difference if I did?

'None whatsoever, but one is ever mindful of the courtesies of life.'

'I don't think you give a rap for them, my lord.'

'You misjudge me, Miss Broughton. Life is very much more comfortable if everyone is happy.'

'How very true! But I don't think someone else's unhappiness would prevent you doing precisely what you set out to do,' Abigail told him.

He sighed as if regretting that she had formed so uncharitable an opinion but there was a gleam in his eye that would have warned Abigail, had she known him better, to step warily. 'I'm sure you're right. So perceptive of you. Do I infer you don't like this toilette?'

'I don't *dis*like it, precisely,' Abigail said thoughtfully. 'It's so very mannish − on the hunting-field it would be most fitting, but on a servant? I'm not convinced.'

'But I am. We're starting a fashion, Miss Broughton. Tell me, do you hunt?'

'In Virginia? What a superfluous question! Of course I don't! It's just that I'm not at all comfortable in a garment of such masculine cut in my present situation.'

Lord Jasper walked carefully round her as if seeing her in a new light. 'Do you know, Miss Broughton, I think you have a point. What a pity it's too late for me to make use of it.'

'What do you mean?' Abigail asked suspiciously. There was something in his voice, a hint of amusement, that led her to think he was not seeing things in quite the same way as she.

'It is very masculine − "mannish", I think, was your original word − and therein lies its charm. My mistake has been in not taking that feature far enough. I should have dressed you in exactly the same way as the manservants with just a very feminine coiffure to give the game away − allied, naturally, to your very feminine figure.'

Abigail stared at him open-mouthed. 'My lord, you can't − you wouldn't!'

'Wouldn't I? Will you lay me odds against it?'

'The indelicacy, my lord! A female on public gaze in ... in breeches!'

'Would your sense of delicacy be less outraged if it were only in private?' he asked.

Abigail blushed. 'Of course not! That would be just as bad. In fact, I'm not at all sure it wouldn't be worse. You can't mean — my lord, please assure me that that is not in your mind.'

Lord Jasper came very close and Abigail was obliged to look up into the cold eyes that held hers as a flame holds a moth. Any hint of amusement in either his eyes or his voice had gone, replaced by a steely and ruthless determination. He took her chin in an unnecessarily hard grasp and forced her head still furtherback.

'Be sure of one thing, Miss Broughton,' he hissed softly. 'So long as you remain my bond-slave, you will do precisely what I require of you.'

Abigail tried to pull away from his grip. 'My lord, you're hurting me.'

'That, too, is the privilege of ownership.'

He meant it, and for the first time, Abigail realised the full implications of her present position. She was as much this man's property as the chair by the fireside or the dogs in the kennels. His power over her was absolute and he could do with her exactly as he chose. It was not a reassuring thought. Fear dilated her pupils and she could feel her pulses throbbing but she forced herself to return his stare, determined that he should not guess what an effort it cost her to do so.

He did, of course, and found a disturbing satisfaction in the knowledge that the mere threat of the exercise of his power could produce such naked fear. But he also admired the courage that made Abigail hold her gaze. He obliged her to continue doing so for a few moments and then released his hold.

'Very well, Miss Broughton. I think we understand each other.'

Abigail rubbed her jaw. It felt numb where he had gripped it.

'If you mean by that that you have made your point, then I'm forced to agree with you, my lord.'

'Good. Tomorrow when my guests arrive we will observe the effect of a female footman. It should be quite entertaining.'

Abigail bobbed the obligatory curtsy and whisked herself out of the room, her dislike of Lord Jasper more deeply entrenched than ever.

Blanche Quenington was a beauty. Tall and statuesque, with a creamy skin, raven-black hair and large, limipd brown eyes, she was fully aware that the combination of her physical and financial attractions made her irresistible. Observing her dispassionately, Abigail noted that Miss Quenington, despite the opulent lines upon which she was built, had cultivated to perfection the role of the flutteringly feminine woman. She spoke in a breathless, little-girl voice, as if overwhelmed by the great big wide world around her and her slightest utterance was accompanied by a fluttering of both her long eye-lashes and her diamond-encrusted fan. She looked out under the one and over the other at any gentleman with whom she was in conversation, in the most fetching manner imaginable. She did not spend a great deal of time talking to the other ladies present but, since they were mostly older than she was, they seemed unresentful, watching her with an amused tolerance, particularly if they had hopeful sons.

Abigail did not much like Miss Quenington but she thought her the ideal wife for Lord Jasper. Her woman's instinct told her that the marshmallow exterior covered a core of pure steel. The arrogant Lord Jasper might find he had met his match.

Her own presence caused no small stir and some frankly curious stares which she found more discomposing than she had expected. She succeeded in appearing unconcerned and since, like any well-trained footman, she spoke as little as possible and only when directly addressed, the novelty of her appearance soon ceased to cause comment. Miss Quenington subjected her to a prolonged and calculating gaze before deciding that such insipid colouring could be no competition, and thenceforth ignored her totally.

Once the guests had relegated Abigail in their own minds to the same level as the other attendants and ignored her in much the same way as they ignored the Chinese wallpaper, she was able to derive considerable amusement from watching and listening.

There had been one name on the guest list that had caused her some consternation when she saw it despite the eagerness with which she had searched for it, but Lance Haworth had not so far appeared and Abigail felt increasingly able to relax as time passed and he still did not arrive. She had not seen him since her disembarkation and, while part of her desperately wanted to do so, she also acknowledged that this evening's circumstances were not the ones she would have chosen for such a meeting. She was not, therefore, altogether disappointed that he had not come. It gave her ample leisure to observe Miss Quenington's technique for enslaving Lord Jasper.

He seemed very ready to be enslaved. It could not be said that he hung on her every word as did some of the younger gentlemen there, but he accepted even her more inane remarks with a bland seriousness that surprised Abigail, who would not have been at all astonished had he given Miss Quenington a biting set-down.

The view from the window of the Summer Hall on to the terrace Miss Quenington found particularly charming, despite the fact that the moon had not yet risen and the lights from the house illuminated nothing beyond the parapet.

'Ah, Lord Jasper,' she sighed. 'How delightful it must be to look out upon such beautiful grounds. I declare, it must remind you of England.'

He smiled. 'It's not a displeasing prospect but I can't truthfully say it reminds me of England.'

Miss Quenington tapped him playfully with her fan. 'How can you say such a thing, Lord Jasper! Why, everyone knows your garden is laid out like that of an English country house!'

'You would find no catalpas in an English garden, Miss Quenington, and walnut trees instead of pecans. The effect is entirely dissimilar.'

'I don't believe it,' she said firmly. 'I'm sure you've arranged the garden here exactly similar to that with which you grew up.'

He bowed politely and Abigail repressed the smile that twitched the corners of her mouth.

Miss Quenington saw nothing amiss in Lord Jasper's non-committal bow. She looked up at him archly. 'I vow there's much I would give to see your ancestral home, Lord Jasper.'

'It's no secret that you have much to give,' Lord Jasper replied, smoothly enough to remove any hint of irony from his voice. 'Let us hope the opportunity may be offered you.'

Blanche Quenington blushed fetchingly and lowered her long lashes momentarily before glancing up at him from beneath their soft curve. 'I should like that above all things, my lord,' she said in her breathless voice, and Abigail felt an unaccountable urge to slap her beautiful, complacent face.

Then Abigail's world turned sharply upside-down. Jabez announced the arrival of Mr Lance Haworth and she moved forward to relieve the late-comer of his cloak, hat and cane.

Lord Jasper wore the velvets and brocades that fashion decreed with a casual elegance that Lance Haworth lacked. The latter's broad shoulders and huge frame were better suited to the leather, linen and worsted of more workaday clothes than to the butterfly colours and metallic embroidery affected in society. He gave a slight start as Abigail moved towards him but that might have been due to nothing more than surprise that a woman should play footman. He betrayed by neither look nor word that he had ever seen her before. Abigail, aware of her heightened colour, could only envy his self-control.

108

Lord Jasper, observing the encounter, drew his own conclusions. His urbanely smooth voice was that of a man who had noticed nothing.

'We'd almost given you up, Haworth,' he said. 'Nothing untoward, I hope.'

'I must apologise for keeping you waiting – a matter of business at the last moment.'

'Say no more, my dear man. Pleasure must never be allowed to interfere with business, else where would the colony be? Miss Quenington, I think I have no need to introduce Mr Haworth?'

'Indeed no. We've been neighbours across the James far too long for that to be necessary.' She fluttered her eyelashes. 'The evening would not have been the same had you not come, Mr Haworth.'

'How could I stay away, knowing you were here?' he replied with what Abigail considered to be quite unnecessary warmth.

Blanche blushed and Abigail wondered maliciously if she could do it to order. 'You shouldn't say such things, Mr Haworth. Lord Jasper will be quite jealous.'

He looked more amused than jealous, Abigail thought, though one could never really tell.

When supper was announced, her presence serving at the table caused a murmur of surprised comment and some disapproving frowns in certain quarters. One or two gentleman made jovial remarks as she bent over to take their dishes to the buffet but the icy stares of their wives ensured that such comments were kept to the minimum. So far as Lance Haworth was concerned, she might have been invisible. He made no attempt to catch her eye and, although Abigail glanced in his direction several times, she caught no hint that he might have been watching her.

She was unsure whether to be relieved or alarmed. His failure to acknowledge her presence undoubtedly eliminated all embarrassment. If he wished to convey the impression that they had never met, he succeeded admirably. But he was also conveying to Abigail the impression that she meant nothing to him – and that was by no means so welcome. It was refined torture for her to find herself so close to the man she loved so passionately and to be unable to communicate in any way. If only she could catch a hint that he was even aware of her: if, for instance, their eyes could momentarily meet, or she should discover him to have been watching her, she would have felt less as if he had deserted her. That he should converse with a servant at such a function was unthinkable; that he seemed unaware of her existence was unbearable.

When the gentlemen rejoined the ladies in the drawing-room Lord Jasper indicated that Abigail alone should stay behind with Jabez to dispense tea and, once that task was completed, she remained unobtrusively available in case anything else should be needed. These hours on her feet, much of the time relatively motionless, were more tiring than Abigail had foreseen and several times she found her eyes closing and her head nodding in the warmth of the crowded room. The interest she had originally found in listening to little snippets of conversation had waned, and although disconnected phrases wafted across her ears, they contained nothing of sufficient significance to catch her attention for long.

The tedium of her post was relieved when it was suggested that the ladies should entertain the company with the aid of Lord Jasper's recently imported pianoforte, the first to be seen in the colony. There were a few protesting murmurs that those accustomed to the clavichord would lack the skill to do justice to this new instrument, but they were soon overruled and Abigail was not at all surprised that Blance Quenington's becoming modesty was overcome sufficiently easily to enable her to be the first to contribute to the evening. She sang two contrasting songs by Purcell in a pure, clear, well-taught voice and Abigail grudgingly admitted that she deserved the compliments showered upon her. After Miss Quenington's performance, the modesty betrayed by the other ladies proved entirely justified. Nevertheless Miss Quenington was rapturously generous in her praise of their efforts.

Jabez caught Abigail's eye and silently directed her attention to the fireplace, where the cheerful blaze which removed any slight chill from the Virginian night had died down to a level which the experienced servant found unacceptable. In obedience to his tacit command, she moved quietly round the room to the hearth. The guests had their backs to the fire in order to attend to the music and she was able to carry out her task unobserved. Blanche Quenington had drifted towards the back of the brightly dressed crowd and now stood close to Lance Haworth, scarcely three feet away from Abigail.

They spoke in undertones but Abigail, her senses finely tuned to anything that involved Lance Haworth, had little difficulty in making out their brief exchange.

'It must be soon.' Lance's voice was charged with urgency.

'You are importunate. I won't be rushed.'

'Does a title mean so much to you? I recall that it was not always so.'

'It is no small consideration, however, and Papa views it very favourably.'

'But he won't force your hand. Blanche, I must have an answer soon.'

She tapped his arm lightly with her fan. 'And so you shall, dear Lance. Just as soon as I've made up my mind.' With a charming ripple of light laughter she moved away from his side before their converse could attract attention. She was soon back at her host's side, absorbed in his attention.

Abigail was glad she could attribute her heightened colour to the surge of flame from the fresh logs she had just put on the fire. What did the exchange between Lance and Miss Quenington mean? Much as Abigail longed to find some innocuous interpretation to put on it, she was unable to do so. The inference was very clear: Lance Haworth must have proposed to Blanche. At the same time it would seem that the lady was still considering an offer from Lord Jasper and his lordship's household was in no doubt that it would be accepted. Abigail hoped with all her heart that they were right. She considered that Lord Jasper and Blanche Quenington deserved each other and were quite probably very well suited. She was also quite sure that becoming Lady Jasper would prove irrestistible to a woman of the sort she judged Miss Quenington to be. Nevertheless it was clear that she was in no hurry to answer either suitor and this raised a question which was crucial to Abigail: when had Lance proposed?

Had the proposal been made before his recent visit to England? If so, then as a gentleman of honour, he could hardly retract it just because someone else had engaged his affections yet he would understandably be anxious for an answer that would solve his dilemma, one way or another.

But that was not quite the impression Abigail had gained from the overheard conversation. Lance had not sounded like a man who hoped for the answer 'no'. She had a chilling, inexplicable feeling that Lance's proposal had been of a more recent date. Did that mean he had abandoned any hope of buying her? It did not cross Abigail's mind that Lance could possibly love her any less than she loved him – after all, during those days on the *Alice Nancy* they had been everything to each other and it was inconceivable that his commitment should be so shallow. Only if she were unattainable could he possibly contemplate marrying another ... surely?'

Perhaps he had approached Lord Jasper and had his offer to buy her rejected. It was also quite possible that Lord Jasper might have named a figure beyond Lance's reach. When she recalled that his lordship had relinquished her father's entire estate for her, it was only to be expected that he would have required a sum of such vastness as to be out of the reach of all but the wealthiest of men – and Abigail had no idea just how wealthy Lance might be.

She turned the whole matter over and over in her mind but reached no conclusions that gave her any comfort: either Lance had already committed himself before they met, or she was beyond his reach. A feeling of grey desolation came over her and she wondered how she could have been so foolish as not to foresee those very possibilities.

Card-tables having been set up in one of the smaller saloons, many of the guests welcomed the opportunity to play whist or loo, and Abigail was detailed to stand ready to fetch refreshment for any player who was loath to leave the game. Abigail had not inherited her father's passion for gaming. She had little understanding of card-games and no interest. Now she found she had developed a profound distaste for the pastime in all its guises, a distaste that she had no difficulty in attributing to her present situation. The little cries of delight and groans of dismay with which the games were punctuated seemed mere affectation and she wondered savagely how some of the ladies would have reacted had the stakes been truly high.

When carriages were finally called, Abigail was surprised to see that, while all the ladies left, many of their menfolk did not. This unusual arrangement was soon explained on her return to the card-room. The cards had been removed and unopened pairs of dice had taken their place. Lord Jasper's elegant assembly was over. The serious gaming had begun.

Jabez coughed discreetly at his master's elbow and whispered to him. Lord Jasper glanced briefly at Abigail and shook his head. 'She remains. It will do her no harm to stay up a few hours more. You may go, however. I want you up and about early. Abigail is perfectly capable of handing people their cloaks when they wish to leave.'

When her master's instruction was relayed to her, Abigail sighed. Bed became more attractive with every passing minute. 'Don't worry,' Jabez whispered. 'Just keep the candles burning — there are fresh ones in this drawer — they don't like the light to get dim and the more they drink, the more it bothers them. Apart from that, there's nothing to do except stay awake.'

'The most difficult thing of all!' Abigail told him, and was rewarded with a quick grin.

'You'll do,' Jabez said, and then she was left in sole attendance.

Had she been able to muster some interest in the game, the time might have passed less slowly and she might have found it easier to stay awake. As it was, she was dimly aware that the jocularity of the first few games had been gradually replaced by an increased tension as the freely flowing brandy encouraged some deep plunging by several of those present. Even so, most men acknowledged their financial limits and withdrew, some to their houses, others to watch, until eventually only two men remained at the table.

Neither seemed drunk. Lord Jasper's eyes held a glitter that Abigail remembered from that night when he had come home with her father but she had no idea whether this was attributable to the brandy or the excitement. Lance Haworth might have been considered entirely sober had he not enunciated his words with more than usual care.

Abigail was so tired that she had barely assimilated the significance of there now being only two active participants and it was not until a tense and threatening silence fell upon the room that her interest was sharply alerted.

'You don't mean that, Haworth,' said a bystander.

'I mean it.' Lance's voice was adamant.

'Lord, man, you can't refuse an I.O.U. from your own host!'

'I have done so, however.'

Lord Jasper's silken tones broke in. 'We must remember, gentlemen, that Mr Haworth lacks our in-bred awareness of the niceties of social custom. There's a limit to the amount of gold I keep on the premises, Mr Haworth. I'm sure you are equally cautious.' He waved an arm in an expansive gesture round the room. 'Perhaps there's an article of furniture or decoration you would accept as a stake?'

The speech was deliberately insulting but Lance Haworth seemed unmoved. 'I think something of that sort might be acceptable.'

'The silver is generally thought to be particularly fine,' Lord Jasper informed him sarcastically. 'It survived the Civil War – no mean achievement.'

'You may keep your silver. You hold a far more acceptable stake than that.'

'I do?'

'There's only one item I'm prepared to accept, Lord Jasper. You've set tongues wagging tonight by putting before the society of Williamsburg a female in the role of footman. I'll accept that slave as a stake.'

A gasp went up from the assembled company which turned as one and stared at Abigail. Only partly aware of what had transpired, she looked from one to the other of the two protagonists. When Lord Jasper beckoned her over, she came and stood by the table.

'Did you hear that, Miss Broughton?' Lord Jasper asked.

'Yes, I think so ... I mean, I'm not sure I understand.'

'Then let me explain. Mr Haworth isn't prepared to accept an I.O.U. from me to continue the game which I am steadily losing. He has, however, expressed a willingness to accept you as a stake instead.' He saw the hope spring into Abigail's eyes. 'I see,' Lord Jasper went on drily. 'I don't have to ask if you object to being the stake.'

Abigail lowered her eyes. 'Do I have the choice, my lord?'

He regarded her in silence for a few moments. 'In the last analysis you don't, of course.' He turned to Lance. 'Very well, Haworth. Abigail Broughton is the stake. I make only one stipulation: win or lose, this is the last throw.'

'Agreed.'

Abigail's fatigue fell away as if she had had ten hours' sleep. Her lack of interest in games of chance disappeared like mist in the sun. None of the spectators objected to the stake. Slaves were a valuable commodity and were not usually gambled away except in an attempt to ward off bankruptcy but it had been done before and it was certainly legal. The fact that this particular slave was white and beautiful gave it a slightly salacious 'edge' that added to the excitement, and they were perfectly willing to allow Abigail to remain beside the table: watching her face could only add to their interest.

Lord Jasper was observed to cast a long and inscrutable look at his slave's face bfore picking up the dice-box and shaking it. Breaths were held as he threw.

A four and a two – six. An indecisive throw that could equally easily be beaten or prove victorious.

Lance Haworth returned the dice to the box and shook it. At no time in the proceedings had he so much as glanced at the beautiful bond-slave who stood so close, watching the fall of the dice with an interest as great as that of either participant. He cast the dice. One of them settled at once. A three. The other rolled almost to the edge of the table, its every turn followed by avid eyes.

Four.

Abigail Broughton now belonged to Lance Haworth.

If Lord Jasper's feelings on the outcome were impossible for the bystanders to gauge, Abigail's were not. Relief mingled with delight flooded across her face, resulting in more than one knowing nudge between spectators. The uncertainties of the evening vanished for Abigail as if they had never been. So this was how Lance had planned to gain possession of her! She had underestimated him; she must also have misinterpreted that exchange with Blanche Quenington. Abigail was too happy to speculate upon an alternative interpretation. It no longer mattered. She was now indisputably Lance Haworth's and she was the happiest woman alive.

Lord Jasper studied her radiant face and then rose from the table. 'An ironic twist, Miss Broughton.' He turned to the victor. 'The hour grows late, Mr Haworth. I'll have the appropriate papers drawn up in the morning and your new acquisition will be brought to you.'

'There are witnesses enough here to the legality of the exchange,'

Lance replied. 'The girl comes with me. Fetch your things – or at least, such as you can carry,' he added, still without so much as a glance at his new slave.

Abigail bobbed a cursy and needed no second bidding. Once out of the room, she picked up her skirts and ran out of the house and across to the dependency where her room was. There she paused. 'Fetch what you can carry,' Lance had said. Did that mean her trunk would follow? It must mean that. And what about her necklace? Did she risk leaving it in its present hiding-place, tucked away in the bottom of the trunk, to follow in a day or two or did she take it with her and keep it safe until she had the trunk again? The latter was undoubtedly the safer course. First, though, she must take off Lord Jasper's livery, something that could not go with her to another man's house. If she was quick, she would have time to unearth the necklace and somehow devise a way to conceal it under her everyday clothes.

Hastily she unfastened the silver buttons of her close-fitting jacket and removed it. She was stepping out of the full skirt when a footstep on the boards outside made her paused. There was a cursory knock at her door. It opened immediately and she looked round to see Lord Jasper standing in the doorway.

'My lord?'

'My apologies for this intrusion, Miss Broughton.' He paused as if assimilating what he had interrupted. 'You don't have to leave behind the clothes I provided. Since Mr Haworth seems somewhat impatient, your time would be better spent collecting together as much of the rest of your wardrobe as you can carry.'

'Thank you, my lord, but this is your livery and hardly appropriate elsewhere.'

'True, but since it will be of no further use in this household, you may as well take it.' He paused again and Abigail had the distinct feeling that he had not come here merely to tell her to take her present costume. She looked at him enquiringly.

'Was there something else, my lord?'

'I fancy our opinion of this night's events would differ. You are clearly overjoyed at the outcome. I am less sanguine about it. I shall make sure the terms of your bondage are clearly set down and suitably witnessed. Fifteen years is a very long time. I'm sure you wouldn't wish them to become transmuted into life.'

'Your concern overwhelms me, my lord.'

'No, it doesn't. You think it both unnecessary and uncharacteristic. It may well be the latter. I do not, however, consider it unnecessary. Things don't always turn out as we plan, you know – a lesson I've just learnt to my cost. I'm well aware that you've held me in abhorrence since the first time we met and that abhorrence has not diminished since you came to Virginia.'

'Are you surprised?' Abigail interrupted. 'With a gamester for a father, I was hardly likely to accept a proposal from another such and to be, in effect, bought in a fit of pique by a rejected suitor and gambled away within a month of my arrival here are not events calculated to promote either admiration or liking!'

'Is that how you see it?'

Abigail's surprise matched his own. 'How else would you have me see it?'

He hesitated as if he were about to answer her and then shrugged instead. 'It's immaterial now though I feel obliged to point out that, as a gamester, I don't place myself in the same class as your father. I mean no disrespect to Sir Thomas when I draw your attention to the fact that he was scarcely noted for his success at the tables.'

'You didn't seem to be winning much yourself, tonight.'

'No one expects to win all the time, Miss Broughton. Look around you. Almost all I possess has been acquired by gambling – of one sort or another. I've never allowed myself to stake all I possess on one throw, however – that way lies madness – and had Mr Haworth accepted I.O.U.'s, this conversation would not be taking place. I simply advise you to bear in mind that in the long term, I win.'

'Then we part in the agreement that you are a successful gamester and my father is not. I'm quite happy to acknowledge that. Are you satisfied?'

'I shan't be satisfied until I'm sure you will not regret your delight at this evening's outcome. Whatever you may think of me, Miss Broughton, I'm concerned for your future welfare at Haworth's hands.'

'You're too kind, my lord! It's not a concern I share. I rather fancy Mr Haworth won't be treating me as a skivvy.'

A sardonic smile lifted the corners of his mouth. 'I'm sure you're right, Miss Broughton. I imagine Mr Haworth has a much more comfortable position for you – to start with, at least. It's when the novelty wears off that you'll need to be careful.'

Before Abigail could think of an appropriately biting retort, steps could be heard on the stairs and Lance's broad frame filled the doorway. 'What keeps you?' he asked. 'Lord Jasper, I trust you're not sullying my property?'

'On the contrary,' his host replied smoothly, 'I'm endeavouring to ensure its well-being.'

'A kindness which is quite unnecessary now that I'm here. Abby, we go.'

'But I've not yet collected my things together,' she protested, glancing at her trunk.

'No matter. Leave them. I'll provide all you need.'

Abigail thought of her necklace. 'If someone can but be sent to fetch my trunk tomorrow, I shall have all I require.'

'No need. Lord Jasper may dispose of it as he will. You'll be better off without it.'

Lord Jasper watched Abigail with interest. For some reason he could not fathom, the loss of her trunk meant far more to her than the value of its contents could possibly merit. Perhaps it contained mementoes of her past life. He could think of nothing else to account for her obvious unease at Lance's declaration.

'Miss Broughton's trunk will remain here untouched until such time as she sends for it personally or is in a position to collect it,' he said.

Abigail looked at him searchingly. 'Do you mean that, my lord?'

'I do.'

Abigail considered the matter briefly. She despised Lord Jasper's way of life. She neither liked nor, in general, was she inclined to trust him. Yet there was something in his voice on this occasion which convinced her that he meant precisely what he said.

'Then thank you, my lord. I'm obliged to you.'

He bowed. 'And for my part, Miss Broughton, I shall watch your career with interest.'

Chapter Six

The events at Lord Jasper's assembly had happened so quickly that Abigail had not time to speculate upon her future, and the journey to the Haworth house was so short that she had still not got beyond congratulating herself on the way things had turned out, when they drew up at the door.

Lance had not spoken to her during the drive. Perhaps he, too, had been overwhelmed when the dice had finally fallen in his favour. The house was in darkness and no one was waiting up for the master. This surprised Abigail but Lance seemed to find nothing untoward in it. He dismissed the carriage and caught her wrist. He teeth gleamed in the moonlight. 'Come,' he said, opening the picket gate and pulling her after him up the short path and into the house through the unlocked door. Abigail went willingly enough, her only problem being to keep up with his long strides, and when the door closed behind them and they stood in the dark hallway, no words were needed to fill the brief pause before he swept her into his arms.

Abigail thought she had reached a pinacle of happiness on board the *Alice Nancy*. She now knew that was nothing compared with the happiness of being once more in the arms of the man she loved, and her kisses were as demanding as his.

He released her only to light the candle that stood on a chest against the wall. Abigail needed no coaxing to follow him up the stairs. Lord Jasper's livery slipped to the floor in a crumpled heap and when Lance carried her naked body to the huge four-poster bed, there was no need for the sensual preliminaries with which he had been accustomed to bring her to the peak of her desire. Abigail welcomed his entry with every fibre she possessed, rejoicing in the pulsing thrust of his manhood as it claimed her innermost places for its own, and when they had reached their mutual climax he stayed within her, the life-giving force drained into her receptive, eager body. Such was the heat of their desire that he stayed within her still until she felt him harden and move once more, thrusting with undiminished vigour, and only when their passion was slaked again did he withdraw. They slept the rest of the night in each other's arms like lost children in some antique tale.

When Abigail awoke, the sun was streaming through the window and she was alone. The wide, deep bed, the strange room and, above all, her feeling of profound contentment puzzled her at first. None of this was what she was accustomed to. Gradually she remembered the events of the previous night and as she recalled her changed fortunes, she snuggled down contentedly beneath the quilt. At last she was where she should be: in Lance Haworth's house. He had chosen a flamboyant – and risky – way of gaining legal possession of her, but his gamble had paid off and now their love need know no bounds. She recalled with a warm half-smile Lord Jasper's concern that Lance should be in no doubt about the terms of her bondage. As if it mattered! She did not doubt for one moment that Lance, secure in the knowledge of their mutual love, would tear it up – or perhaps throw it on the fire – a symbolic acknowledgement that only her love enslaved her.

With warmly consoling and entirely delightful thoughts such as these, Abigail lay in that cosy in-between world of just awake but not yet up. A tap at the door, followed by the appearance of a young and rather untidy black girl, broke into her day-dreams.

'Awake at last – and about time, too!' the girl commented. 'You're to get washed and dressed and come down for something to eat. Then they'll sort out what's to be done with you.'

It was not an auspicious beginning and combined with the cold water in the ewer effectively to dispell the wilder flights of fancy in which Abigail had been indulging herself. She reminded herself that, no matter what might eventually come to pass, for the time being she was still a bond-slave. Since the only clothes she had with her were those she had been wearing the previous night, she had no choice but to put them back on and was not surprised that the slaves in the kitchen should watch her in silent and sullen curiosity. A white slave was sufficiently unusual to arouse interest; one dressed in magnificent and inappropriate velvet raised several questions.

Abigail was somewhat annoyed that Lance appeared to have given very little thought to the impression created by the sudden appearance of a white woman in his house with only the clothes she stood up in – and those wholly inappropriate. He really should have given some explanation, and the niggling thought that perhaps his household would find nothing at all unusual in the situation did nothing to reassure her.

119

Her curiosity about her fellows was at least as great as theirs in her. After all, in whatever capacity she was here, this was where she would be living. She soon realised that there was something subtly different about these slaves when compared with those in Lord Jasper's household. Indeed, now that she came to think about it, Lord Jasper's slaves displayed a more independent spirit than these seemed to, even on so very short an acquaintance. There was something else, too: a degree − no, rather a hint − a carelessness in their appearance and in the appearance of the kitchen itself which suggested that Lance Haworth suffered lower standards than Lord Jasper. Abigail's immediate thought was to attribute it to the lack of a mistress in the house, but then she remembered that that consideration applied equally well to Lord Jasper's menage. She recalled the derision with which Jabez, Jubilation and Mama Lou had spoken of Lance's slaves. She was still sure they had overstated the case, but this must be what they had meant.

Lance had a butler but Noah, unlike Jabez, had no intention of demeaning himself by conducting another slave to his master, so it was the black girl, Jemima, who led the way through the comfortably furnished but slightly old-fashioned rooms to the dining-parlour. Lance sat at an oak table with a highly polished top and unpolished legs, a bottle of rum and a glass in front of him. He dismissed Jemima with a nod and swirled the rum round in the glass before leaning back in his chair to study Abigail.

'Well, Abby,' he said at last. 'Our paths seem to have crossed again.'

'I'm glad,' she said simply.

He smiled then, his white teeth gleaming. 'D'you know, I had the feeling last night that that might be the case,' he said, and Abigail supposed he could be excused a degree of complacency. 'Of course,' he went on, 'we can't return to quite the level of intimacy we enjoyed on the *Alice Nancy*.'

Abigail's heart stood still. 'No?' she asked.

'Hardly. It won't do to attract too much gossip. Particularly right now. If you were black it wouldn't occasion any gossip at all, of course, but you're not. We must be circumspect in our behaviour.'

He rose from his chair and came over to Abigail. He towered over her and when he lifted her chin, she felt her whole body tremble with a desire that a night's indulgence had done nothing to abate.

'So,' he murmured, 'the passions we gratified so thoroughly are not diminished.'

He pulled her to him and sank his mouth on hers, his hands and body alike relentlessly increasing the longing she felt to be one with

120

him once more, until she wondered if she could bear the agony of suspense and yearning he induced.

The response of her eager body left him in no doubt at all that she was his in any way and to any extent he chose, but he had more pressing considerations than the further gratification of the desire he felt for this beautiful creature. Besides, he owned her now. There was no need to take advantage of the odd snatched meeting. Abigail was going nowhere. She would be here when he had time to enjoy her to the full and, if he was any judge of women, the waiting would only increase her longing and the depth and passion of her response.

So he drew back with a light, dismissive kiss. 'Not now,' he told her. 'We have all the time in the world at our disposal but we must be careful. I shall see to it that you have a room to yourself. That will be enough to cause comment but when it's observed that I don't visit you there, the comment will die down and we can then resume life, albeit discreetly, on a footing similar to that which we enjoyed before. Meanwhile, make yourself useful.'

Abigail returned to the kitchen, her mind in confusion. What did it matter if he were known to visit her? Everyone in the household must know in whose bed she woke up that morning. What was she to make of his words? One thing seemed abundantly clear: he had no immediate plans to legitimise their relationship. She could not but feel uneasy about this. She had never doubted, when he had mentioned on board ship the possibility of her changing hands, that he had anything less than marriage in mind, and his actions at Lord Jasper's little gaming party had confirmed this belief. His words, however, were unambiguous. He expected her to continue as his mistress and to do so with complete discretion. The exchange overheard between Lance and Miss Quenington crept unwelcome into her mind. Did that have any bearing on his expectations? Or was it simply that he could make no more definite proposal to Abigail until he had had Blanche's answer? She had no idea but the recollection of that incident did nothing to increase her confidence in what the future held.

Because her certainties of the previous night had been replaced with confusion, Abigail felt a rising indignation that Lance should so misunderstand her feelings and misjudge her character as to assume that the life of a discreet mistress would be acceptable to her. Yet a small inner voice reminded her that there had been little in her ship-board behaviour towards him to suggest she was a woman of high moral principles. When her indignation was at its peak, she vowed he would go away disappointed from any visit to her room but even as she promised herself that she would spurn him, she knew she could not. Had she and Lance never again met after this disembarkation, she would gradually have come to accept what had passed between them as a happy memory. Having now once more felt the ecstacy of his manhood within her, she knew she could deny him nothing.

She reminded herself that, as a bond-slave, the colonists would not expect her to have the standards of the class into which she had been born — would probably not believe that she had been born into the lesser aristocracy at all — and it was highly unlikely that any word of her ambiguous position in Lance's household would get back to her family, which was at least something to be grateful for.

In the ensuing days Abigail found her place in the household scheme and it was not dissimilar to her role in Lord Jasper's house, though everywhere here she found standards more lax. Since the whole household knew where she had spent the first night, the allocation to her of a room of her own occasioned less comment than their master's failure to vist her there. But that soon died down, and she lay there night after night hoping that every creaking board and banister heralded his arrival.

Eventually it did and she gave herself once more to the delights she had craved through so many lonely nights. Sometimes he came to her; at others he let her know during the day that he expected her to attend on him. He took a particular pleasure in initiating her in the many ways of giving and receiving pleasure. Abigail proved an apt pupil, luxuriating in the sensual delights of his instruction when he sought her company and contenting herself when he didn't with the thought that she needed sleep.

Such clouds as there were in a clear blue sky at first were small ones. At no time did Lance ever refer to marriage and Abigail, tempted though she was to raise the subject, pushed the temptation away, something in the pit of her stomach telling her to leave well alone. Far more depressing was the continual linking of Lance's name with that of Blanche Quenington. At first when her name was mentioned, it was accompanied by a quick glance at Abigail and a sly smirk, as if the speaker's real purpose in mentioning it at all were to watch her reaction. Abigail knew this and very quickly learnt to school her features so that any pain she felt was unobservable. As a consequence, the references to Williamsburg's heiress became less frequent but this was hardly a relief, since it was soon clear that there was still a serious prospect of Blanche's marrying Lance Haworth. No other woman's name was ever linked with his, and somehow or other word always got back to the Haworth slaves of those occasions when the couple had sat together at an evening party, played cards together or had done nothing more significant than bump into one another outside a shop. The slaves' curiosity was natural. Abigail just wished that more than one name would crop up from time to time. It was another topic which instinct told her not to raise, despite her desperate curiosity to know just how things stood between Lance and Blanche.

Another matter hovered on the horizon and grew steadily stronger, though Abigail was uncertain whether to regard it as a cloud or a ray of light. Nature did not appear to be running its normal, regular course. It was entirely possible that the very considerable upheaval in her life – an upheaval which included a change of climate and diet, as well as of physical activity – might well be sufficient to throw matters out of kilter, and at first Abigail was in daily expectation that they would right themselves. She told herself that irregularity was to be expected in the circumstances and tried to put all thought of any other possibility out of her mind. She wanted to be quite sure of the cause before she mentioned it to Lance.

There was nothing Abigail wanted more than to bear his child, living, tangible proof of their love for one another, but Lance's failure to mention the possibility of marriage and the continued linking of his name with Blanche's made her uncertain of his reaction. It was difficult to believe that he might not be as delighted as she was and impossible to think that he would not wish to legitimise his child by marrying its mother. Nonetheless, she had to be sure. If she were mistaken and he married her because he thought her increasing, his anger if she proved wrong was something she preferred not to contemplate. She had once or twice seen him enraged and had been heartily thankful that his fury had not been directed at her. So Abigail kept her secret to herself, waiting until she was certain and the right moment should occur to tell Lance.

One unexpected skill that Abigail had discovered in Lord Jasper's service was that of marketing. At home in England it had not been something Sir Thomas felt it appropriate for his daughter to do. She could scrub a floor, but no one saw that. Marketing was something left to the servants, even if one's financial state had temporarily reduced the indoor staff to one maid – economies never being allowed to affect the stables: Sir Thomas had his standards.

Jubilation had sent her out when she had no one else to spare and Abigail discovered in herself a most unladylike propensity for bargaining. She found she enjoyed the verbal cut and thrust involved in getting items for the lowest possible price and, as a consequence, had soon found herself doing the bulk of the household marketing. She was perfectly willing to put this skill at the disposal of the Haworth household. Noah had first resented the idea that any white woman, sold into bondage from what he soon realised must be a very unsuitable background, could possibly be better at the job than someone bred and trained into it but he grudgingly allowed her to try and soon discovered, as Lord Jasper's household had done before him, that she drove a harder bargain than he would have believed possible. Consequently, Abigail was soon doing most of the Haworth shopping.

She was returning from one of her more successful forays, turning from the market square into Duke of Gloucester Street, when she encountered Lord Jasper for the first time since she had left his ownership.

He drew rein in front of her as she was about to cross the road and she had no alternative but to stop. 'Miss Broughton,' he remarked with politeness he might have accorded her had they chanced to meet in Hyde Park. 'It must be several weeks since we last met. I trust you're well?'

'Perfectly, my lord. And you? I had heard you had returned to your plantation. Rumour would appear to have been mistaken.'

'Not at all − I had done so and am but recently returned to Williamsburg. There's unfinished business here I have to attend to.' His voice was entirely casual but there was nothing casual about the scrutiny of his cold blue eyes. There was a pallor about Abigail's cheeks and under her eyes were the shadows that betokened lack of sleep.

'How does the work compare in your new position?' he asked.

'Very similar, my lord, except that I'm not expected to play footman.' There was a note of asperity in her voice which provoked a chuckle from Lord Jasper.

'How very wise of Mr Haworth! I have often considered that role a mistake − one I have frequently regretted making.'

'Good gracious,' Abigail exclaimed. 'I didn't think Lord Jasper Cuddesdon ever made mistakes − or, at least, never admitted to them. Didn't you set a fashion after all?'

'I flatter myself I make remarkably few mistakes,' he replied, unperturbed by her sarcasm, 'but that was certainly one of them and I'm not at all ashamed to admit it. As to its setting a fashion, Jabez was right: it was doomed from the start. I knew it then but it was a whim I wished to satisfy.'

'Are people's lives only there to be played with to satisfy your whims?' Abigail asked, unable to repress a note of bitterness.

'My mistake lay in not appreciating that that was what I was doing.' He paused, and when he continued his voice had softened in a way Abigail could not recall ever having detected before. 'Miss Broughton, you say you are perfectly well but I don't think that's so.

You're no longer my property and will be perfectly within your rights to send me about my business with no more ado, but I feel some responsibility for you and would know the truth.'

'Don't you consider it a shade late in the day to acquire a sense of responsibility or to express concern for my welfare?'

'A rebuke I deserve. Very well. Call it another whim, if you like, but tell me how things stand.'

'I am well-treated, well-housed and not over-worked. Does that satisfy you?'

'It must do so if that's all you wish to say. I fancy your expectations were rather higher when Mr Haworth acquired possession of you.'

Abigail's heightened colour told him he had struck a nerve but the unconscious tilt of her chin and almost imperceptible tightening of her mouth told him that the innate dignity he had admired in the past was undiminished.

'As you said, my lord, I'm no longer your property so you need concern yourself no more.'

'My *congé,* I perceive. There's just one matter I would mention before I go: your trunk is still safely stowed in one of my attics. Should you require it, you have only to say so.'

Abigail hesitated. Lance had said she had no further need of it and had seen to it that she was perfectly adequately supplied with clothes, but it contained more than that. She had a feeling that Lance would not allow her to send for it but, from the way Lord Jasper spoke, she rather thought he would be willing to have it delivered if she asked him. Should she do so? It was a temptation. Then she mentally reviewed Lance Haworth's houshold. Her room could be bolted from the inside but there was no way of securing it when she left. Bearing in mind the general laxity of most of the house-slaves and the curiosity the arrival of a trunk would inevitably arouse, perhaps it would be wiser to leave it where it was. She had no doubt it was perfectly safe at the Cuddesdon house.

'Would it be terribly inconvenient if I asked if it could stay in your care, Lord Jasper?'

His face was enigmatic, his voice expressionless. 'Not at all, Miss Broughton. It would be my pleasure. It will be there whenever you need it.' He paused and looked her over briefly. 'I, too, shall be there if you should need assistance at any time.'

'An unlikely eventuality, my lord, but thank you for the offer, all the same.'

He bowed. 'I hope you're right. Good day, Miss Broughton.'

Abigail hurried home after that encounter. Lord Jasper had not lost the power to surprise her. He had seemed, in his cold and unemotional way, genuinely concerned for her well-being. She did not like the man and could not imagine sinking sufficiently low to necessitate an appeal for help to him. She could just imagine the sardonic comments with which that would be met. No, matters were unlikely to get to such a pass, but perhaps she should waste no more time before confronting Lance with the news that would surely render superfluous any offers from Lord Jasper.

She had learnt early in her sojourn in the Haworth house that irregularity was the hallmark of Lance's way of life. He rarely ate an evening meal at home and seldom went to bed on the day he got up. To Abigail, ever alert to the possibility of a visit from him, it sometimes seemed as if he frequently did not go to bed at all or, if he did, it was in someone else's house. The only thing upon which any dependence could be placed was the reasonable certainty that, sometime before ten in the morning, he would attend to essential business in his office off the hall.

Having made up her mind that he must be told – and soon – Abigail hoped that this would be one of the days when he dined at. home. Somehow it seemed more fitting that such news should be broken in the soft light of evening than in the harsh morning glare. As she came through the kitchen door and saw Cook rocking away in her chair, fan in hand, she guessed that dinner was not today's foremost priority.

'That you, Abby?' Cook asked. 'Hope what you've got'll keep. Mas' Haworth's done sent a message he's eating at Quenington's tonight.'

Abigail sighed. Unless Lance paid her vist on his return, the harsh morning glare it would have to be.

There was no visit, though Abigail lay awake straining her ears for the sound of his return, hoping for the opportunity to tell him of her condition within the warmth and intimacy of either her bed or his. She heard him finally come home and his steps on the stairs but they turned to his own room and she heard his door close with a depressing finality. Sleep came late because her mind insisted on going over and over what she judged to be the best way of breaking her news. It did not occur to her that there was any significance in the fact that she awaited the revelation with such trepidation.

Lance Haworth was in a particularly begin mood when Abigail entered his offce, smoothing her hands down her apron like some nervous scullery maid. A young man who, to judge by his clothes, was one of Lance's clerks, was with his master but he seemed unconcerned at the interruption and beckoned her forward when she hesitated at the door.

'Come in, come in. I've only Stephen with me and our business can wait. What is it?'

'I'd like a few words with you, sir. Alone.'

Lance's eyebrows shot up. 'Intriguing! Off with you, Stephen, and no listening at keyholes!' The door closed behind the clerk. 'Well, what is it?'

Abigail looked at the door. She had no desire to have her news spread throughout the house just yet. 'Will he?' she asked apprehensively.

'What? Listen at keyholes? I'd be very much surprised if he did. Young Stephen's got more sense than to risk a beating, for that's what he'd get. Now what do you want? I hope it's straightforward – I've a lot to tie up today, but so long as it isn't complicated ... I haven't seen you for a few nights, have I? I've been meaning to have a chat with you – I nearly came to you last night, as a matter of fact – but something's always cropped up, you know how it is.' He glanced at her with rather more perception than usual. 'I must say, you're beginning to look a bit hagged. I suppose you're finding the climate hard to take. Some people take longer to get used to it than others.'

Abigail felt her courage diminishing with every insensitive word and it was with difficulty she resisted the impulse to turn and flee.

'May I sit down?' she asked.

'Why, yes, I suppose so.' Lance's surprise was undisguised. Abigail might be his mistress but she was still a slave and slaves, bond or freehold, did not customarily ask to sit down in their master's presence.

'I, too, had been hoping to see you,' Abigail told him, 'but as you say, there has been no opportunity and I can leave it no longer. It's a simple enough matter. Lance – I bear your child.'

There was a long, stunned silence. Lance stared at her, the smile wiped off his face and the colour draining away under his tan.

'You *what*?'

'I'm carrying your child.' Abigail's voice seemed very small.

'You're mistaken. The change of climate, routine, food – all have conspired to throw things off-course. It's not unusual, I believe.'

'I know that, and it's what I thought myself at first, but it's not so, Lance. I have no doubt about it.'

'How far gone do you reckon to be?'

'About three months, as far as I can judge.'

'A nicely vague estimate. It takes you conveniently back to your change of ownership.'

Abigail smiled doubtfully. 'I know. I can't help feeling it is a fitting outcome of so happy a night, if indeed it stems from then.'

'Very touching,' Lance sneered. 'Did you think that would convince me? Do you take me for a sentimental fool?'

'What do you mean?'

'Don't play the naive innocent with me, girl! Cuddesdon was willing enough to stake you. He'd taken his fill and lost interest, I suppose. I wonder if he also guessed he was shifting a bastard onto someone else's shoulder's?'

Abigail's face could not have looked more shaken if he had slapped her. 'Lance, you can't possibly believe such a thing! You know I had been with no other man when you took me − you can't in all honesty pretend otherwise − and I swear to you Lord Jasper has never so much as laid a finger on me. There has only ever been you! Surely you believe that?'

Lance knew that if he had ever had any suspicions on that score, he would never have bothered to win her. To take the other man's leavings would have been to make himself the butt of snide nudges and whispers. He had no very clear idea what had induced Lord Jasper to gain possession of Abigail in the first place, but Lance had had the satisfaction of taking her virginity before his lordship had a chance and had then, because he suspected that Lord Jasper valued this possession, deprived him of it permanently. Lord Jasper was a strange man and one against whom it was wisest to move with great caution, if at all. It was perfectly credible that he had never exercised his rights over Abigail, though Lance suspected that that situation might not have lasted much longer. He entirely believed Abigail's protestations but his instinct for self-preservation precluded any overt admission, so he withdrew nothing.

'I admit I've wanted to believe that and I accept that I was the first, but you'll not deny you acquired a taste for it and at the Cuddesdon house you had your own room. To what purpose was that if not to facilitate his lordship's nocturnal visits? Don't we have precisely the same arrangement here? I've not noticed you locking me out.'

Abigail flushed, angry at an imputation both untrue and distasteful. 'If your spies have told you I had a room to myself, they will also have told you that the door remained firmly locked. I confess I was more than half afraid Lord Jasper would come one night, but in all honesty I have to admit that he made no attempt to do so. No other man than you has knowledge of me and I don't believe you doubt that. This is your child I bear, yours and no one else's.'

She stretched out her hand imploringly across the desk that separated them. 'Lance. Lance, I didn't think it would be like this,' she whispered. 'I love you − I have always loved you and I know I

128

always will. There could be no one else. I thought you'd be pleased at the prospect of a child, perhaps a son.'

Lance stared at her and then threw back his head and roared with laughter. 'Pleased with another bastard? My dear Abby, the plantation is full of them! An exaggeration,' he corrected hurriedly, 'but yours is far from the first. It will be unique only in having a white mother.'

Abigail stared at him in stunned dismay. 'What are you saying?' she whispered.

'Merely that you are not the first and you almost certainly won't be the last whether the father is me or Lord Jasper.'

Abigail shook her head. 'This has nothing to do with Lord Jasper, Lance. It's just you and me. What do we do?'

Lance's face hardened. 'I wonder what ideas were running around in that pretty head?' he speculated. 'You can hardly had deluded yourself that I might marry you.' He stared at her. 'By God, I believe that's precisely how you did delude yourself! You can put that idea out of your head right away. Lance Haworth weds no bond-slave. In fact,' he continued complacently, 'Lance Haworth marries Blanche Quenington.'

'Blanche!'

'Why the amazement? She offers all I want: beauty, fortune and an old-established Virginian family. There were a few nasty weeks when I thought the lure of Lord Jasper's title would prove too much for her, but maybe she doesn't fancy spending the rest of her life with that cold fish. Whatever the reason, she accepted me yesterday and the wedding will not be long delayed. I had intended to let you know. It's been fun but, for the time being, at least, I'm going to have to make other arrangements for you. Frankly, Abby, this is a damnably awkward time to spring this. Haven't you tried to get rid of it?'

Abigail shook her head in mute horror.

He looked at her as if he were going to pursue the suggestion but thought better of it. 'Well, I'm sure of this: I'm not having you staying around here visibly increasing. What Blanche finds out after we're married is one thing, but she's learning nothing until her fortune is secured. I'm still not entirely convinced the child is mine but you are, and if she gets wind of it I don't doubt she'll believe it, too. There's little I can do about that except get you out of the way for the time being.' He rose from his seat and paced up and down the office. Eventually the glimmer of a smile returned. 'I think I've found the solution. Yes, it will work very well.'

'I won't get rid of it, Lance,' Abigail warned.

'You won't have to. There'll be no need for that, no need at all.'

Abigail looked at him suspiciously. 'What are you planning, Lance? What's in your mind?'

He grinned, his teeth gleaming under his moustache. 'The first thing is to get you out of Williamsburg,' he said. 'I've business up at Kingswood myself and there's a craft hove-to in Jamestown to take me up the tidewater. No reason why it can't take both of us. Get your things together, Abby, we're going to the plantation.'

If the rush to get her few possessions together gave Abigail no time to think, the same could not be said for the slow journey up-river but, despite the lack both of occupation and converse, her mind was in such a turmoil that she had no better idea of her position when she arrived than she had when they left.

Ezra Vatsetter rode down to meet them, his presence reminding Abigail how much she had disliked him on their previous brief acquaintance. His eyes, pale and watery, travelled lingeringly over her body in a way that made Abigail momentarily doubt whether she was adequately clothed. Lance watched his overseer's glance and smiled.

'Put her up in front of you, Vatsetter,' he said. 'She's not used to walking in this heat.'

The overseer needed no urging and, while Lance swung himself into the saddle of the big horse his overseer had brought with him, Ezra Vatsetter lifted Abigail on to the pommel of his own saddle and then swung himself up behind her. It would not have been a comfortable ride at the best of times but with the hand that held the reins resting on her thigh and the other round her waist in a clasp that was certainly tighter than was entirely necessary, Abigail found it embarrassing as well as uncomfortable.

Neither factor was sufficient to lessen her interest in her surroundings. This was her first visit to a plantation and she was curious to see how it differed from the provincial urbanity of Williamsburg. She was also curious to see what sort of a place it was where she was destined to stay. The house itself proved to be a handsome one. Or, rather, it had been handsome. Like so much connected with Lance Haworth, it betrayed that slight, insidious edge of neglect that could so easily slip into decay. It was constructed largely of timber, with which the plantation was amply provided, on brick footings. Off to one side was a veritable village of small wooden houses − little more than shacks − set neatly enough on either side of a path but, like the house itself, betraying a lack of care, of pride of ownership, that characterised Lance Haworth's property. She had never seen Lord Jasper's plantation but she doubted very much that it would show any sign of neglect whatever.

When they drew to a halt in front of the house, Lance swung himself out of the saddle and threw the reins to his overseer. He nodded towards Abigail. 'Find her a cabin,' he said. 'As good a one as you've got empty, mind. Then come and see me while she makes herself at home. Make sure someone gets her some decent bedding: there'll be some in the house she can have. Don't keep me waiting, though. I've a proposition to put to you.'

Somewhat apart from the other cabins was a more substantial house with a large, overgrown garden behind an unpainted picket fence. This, Ezra told her, was the overseer's house. He rode on until they came to a cabin which appeared to be empty. He drew up in front of it and studied it.

'Roof looks sound enough,' he commented. 'This'll do, I reckon. What's Mr Haworth got in mind for you?'

'I've no idea,' Abigail told him. 'I didn't even know I was coming until this morning.'

'Ah, well, we'll find out soon enough, I reckon. They could do with someone useful in the house and I don't reckon you'd be much use anywhere else.' He looked her over and grinned. 'Except the bedchamber.'

Laughing uproariously at this sally, he helped her down from the horse and called out to the girl standing at the door of a nearby cottage. 'Go up to the house, Glory, and get this one some bedding. Decent stuff. Tell 'em it's Mas' Haworth's orders.' He turned back to Abigail. 'I'll get your baggage sent over.' His eyes narrowed. 'I didn't see no trunk this time but you had one when you docked, didn't you?'

Abigail was instantly wary. It was an odd thing for him to have noticed or remembered. Her possession – or otherwise – of a trunk had nothing whatever to do with this unpleasant man but she instinctively felt that the less he knew about it, the better. She shrugged. 'I had one,' she agreed. 'It proved totally unnecessary and I got rid of it.'

He laughed nastily. 'Not a thing a slave's likely to have much use for, a trunk. Still, you wasn't to know that when you set out, I suppose.'

She was not sorry to see him ride off in obedience to his instructions, leaving her to investigate her new home. It didn't take long. The 'cottage' consisted of one room. The walls were timber, the floor was dirt and the roof was a rough thatch. The only thing to raise it above the level of an animal shelter was a brick chimney on one end wall. Abigail looked out of the door. A cluster of those cabins nearest to the big house were similarly equipped but the majority, all of which

131

were farther off, lacked this refinement. She wondered whether the original owner had provided his work-force with a safe hearth whereas Lance, coming later, had only felt the need to provide basic shelter for his slaves.

The place was equipped with a table, chairs and a bed, all roughly hewn from wood. An iron cauldron stood on the hearth with some iron utensils – a ladle, a rough, long-handled, two-pronged fork, and a poker – inside it. There were some wooden bowls and trenchers but no plates or drinking vessels. Abigail supposed the bowls would also serve the latter function. In one corner she found a besom.

When Glory returned, she dropped an armful of unfolded blankets on the bed. 'There you are. That'll do you, I reckon.'

When Abigail had sorted out the heap she had just two blankets, now neatly folded. She looked at Glory. 'Is this all there is? No sheets? No pillow?'

Glory grinned. 'My, where've you been all yo' life? 'Course there ain't no sheets or pillows. Two blankets, that's yo' allowance – and them's two good ones, 'cause I sorted them myself. What's yo' name?'

'Abby,' Abigail told her.

'Well, then, Abby, you come with me and I'll show you where the straw is. Bring a pail and we'll get water, too.'

She tut-tutted when she discovered that there was no pail in the cottage. 'Bring the stew-pot, then,' she said. 'Get hold of Mas' Vatsetter as soon as you can and ask him for pail. He'll rant at you for there not being one. Don't argue or make excuses. Bow yo' head and look sorry and when he's done shoutin', he'll get you a pail.'

'He doesn't sound very reasonable,' Abigail suggested cautiously.

Glory threw back her head and roared with laughter. 'Reasonable? Mas' Vatsetter? He ain't never heard the word.' She dropped her voice and glanced instinctively around as if he might be lurking somewhere near even though they both knew he had gone to the house. 'Watch yo' step with him, Abby. He's a nasty man, a very nasty man. Don't never argue with him. You say "Yes, sah. No, sah" no matter what he says. That way maybe he'll take no notice of you at all.' She looked Abigail up and down. 'Maybe,' she concluded doubtfully.

She showed Abigail the barn where straw was stored, and the well. Both were situated with the convenience of the stables in mind rather than that of the slaves. Abigail collected as much straw as she could carry while Glory filled the cauldron. When they returned to the cottage, the doorway was filled by a tall, powerfully built young man a few years older than Abigail.

'Who's this?' he said to Glory.

'They call her Abby,' the girl replied. She turned to her companion. 'Iago's my brother,' she said.

'What's the likes of her doin' here?' he asked, still ignoring the subject of his questioning.

'She's one of us.'

'Her? Never! She ain't never done a day's work in her life.'

Abigail decided she had had enough of being spoken across. 'On the contrary, I'm accustomed to working very hard — though not outside,' she added in the interests of strict accuracy.

'You're no slave,' he insisted.

Since this was the first remark he had addressed directly to her, Abigail felt she was making progress. 'I'm a bond-slave,' she said, and explained in as matter-of-fact a way as she could how she came to be in so unenviable a position.

Iago stared at her incredulously. 'And yo' father's a white man?' She nodded. 'In England?' She nodded again. Iago shook his head. 'If that don't beat all. What sort of man sells his daughter into the sort of life you'll lead? No black man would do it. Not if he got the choice, that is,' he added bitterly.

'A very selfish man — and one with, I think, very little imagination,' Abigail told him. It was the first time in her life she had ever openly criticised her father and she was shocked to hear herself doing so even though she knew she spoke no less than the truth. She looked from one to the other of her companions. There was no mistaking the family likeness and it was obviously a very handsome family. She estimated Glory's age at fifteen or sixteen with looks that were simply a softened, feminine version of her brother's. 'You're brother and sister?' Abigail continued. 'That must mean your parents are on Kingswood as well, I suppose.'

The two black slaves glanced at each other and it was Iago who answered. 'They were. Had been all their lives. Mas' Haworth reckoned when he took over that they was too old to be much use so he sold them while there was still some work to be got out of them.'

Abigail nearly said, 'That's dreadful,' and stopped herself just in time. Such expressions were so inadequate as to be offensive. Instead she asked, 'Did they go together?'

'No.'

A clatter of hooves broke into the silence that followed Iago's bald statement and Abigail was almost glad to see Ezra Vatsetter reappear.

'You're to join us up at the house,' he said. 'Now.'

He clearly had no intention this time of letting her ride. She found that Glory and her brother had melted away with the overseer's

133

arrival and Abigail set off in his wake.

At the house the overseer waited for her in the kitchen, tapping his whip impatiently against his boot. He made no comment, however, but with a curt, 'Follow me,' led her to Lance's office and preceded her through the door.

Lance was seated behind his desk, his fingertips pressed together, smiling with all the complacency of the proverbial cream-stealing cat. Abigail's heart leapt as it always did when she saw him but, even so, that smile made her apprehensive and very wary.

'Ezra and I have been discussing what's to be done about you,' Lance began. 'I think we've found a very satisfactory solution.'

'Indeed?' Abigail's tone was frosty. 'Am I to be told what it is?'

Lance was impervious to sarcasm. 'Of course, since it concerns you intimately. You've only seen Williamsburg until now. You've probably given no thought at all to the position of men like Ezra, here. They spend most of their lives on the plantation and the only white people they see from one year's end to the next are the plantation owner and his family. You follow me?'

Abigail did, but she was unable to see the relevance to her present situation. Enlightenment was soon to dawn, however.

'Ezra is of a mind to be married,' Lance went on. 'He can't marry a black woman yet where is he going to find a white one appropriate to his position? Now, he knows you're with child and that there's some question as to its paternity – '

'There's no question about it at all,' Abigail interjected. 'The child is yours and I'll not stand silently by while you imply otherwise.'

Lance shrugged. 'It's immaterial. What we all know is that it can't possibly be Ezra's. Despite that, he's willing to take you to wife – '

'No!' the cry was wrenched from her heart.

' – and to claim the child as his own,' Lance continued inexorably. 'Of course, it will be born a month or two early, but it won't be the first time that's happened. You'll be an honest woman with a good house instead of a slave's shack, and the child will be legitimate. I'd say it's an arrangement that takes care of you rather well, don't you agree?'

Abigail looked at the overseer. The short, stocky figure, the pale, watery eyes, the grizzled red hair, the generally unwashed, neglected appearance. She shuddered. 'Do I have the power to refuse?' she asked.

Lance's eyes narrowed and his smile disappeared. He leant across the desk towards her. 'The preacher's been sent for,' he said. 'You can tell him you're unwilling and he'll refuse to marry you, though he's none too scrupulous and I daresay I can close his ears with gold.

134

But if you do that, I can guarantee you one thing, Abigail Broughton: your child will not be born alive, even if you survive the treatment Ezra will be empowered to mete out to you long enough to be delivered of it. There will be no white bastards on this plantation when I bring my bride here.'

Abigail stared at him uncomprehendingly. How could Lance talk like this after they had been so much to each other? He mentioned his bride, yet Abigail knew he could not love Blanche Quenington, not when she remembered how close they had been. The only explanation must be the lure of Blanche's fortune: Lance would automatically inherit the entire Quenington estate when his father-in-law died. She told herself his brutal threat was as much to ensure the future for his child as to force her into this marriage and yet, even as she told herself this, deep down was a dreadful fear that he meant every word of it. A preacher had been sent for. She knew that the plantations relied on a travelling preacher to minister to their spiritual needs when they were too far from a church. The preacher could be anywhere. It might well take some time to fetch him. Surely it would be a relatively simple matter to steal a boat and go downstream to Jamestown?

Lance studied her shrewdly. 'If you're making plans to run away, abandon them,' he said. 'If you head for the wilderness, you'll be taken by Indians − always assuming you survive the wild animals. If you head downstream, you'll probably drown and, if you don't, you'll be picked up at Jamestown, if you get that far. As for going upstream ...' he paused and looked her over. 'No, you'd never be able to row against the current for long enough to get anywhere. The preacher, on the other hand, may well be back here by nightfall − tomorrow at the latest.'

Abigail knew she had no choice. Her only chance lay in escape. Had she been in the colony for longer, there might have been a possibility of her surviving but she knew nothing whatever of the terrain beyond the limits of settlement. Williamsburg differed little in essence from any English provincial town. Different trees grew there and there were subtle differences in architecture but it was a safe, civilised society. Nonetheless, she knew its citizens did not expect to travel much beyond its boundaries and certainly not beyond the limits of cultivated land. There were wild animals, there was the permanent menace of the native Americans of whom Abigail had heard much and seen nothing, there was − or so it was said − the ever-present threat of runaway slaves who would assuredly murder to prevent identification.

She told herself that a marriage such as Lance had set up for her was no different in essence to the marriages of convenience which

English fathers arranged for their offspring. Furthermore, she rather thought this particular marriage might have an advantage that had not so far been mentioned. She could hardly marry one man yet remain the property of another. Surely, she must become entirely the responsibility of her husband? She was fairly certain that Ezra Vatsetter would choose to interpret this as meaning she belonged to him, unable to distinguish between the wife's person and her property. Abigail could not see how she could possible remain a bond-slave if she were married to Vatsetter. It was a point upon which she would have liked clarification but a suddenly sharpened instinct for self-preservation stopped her asking for it. If the thought hadn't occurred to either man, she had no wish to raise it and if her guess was correct and they were aware that marriage would change her circumstances, then it was probably to her advantage not to let them know she was aware of it, too. It was the sort of thing Iago might know. She would find an opportunity to ask him.

Abigail lifted her chin and straightened her shoulders. She looked Lance directly in the eye. 'Very well, Mr Haworth. I'll marry your overseer.'

He looked at her suspiciously. It had been too easy. He had expected a scene. 'Just like that?' he asked.

She shrugged. 'Even if I could run away, I'll soon be too big to fend for myself in the wilderness and Williamsburg's too small to escape you for long, even if I managed to reach there.'

'You show more sense than I gave you credit for. All the same, I'll make sure someone keeps an eye on you until the knot's tied.'

Abigail glanced at her future husband with distaste, then turned back to her former lover. 'There's just one favour I'd ask, sir,' she said.

'Go on.' Displeasure figured large in Lance's voice.

'Mr Vatsetter doesn't come near me until we're wed.'

She saw Ezra frown but Lance threw back his head and laughed. 'You heard her, Ezra. Keep your hands to yourself until it's legal. You'll have to get your relief elsewhere in the meantime.'

The overseer's scowl deepened but Abigail knew he would obey his orders.

Chapter Seven

The preacher did not arrive before nightfall. Nor was there any sign of either the preacher or the man sent to fetch him on the following day. It was not until mid-morning of the next day that the messenger returned – alone. Abigail put her hands behind her back and crossed her fingers. Perhaps the preacher had had a nasty accident ... It was a short-lived surge of hope.

'I found him, right enough,' the slave said. He was an old man, and an injury to one foot ensured that he could be trusted to return to the plantation where he could be sure of food and shelter. 'Took longer than we reckoned. He'd gone up into the hills where old Martha Benson's dying, so they say. That's where he is, though, well-soused in Mis' Benson's liquor and lookin' for the hoard of gold she's s'posed to have hid thereabouts. Don't reckon he'll find anything, meself. He puts his hand on his heart, real earnest, and says as soon as she's shook off this mortal coil, he'll be right along. Let's hope his mule can find the way, 'cause I don't reckon *he's* goin' to be in any fit state to, and that's a fact.'

Lance was annoyed and Ezra was furious. Abigail tried to conceal her delight but was not entirely successful. Ezra paused beside her on his way out of the office where they had met to hear the news.

'You're mighty pleased with how things have turned out, I dare say,' he snarled. 'I'm not a patient man and right now my patience is wearing thin – and so's my temper. Maybe I'll not wait any longer. Maybe I'll pay you a visit tonight.'

'No, you won't,' Lance interrupted. 'It'll do you no harm to wait another day or two. Get your relief elsewhere. You've always managed to before.'

Ezra threw him a fulminating look and turned on his heel, muttering under his breath as he left the room.

Lance waited until the door had shut behind him. 'Keep out of his way, Abby. He's not a nice man to cross and right now he's disappointed.'

'And this is the man you want to see become father of your child?' Abigail asked bitterly.

'Once you're married, it will be his child,' Lance pointed out. 'That's the law and it won't be me arguing with it.'

Abigail went back to her cottage with a sinking heart despite the respite afforded by the preacher's attendance on Martha Benson. Her existence was proving a very lonely one. Word had spread rapidly through the slave quarters that she was to marry Ezra Vatsetter. They had been prepared to regard her as a curiosity but one of themselves. The impending marriage placed her firmly, in their estimation, on the other side of the picket fence. She was shunned by all expect Glory, who had taken a liking to the slightly built white woman, and Iago who, while he had no knowledge of her condition, could at least appreciate that marriage even to so unsavoury a character as the overseer might be preferable to a life in the tobacco fields. He spoke, if only to pass the time of day; Glory would have chattered but she had her own work to do, so Abigail was left entirely to her own devices expect for the fact that she was conscious she was never entirely unobserved. No one bothered to find her any work: once she was married, her work would be in looking after her husband and since that might be a situation to arise at any moment, there was not much point in finding her any employment. So she stayed in her cabin, out of the hot sun and entirely alone, until dusk when Iago put his head briefly round the door.

'He's been drinkin' hard all afternoon,' he warned, and Abigail knew he was not referring to Lance. 'You'll lie low if you've got any sense.'

'Surely he won't dare come here — not when Mr Haworth has told him not to?' Abigail said.

'I wouldn't take no bets on it. I know the man, and he's sure as hell goin' to break out some way.'

He disappeared with these pessimistic words and Abigail sat on in the deepening gloom, afraid to light a candle and hesitant to stoke the fire for fear of reminding Ezra of her presence.

She lay down and tried to sleep but fear of being awoken by the bursting in of her door kept her awake and finally she gave up the attempt. She stood with her door partly open. It was a warm night with clear skies and the thin light of a sickle moon was just enough to touch the thatched roofs with silver and transform the hovels for a few brief hours into something exquisitely strange. Apart from the moon, there was no light anywhere. The little shacks were in

138

darkness, the windows of the big house were blank and dark, there was no crack of light from the overseer's house. The plantation slept. Or so it seemed at first. As Abigail stood there, her ears gradually became attuned to the sounds of the night. The monotonous scraping of crickets, the occasional call of an unfamiliar nightbird, the sporadic scuttering of small animals – mice? – in the grasses. Then she picked up more distant sounds: the barking of a dog a long way off, the nearer, pleasantly homely clump and rustle of a horse shifting his weight from one leg to the other in his deep straw bed. The stable doors must be open, she thought, because she could even make out the unmistakable sound of jaws munching hay. Not everything on the plantation slept.

Then she became aware of an alien sound, one that somehow did not fit in with the unhurried calm of the other night-noises. It came from the barn where the straw was stored and it sounded as if something large had got in there among the straw and hay. A horse, perhaps, that had not been securely tied or, more probably, one of the house-cows had wandered in. Either way, no one would be grateful for the ensuing havoc which the morning would reveal. She slipped out of her cabin and ran the short distance along the dirt track to the barn.

The entrance was on the opposite side to the slave-quarters and, as Abigail rounded the corner, she could hear very clearly not only the frantic rustling of straw but also a muffled moaning, as if someone was trying to cry out but could not. When she had fully rounded the end of the barn and faced its open door, a patch of light thrown by a lantern told her that the source must be human. A cautious woman would have retreated at this point but Abigail was not inclined to be cautious. For good or ill – and quite probably the latter – Kingswood was now her home and, since no one had a legitimate reason for being in a barn at dead of night, it followed that they must be sent packing. If Kingswood had been Merefield, she would not have hesitated to send them about their business. It did not occur to her to hesitate now. She whisked up her skirts and marched determinedly into the barn.

'I don't know what on earth you think . . .' she began and her voice petered out.

There were two people in the barn, one of them black and female. The other was unmistakably Ezra Vatsetter. He had obviously had no hesitation in taking his employer's advice and it was equally apparent that his partner was very far from willing. When she realised that her assailant's attention had been distracted, the woman made a renewed attempt to get out from under him, but the overseer's attention had not been quite so totally diverted. As soon as he felt her try to twist away, he raised one fist and struck her a mighty blow across the side of her head and at the same time thrust himself still deeper inside her until she cried out in pain, there being no hand this time to muffle her cry.

Abigail was aghast. She threw herself on the overseer, flailing at him with the only weapons she possessed, her fists. 'Leave her!' she cried out, regardless of how her voice might carry in the still night air. 'Leave her! What sort of a monster are you? Can't you see you're hurting her? For pity's sake, leave her!'

Vatsetter looked up at her and sneered. 'So we're jealous after all, are we? Well, well, well — whoever would've thought it? Maybe it'll be worth waiting for the preacher-man, after all. Or maybe you'd rather I visited you later on tonight?'

Abigail scarcely heard him. Her attention was rivetted on the girl who now crept into a corner of the mound of straw and lay, battered and bleeding, and crouched over in a mixture of pain and shame. It was Glory.

'What have you done?' she demanded.

The overseer laughed shortly. 'I'd have thought that was obvious,' he commented then, seeing Abigail was still staring at Glory, he added, 'Don't worry about her. It's all some of these women are good for. She had to have it sooner or later. There aren't many advantages to this job, but that's one of them.'

Abigail glanced at him briefly and in disgust. 'Get out,' she said. 'Get out and leave her with me.'

His mouth opened to protest that Ezra Vatsetter took no orders from a woman but there was something in her manner and her voice that made him think better of it. He despised himself for so tamely doing as he was told and almost simultaneously reminded himself that it couldn't be long before the preacher was here and then they'd see who was master. That prospect made him feel much better about it and he stumbled out of the barn without another word, giving no thought to the fact that he passed Iago on the way.

When Glory's brother entered the barn and saw Abigail bending over his sister, attempting to cover her with the only garment she had, a totally inadequate apron, he needed no explanation.

'Go to my cabin,' she told him. 'There's a good warm cloak behind the door. Bring it here. A blanket, too. Bring a blanket from the bed.'

Iago seemed to hesitate briefly before doing as he was told but was quickly back with the cloak and blanket. Between them, they wrapped these round the girl who was by now shivering uncontrollably, Iago picked her up in his arms as if she had been no weight at all.

'Leave this to me,' he said. 'I'll bring your things back to you as soon as I've got her settled down.'

Abigail looked up at him across the human bundle in his arms. 'I'm sorry,' she whispered. 'I'm so sorry.'

He seemed surprised. 'Why? It happens all the time. You had no hand in it.'

'He threatened to come to me,' Abigail told him. 'La – , Mr Haworth told him to leave me alone until after we were married. He told him to get his relief elsewhere. If I hadn't been so anxious to . . . to postpone the inevitable, this wouldn't have happened.'

'Yes, it would – sooner or later. He's been watching Glory for some time now. Besides, out here you've got to look out for yourself. If you're a slave, you soon find no one else will.'

It was a long time before he returned Abigail's cloak and blanket and he did so without comment. Abigail found that any desire to sleep had left her completely and she spent what was left of the night in far from happy contemplation of what a future married to Ezra Vatsetter might hold.

Next morning she sought out Lance Haworth before he set out on his daily ride. She was fortunate in finding him alone. Briefly and without dwelling on the details, she recounted the events of the previous night. He seemed more puzzled than surprised.

'Why are you telling me this, Abby? After all, you didn't want him visiting you. What did you expect him to do?'

'But you don't understand, Lance. This wasn't a man seeking satisfaction with a willing partner. Glory was forced into it. Lance, she was bruised and bleeding.'

He shrugged. 'Some women prefer it like that.'

'Some women . . . Oh, come, Lance, you can't believe so preposterous a statement!'

'No? I fancy my experience is more extensive than yours. In any case, slaves expect it. After all, it's one of the reasons for buying women in the first place.'

Abigail suddenly felt very cold inside. 'Is that why you bought me?' she asked.

'Not entirely.' He grinned. 'No, there were other considerations. You might as well accustom yourself to the idea of Ezra's finding satisfaction elsewhere, especially since your present condition will soon limit your own usefulness in that direction. Such episodes have no significance, you know.'

'So far as I'm concerned, he can find his satisfaction where he likes,' Abigail retorted. 'I'd prefer him to pick willing partners, however, and I'm more than a little worried that he will use the

141

same brutality on me as he did on Glory.'

'Offer him no resistance and he'll have no cause, will he?' He stood up and picked up his beaver and his whip. 'I've wasted enough time on this silly business. I've a plantation to see to. I suggest you go back to your cabin. Visit Glory if you're concerned about her, though I dare say she's back in the fields, not half as bothered as you seem to think.'

Glory was not back in the fields. She was lying on the bed in her cabin, curled over like a baby and staring vacantly at the wall. Her face was swollen and bruised and blood had congealed round a cut near her eye. Abigail bathed it as gently as she could and spoke soothingly to her, as one speaks to an unhappy child, but there was no response. Glory offered no resistance to Abigail's ministering hands, indeed, she seemed oblivious of their efforts, but Abigail was unable to coax her into drinking either some water or some warmed milk.

It was while she was trying to persuade her to sip the latter that Abigail was aware by the sudden darkening of the little room that they were no longer alone. She looked up to see Iago's tall figure in the doorway.

'I thought maybe you'd be here,' he commented. 'I was sent to look for you. Preacher-man's here. You're to go up to the house.'

Abigail ignored his news. 'Has she been like this all night?' she asked.

'What was left of it. She's took it bad. No woman don't welcome it − leastways, none that I've ever known − but I ain't seen no one take it like Glory has.'

'Will she be all right?' Abigail asked anxiously.

'Who knows? No reason why not, I suppose. Others have learned to live with it. Glory's always had a bit more imagination than most, though. Maybe that makes it worse. What do you think?'

Abigail shivered. 'It can hardly help.' She glanced at him curiously. 'You're her brother. Doesn't it make you angry?'

'Slaves ain't got no rights to be angry − not with white men, at any rate. I tells myself I'll bide my time, that one day ... but the truth is, I ain't succeeded in convincing myself.' There was bitterness, not resignation, in his voice and Abigail knew that if Iago ever found an opportunity to revenge himself for wrongs done, he would take it. He did not expect such an opportunity, but he wouldn't flinch from it if it arose. He changed the subject suddenly. 'You'd better be gone. They're expecting you at the house. Don't do no good to keep them waiting. Don't worry about Glory. I'll take care of her.'

Abigail stood up. 'I'm sure you will.' She sighed. 'Wish me luck, Iago. I need it.'

He stood between her and the door. 'I ain't met many white women,' he said, 'and none like you. What for are you marrying the likes of Vatsetter? He don't seem your sort, for all he's free and you're a slave.'

'As you say: I'm a slave. I've no choice but to marry him and make the best of it.'

'There ain't no best to be made. He's an evil man.'

'As I discovered last night. I'll survive,' she added grimly.

Iago looked at her in silence for a moment and then stood aside. 'I reckon you will,' he said.

It was not the sort of wedding any woman dreams of. Abigail suspected that even her father would have been horrified had he been privileged to witness it. The minister had a fine air of pomposity and a resonant voice. He also had several days' growth of beard and difficulty enunciating his words with the clarity expected of his profession. Neither the bride nor the groom had taken any particular care with their appearance, the former because she had been summoned at such short notice, the latter because it would never have occurred to him to do so. Parliament's new law requiring the banns to be read in church for three consecutive Sundays before a marriage could take place was observed in the colony's towns but largely disregarded on the plantations among the handful of free white citizens who might otherwise have been affected by it. It was considered that two independent witnesses was perfectly sufficient guarantee the ceremony had taken place, and even that requirement could be difficult to fulfil. On this occasion Lance Haworth, more anxious than anyone else to ensure there should be no grounds for future doubt about the validity of the ceremony, was one witness and the preacher's down-trodden wife, the other. The ceremony itself was as brief as the minister could decently make it and it had occurred to no one to provide any sort of wedding-breakfast. Only one concession to the event was made.

'Well, Ezra,' Lance said as soon as the preacher had declared his overseer and his mistress man and wife, 'I suppose you'd better have the rest of the day off. Show your bride her new home.' He turned to Abigail. 'You'll find it a considerable improvement on your cabin.'

Abigail wondered whether she was supposed to exhibit gratitude but since she felt none, either for the gift of the husband or his house, she said nothing but turned and followed her new husband out of the house.

There was no denying the overseer's house was indeed an improvement over any slave's cabin, or would have been, had it been kept in any sort of order. The furniture was minimal and there had been little attempt to keep it neat and tidy. Abigail told herself this was no disadvantage: it meant she would have plenty to occupy both her mind and her hands for some time to come, and that could only be an advantage.

'Shall I get us a meal?' she began doubtfully, uncertain whether her husband — she had to force herself to think of him as that, even in her thoughts — kept enough food in stock to make implementation of such a suggestion feasible.

'Later,' he said, and grinned unpleasantly. 'Much later.' He caught one of her wrists and pulled her towards him, sinking his full, moist mouth on hers. Abigail tensed at his touch. She longed to push him away, to scream, yet she dared not. This man was her husband. He was doing nothing he had not every right to do. She had to submit but she could not be made to enjoy her duties. He released her mouth and her wrist. 'We've the rest of the day and all night before us, and I've had an eye for you since you landed at Norfolk,' he said. He nodded his head towards the door that closed off the bottom of the stairs. 'Up there.' The bed was a large, curtainless four-poster left over from some previous overseer's occupancy. Together with a chair and a chest, it filled the room. Ezra closed the door behind them, placed the chair just in front of it and sat on it.

'Over there,' he said, nodding towards the head of the bed. 'Stand there. Now let me look at you.'

Abigail did as she was bid.

'Turn round. Slowly.'

Abigail obeyed.

'Now get undressed.'

She hesitated. 'In front of you?' she asked.

'Why not? I'm your husband, aren't I? Slowly.'

She took off her apron and folded it neatly before laying it on top of the chest. Then she removed her cap and shook her hair free. She stepped out of her shoes before undoing the front-lacing of her plain, brown dress. That done, she hesitated and glanced across at Ezra.

'Slip it down and step out of it,' he said.

She did so, and stood before him in her plain white shift.

'Go on.'

She loosened the ribbon at the neck and then, after another momentary hesitation, slipped it off her shoulders and let it slide to the ground. She heard his sharp intake of breath as she stood naked before him.

'Turn round — slowly,' he ordered.

Abigail did as she was told.

144

He rose from his seat then and came across to her. He stood in front of her and ran his hands over her entire body. Her nipples hardened at his touch but it was with fear, not desire. Nevertheless, that involuntary tensing excited him and he bit them hard, till she cried out.

'Enough of this,' he said. 'I'll wait no longer.' He pushed her down on to the bed and without further preamble entered her, thrusting with a savage, relentless power in which consideration for his partner played no part at all. As soon as he was spent, he withdrew.

Abigail, whose revulsion increased at every thrust, forced herself to submit but made no attempt to pretend to a response she did not feel. If he noticed, he made no comment and it crossed her mind that there was a strong possibility he had never experienced anything else and therefore took her lack of enthusiasm for granted.

Abigail had made up her mind that he would detect no sign of weakness in her but long before morning she was exhausted, bruised and sore – and more than a little afraid for the well-being of the child she carried, a child conceived in love, not duty.

'Please,' she begged, more than half afraid of the possible violence of his reaction, 'no more – not tonight. It hurts so much now – and we must consider the child. Were it not for that, we'd not be wed.'

'Had enough, have you?' he said with satisfaction. 'I knew I could exhaust you. I've no regard for the child, mind, and won't have for any that's not my own, but it got me a wife any man would be proud to be seen with, so I guess I owe it that much.' There was nothing complimentary in his tone, just the self-congratulation of a man who had acquired a mare or a boar or an ox-team that someone else had wanted. It was a chilling comparison, but it illustrated his weakness and if Abigail was somehow to be able to turn this disastrous sequence of events to her advantage, it was his weaknesses she must get to know.

For the longest week of Abigail's life, he gave her no respite and she dreaded the onset of darkness which brought with it his nightly demands. By the end of a week she both looked and felt haggard and exhausted. There was no sign of any diminution in Ezra's lust for her and she become increasingly concerned for the well-being of the child she carried. She might not be able to understand Lance's willingness to let another man accept his child but that could not change the fact that it *was* his child she bore, a child that represented the love they had shared and whose existence she was therefore not prepared to hazard. For the child's sake, Ezra must stop and, having made up her mind to it, there was nothing to be gained by postponing the unpleasant task of telling him so.

He sat down for his supper and, as she stood beside him ladling broth into his bowl, he reached under her skirt, as he always did, and began fondling her. She always flinched at his touch, an involuntary reaction which seemed to excite rather than disgust him. On this occasion she pulled away.

'No,' she said. 'No more. Not for the present.'

His face darkened with anger. He stood up, his chair clattering to the floor, so great was the force with which he thrust it back. He caught her wrist and twisted her arm behind her back so that she was forced to come closer to him in order to lessen the pain.

'I decide when we stop. Not you. You've raised no objections so far. Why the sudden change?'

'I'm your wife,' she told him. 'I had a duty to you and I've fulfilled it — over and over again. That you can't deny. But I tell you this, Ezra Vatsetter: I'll not risk the child I bear just for your gratification, and without that child we'd not be man and wife. Leave me in peace until it's born. You'll not find me shirking my duties after that.'

He studied her with narrowed, suspicious eyes, as if he suspected that more lay behind her words than was overt.

'And what do I do for the next few months?' he demanded.

'Exactly what you did before, I imagine,' Abigail told him. 'You'll not hear me complaining if you choose to satisfy yourself elsewhere,' she added, reflecting that those were the truest words she had ever spoken.

He released her with a grunt, dimly aware that, while he might possess her legally and physically, there was some part of this beautiful, fragile creature that eluded him. Nor could he quite come to terms with the innate dignity upon which she seemed able to draw and which he found so disconcerting.

'Very well, then,' he said grudgingly. 'On that understanding — and an undertaking that you'll not dredge up other excuses once you're safely delivered — maybe I'll rest content for the time being.'

Abigail gave him the undertaking he required because she could see no alternative to it and was more than a little surprised that he resumed his seat and his supper not only with no further argument but also no further attempt to touch her while he ate. When the meal was finished, he snatched up his battered brown tricorne, slapped it on his head and left the house. He returned in the small hours of the night and threw himself into bed beside her with no thought for whether or not she might have been asleep. Abigail was not, but she stiffened in fearful expectation of what might ensue now that he was back beside her. Her fears proved groundless. He slept until dawn and made no reference to any aspect of the night's events. When the next two

146

nights followed the same pattern, Abigail felt able to heave a very cautious sigh of relief. Whatever else might characterise the man she had been obliged to marry, he seemed to be a man of his word.

Some time after dawn on the third day, the body of Glory was found hanging from a rafter in the barn. She was naked and had been badly beaten, some of the wounds and bruises being old ones. A stool, identified as being from her cabin, lay overturned a little way from her feet. No one doubted that she had taken her own life and no one doubted that she had managed it inexpertly with the consequence that her actual death had been slow and agonising.

Abigail sought out Iago to express to him her deep regret at the loss of his sister who had meant so much to him. His words were guarded, his manner wary and there was something unpleasantly close to hatred in his eyes.

Abigail could think of no reason for either the wariness or the hatred — none that related to her, at all events — so she decided to ignore both. 'Did she never recover from the pain and shame of that night?' she asked. 'To be sure, it would be no easy matter to do so, but I had thought she was just beginning to ... to live with the memory of it.'

'Maybe she was. Maybe she would've done — if she'd been let alone. Only she wasn't, was she? Your husband decided to make her pay for what you refused him. Oh, I can't blame you for wanting him elsewhere but did it have to be with Glory? He hurt her and humiliated her. He did things she couldn't bring herself to describe. Is it any surprise she hanged herself?'

Abigail stared at him, aghast, then buried her face in her hands. 'Is that what happened?' she asked. 'I knew he wasn't with me. I guessed he must be elsewhere, but I had no idea ... There was no hint, no word ...'

'Did you ask?'

'No, I didn't.' She coloured. 'To tell the truth, I was so relieved to be free of him that I didn't care. It never crossed my mind he would go back to Glory.'

'Would it have made any difference if it had?'

Abigail was about to protest that of course it would but she hesitated. 'I don't know,' she said. 'I'd like to think I'd have done something — or tried to — but I don't know.'

Iago shrugged and Abigail fancied his manner towards her softened infinitesimally. 'I suppose that's an honest answer,' he said at last. 'He told Glory you'd made him keep away. I guess you had your reasons.'

'I had. Whether they warranted Glory's life is another matter.'

'It's done now, and I've another score to settle. Sometime.'

Abigail glanced round anxiously. 'That's not a thing to say out loud – and you know it.'

'I know it, and right now I don't much care. I'll bide my time and maybe I'll get my chance yet. Always assuming the overseer's wife don't pull the rug out from under me first.'

'The overseer's wife will keep her own counsel,' Abigail told him and was rewarded with the merest ghost of a smile.

It was not long before the reasons for Glory's suicide were known or guessed at among the slaves and the air of resignation with which they went about their daily lives subtly changed to one of sullenness. There were mutterings about what could be done to dispose of the overseer once and for all and there was nothing impossible about the suggestions, Vatsetter being just one white man outnumbered by black. But even as they muttered, the slaves knew they would do nothing about it: the habit of obedience died hard and there was the additional knowledge that retribution would be exacted by every plantation owner in the colony and it would be swift and final, a lesson to every other slave in Virginia not to dream of tangling with a white man. Nevertheless, the very act of muttering relieved a little of their bad feeling and it was commented upon – though never in his hearing – that Iago, who never joined in the general condemnation of the overseer, was taking things mighty calmly.

The overseer himself cared not one jot whether Glory was alive or dead but he had been in the colony long enough to realise that the unrest he sensed about him would die down more quickly if he gave it no fuel. He accordingly slept at home where, somewhat to Abigail's surprise, he made no demands upon his wife except to assume that a meal would be on the table when he wanted it and the house would be better looked after than it had been before his marriage. He also ventured to suggest to Lance that perhaps bread and circuses were what was needed, a substantial diverson to take the slaves' minds off 'other matters'.

The excuse – Haworth's forthcoming wedding – was at hand. Lance and Blanche were getting married in Williamsburg to enable as much of the capital's society as possible to be present. This was primarily the bride's wish but it was one which her father was perfectly willing to indulge and to which her groom raised no objection: after all, it was not a frequent occurrence for a former indentured servant to have a wedding attended by the cream of Virginian society.

So far as the plantation slaves were concerned, it had been Lance's original intention to do no more than make a barrel of rum available to them and to resign himself to the loss of the following day's work. He was annoyed at the death of Glory: she had had the makings of a handsome woman, one who would have fetched a very nice price in a year or two, and that profit was now lost. Still, these things happened and Vatsetter could hardly have been expected to foresee her suicide. The overseer was right: if he made a more generous event out of his wedding-day, the blacks would soon forget their disgruntlement in anticipation of the festivities and, later, enjoyment of them. True, he would lose a couple of days' work, perhaps more, but then it would all be forgotten. He would not be there himself, of course, but he doubted whether his absence would cast a cloud over the celebration.

Ezra wasted no time in making sure that his wife knew that the marriage of her lover was to be celebrated in some style on the plantation but was denied the gratification of seeing her upset by the news. Abigail was fast learning to school her features so that every emotion no longer flitted revealingly across them. The news cut her deeply. She had known the wedding was inevitable, that celebrations were to be expected, but such prior knowledge did nothing to ease her anguish. It was news she must learn to live with, just as she would later have to live with the daily sight of Blanche Quenington in the position she had once expected to occupy herself.

Determined that no one, least of all Ezra or Lance, should have any idea of the depth of her inner misery, she went up to the house and set about doing what she could to ensure the celebrations would be something that no one would forget.

The appearance of the overseer's wife fired with the enthusiasm of the born organiser was not entirely welcomed by the rest of the household, but when they saw that Mis' Vatsetter not only had very clear ideas as to what they should do but also how they should go about it, it was tacitly agreed that she might as well be allowed to take command since that meant that everyone else had only to follow instructions and the blame, should failure ensue, would be entirely hers.

Abigail was by now uncomfortably aware that her girth was visibly increasing. She eased her lacing and hoped no one had noticed, though on more than one occasion she caught Ezra eyeing her shrewdly. One night after he had clambered into bed beside her, he put his hand under her night-shift and slid it up to her belly. She shuddered at his touch, fearing what it might portend, but all he said was, 'I'll be glad when this is over. Then you'll really know you've a husband.' He withdrew his hand, turned his back on her and went to sleep.

Ezra was not the only person to comment. She made her way to the

149

saw-mill where trestles were being made to support the long tables. The work was progressing satisfactorily and Iago, sweat glistening on his rich brown skin, gave her his hand to help her across some carelessly dropped planks.

'Your man sho' ain't wasted much time, has he?' he asked. 'In fact, if I didn't know when you came to Kingswood, I'd have said he'd been a touch premature.'

Abigail coloured. 'You know better than that, Iago,' she said.

'Do I? I'll grant you this, Mis' Vatsetter: I don't reckon you let your husband near you till you had to.' With these cryptic words he released her hand and returned to his work, leaving Abigail to speculate upon his precise meaning.

As the days leading up to the wedding passed, Ezra became short-tempered and uneasy, as if he were afraid the marriage might not take place. Abigail caught him eyeing her from time to time in a way she could not like. It was almost as if, as the wedding approached, he had an increasing need to re-establish his own conjugal rights to force her to acknowledge once more that she was his and not Lance Haworth's.

The day before the wedding celebrations, he came home unexpectedly in the middle of the morning and found her upstairs making the bed. Her lack of pleasure at seeing him was briefly apparent before she schooled her expression to welcome him. He was not deceived.

'You need to pretend better than that,' he told her. 'Haven't you realised that half my pleasure lies in having you against your will? Your dislike – and your fear of what I may do – excite me more than any amorous welcome would do.'

'I'll try to bear that in mind,' Abigail told him, and meant it.

He reached out as if to touch her and then, almost before she had had time to steel herself, thought better of it and left her to her chores. Abigail was both relieved and puzzled. Her short acquaintance with Ezra Vatsetter showed him to be a man not accustomed to denying himself such pleasures as were available to him. He had shared her bed since Glory's death and made no demands in that time and Abigail was unsure how long this relatively happy state of affairs could continue. Perhaps, once the celebrations were over and some of the resentment over Glory's suicide had died down, he would once more transfer his attentions to one of the plantation women, some of whom were likely to be more resigned to his demands than Glory had been. Her fear was that, unwilling to hold himself in check, he would sooner or later force himself on her once more, despite her condition.

The celebrations started early next day and rum figured prominently in them. Lance had returned to Williamsburg for the

150

ceremony but his absence was scarcely noticed, although one or two voices were heard to mutter that it was a pity he hadn't seen fit to take his overseer with him. Abigail had seen to it that the refreshments were lavish and arranged on the long trestle tables she had had made for the purpose, in the manner of similar feasts on any English estate. She had argued that to do it this way made a far more memorable occasion of the event than would have been achieved by Lance's original idea of declaring a holiday, providing a barrel of rum, and leaving it at that and, since the object of the exercise was largely to try to erase the recollection of Glory's suicide, Lance had dipped into his coffers without too much reluctance.

Where there is food and drink in plenty, music soon follows with dancing in its wake. One of the house-slaves proved to be a fiddler of no mean ability. His instrument was home-made and its tone coarser than those heard in the drawing-rooms of England but it was somehow right in the warm Virginia air and its music was soon enriched with the sound of pipes and drums as others brought out their instruments and their talents.

By the middle of the afternoon, the combination of good food, good music and plentiful liquor was having its inevitable result. Apart from Abigail, who had no desire to lose command of her senses and, in any case, disliked rum, the only other noticeably abstemious reveller was Iago. He ate, he sang, he danced – and was much in demand for his excellence in the last – but he drank scarcely at all. The same could not be said for Ezra. Abigail could only wonder that her husband was still on his feet. She looked at him in disgust. His pale, repellant eyes had become positively watery and his always-moist mouth now drooled as he tried to converse with his table-companion. He glanced up and when his eyes focussed on her and he saw she was looking at him, he staggered to his feet and blundered over to her.

'And how's my lady wife?' He enunciated with great care and spoke with exaggerated courtesy.

'I'm very well and have no desire to separate you from your companions,' she replied with perfect truth.

'Howarth marries the Quenington woman today,' he went on.

'Indeed, he does, and that's precisely why we're celebrating.'

'They'll be married by now and that's the end of any ideas *you* may have had.'

Abigail coloured but maintained the appearance of good humour. 'I wish them well and no other idea of mine could possibly be of interest or value to them,' she said.

He narrowed his eyes as if to sharpen their focus. 'You may try to

151

put a good face on it, but we two know better, don't we?'

'Now you're talking nonsense,' Abigail told him. Her tone was the tolerant one of somebody humouring a fractious child.

It was the wrong tone to take: Ezra was not yet too drunk to notice when he was being patronised. He caught her wrist in a strong grasp that did not waver though he swayed on his feet as if the effort had nearly cost him his balance. 'Nonsense, is it? We'll see about that. Come on.' He staggered away from the tables and in the general direction of the barn, dragging Abigail with him.

She flexed her wrist once or twice but the grip was too strong to slide out of it. On the other hand, Ezra was sufficifently unsteady on his feet for it to have been quite a simple matter to push him off balance and thus oblige him to loosen his hold. Abigail toyed with the idea and then abandoned it. His temper was uncertain at the best of times, and when he was half-inebriated was not the best of times. If she made a public fool of him by pushing him over, he was sober enough to recognise what she had done and drunk enough to take immediate and violent revenge for the humiliation. She followed him.

Several people saw them go but thought little of it. The overseer's capacity for rum was legendary and, though he must be approaching his limit, he was still some way from being legless.

Abigail submitted to the indignity of being half-dragged across the garden where the tables had been set up, across the empty stable-yard and over to the adjacent barn. The sounds of festivity could still be heard but their clear passage had been interrupted by the succession of intervening buildings so that it was only the generality of festive noise that could be heard, not the particularity.

When they reached the barn, Ezra braced himself against the lintel of the door with one hand while the other, which still grasped Abigail's wrist, pulled her forward, past him, and flung her over on to the loose straw in the bay opposite. The action was unexpected and caught her off-balance so that she stumbled and fell, only grateful that the straw was there to cushion her fall. She was out of breath and found herself instinctively clutching her belly. It was a gesture that did not go unnoticed.

'We mustn't let anything happen to the child, must we?' he sneered bitterly. 'Whatever else happens, the master's bastard must be protected.' He staggered over to her and stood peering down at her. 'As if he cared! He cares about as much as I do. Lance Haworth's only concern is that nothing stop this marriage. By God, how he needs this marriage ! Your news must have been a mighty blow to him. Neither he nor I gives a damn what happens to it. I'll tell you what I care about. I care about having a wife I can't touch. And why can't

I touch her? Because she's carrying another man's child. What sort of reason is that?' Tears welled in his already moist eyes and Abigail realised he was fast becoming maudlin. Perhaps, if she could but keep him going in this vein, it would be only a matter of time before the rum finally conquered all. Already the effort of coherent speech was making him sway on his feet, but he was not finished yet. 'I'll tell you what sort of a reason that is. It's no reason at all. You're my wife and Lance Haworth's got one of his own so there's no need for this thing you're carrying to be born at all. This is as good a place as any to teach you who's master in my household.' He laughed. 'It was here I taught that nigger her duty and you can learn the same lesson the same way.'

Abigail's stomach lurched sickeningly. His meaning was unmistakable and she had no way of knowing whether he was yet too drunk to carry out his threat. At least if she got to her feet, it should be perfectly possible to duck away from him while he was so unsteady on his feet. She stood up cautiously and was barely upright again when a savage blow caught her on the side of the face and sent her reeling. She stumbled backwards against the partition of the bay and only its wooden walls prevented her from falling. Another blow followed the first and this time she was prevented from falling by the shaft of a pitchfork left carelessly in the bay and half hidden by the loose straw.

Ezra determined to press home his advantage. He lurched across the short distance between them and made a grab for her arm. He missed but caught her shoulder instead and Abigail felt the sleeve rip where it joined the bodice. She flung up that arm to ward him off, conscious now of the warm, sweet stickiness of blood in her mouth and the fact that, for some reason she was unable to determine, she could see only imperfectly.

'You'll not push me away. Not this time, not ever again,' he told her. 'I'll take it by force – for that's how I like it – until you crawl and beg for mercy, and then I'll take it again until I'm empty. And if I have to beat you unconscious or tie you up to keep you available, then that's what I'll do.'

A third and a fourth blow in rapid succession loosed her hold on the supporting pitchfork and left her spreadeagled on her face in the straw. She felt a boot strike the small of her back and, as she struggled to her knees, he laughed.

'So you want it like that, do you? Who'd've thought it!' he sneered and before Abigail realised what he meant, he had flung himself on her, the weight of his body forcing her knees from under her while he displayed a remarkable dexterity in simultaneously forcing her legs apart.

As she realised what he was about, Abigail's efforts to evade him became desperate. He must, of necessity, fumble both with his breeches and her skirts and in those brief moments when his weight on her was less, she twisted to one side, her hands groping for support and one of them finding once more the pitchfork handle. So quickly had she seized the limited opportunity offered, that she was almost on her feet before Ezra fully realised what had happened. He could move with neither speed nor precision but he grabbed her ankle, a sure lever to yank her off her feet once more.

But Abigail was standing now and, although a mist prevented her from seeing clearly, she had no difficulty feeling his grasp and guessing his intent.

It was pure instinct that made her raise the pitchfork. Ezra saw its prongs gleaming in the light from the doorway.

'Don't waste your time threatening me,' he warned her, reaching up for it. 'You'll only make me more determined.'

With all the force she could muster, Abigail brought the implement down. There was a moment when something blocked its passage and she had to lean harder on the shaft to force it through. After that, it slid easily until it stopped because the prongs had run out of length. She let go. Instead of clattering to the floor, the pitchfork remained upright, swaying slightly. Abigail put the back of her hand up to one eye to rub away the mist that impaired its vision. The hand came away wet and when she glanced down at it in surprise, found it was blood, not tears. At least Ezra had finally realised she meant what she said and was not merely playing perverse games. She looked at him. There was a surprised expression on his face and he was gurgling as if he was trying to say something but could not get the words out. The rum was finally having its effect. Then she realised that the gurgling was caused by thick clots of blood oozing sporadically from the corner of his mouth. She stepped back. A dark stain was spreading over his shirt around the prongs of the pitchfork. So that was why it hadn't fallen over when she let go of it! It was strange how explanations were often extremely simple. It was several second before an even simpler explanation of Ezra's inertia occurred to her.

Abigail stepped back. Was he dead or merely dying? Such a very short time ago he had been horribly, repulsively, alive. Could it happen so quickly? A far more chilling thought superseded this one. If Ezra was dead – or merely dying – the reason was the pitchfork but the cause was the person who had used it. Perhaps she should remove it? Then all would be well and Ezra might even have learnt his lesson. She reached for the shaft. It felt sticky and unpleasant now. Some blood must have got on to it. Abigail shuddered. She was sure she should remove it but suddenly the very idea of doing so made her flesh creep. Someone else must do so or Ezra would die. She didn't really mind if he did, but she didn't want to be responsible for it. She must fetch someone – and quickly or it might be too late.

She backed steadily away from Ezra's body. Something in the way he lay there drew her gaze and made it quite impossible for her to turn round and leave the barn normally. While she could see him, she must look. Only when her egress was blocked did she prise her attention away from her husband. She had backed into Iago. She heaved a sigh of relief. Who better could she have found to help her? Iago would not ask inane questions or demand endless explanations. Her face broke into a welcoming smile and one hand caught at his arm while the other pointed towards Ezra.

'I'm so glad it's you, Iago,' she said, quite unaware that the neat figure of the overseer's wife had been transformed almost beyond recognition. Her face was swollen and bleeding, and there was blood on her hands, her torn dress and her apron. Straw was caught in her hair and her dress and she crouched and walked painfully, like one whose back has been injured. 'If someone doesn't remove that pitchfork I think Ezra may die, and that would never do. Would you remove it, please?'

Iago pushed past her and bent over the man in the straw. The overseer wasn't dead yet but in Iago's judgement, it was only a matter of time. Removing the pitchfork which, so far as he could tell, had penetrated the lung, would only hasten the end. He looked up.

'What happened?' he asked.

Abigail shrugged and seemed puzzled. 'I don't really know. He was drunk, of course. He said he'd teach me who was master, as he'd taught Glory. I didn't want to risk the baby but he was insisting. I only meant him to leave me alone. That's all.'

'Well, you've sure succeeded in that,' the slave said grimly. He took hold of the pitchfork and pulled. The body came up with it initially, until Iago put his foot on its chest to hold it down.

'Is he dead – or are we in time?' Abigail insisted.

'No, he's not, but he soon will be. You can thank the Lord everyone's eating and drinking and minding their own business. This man of yours needs to disappear.' He picked the detested overseer up in his arms and strode towards the door.

'Yes,' Abigail said. 'You're right. Take him to the house. How long will it take to fetch a doctor?'

'He don't need no doctor,' Iago said shortly, hastening as fast as his burden would allow away from the barn, the stables, the cabins and the cowsheds, casting anxious glances around him in case they were observed. Abigail, uncomprehending, trotted at his heels. Not

155

till he reached the pigsties did Iago pause and then it was briefly, to ensure there were no witnesses. With one deft heave, he tipped Ezra Vatsetter over the low wall and into the trough where the bulk of the overseer's form was submerged in the swill. Then he took Abigail's arm and led her firmly away. Hogs enjoy their food, but they are noisy, sometimes messy, feeders and it might be better for Abigail's sanity if she were elsewhere for the next few hours.

He hurried her back to her house, relieved that there was still no sign they might have been observed. He pushed her inside and shut the door behind them. He looked around him. He had never been inside the overseer's house before.

'Where do you keep your clothes?' he asked.

'Upstairs. Is he dead?'

'He is now. Nothing you could do to stop it. Come on, then – upstairs.'

Iago threw open the chest and found a grey dress not dissimilar to the torn and bloody one Abigail was wearing. He poured some water from the ewer into the bowl. 'Get this on and clean yourself up,' he told her. 'Give me the dress you're wearing and I'll burn it.' He glanced down at his own garments. These were his working clothes and he had no others. If he covered the blood with mud, maybe no one would notice. 'I'll get the fire going. Then I'll be back for that dress,' he told her.

When he returned up the stairs five minutes later he found her discarded gown in a crumpled heap outside the door. Thank the Lord, he thought. At least she can still follow instructions. It took skill to destroy the dress because the heavy cloth was all too prone to smother the flames but he kept at the task until nothing but charred and unidentifiable fragments remained. He realised with some alarm that there was still no sign of Abigail.

When he investigated, he found that she had dressed herself again and had made an inadequate attempt to wash her face but she was now sitting on the edge of the bed, her expression quite blank. He took the cloth, dipped it in the basin and carefully wiped her face clean, ignoring the involuntary wince she gave whenever he touched the bruises and cuts inflicted by her late husband. Then he wiped her hands, finger by finger, as one wipes a child's. He removed the straw, wisp by wisp, from her hair and made a heavy handed attempt to brush it into some sort of order.

'Now, Mis' Vatsetter, we go back to the party.'

Abigail turned and stared at him. 'Is he dead?'

'He's dead, but there ain't no call for you to tell anyone.'

'It's my fault, isn't it?'

156

'No, ma'am. It he'd treated you decent, it wouldn't never have happened.'

'That's true, I suppose.' She spoke with a calm that worried Iago far more than hysterics would have done. It was easy to knock someone out of hysterics. Then, to his relief, he saw tears well up in her eyes and she began to shake uncontrollably. This was a more natural reaction. He hesitated — there were liberties slaves didn't take — then put his arms round her and let her cry against his shoulder, great body-shattering sobs that an outsider might take for a widow's grief. Iago knew their cause was an unpalatable combination of relief and guilt and the sooner Mis' Vatsetter came to terms with that mixture, the safer it would be for both of them.

Abigail wept for a long time, her agony unconsciously eased by the fact that she did not have to bear it in solitude. When the sobs finally ceased and Abigail looked up at Iago, she appeared to be in complete command of herself again.

'What do we do now?' she asked.

'We go back to the party.'

'And Ezra? The bruises on my face? How do I account for them?'

'The truth, only maybe not quite all of it. They all know what he's like with women. A few bruises won't seem strange. It's my guess no one'll even comment. As for Vatsetter — Well, he drunk some more and staggered out of the house after he'd done what he wanted to with you, and you — why, you don't much care where he went or how long he stays there, just as long as he leaves you alone for a while.'

'That's true enough,' Abigail admitted bitterly. 'But won't they start looking for him?'

'Not today, and not tomorrow, I don't reckon. No one ain't going to be in any fit state to work tomorrow and they sure ain't going to go looking for the overseer so's he can make them. No one ain't planning on feeding the hogs tomorrow, either, not judging by how full the trough was. No, I reckon we've got two clear days before anyone suspicions he's dead. Two days to fix it in their minds that he was real drunk after he dragged you off here — and that's something they all saw, remember. There's just one thing you've got to keep in your mind, Mis' Vatsetter.'

'And what's that?'

'If the whole story gets out, we both stand to hang. You with a trial, me without. Now I don't know about you, but I ain't got no intention of hanging, not for the likes of white scum like Ezra Vatsetter.'

'You'll have no argument from me on that score,' Abigail told him. 'We'll have to be very careful, I think.'

'More careful than you've ever been in your short life.'

157

Chapter Eight

Iago's assessment of the situation appeared next day to be cynically accurate. The plantation slaves were in no fit state to work and had no inclination to seek out their overseer once they realised he was not about. The respite was welcome, both on its own account and as an aid to recovery from the previous day's excesses. No one was surprised that Mis' Vatsetter, too, remained indoors. Her husband had seemed mighty determined when he hauled her away. It would be interesting to see how long it would be before the bruises faded on that pale, impractical skin.

The next day began similarly, though the overseer's untypically prolonged absence gave rise to some unease amongst the more fully recovered members of the little community. There was the unpleasant possibility that he was lying concealed somewhere, watching the inactivity and anticipating with some relish the prospect of exacting retribution for idleness. Unease was goaded into activity when word raced through the slave quarters that Mas' Haworth and his new bride had just hove to at the little jetty.

They were entirely unexpected. Conditions in the colony were such that the wedding-journeys favoured in England were scarcely practical and Blanche Haworth's known preference for the social life of the capital had led everyone to assume that the couple would remain there for the foreseeable future. The house-slaves, in particular, rushed to make good, even at this short notice, any deficiencies in their management: Lance Haworth might be unlikely to notice or comment upon any shortcomings but they were disinclined to place a similar dependency upon his bride.

Lance's first action was to send a boy to the overseer's house with instructions for Ezra to wait upon his employer without delay. He was not pleased to receive instead a message from his overseer's wife to the effect that she had not seen her husband since the day of the wedding. Neither, the messenger added helpfully, had anyone else.'

Lance scowled. He was safely married to Blanche but if, in the not too distant future he was going to need to persuade her father to invest in Kingswood, he must create the impression of a well-run and profitable enterprise, and an actively present overseer was an essential ingredient in that creation. He told the boy to fetch Mis' Vatsetter.

Blanche was well aware who Mrs Vatsetter was. The gossiping tabbies of Williamsburg had not been slow to pass on to her the information their husbands had brought home following Lord Jasper's reception. Lance had dismissed her jealously pointed remarks but had taken very good care to let his intended bride know that his acquisition had decided to marry his overseer. The news had gone some way to putting Blanche's mind at rest but she was no fool and she had no intention of leaving her husband to speak to the overseer's beautiful − if somewhat insipid − wife alone.

Her mind was considerably eased by Abigail's appearance. Gone was the fragile beauty immaculately gowned in midnight blue velvet that she remembered from Lord Jasper's reception. The plain grey stuff gown loosely laced over a noticeably increasing girth was neat enough, but neither immaculate nor fashionable, and there was no disguising the cuts on her face and the lurid, multi-coloured bruises accompanying them. Nor was there any disguising Blanche's involuntary smile of relief. Abigail Vatsetter, clearly pregnant by the uncouth oaf she had elected to marry, was no threat to Blanche Quenington Haworth.

Abigail's appearance was, however, a shock to Lance. Had she looked like that on the *Alice Nancy,* Eden Paisley would have been welcome to her. It seemed a pity to see such beauty marred but doubtless Ezra had had his reasons.

'They tell me you haven't seen your husband since the day before yesterday,' he began.

'Not since the afternoon,' Abigail confirmed with perfect truth.

'And neither has anyone else?'

'They must speak for themselves but I can't imagine why anyone should lie,' she replied.

Lance frowned. 'Why should he have disappeared?'

'Initially, I imagine, to sleep off the effects of too much rum,' Abigail told him.

'He celebrated well, I take it?'

'Doubtless he would express it so. Three sheets to the wind describes it better, I think.'

'And you've no idea where he went?'

'None at all. You know him better than I. Your own guess on the

159

subject would have more value than mine.'

Lance tapped the arm of his chair impatiently. There was a pertness in her manner that came uncomfortably close to insolence. It bothered him, yet there was nothing in her words to indicate why it should.

He dismissed her. 'Send him straight to me if he returns,' he said. 'Iago should be outside. Send him in as you go.'

Abigail glanced anxiously at the slave as she delivered her instructions but he made no reply and neither his face nor his manner gave her any indication of what was going on in his mind.

She left the house with a firm step that implied a confidence she was far from feeling, her troubled frown giving far more accurate reflection of her true feelings, though an observer would have attributed it to natural concern for a missing husband. Once her own door closed behind her, however, she sank on to the nearest chair and found she was shaking uncontrollably. What would Iago tell them? Could she really trust him? Or might he use his knowledge of what she had done to negotiate by some means an improvement in his present lot? She told herself that the slave's own involvement was too great for that, but a nagging doubt at the back of her mind suggested that a sufficiently ruthless liar would be able to manipulate so inconvenient a truth, especially if no trace of Ezra's body was ever found. She had no idea how much the pigs could be expected to devour. She thought it unlikely there would be nothing left and her only real hope could be that such remains as there were would be unidentifiable. Even that eventuality would leave the question of whose they were. She rested her hands on her belly. Did they hang women who were with child? She wanted this child of Lance's so badly and had already suffered considerably in its interest. Perhaps they would let it be born and then hang her.

Such thoughts did little to comfort her but at last the shaking diminished and Abigail thought she felt almost calm. Reflecting that there is nothing like hard work to occupy mind and body, she decided to clean the little house from top to bottom but when she started, she found she was quite unable to concentrate on any task. The slightest sound brought her eyes to the door and she could feel the colour draining from her face whenever someone passed by. Her sense of isolation was increased by the fact that no one called by to see how she did or to tell her what progress was being made in the hunt for the overseer. It was true she was unsure how she would cope with a visitor, but it was more than a little unnerving not to have one.

Night fell, and she forced herself to prepare something to eat, but when it was ready she had no appetite. When she finally took herself off to bed, sleep − which had not come easy these last few nights − proved impossible and she rose with the first light of dawn, heavy eyed and heavier headed.

She felt no more inclined to eat breakfast than she had to eat supper but she reminded herself that there was the child to consider and forced herself to swallow some bread and cheese. She had started to carve herself a slice of ham but although that particular pig had been slaughtered before she came to the plantation, she felt a sudden aversion to it.

The morning was well advanced and Abigail had nothing to show for it beyond deepening anxiety and melancholia, when she heard the sound she had been dreading all the previous day. She opened the door to find Lance and behind him Iago, with two or three other plantation slaves behind him, filling the doorway. Abigail had no idea how she looked and Lance was surprised − and more than a little piqued − that she looked as distraught as would normally be expected of any wife whose husband was unaccountably missing. It was not a reaction he would have expected from Abigail, given the circumstances of her marriage. There was no understanding women.

'May we come in, Mrs Vatsetter?' he asked, formally polite.

Abigail gave no answer but stood aside to admit them. Her eyes searched Iago's face but it told her nothing.

Lance held out his hand and opened it, palm uppermost. A somewhat battered tin button lay there.

'Do you know this, Mrs Vatsetter?' he asked.

Abigail took it and studied it. She knew it very well. It had a lion crudely stamped in the middle, damaged but recognisable. It was one of a set Ezra had bought from a pedlar and which she had but recently sewn on to his 'best' coat.

'Yes. It's one of Ezra's,' she said.

'Do you know when he was last wearing it?'

'At the wedding-party. He had the set sewn on his good coat to mark the occasion.'

Lance nodded. 'That's more or less what others have said. Sit down, Mrs Vatsetter.' Abigail did so, her eyes fastened on his face with an apprehension he found entirely understandable. 'I think we've found Ezra,' Lance went on. He paused both to let this sink in and to gauge her reaction. There seemed to be none. 'Mrs Vatsetter, this is not going to be very pleasant for either of us,' he continued. 'How drunk was Ezra after that celebration?'

'Very. As drunk as I'd ever seen him − perhaps more. Why?'

'This button was found in the bottom of the pig trough when the hogman went to feed them this morning. It wasn't the only thing he found.' Lance hesitated again, reluctant to be specific. 'There were two thigh-bones and the remains of a skull. It could be anyone, of course, but no one else is missing and this button would appear to clinch the matter. We think whoever it was must have overbalanced into the trough in so drunken a state that he neither knew what had happened nor was in any condition to right himself. He would have drowned, and then ... well, hogs aren't selective feeders.'

Abigail stared at him. 'You think it was a drunken accident?' she said.

'I certainly don't imagine he dived involuntarily,' Lance said, surprised. 'And, while there may well be those who would be happy to see him dead, I doubt whether they would pick so uncertain a means of killing him. Would you?'

'I suppose not.' Abigail's tone was doubtful. Lance did not find anything strange in this − after all, she must have discovered that her husband was not universally popular − but Abigail's doubt was due to sheer disbelief that the truth could so easily have escaped discovery. She glanced past Lance at Iago but again his face told her nothing. She rose from her seat and turned away from her vistors to lean against the mantelshelf. 'Please leave me,' she said.

Lance hesitated. He was not a sensitive man but it occurred to him that she seemed remarkably self-possessed for one who had been so suddenly and gruesomely widowed. 'Shall I send someone to you?' he asked. 'One of the women, perhaps?'

'No.'

Iago touched his arm respectfully. 'Best we come away, Mas' Haworth. Sudden death takes people different ways and there ain't no accounting for it, most of the time.'

Lance nodded. 'Send to the house if you need anything, Mrs Vatsetter,' he told her. 'We'll discuss your future later. I'll send for the preacher and we'll give such remains as there are a decent burial. You can leave that to me.'

Abigail, her back still towards them, nodded and, after a further brief hesitation because this seemed an oddly unsatisfactory way to end a difficult interview, Lance and his companions left the overseer's house.

Abigail waited until the sound of their footsteps died away and then sank back on to her chair again, buried her head in her hands and burst into tears. They were tears of sheer relief. Iago had proved himself trustworthy; no suspicion of the truth about the way in which Ezra had met his death had been hinted at, and the finding of that one button was really most fortuitous because it meant her widowed status was undisputed. It left only the question of whether she was a free woman or whether she must revert to her bonded status following her husband's death. Abigail was sure it must be the former but it was the sort of thing Iago would know. She would ask him but must pick her time carefully. It would never do for anyone to suspect there had been anything between them other than the formal relations between a slave and overseer's wife.

Lance gave her two days to grieve and then sent for her.

'Your situation is scarcely enviable,' he began, an observation she could not dispute. 'I've been giving it much thought over the last two days and, although I appreciate that you may not be entirely ready to discuss it, the fact remains that I need a new overseer and he will require your house, so talk we must.'

Abigail inclined her head in acquiescence with his assessment of the position. 'And what conclusion did you come to?' she asked.

'I've posted notices in both Williamsburg and Norfolk inviting men to apply for the post,' he told her. 'In a few days' time I shall go to the capital to interview them. I have indicated that the widow of their predecessor, a white woman of good birth, is available as a wife, should that be appropriate.'

Abigail stood very still. 'Without consulting me?'

'To what end? The alternative is labour in the fields and a return to a slave's cabin. At least you would remain well housed.'

'My marriage to Ezra made me a free woman,' Abigail told him, knowing it was a bluff but hoping she might have hit the nail very squarely on the head.

Lance flushed angrily. 'Who told you that? You married at my instigation and you reverted to my ownership when Ezra died. Only if he had lived until your bondage was up would you have been free. No, Abigail, you remain a bond-slave unless you can buy your freedom.'

'And how much will that be?'

Lance looked at her through narrowed eyes. Was it possible Ezra had had some hoard of gold which his widow had discovered? No – a few golden guineas, maybe, but not enough to think in terms of buying her freedom. 'The amount of the I.O.U. I refused to accept from Lord Jasper was four thousand guineas. That would seem to be a fair price,' he said.

Abigail tried not to let her dismay show. 'Surely not. I was not then pregnant by you, was I? My value must be lower now.'

'On the contrary, it proves you are not barren, a great advantage out here. Furthermore, you have had a certain degree of training in household matters.' He smiled unpleasantly. 'I'm glad you questioned the price, Abigail. Four thousand is too low. Five would be a fairer price. For five thousand guineas, you will be free. Otherwise you marry the new overseer should he lack a wife.'

When Abigail left the house, she sought out Iago and drew him to one side, a little apart from his fellows. Briefly she told him the gist of her converse with Lance. 'Is he right, Iago? Am I really his bond-slave once more?'

Iago shrugged. 'I don't know much about the laws concerning bond-slaves,' he admitted. 'It don't seem right, though. No point in arguing about it, all the same. If you get into court – always assuming you can raise the money for it – I don't reckon any magistrate in the colony'll back a slave against its master.'

Upon reflection, Abigail conceded that he was right.

She returned to her house in the lowest of spirits. It was not only the discovery that she was still not free, but the scarcely acknowledged discovery that, despite his treatment of her, she still loved Lance Haworth. It hurt to be in the same room as he and not to feel his arms around her. It hurt still more to have him thus callously disposing of her without reference to her own feelings in the matter. She told herself that perhaps he did so because this was the only way he could keep her near him; that perhaps, when Blanche tired of the plantation and wanted to return to the excitement of Williamsburg, he would remain at Kingswood and they could resume the relationship they had once shared. That would hardly be advisable if she were married to his overseer. It began to look as if her only chance of happiness would be to make a life for herself and her child away from here, to divert her love for Lance into the care his child would need. She had the means of buying her freedom. She would have preferred to be able to pass her mother's necklace on to the child she carried, but perhaps the use she could make of the money it would fetch would be of greater value to her baby. Five thousand guineas was a sum so large she could barely imagine it but she knew the necklace must be worth even more. There was one insuperable problem. It was still in Williamsburg.

She toyed with the idea of seeking permission to go to the capital, and rejected it. Lance would not risk her running away and, at the very least, would demand an explanation. Abigail had a very strong suspicion that a slave's possessions might well belong to its master. Since most slaves had few possessions, and none of value, there was rarely a conflict but she was by no means sure that would apply to any master, however generous, who discovered the Broughton necklace in his slave's possession – and Lance betrayed little sign of generosity. She had the means to buy her freedom but not the opportunity. It was a galling discovery.

The solution to her dilemma came unexpectedly and from the most

164

unlikely source. Lance decided to take her to Williamsburg with him so that any prospective overseer would have an opportunity of seeing his potential wife.

'We can't disguise the fact that you're increasing,' he said in the matter-of-fact tones of someone selling a horse. 'That may or may not be a disadvantage – probably, on balance, not. But at least he'll be able to see you're better quality merchandise than he is otherwise likely to find.'

'Thank you,' Abigail said with heavy irony. 'Have you mentioned this scheme to Mrs Haworth?'

'Mrs Haworth will be coming too,' Lance said stiffly. 'She visits the dressmaker.'

Abigail smiled to herself. Blanche was no fool, then, and her presence might well make it easier for Abigail to slip out since it was unlikely Lance would be in a position to keep her close. She decided to prepare the ground. 'I have a little money that Ezra left,' she said. 'May I have permission while we're there to buy one or two things for the house?'

'I suppose so.' Lance seemed surprised. 'As long as you don't give his replacement the idea you're extravagant.'

'Ezra's legacy was not of a size to make that a likely eventuality,' she said drily, thinking of the handful of shillings and sixpences she had found. It had amounted to two pounds, three and four-pence three-farthings – a useful sum for housekeeping but hardly justification for an orgy of spending.

The journey downriver was fast and the Kingswood party was obviously expected at Jamestown, for a carriage awaited the Haworths and there was a waggon to carry the baggage and Abigail. There was a discernible improvement in the Haworth house which Abigail had no hesitation in attributing to Blanche. The house-slaves seemed a little more on their toes and someone had insisted that the legs of the furniture were polished as well as the tops. Abigail's old room had been allocated to Blanche's maid, and upon reflection Abigail decided that this was probably no bad thing. On this visit she shared a room with other female house-slaves and bore their curious stares with every appearance of equanimity.

It proved harder than she had anticipated to be back once more in the house where she had known so much happiness. That part of her life was over, she reminded herself, and it would certainly remain so as long as Blanche lived.

She permitted herself the luxury of a brief day-dream in which Blanche's sudden demise figured prominently and then told herself not to be silly. She had loved Lance. She still did love him and could not imagine a time when she would feel differently about him, even though his actions made it perfectly clear that his own feelings were by no means so deep. She carried his child and, since there would be no man to replace its father in her affections, she must channel her affections towards this palpable proof of the love there had once been between then. Of one thing Abigail was convinced: whether Lance was hiding his true feelings for practical reasons or whether his feelings towards her had undergone a change, she did not doubt that, at the height of their liaison, he had loved her. That conviction and the memory of those brief weeks must be treasured and nurtured because she would be living on them for a long, long time.

Chapter Nine

Abigail had no intention of presenting herself at the Cuddesdon house looking anything other than confident and spirited. Since all she was going for was her necklace, there was no need to see Lord Jasper at all and she certainly had no intention of doing so if it could be avoided. She suspected that it might not be possible to do so, however, and was determined to present an entirely self-confident appearance. So, on her first morning back in Williamsburg and with permission to go out to buy things for the overseer's house, she arranged her curls with more care than she had taken for months, flung a shawl round her shoulders and shortly after a cursory glance in one or two shop-windows, presented herself in the kitchen of the Cuddesdon house.

Mama Lou was making pastry when Abigail appeared at the kitchen door. She threw up her floured hands in amazement. 'Glory be, where did you come from?' she exclaimed.

'Only the Haworth House. No, Mama Lou, don't wipe your hands clean: I'm not stopping. I've come to collect something from my trunk. Do you know where it is?'

'Sure. In the attic and his lordship has the key. Jabez'll be by in a moment. He knows all about it. Pour yourself some milk and set yourself down and tell me how's things with you.' She watched Abigail carry out the first part of her instructions and then, as the white girl sat down on the wooden rocking chair, she added, 'You don't look as well as you did here, girl, and if you're increasing, you should look better. Haworth house not suit you?'

'I've not been there much, but the Haworths treat me well enough,' Abigail told her. 'The house isn't run like this one,' she added. 'The tight supervision isn't there, and it shows — though it's improved since Mr Haworth married.'

Mama Lou nodded knowingly. ''Tis easy enough to grumble about

Jabez and Jubilation for neither of them lets a speck of dust pass unnoticed, but there's no denying they knows their work — and they does it well.'

'I wonder if Lord Jasper realises how lucky he is in his household?' Abigail said.

'Lucky? I don't know as how luck enters into it. His lordship knows how to get the best out of his people. I don't know how he does it for he surely don't seem to try, but there's not a soul working for him who'd gladly leave and that I *do* know.'

Except me, Abigail thought. I couldn't leave fast enough — and now where am I? 'Will Jabez be long?' she asked.

'Jabez is right here.' Abigail turned to see the huge negro smiling in the doorway. 'Is this a social call or have you come for your things? We heard you'd married,' he added accusingly.

'And am suddenly widowed,' she told them. 'You've no idea how pleased I am to see you both,' she added warmly, genuinely touched that they should seem so much like old friends. 'The truth is, though, that I've come to get something from my trunk.'

'Ay, well, his lordship done padlock it and put it in the attic and then locked *that*,' Jabez told her. 'As if we're all thieves, I told him and he said, not at all, it behoved us to take extra care of someone else's property, which is true enough, I suppose. But he's got both keys and there ain't no one can't get it without going to him first — not even you.'

'Where is Lord Jasper?' Abigail asked anxiously. 'I need to get to my trunk rather urgently. Will he be long?'

'Lord, Abby, he ain't going to be any time at all — he's in the library and he's not going nowhere yet awhile,' Jabez told her. 'There's no rush. Plenty of time for a good visit.'

'A good visit must wait,' Abigail said, getting to her feet and putting her empty glass on the dresser. 'It really is urgent, Jabez. Will you take me to him?'

Jabez opened the library door and stood aside to let Abigail enter. 'Abigail Brough – Vatsetter, I suppose. She says it's urgent,' he added unceremoniously.

Lord Jasper looked up from the book he was reading and raised his eyebrows. Then, laying the volume aside, he rose. 'So soon?' he murmured, and gestured to the chair opposite his own. 'Please sit down, Mrs Vatsetter.'

'Thank you, Lord Jasper, but there's no need. I've no wish to incommode you by staying. I only want to collect something from my trunk.'

'You incommode me by standing, Mrs Vatsetter. I infinitely prefer to sit but can scarcely do so while you refuse.'

Flushing with annoyance at his unfailing ability to put her at a disadvantage, Aibgail took the seat he had indicated. Lord Jasper resumed his chair, commenting, 'They say standing puts a strain on the heart, you know, and one does not like to take unnecessary risks.'

'There can be little fear of that,' Abigail replied with some asperity. 'I don't think your heart is likely to suffer much strain.'

Lord Jasper's eyes narrowed. Women – even unhappily married ones – tended to bloom while they were increasing. Abigail was not. She looked like a woman covering desperation with bravado. He wondered just what had been happening to bring this about. He had heard of Vatsetter's sudden death but doubted whether Abigail had been a willing bride or was a grieving widow. However, he knew her well enough to suspect that direct questioning, whether sympathetic or astringent, would be unlikely to tell him. 'A waspish tongue is unbecoming in the extreme,' he said. 'You should learn to cultivate a more conciliatory manner.'

'To what end?' Abigail snapped. 'My lord, I didn't come here for a verbal fencing match. I didn't even come to see you. Only the fact that you hold the keys to the attic and my trunk has made this interview necessary. Please, my lord, I've no time to waste.'

Her final words were an entreaty at considerable variance with the spirit of her earlier words and Lord Jasper had a shrewd idea that tears were not far off. He rose from his chair and, taking a small key from his waistcoat pocket, unlocked a drawer in the large desk that stood by the window. From this he extracted two more keys which he dropped into Abigail's lap.

'You know where the attic is,' he told her. 'All I require is that you return the keys to me personally when you've finished.'

'Of course.' Abigail was surprised. For some reason she had expected that he would want to come with her. She stood up and then hesitated, looking at him with an expression he could not quite fathom. 'Thank you, my lord.'

'Not at all,' he said politely. Now what was all that about? he thought as the door closed behind her. The only thing she had brought with her in which to carry things was her shawl, and that would not prove very capacious. Whatever had happened, Abigail Vatsetter was, in his estimation, very near the end of her tether. She would need watching. She must not be allowed to do anything foolish.

Abigail ran up to the attic, fumbling nervously with the key in her haste to open the door. Once inside and kneeling beside the wooden trunk, she made herself pause before tackling the padlock. There was really no need to be in such a rush. It was so long since she had opened the trunk that she had almost forgotten its contents and she turned the garments over, her hands lingering wistfully on the luxurious fabric of her Court dress. She sighed. There was precious little hope that she would ever wear that again!

Eventually she found what she sought. She opened the pouch which housed her mother's necklace and sat back on her heels with the jewel in her hands. It was so beautiful. The diamonds were said to be of exceptional quality and they shot facets of fire across the room as the sunlight caught them, while the sapphires that they surrounded and linked gleamed like a cloudless starlit sky.

As she looked at the necklace, Abigail could not repress a pang of regret that she must part with it, but part with it she would have to, and for as high a price as she could. It would be wonderful to hope that one day she might be able to buy it back but that, she knew, was a dream even more fantastical than the one that Lance might marry her.

She put the necklace back in it pouch and dropped it in the purse that hung at her waist. It scarcely seemed necessary to lock the trunk again now that its treasure was gone but she did so since, if she did not, it would arouse comment. She locked the attic door and returned to the library. It was only reasonable that Lord Jasper should want to receive the keys from her own hands but she hoped he would not detain her – she must waste no time in obtaining the wherewithal to buy her freedom.

When she entered the library, it was obvious she was to be detained: a tea-tray had been sent for and it bore two cups.

'Sit down,' Lord Jasper commanded.

Abigail opened her mouth to protest, then shut it again. She wanted to be away from here as soon as possible and she suspected that arguing with her host was not the way to expedite matters. So she obeyed his instruction and accepted with murmured thanks the cup of tea he offered.

Lord Jasper noted the fact that her shawl was still round her shoulders and she was carrying nothing bulky.

'So you came for the necklace,' he commented.

Abigail spluttered in a most unmannerly way over her tea and stared at him. 'What do you know about my necklace?'

A sardonic smile twisted his lips. 'Come, my dear, don't be naive! When you were so concerned about the safety of your trunk – on the occasion of that fateful game of dice, you remember – I couldn't believe you were worried only about clothes, something any master,

170

and certainly any lover would expect to provide. Naturally, I went through the trunk to discover what it was that occasioned such concern.'

'Naturally.' Abigail's voice was as acid as she could make it.

'For what reason do you think I had it padlocked, placed in a locked room and kept both keys myself? Do you imagine I customarily take such care of a slave's belongings?'

'No, I suppose not,' Abigail admitted grudgingly.

'I have no reason to distrust my servants, as you have good cause to know, but nevertheless there was the possibility your trunk might remain here indefinitely, and who knows what might happen if it were judged to be unwanted or forgotten?'

Everything he said was true enough, but Abigail was still not happy that he should have taken it upon himself to go through her things in that way.

'What do you want it for?' he asked suddenly.

Abigail stiffened. Was this man determined to leave her no privacy at all? 'I'm grateful to you for keeping it safe, my lord,' she began diplomatically and then became flustered by the cynicism of his expression and finished badly, 'but it is really none of your business.'

He shook his head sadly. 'So blunt, Mrs Vatsetter! You really should learn to phrase things more circumspectly. If a man's servant comes to my house and removes an extremely valuable item which is in my care, don't you think that becomes my business?'

'Not when the item belongs to the one who removes it,' Abigail retorted. 'At least, handing it over may be your business but not what the rightful owner does with it subsequently.'

'Then gratify my curiosity.'

'Why should I?'

'Why should you not? Will you suffer by doing so?'

Abigail thought about that. She was very loath to tell Lord Jasper anything at all that wasn't absolutely necessary: she did not like him and she liked still less his disconcerting ability to comprehend precisely what was going on in her mind. She could not immediately perceive any disadvantage in telling him since she was no longer his property, but she suspected there might be one and merely shook her head.

Lord Jasper put his fingers together and stared up at the ceiling as if in rapt contemplation. 'Let me see,' he began. 'Lance Haworth has a desire to see you in jewels but perhaps not to be put to the expensive inconvenience of buying them himself.'

Abigail's colour rose with anger. 'Don't be ridiculous,' she snapped. 'I shall use them to buy my freedom.'

171

'Aah, so that's it! Widowed and with no other means of support, you put yourself once more in Haworth's pocket – only to find his passion for you is spent. Or is he finding it difficult to keep his mistress and his wife in the same house?'

Abigail leapt from her seat, her eyes blazing, and brought her hand down in a stinging slap across his face.

Although her action took him totally by surprise, his reflexes were remarkably quick for so apparently indolent a man. Almost before she realised what she had done, he had caught her upraised hand in an iron grip and forced it down, rising from his chair as he did so. He towered over her and his fingers bit painfully into her wrist. Abigail tried to pull away but so firm was his grasp that she could not even move to arm's length. His cold eyes mesmerised her into gazing back at him.

'So Lance Haworth hasn't beaten the spirit out of you,' he said.

'He's never tried,' Abigail exclaimed.

'Really? You've been quite remarkably lucky, then, or perhaps you married Vatsetter just in time – though he himself was quite a by-word, but doubtless you discovered that for yourself.'

His finger traced the last lingering remnants of the bruise on her face before throwing her shawl to one side and pulling out the linen fichu at the neck of her dress. He studied the white skin of her neck and shoulders without comment. 'Unlace your bodice,' he ordered.

'No, my lord. I will not!'

'Then I'll do it for you.' His free hand had no difficulty with the front lacing of the simple grey dress and once it was undone, he pulled the bodice and its underlying chemise briskly off one shoulder. Abigail was self-consciously aware of the firm curve of the breast thus revealed and its involuntary tightening as Lord Jasper's long fingers ran lightly over the surface of her exposed flesh. 'Your husband, I assume,' he said at last and paused, looking down at her, his finger still stroking her breast almost absentmindedly. Suddenly his mouth descended on the nipple until she cried out in pain. He pulled her struggling body towards him and his mouth met hers with an angry lust that frightened her more than anything that had gone before because it was so much at variance with the Lord Jasper she thought she knew – unsympathetic and caustic, maybe, but always in complete control of himself.

Abigail tore her mouth away. 'No, my lord!' she gasped. 'No!'

He paused and stared down at her. 'I believe you mean it,' he said and Abigail thought she detected surprise and regret in his voice. He gently pulled her bodice back over her shoulder. 'Lance Haworth is a bigger fool than I thought if he is really letting you go.' He watched her relace her bodice and when next he spoke his voice was softer, warmer. 'Are you sure he'll let you buy your freedom?'

'Why shouldn't he? He's set a price on it.'

'How much?'

Abigail was tempted to tell him that this, too, was none of his concern but his onslaught, so totally unexpected, left her disinclined to cross swords with him again just yet. Besides, what harm could it do?

'Five thousand guineas,' she said.

He whistled. 'An exorbitant price. You should feel flattered.'

'You paid a higher one for me,' Abigail pointed out. 'You could have had my father's entire estate.'

'That was quite different. I don't wish to lower you in your own estimation, Mrs Vatsetter, but your market value now is less than a tenth of Haworth's price. Perhaps he hopes you'll not be able to raise so much.'

She looked anxiously at Lord Jasper. 'The necklace should be worth that much, don't you think?'

He held out his hand and Abigail took the jewel from her purse and gave it to him. He examined it closely. 'At least that,' he said at last, 'though I doubt whether you will be offered anything like as much.'

'You underestimate me, my lord. I'm a very skilled bargainer!'

'No doubt, but your position is known. What freeman is going to believe you came by this honestly?'

Abigail stared at him aghast. 'But you know I did!'

'*I* know you did, yes, but I'm not buying it. Do you really imagine a jeweller is going to believe your story? With this in your possession, why on earth should you have become a bond-slave in the first place?'

'You know the reason!'

'Of course I do but, loath as I am to repeat myself, I'm not the jeweller to whom you hope to sell it. It's well known you were my slave originally and this is just the sort of household where you might lay your hands on such a piece, hoping to dispose of it at a later date. I fancy your intended buyer might think along such lines, don't you?'

Abigail's brow cleared. 'Then there's no problem, my lord: he would consult you and you would naturally be able to put his mind at rest.'

'Would I?'

'You know you would − after all, you know the truth!'

'I would certainly be able to do so. Whether I might be willing to is quite another matter.'

Abigail stared at him, the colour draining from her face. 'You can't mean that. Surely you wouldn't be so cruel?'

'No? Do you know me so well that you can be sure of that?'

'No man of honour would do such a thing!'

'Indeed he would not — but what leads you to assume I am a man of honour?' Perceiving that no instances of his honourable behaviour sprang instantly to Abigail's mind, he hammered the point home. 'Would a man of honour accept another man's daughter as a gaming-stake? Would a man of honour dispose of her as easily and in the same way? A man of honour would not, I fancy, have gone through your trunk to see what it contained that was so important — and a man of honour would not be banished by his family to some far-flung colony. I won't refer to my behaviour in this room just now,' he added blandly. 'You can judge that for yourself.'

'Did your family really banish you?' Abigail asked curiously, momentarily diverted from the more important matter.

'Most assuredly they did. Wastrel younger sons who seduce clergymen's daughter's aren't generally encouraged, you know.'

'Is that what you did? I had heard you'd killed a man.'

'Intrigued, Mrs Vatsetter? Rumour exaggerates, I'm afraid. I can't say I recall actually killing anyone, though I've often been tempted. It was all a long time ago and I compounded my sin by refusing to marry the girl. I told you I wasn't a man of honour.'

'All the same, it was a harsh punishment.'

'You needn't feel obliged to pity me: I certainly don't pity myself. The opportunities this colony offered me were very much to my liking and I could hardly have turned them to better advantage. As you have observed, I'm even welcomed back in England — provided I don't stay too long.'

'Pity isn't the emotion that sprang to my mind,' Abigail assured him. 'Particularly when you have just threatened to let me be branded a thief.'

Lord Jasper shrugged his shoulders and moved over to the window. 'It's irrelevant, you know. Even if you were believed — and I don't think you would be — you'd not be able to get half the sum you need.'

'But you've already said the necklace is worth at least five thousand guineas!' Abigail exclaimed.

'Considerably more in the normal way of things, but not only do you have to convince the buyer that the necklace is yours to sell, you also need the money urgently. That immediately puts you at a grave disadvantage.'

Abigail sank back into her chair dejectedly. 'What do I do, my lord?'

174

He came back to the fireplace and rested one arm long the mantel, looking down at her.

'You could try trusting me,' he suggested.

'Why should I? You've made it abundantly clear you're not a man of honour.'

'Because you've no choice. I can achieve what you cannot.'

'How so, my lord?'

'Let me take the necklace. No one will query my right to it: I bought it in London for a mistress and tired of her before presenting it. There's more than one man in Williamsburg who owes me a favour or two. I can get your five thousand guineas for you.'

Abigail was obliged to admit that he was probably right and since he had not taken the necklace in all these weeks, he was unlikely to make off with the money now, especially since, of all people in the capital, he could have no need of it. It was not consideration of Lord Jasper's honesty that made her pause, but the fact that so much depended on this transaction. She was loath to leave it to someone whose sense of urgency might not match her own.

'How long would it take you?' she asked anxiously.

'How long do you have?'

'I'm not precisely sure. Mr Haworth spoke of sending me back upriver on the next boat. He intends me to marry his new overseer.'

Lord Jasper frowned but made no comment on the last piece of information. 'The *Sparrowhawk* returned to Norfolk yesterday. It will be back at Jamestown the day after tomorrow and is expected to return to Kingswood on that day's afternoon tide. I'd have liked longer but it will suffice.'

'Are you sure? Forgive me, my lord, but you can't imagine how much I depend upon it and if there's any doubt, I'd be happier negotiating the sale myself.' Abigail's blue eyes pleaded with him and Lord Jasper knew it was the thought of an impending and unsought marriage that lent such desperation to her quest.

'You think me devoid of imagination, do you? You're mistaken, Mrs Vatsetter, but it would be a far worse mistake to undertake this business yourself. Return here tomorrow afternoon. If I manage as well as I plan to do, you can be free of Lance Haworth by evening. Will that suit you?'

'Admirably.' Abigail rose from her chair, the necklace in her hand. She stared at it silently for a few minutes. This was the last time she would ever see it, her last link with her late beloved mother. 'I'm so sorry,' she whispered, and held it resolutely out to Lord Jasper who took it without comment, not so much as a flicker of an eyelash betraying that he had heard the almost inaudible cry that revealed another facet of this intriguing situation.

He slipped the necklace into his pocket. 'Tomorrow afternoon,' he reminded her. 'As late as you can manage.'

A brief, rueful smile touched her lips. 'I'll not forget, Lord Jasper.' She hesitated. She could not like this cold, austere man whose only gratification seemed to come from putting her at a disadvantage of one sort or another, yet despite his coldness he was proposing to put himself to some inconvenience on her behalf. 'Thank you, my lord,' she added and turned towards the door.

'Thank me tomorrow when you may have cause,' he told her. He was close behind her and reached past her to open the door but paused with his hand on the brightly polished knob. 'You can trust me, you know,' he said and Abigail looked up at him suddenly, surprised at the note of what might almost have been warmth in his voice. She smiled fleetingly.

'Am I not doing so?' she asked.

Over the next twenty-four hours doubt, uncertainty, despair and sheer panic vied with each other, and Abigail went about in such a remote, detached manner as to occasion the comment of even Lance Haworth's most unobservant slave.

All Lord Jasper's arguments had made sense. He was far more likely than she to be able both to sell the necklace quickly and to get a good price for it. Her head told her she had done the right – possibly the only – thing. Her heart was not so easily satisfied. She had handed it over to him with no guarantee of receiving the sum she needed or, indeed, any sum at all. It had not occurred to her at the time to ask for a receipt so she had no record that the necklace had ever been hers. She was sure Lord Jasper had no need of the money represented by the necklace but he was a gamester of the worst sort, as she knew to her cost.

She remembered the ruses to which her father would sink to get hold of anything that could be turned into a stake, and she remembered the ruses to which she had sometimes sunk in order to keep that necklace out of his hands. The only difference between the two men, so far as she could see, was that Lord Jasper was successful. But success at the tables was a transient thing. She was in no position to know whether or not his luck was still holding. If it had turned, how very useful her necklace would prove! And if his luck still held, he might even think to win the money she needed by staking the necklace instead of selling it.

Abigail shuddered. Surely he could not be planning to take such a risk when so much depended on the outcome?

Don't be naive, she told herself. That's exactly how a gambler's mind works. Surely you've learnt that by now? She recalled his parting words and, more importantly, the tone in which they were uttered: ' "You can trust me, you know",' he had said and, in spite of her dislike and mistrust of the man, she almost believed him.

Then she thought of the one eventuality she had not considered: what if he sold the necklace but failed to get the price she needed? What if he only obtained three, or four, or four and a half thousand guineas? It would still be a vast sum, but would she be able to beat Lance down to the sum she had? Four thousand was what he had originally demanded so perhaps she might be able to bargain down to that, but what if he refused to accept anything less than the stated price or could only be beaten down down to a figure that was still in excess of what she had? What happened then?

There was one line of thought she dared not pursue. Once she had bought her freedom − an eventuality that seemed the more unlikely the more she thought about it − what then? She would be destitute. Destitute and pregnant. No, that was not something to be thought about until her freedom had been regained. Only then would she consider what options lay before her. All she could hope now was that if she occupied herself with work, she would have no further energy to think.

Abigail immersed herself in tasks of one sort or another for the rest of the day and succeeded in putting her problems out of her mind for at least part of the time, but when she lay in her lonely bed that night it was a very different story. She tossed and turned, her mind churning impotently over the same arguments again and again, arguments for which the daylight hours had already failed to provide answers. Once in the night a man's step halted outside the room, or so she thought. For a brief, ecstatic moment she thought it was Lance, filled with remorse and a change of heart. But the steps went away again and she never knew whose they were or considered the improbability of Lance's visiting her in a shared room. She was never even sure that they weren't a figment of her overwrought imagination.

Sleep, of a sort, came at last but she awoke heavy-eyed and downcast and Noah's first words did nothing to raise her spirits.

'Mas' Haworth says you're to wait on him at breakfast.'

'Must I?' Abigail didn't think she could face her master until she knew how successful Lord Jasper had been.

'Don't be a fool, girl. You don't have no choice.'

Lance Haworth had never favoured the practice of serving oneself at breakfast from side-dishes heated over candle-holders or spirit-lamps. He invariably insisted upon being served. Abigail had always told herself it was quite understandable in a man who had risen from nothing but today, of all days, she had no desire to pander to his wishes. She knew she had no choice and one look at Lance's face as she entered the room was enough to dispel any momentary delusion she might have had that he had sent for her in order to retract his commands of the previous day. Of Mrs Haworth there was no sign.

'Sleep well?' he mocked.

Since Abigail knew the answer to his question was written clearly on her face, she ignored his inquiry, a fact which irked him.

'Don't be sullen with me, my girl. You're still mine, you know, and while you remain so, you will act accordingly.'

There was a cruel edge to his voice which made Abigail flinch inwardly but she maintained her outward composure. 'My apologies, Mr Haworth. No, I did not sleep well.'

'The *Sparrowhawk* sails tomorrow. Contenders for your hand will be here late this evening to look you over. You will then return to Kingswood while I make the final choice. If you leave here at dawn, you'll be in Jamestown in time. There's a waggon going to relieve the *Sparrowhawk* of some of her rum. You can ride on that.'

'Unless I've bought my freedom,' Abigail reminded him.

His eyes opened wide and then he laughed in genuine amusement. 'I'd forgotten – of course, there remains that possibility! How much have you raised so far?'

'None.' He would not be allowed to guess the effort that admission caused her.

'None at all? Dear me – the outlook isn't very cheerful, is it? But never let it be said that I'm less than generous: when your chores are completed, you may be excused further work until tonight.'

Abigail bit back the acid retort that hovered on her tongue. Instead, she bobbed a quick curtsy. 'Thank you, sir.'

He looked at her suspiciously. 'And remember – I'll take no money that comes from Lord Jasper. If you cajole the money out of him, our agreement is null and void. Do you understand?'

'Perfectly, sir.'

He did not seem entirely convinced but he let the matter drop and Abigail completed her duties as quickly as she could in order to leave his presence.

Lance had given her something else to worry about. Abigail knew that, in referring to Lord Jasper, he had in mind that she might, by some means unspecified, persuade his lordship into giving or, more probably, lending her the money, perhaps even into buying her back.

Lord Jasper would be doing none of those things but if everything went according to plan, she would undoubtedly be obtaining her release with his help. If Lance discovered that, would he consider his offer void? Abigail suspected that he would. Williamsburg was a small town of some three hundred houses and two thousand souls. Lance would have no difficulty tracking her down if he decided to do so.

She took advantage of his offer but, since Lord Jasper had told her not to return until as late in the afternoon as possible, that left her at an unenviably loose end: unenviable because she was free to think. Abigail thought it wisest to leave the Haworth house when her work was done. There was nothing for her to do but roam the streets, stroll round the market and gaze in shop windows but that at least might be interpreted by Lance − if word of her whereabouts got back to him − as part of her efforts to find five thousand guineas. It would be very difficult, having already admitted a singular lack of success, to sit in her room for most of the day, go out for a brief walk and return with so large a sum of money.

By the time she judged the afternoon far enough advanced for her visit to the Cuddesdon house, she was exhausted. As she turned in at the ornate gates, she forced herself to straighten her shoulders and to walk more briskly. She had no desire to let Lord Jasper see how low fatigue and anxiety had brought her.

She was clearly awaited for, as she turned to make for the kitchen dependency intending to ask Jabez to announce her, the front door opened and he stood at the top of the steps.

'You're to come this way, Ab ... Mrs Vatsetter,' he corrected himself.

Jabez' face was a mask of inscrutable politeness that told Abigail nothing but which led her to think that perhaps he had heard something to her detriment and this was his way of telling her so. She sighed. She had few enough friends as it was.

Lord Jasper was in the library and turned as Abigail entered. He noted her pale, drawn face with the dark shadows under eyes that should sparkle but were now dull and lifeless. He noted, too, the almost defiant lift she gave her chin and shoulders as she entered. The girl has pride, he thought. I wonder how long it will serve her?

Dismissing Jabez with instructions to bring in the tea-tray, he led Abigail to the huge upholstered wing chair that he normally regarded as his own. Then he turned to a crystal decanter and poured a rich, dark liquid into a small glass which he handed her.

'Drink this,' he commanded.

179

Abigail took it doubtfully and sniffed it, wrinkling her nose with some distaste. 'Rum?' she asked.

'Yes.'

She held the glass out to him. 'No, thank you, my lord. I don't like it.'

'I care not whether you like it or loathe it,' he replied. 'Just drink it. You look as if the last twenty-four hours have nearly done for you. This will revive you, if only temporarily. When Jabez brings the tea-tray you may return to the more elegant beverage – and Mama Lou has made some . . . "cookies", I think she called them. She says you like them.'

Abigail smiled in spite of herself. 'They're never sent up to the drawing-room, my lord, and I promise you, that is elegant society's loss.' She sipped the rum and grimaced as the fiery liquid hit the back of her throat.

'And the rest,' Lord Jasper commanded. 'Forget the immediate effect and drink it down.'

Abigail did so and felt the warmth seep into every corner of her body and with the warmth came an involuntary relaxation of the tension she felt. Lord Jasper said nothing but watched the colour return to her cheeks. When Jabez entered with the tea things and Mama Lou's cookies, he set them down without a word and was dismissed with a single elegant wave of his master's hand.

'Better?' Lord Jasper inquired.

Abigail nodded.

'Good. Business first – or tea?'

'Business,' Abigail told him without an instant's hesitation. 'Tea can wait.'

'A woman after my own heart,' Lord Jasper said lightly and went to his desk. He unlocked a drawer and took out a heavy pouch which he brought over and dropped into Abigail's lap. 'Your freedom, Mrs Vatsetter.'

'All of it?' she asked doubtfully.

'All of it.'

'Five thousand guineas?' Abigail could not quite believe it had been so easy.

'No, not five thousand guineas,' Lord Jasper said and then, seeing the despair return to Abigail's face despite his earlier assurance, he relented. 'That was cruel and this is no time for cruelty. You see, it occurred to me that with five thousand guineas you would be free, but destitute. So I set out to get a little more. That purse contains exactly five thousand one hundred guineas.'

Abigail's face lit up and she stared at him in wonder. 'Five thousand, one hundred? You mean I have one hundred guineas to spare?'

Her delighted disbelief was infectious and Lord Jasper felt a wave of sympathetic warmth towards her. 'You have a hundred guinea stake with which to gamble the rest of your life.'

Abigail shook her head. 'I'm no gambler. The money will be put to good use.'

'If you use it only to support yourself, it will be gone in a year – two at the most,' he warned.

'I know that. No, it must work for me – and now, my lord, if you will forgive my presumption, may I have some tea?'

Lord Jasper was tempted to ask her how she proposed making her hundred guineas work for her. He thought it quite likely she had no idea because she had been in no expectation of having a surplus from her planned sale and therefore had very possibly given it no specific thought. He was also still of the opinion that there was something behind this whole affair of which he knew nothing and he was curious to discover whether Abigail, in her present rum-and guinea-induced euphoria, would happen to mention it.

She did not and he began to think that perhaps he had been mistaken. Abigail drank her tea and ate Mama Lou's cookies without referring further to her situation. When she had finished, she declined further refreshment.

'I must go, Lord Jasper. I can't wait to see the surprise on Mr Haworth's face when I hand him this.' She patted the heavy purse.

'If you take my advice, you'll not be in too much of a hurry,' Lord Jasper replied. 'I suggest you sit down again and take a hundred guineas out of that purse and put it in your own. It would be foolish to let Haworth know you have more than he thinks.'

Abigail opened her mouth to accuse him of cynicism and then recalled how Lance had pushed his original demand up. She closed it again. It was a sensible precaution – and it put her in mind of another.

'My lord,' she began hesitantly, and for a moment Lord Jasper wondered if he was going to be told the full story. 'You've been very kind and I'm loath to ask more of you but there is one favour I would beg ...'

'Which is ...?'

'To say nothing of your part in this. Particularly not in Mr Haworth's hearing.'

'As you wish, though I was hardly likely to shout it from the roof-tops. May I inquire why you feel my reticence is called for?'

181

Briefly, Abigail explained. 'And so you see, I'm dreadfully afraid he might choose to misinterpret it.'

'Knowing Lance Haworth as I do, I should think it entirely probable. Rest assured he will learn nothing through me.'

'Thank you, my lord,' Abigail said simply. 'Now I really must be gone. There's much to be done.' She rose to her feet for the second time and turned to the door, to find Lord Jasper there before her, barring the way.

'Not just yet,' he said. 'There's one more thing. I'm not a fool, Mrs Vatsetter. I'm very well aware that you hold me in dislike – even abhorrence – and I imagine there's little I can do about it, but at least I've proved that you can trust me. Please accept my assurance that you can safely continue to do so. If I can be of any assistance at any time, you've only to ask. Will you remember that?'

There was genuine concern in his voice which Abigail had never noticed before. She looked up at him, puzzled.

'I shall remember it,' she told him, and could not resist adding, 'There has been nothing in your behaviour this afternoon to elicit dislike, my lord.'

'Ah, perhaps not, but yesterday was different, was it not?'

Abigail's eyes gleamed. 'Yesterday was another matter altogether. Good day, my lord.'

He opened the door with a short laugh. 'Good day, Abigail – and good luck. I fancy you'll need it.'

Abigail paused outside the room where Noah had grudgingly told her Lance was sitting over a brandy. She smoothed her skirt and took a deep breath before opening the door. He stared at her for a moment as if he didn't quite believe his eyes.

'So you're back, are you? I heard you were out all day. What do you want?'

'My freedom,' Abigail reminded him, wondering how full the brandy decanter had been when it was set before him.

His eyes narrowed and an unpleasantly calculating look that she had never seen before entered them. 'What was the price I set on it?'

'Five thousand guineas.'

'Are you telling me you've managed to lay your hands on such a sum in only twenty-four hours?' Abigail nodded. 'How did you do it?' he asked suspiciously.

'That is surely irrelevant,' Abigail said. 'It's done and the money is here.' She held up the heavy purse as she spoke.

Lance studied it consideringly. 'Yesterday I was taken by surprise,' he said at last and his white teeth flashed in one of his charming smiles. 'I'm not at all sure I want to let you go so easily.'

He paused and Abigail's heart leapt with joy. She had been right, after all. Now that he was faced with the prospect of losing her, Lance had realised how much she – and her unborn child – meant to him. A day's anguish and worry had been unnecessary, but that was something easily forgiven. Her face lit up with the happiness in her heart and she took a step towards him, her hand outstretched. His next words brought her up short.

'I underestimated your value, my dear. A bond-slave you may be, and pregnant, but you are without doubt one of the most beautiful women in Virginia. Five thousand is scarcely recompense enough. Let's say six.'

The colour drained from Abigail's face and a fury such as she had never known before overcame her.

'No!' she cried. 'You *shall* not reneague on the agreement!'

She brought her fist down on the table and the decanter bounced. As if she had noticed it for the first time, Abigail grabbed it by the neck and, oblivious to the probable consequences, brought it down on the table to emphasise her point. 'I've kept my part of the bargain. You'll keep yours.'

The crystal base of the decanter shattered under the blow and Abigail was left holding the neck and shoulders with their jagged edge. She was not even aware she held a formidable weapon until she saw the fear in Lance's handsome face as he half rose from his chair.

'Sit down,' she commanded, raising the remnants of the decanter until it was aligned with his face. He sat, his eyes riveted to the broken glass. 'Now write out the document that makes me free.'

'I can't. Not in here, at least. Come into my office – I've writing materials there.'

Abigail thought quickly. He was a big man and immensely strong. It would be all too easy for her to lose her present precarious advantage if they moved. 'No,' she said. 'Ring for Noah. He can bring whatever you need – and give him no hint that anything is amiss. I don't doubt that you could overpower me between you, but before you succeeded, I vow your face would be slashed to ribbons.'

She knew the decanter was her trunp. If she lost that, she lost both her freedom and her money – and that would be the least of her losses. The knowledge gave an edge to her voice that told Lance this was not an occasion when he could coax and charm a woman into doing what suited him.

So he nodded and rang the little bell that lay beside him on the table. When Noah came in, all he saw was his master at the table and opposite him the white bond-slave, her eyes fixed on their master, her

183

hands hidden in the folds of her skirt. He looked at the broken glass that lay scattered across the table and the floor.

'Sir?' he queried.

'I broke the decanter,' Lance said hastily, glancing at Abigail's grimly determined face. 'Fetch me paper, quill, ink and sand – and the scales. I've business here but it won't take much longer. Then you can send someone to clear up.'

Noah looked curiously from one to the other but their faces told him nothing and he returned shortly with the items Lance had required. 'I'll come back with another bottle of brandy,' he suggested.

'No need,' Lance assured him hurriedly. 'Leave it till tomorrow.'

'Now write,' Abigail commanded as the door closed behind the slave. She raised the jagged glass from behind her skirt. Lance pulled the paper towards him, dipped the quill in the inkpot and wrote. When he had finished, he held out his hand for the money-pouch.

Abigail shook her head. 'No, Mr Haworth. Not until I have that document in my own hands and have read it through.'

'Are you suggesting I can't be trusted?' Lance's voice was indignant.

'Does that surprise you?' Abigail took the reluctantly proffered paper and glanced at it. A movement from Lance Haworth reminded her that her business was not yet safely concluded and she tightened her hold on the decanter's remains. The document took longer to read with half her attention on Lance, but at least it precluded sudden action on his part. Satisfied that the paper was all she hoped for, she tucked it into the bosom of her dress and threw the pouch onto the table. Lance drew the scales towards him and emptied the gleaming gold coins into the brass pan. After a few moments adjusting the brass counterweights until the balance was reached, he tipped the coins back into the pouch.

'Very well, Mrs Vatsetter. You drive a hard bargain but you're free – unless I discover you had this money from Lord Jasper.'

'You'll not do so for he had no hand in it.' Abigail lied without a qualm. Lance's behaviour did not entitle him to the truth unless it served her purpose. 'I'll be gone in the morning.'

'No, my dear. You'll be gone within the half-hour. I run no lodging-house for destitute wenches here.'

She stared at him. Could he really be so cruel? 'But Lance ... Mr Haworth, you've not thought. It will soon be dark and I must first put my things together.'

'That'll not take long. As I recall, you came here with only what you wore and what you could bundle into a shawl. Half an hour should suffice.'

Abigail was at the door before she remembered that she still held the top of the decanter. She turned and flung it into the hearth where it broke on the flags. She left without farewells and with bitterness in her heart.

Chapter Ten

Half an hour was more than enough time in which to scoop such few belongings as she had brought to Williamsburg into a knotted shawl. Even finding a place to sleep proved less difficult than she had expected: the Raleigh Tavern, just two blocks down the street from the Haworth house, was a popular and respectable hostelry which would not normally have dreamed of accommodating an unescorted female. However, Willimasburg's size was such that Abigail's history was well known and there was a degree of sympathy for her predicament. The landlord accepted without question her statement that she was free from bondage with the comment, 'You're the first Haworth's ever let go, that's for sure. It so happens you're in luck: our Bathsheba's gone sick. If you'll clear up the taproom in the morning, there's a bed for you under the eaves.'

Abigail accepted his offer with alacrity and asked hopefully if there might be work for her on a more permanent basis − in the adjoining bakery, perhaps?

The landlord shook his head. 'That's skilled work and heavy, and I don't aim to let Bathsheba be ill for long so there's nothing for you in the tavern.' He looked at her with some sympathy. 'In a town serviced by slaves, I don't reckon there's going to be much work for a free woman − not less'n she's strong and plain.'

The next day was to prove him all too right. Abigail started with the shops and then the various hostelries. Shopkeepers expressed sympathy but even those prepared to employ a woman who was visibly increasing had less enthusiastic wives. If Mrs Vatsetter had been a plain woman, it would have been a different matter but she wouldn't always be pregnant. The respectable taverns did not want her either and the proposition that was put to her by the landlord of one singularly insalubrious hostelry sent her back into the street flushed with indignation.

She had only one stroke of luck: she learnt that there was a small cabin off Nicholson Street, close to the gaol. Its former tenants had gone up-river to scratch a living from the wilderness beyond the tidewater. The owner was dubious about letting it to Abigail but was eventually convinced that she had no intention of turning it into a house of ill-repute and finally gave her the key.

When Abigail stood in the open doorway of the little cabin and looked about her, she could barely repress a smile: anyone who sought to run a house of ill-repute in this hovel was destined for bankruptcy. Even Lance's slaves were better housed. There were two rooms, one of them considerably larger than the other.The previous occupants had obviously not thought it worth their while to take the bulky, rough-hewn furniture. There was a table which was little more than two planks supported on cumbersome trestles, and a chair of split logs. Planks on wooden brackets against the wall would serve as dresser shelves and the smaller of the two rooms − little more than a space beneath the sloping roof − was almost completely filled with a box-like bed. Even the bedding had been left, though Abigail had no intention of sleeping on dank straw that was compressed into a near solid mat, the result of being slept on and never tedded. The whole place was filthy and Abigail was hard put to it to decide how much had accumulated since the previous tenants had left and how much had been left by them. Still, a broom and some rags were soon come by. A more considerable problem was the hearth, which was empty of everything save ashes: no dogs, no hooks, no pot and no spit.

Having acquired a roof over her head at the end of a long day, the last thing Abigail wanted was to go out foraging for necessities but she had no choice: she could not sleep here in its present condition.

When she returned to the cabin, she brought with her a besom, a pail, a tallow candle, a tinderbox and the promise of fire-irons from the blacksmith next day, together with straw from the ostler at the Raleigh. She had been able to buy a loaf at the tavern's bake-house, and the landlord, taking pity on the fatigue fast overwhelming her, found a pewter tankard that was somewhat past its best and gave it to her. That night she slept on the table wrapped in her cloak, knowing that next day she must spend more of her precious resources on such necessities as cooking and eating utensils.

She awoke early and set to work brushing the accumulated dirt from the earthen floor and out of the door. She managed to set fire to the dank straw and scrubbed the wooden box-bed as if her life depended on it. She found that the windows not only boasted the refinement of glass panes, but by some miracle, none of those panes were broken. Once they had been washed, the cabin became brighter and more cheerful.

Abigail's purse became lighter, too. A hundred guineas might be a great deal of money but it disappeared with alarming rapidity when one had nothing but what one stood up in. Abigail knew she must find some way to support herself and her unborn child as a matter of some urgency, and when the child was born she would need money in reserve to sustain them both until she could resume work. She reckoned this might be as long as a week or even ten days.

The solution came to her as she sat sewing rough cotton ticking into a mattress-cover to take the fresh, sweetly scented straw that the Raleigh's ostler, Nick Camberwell, had dropped off the dray for her. She was a good needlewoman. She had mended linen in both the Cuddesdon and Haworth households and she knew she was better than that. She had the ability to become a first-class dressmaker, and that was something Williamsburg lacked. There was a milliner who made garments as well as hats and stocked the fabrics and haberdashery needed in the town, but most women made their own clothes or had maids to do it for them. She looked about her and was immediately depressed. What woman of any standing would order garments from a mantuamaker who lived in such surroundings?

Telling herself firmly to shake off this self-defeating mood, she looked about her more critically. How could this cabin be made more confidence-inspiring but with a minimum of expense? The answer was delightfully simple: beeswax and elbow-grease, so that it smelt clean; flowers from the fields so that it smelt fresh; a fire in the hearth so that it looked welcoming; curtains at the windows so that it looked civilised. Only the last would make inroads into her capital but they would all make the world of difference.

This left her with two major problems and she did not know which came first. One was to find customers. The other was the purchase of a sufficiently large selection of fabrics from which those customers might choose. Abigail was unwilling to spend what would be the greater part of her remaining money on materials for customers who did not yet exist. She knew that a dressmaker's reputation was built up on recommendation, yet who would come to her without seeing her work?

Suddenly she remembered her Court dress, folded away in her trunk. She could display it in her window. The idea was soon discarded: not only was the window too small, but no one of any elegance was likely to pass it – this cabin was not in a fashionable part of the town. However, that gown remined the only example of her handiwork likely to interest the sort of clients she wished to attract, so she must get it back. Tomorrow she would set about transforming the cabin. The day after that she would go and see Jabez. Perhaps he would be willing to spare a boy and a barrow to bring it to her.

Jabez anticipated no problem beyond the fact that it would be two or three days before someone could be spared. To Abigail, anxious to make a start, this was no small disappointment. Then she recalled that all she needed at this stage was that one gown which she could perfectly easily carry home herself if Lord Jasper would let her have the keys.

It soon became clear that, with the necklace gone, his lordship did not consider the trunk warranted quite such stringent security and Jabez returned from his office with the keys. Abigail took them from him and ran upstairs, grateful that this time she need not face Lord Jasper and his searching questions.

She knelt down beside the trunk and unlocked it, removing the workaday dresses until she came to the delicate harebell blue she sought. She lifted it tenderly from the trunk, removing the tissue with which her maid had sought to prevent its creasing, so long ago. She could not resist the impulse to hold it against her and move as if to music only she could hear.

'Very touching,' said a dry voice behind her.

Abigail spun round to see Lord Jasper's tall form in the doorway. She coloured with embarrassment that he should have caught her in so unguarded a moment. 'My lord! I didn't know you were there!'

'So I imagined. Don't blush, Mrs Vatsetter: you present a charming picture. Pray continue.'

'Don't be silly,' Abigail said crossly, annoyance replacing embarrassment. 'I thought I was alone.'

'And besides, I've broken the spell, haven't I?'

Abigail wondered if she detected a note of bitterness in his voice but since she could conceive of no reason for one, she decided she must be mistaken so she said simply, 'Yes, my lord. You have.'

'Jabez tells me you're anxious to relieve me of responsibility for your trunk. I see you can't wait to take possession of at least one of its contents. Tell me, do you propose to live on the memory of past glories or are you going to put us all in the shade by promenading through Williamsburg in this magnificence?'

'Neither,' Abigail told him, nettled. 'I'm going to set myself up in business.'

'In a Court dress?' His polite astonishment was more annoying than rank disbelief. 'One hardly likes to inquire too closely into the nature of your proposed business, particularly in view of your condition, though perhaps I should advise you that most gentlemen prefer a lady to be under- rather than over-dressed.'

'I bow to your superior knowledge,' Abigail said acidly. 'However, my intended business requires nothing of gentlemen save that they pay the bills.'

'That was what I imagined – after all, their wives would be unlikely to do so.'

'My lord, you may choose wilfully to misunderstand me but you must know I have no such intention as it pleases you to imply.'

'You disappoint me. I had hoped to be the first to . . . er . . . sample the goods.'

Abigail compressed her lips, determined that this time he would not succeed in goading her into unbecoming behaviour.

Lord Jasper laughed appreciatively at her efforts and came into the room. He looked down at her and his finger carelessly brushed her cheek. 'So you're learning to bite your tongue, are you? Very well, I shall stop teasing you – for the time being, anyway. Tell me seriously – what is the nature of your proposed business?'

'Dressmaking.'

'Dressmaking! I know you were a useful seamstress here – Jubilation said the best she'd had – but surely dressmaking calls for skills beyond the ability to hem a sheet or mend a tear? How good are you?'

Abigail held out her Court gown by way of an answer.

He stared at it and then at her. 'You made this?' His disbelief was unmistakable and when she nodded, he took the dress from her and examined it with a thoroughness that surprised her. 'How much of it did your maid do?' he asked finally.

'None.'

'None at all? Come, Mrs Vatsetter, do you expect me to believe you did this unaided?'

'Not entirely. My aunt's maid fitted it for me – it's very difficult to fit oneself, you understand – and Lady Fawler sent it out for the embroidering, though I could have done that, too, and of course I took the design from a fashion-plate. She was doubtful whether I could do it but she had spent so much on my Season and I was determined to save her money on at least one item.'

'But you did all the cutting-out and all the sewing?'

Abigail nodded.

'Then grant me leave, Mrs Vatsetter, to inform you that you are a remarkable woman.'

Abigail flushed with pleasure at such a compliment from so

unexpected a quarter. 'It was a matter of necessity, my lord. Papa's funds were at a low ebb most of the time and either I made clothes myself or I went without. Pap's funds were rarely at what one might call a high ebb.'

'I can imagine,' Lord Jasper said drily. He perched on the corner of the trunk, one long booted leg swinging carelessly against its brass bindings. 'How do you propose to set about establishing yourself?'

Abigail hesitated. Lord Jasper seemed to be taking her idea perfectly seriously and had laid aside his usual sarcastic tone but she dreaded the cutting set-down he could administer at the drop of an ill-chosen phrase. What was more, his question covered the very point she had not yet satisfactorily resolved, thus providing him with a superb opportunity for doing so. On the other hand, his advice concerning her final dealings with Lance Haworth had proved remarkably sound so perhaps, if she were open with him, he might have further advice for her. She described her dilemma.

'Have you considered the further problem of Mrs Hunter?' he asked when she had done.

'The milliner? In what way is she a problem?'

'I understand she supplies fabrics and makes the occasional toilette.'

'She does, but my work is better.'

'That will hardly compensate her for losing business. Furthermore, she's an established citizen, not some bond-slave who has served in the households of two unmarried men, married and become widowed with remarkable rapidity to a third and, by some mysterious means, succeeded in amassing sufficient funds to buy her freedom. Get in Mrs Hunter's way and you go to the wall.'

Abigail stared at him miserably. These were things that had never occurred to her, fool that she was. 'What do I do?' she asked.

'You have a choice. Give up or get Mrs Hunter on your side.'

'That's no choice, my lord, for I can't give up. If I do, I starve and I can see no other way – no other respectable way,' she added hastily to forestall his probable reply – 'by which I may earn a living.'

'You must still have the greater part of that hundred guineas. Why not use it to buy your passage home? You could travel in comfort and still have change.'

It suddenly struck Abigail that that was a solution she hadn't thought of. She considered it briefly before shaking her head. 'No, my lord. What is there for me in England? My father has already sold me to pay one lot of debts. I don't imagine he has reformed and I've no intention of being sold again when it next becomes expedient.' She did not add that a daughter returning from the colonies heavy with

191

child was hardly likely to be welcomed with open arms. 'How do you suggest I get Mrs Hunter on my side?'

'Tell her what you propose. Show her that gown. Offer to buy your fabrics exclusively through her – but insist on a discount – and offset that by offering her a small percentage on any customer she refers to you. If your trade flourishes, so will hers, and if your work is as superior to hers as you think it is, she'll be quick enough to recognise that, unless she co-operates, that side of her business will soon vanish.'

Abigail thought about it. She could find no flaw in his advice which seemed to sew up all the loop-holes very tightly. 'Thank you, my lord. I shall follow that advice.' She looked at him speculatively. 'I think you've become a very shrewd businessman,' she said.

'A penniless and dissolute younger son has little choice if he's to survive,' Lord Jasper told her. 'My father shudders if it's mentioned, however: he can't quite rid himself of the suspicion that I might have made my fortune from trade.'

Abigail laughed at that and it flashed across Lord Jasper's mind that that was the first carefree sound he had heard from her.

'I hope I may be as lucky,' she said.

'Luck, Mrs Vatsetter, has little to do with it, believe me. If you can turn a circumstance to your own advantage, you win. Others may call it luck. I don't. It so happens that you've bought your freedom at the best time to make use of your particular skill. I trust you won't waste the opportunity.'

'I'd not realised there was one,' Abigail confessed.

'So you'd not heard of the Newington wedding?'

Abigail shook her head. 'Tell me about it. How will it help me?'

'William Newington is determined to make his daughter's wedding the event of the decade. No expense is to be spared. There isn't a woman in Williamsburg who won't want a new toilette for the occasion. It could be the making of you.'

'But only if the ladies of Williamsburg know about me.'

'The sooner you see Mrs Hunter, the sooner they will do so.' He took the gown from her hands and tossed it lightly into the trunk. 'Leave it. Jabez will bring the trunk round to you straight away.'

'He said he couldn't spare a boy for a day or two,' Abigail demurred. 'The other things can wait but I must take this gown,' and she reached down for it.

Lord Jasper caught her wrist. 'And I say Jabez will bring it straight away. Jabez is an admirable man but my orders still take precedence.'

For a moment they stood together and as Abigail obeyed an instinctive compulsion to look up into Lord Jasper's eyes, she thought she saw there something beyond his customary mocking smile. The fleeting impression was soon gone and she was aware only of the purely physical discomfort of her wrist.

'You're hurting me, Lord Jasper.' He released her at once and she rubbed her wrist. 'Thank you – and thank you also for sending Jabez.'

'Think nothing of it,' he told her with studied politeness as he followed her out of the room. 'I'll also endeavour to pass the word to as many ladies as I can that there is a brilliantly clever new dressmaker in town whose work has been presented at Court. That should help.'

Abigail paused at the head of the stairs and looked back at him over her shoulder. 'For a commission, Lord Jasper?'

'You learn quickly. Naturally – for a commission, the precise terms of which I shall give some thought to.'

It needed only a very brief examination of Abigail's Court dress to convince Mrs Hunter that it would be more advantageous to work with Mrs Vatsetter than against her. She herself suggested that Abigail's gown should be displayed in her own window and drew the younger woman's attention to the stock of silks and satins, taffetas and brocades, that she had been buying up in anticipation of the forthcoming nuptials.

'Though whatever induced her to take the Bolton boy, I'll never know,' Mrs Hunter rattled on. 'A nice enough young man, to be sure, but she'd have done better to try for Lord Jasper. His lordship's always very much the gentleman, which can't be said for many, these days.' She shot Abigail a sideways glance. 'But you'll know all about that – more than most of us, I don't doubt.'

'I worked in Lord Jasper's house,' Abigail said stiffly. 'He treats his servants well.'

'You wouldn't believe the caps that have been set at him,' Mrs Hunter went on. 'Of course, there's a coldness about him that the younger girls don't like and no one can accuse him of seeking to ingratiate himself with anyone but then, with a fortune and a title, he doesn't need to.'

Abigail agreed that this was indeed so and eventually succeeded in stilling Mrs Hunter's prattling tongue with a mutually acceptable arrangement which sent her home in high hopes.

Her optimism was sorely tried during the ensuing week when day succeeded day and not a soul expressed an interest. Abigail dared not go out in case a potential customer called, yet there was too little to do within four very small walls to keep her mind off her situation, a situation which became less enviable as every passing day brought no

193

prospect of income. She spent much of her time sewing baby clothes and wondering what was to become of the two of them if her skill had not established a clientele before the child was born.

For six days her melancholy deepened and then she had a visitor. Tucked away at this end of town, few horses and fewer carriages passed her door and none drew up. Abigail therefore glanced up from her sewing when hooves stopped outside. Surely she had not heard carriage wheels? There was a heavy knock on the door. Flinging the tiny garment she was making on to the table, Abigail rushed to open it and the welcoming smile with which she did so was soon replaced by disappointment when she saw her visitor was Lord Jasper. He was already leaning out of his saddle to strike the door again with the leather-bound knob of his whip when she opened it. He straightened in the saddle and his whip touched his forehead in salute instead.

'You seem displeased. Shall I go away?'

'Not displeased, my lord. Just disappointed,' Abigail told him. 'I hoped you might be a customer.'

'Then I trust the lack of displeasure indicates that I've risen in your estimation at last. Is business less than brisk?'

'That's one way of expressing it. "Non-existent" is another.'

'Dear me. May I come in?'

Abigail hesitated.

'If we leave the door open, I don't think your reputation will be compromised,' Lord Jasper told her with a solemnity that made Abigail wonder if he were mocking her.

He cast a far from uninterested glance around the room and Abigail had the impression that little escaped him. It crossed her mind that his coat sat less easily across his shoulders than was usual in so fastidious a dresser, and bulged oddly on his chest.

'I hope you'll not be offended if I bring you a small present.' be began.

'A present? For me?' Abigail could not help sounding ungratefully suspicious. She had long ceased expecting such things and had never anticipated one from this source.

'Sometimes I have moods of unparalleled generosity,' he told her.

'Indeed? Not very frequently, I imagine.'

'I thought you'd learnt to bite your tongue?' he said affably and started to unbutton his coat. The cause of the strange bulge was soon apparent when he deposited unceremoniously on the floor a gangly puppy with long pendant ears and a black-and-tan coat that felt like silk and gleamed like satin.

'A puppy!' Abigail exclaimed, not entirely with delight. 'He's entrancing, of course − they always are − but what do I want with a puppy?'

Lord Jasper looked around the room apologetically, though his eyes expressed no particular interest in what they saw. 'Perhaps it wasn't such a good idea. Perhaps you've enough without this.'

Uncertainty was so uncharacteristic of him that Abigail's curiosity was aroused. 'Why did you think it would be a good idea?' she asked.

'Aren't you aware of the comment you've provoked? First you buy your freedom. Then you take a house and set up in business. It hasn't gone unremarked.'

'I suppose not, but it hardly explains the puppy.'

'Some of the comments have been . . . shall we say . . . ribald? You're alone here in a little-frequented part of the town. The presence of a large dog may well deter unwelcome visitors.'

'Undoubtedly,' Abigail agreed. 'You have perhaps not perceived that this is *not* a large dog.'

'But it will be − and its baying will carry.'

'What is it? It looks like a bloodhound, and yet somehow not quite.'

'Jem Steventon was given it by a grateful mountain man − the details need not concern us. I've heard of these dogs but they're seldom seen. The mountain people use them for hunting racoon and 'possum and value them highly. Goodness only knows what has gone into their make-up, though bloodhound must predominate. The build is lighter and the lines cleaner. They're not regarded as a gentleman's dog,' he added.

'That must be why Mr Steventon gave it to you,' Abigail said sweetly.

Lord Jasper replied with a smile as sweet. 'It's why I'm passing him on to you, Mrs Vatsetter.' He paused and went on seriously, 'Do you want him? I'll take him away if you don't and not be the least offended.'

Abigail was not particularly concerned whether or not he was. Perhaps a dog was not such a bad idea and it would certainly be company. On the other hand it would require feeding. Sadly she shook her head. 'I would like him, my lord, but with no business I shall be hard put to it to feed myself.'

'As bad as that, is it?' She nodded. 'Then take the puppy − its antics will cheer you up. After all, it's early days yet. Don't give up so easily.'

Abigail went to the door with him, the puppy in her arms. She watched him mount. 'Thank you for the present − and for your thoughtfulness.'

'Which was unexpected,' he said, finishing her unspoken thought. Abigail smiled reluctantly. 'It's not a virtue you display very often.'

'But you see, today I'm in a particularly benign mood. Good day, Mrs Vatsetter.'

He set his heels into his horse's sides and Abigail did not see the frown that replaced his enigmatic parting smile.

Next day Abigail's first customer arrived. She could hardly believe it when a carriage halted at the door, and her powers of belief were further stretched when she saw who alighted. Mrs Ludwell-Paradise might not be young but the notorious widow did not believe in letting either age or widowhood stand in the way of enjoyment. She was rich and flaunted it, and on that account would not have been received in the best circles in her native London. She came straight to the point.

'If that gown in Mrs Hunter's window is really your own work, you may make me a morning-toilette. If I'm satisfied with it, you have my future patronage.'

Abigail knew full well that Mrs Ludwell-Paradise's patronage guaranteed success: others would flock to follow her example. She was less happy with her new patroness' choice of fabric, for the lady selected a charming sprig muslin which, while it would look delightful on a girl enjoying her first season, was rather less suitable for a lady of considerably more mature years.

'Lord, girl,' Mrs Ludwell-Paradise said, chuckling at Abigail's tactful efforts to dissuade her. 'I know it's too young, but I take care to sit with the light behind me, don't you know — very flattering.'

'But surely the illusion is destroyed when you move?' Abigail asked, fascinated.

'It would be if I did, but I don't. Servants show guests in and out and serve whatever needs to be served. I recline on a day-bed. If anything's needed, however small, I ring. The illusion remains intact.'

Abigail laughed. She couldn't help liking this extraordinarily forthright woman. She suspected that many might resort to the same ruses but few would admit it so freely.

Mrs Ludwell-Paradise was delighted with the toilette and, to Abigail's relief, paid promptly. 'If you're seeking to establish yourself, you can't afford late payers,' she said. 'Others won't see it like that. Offer them a discount for paying on time — that'll draw them.' She looked at Abigail speculatively. 'Jasper was right — you're good, but you'll need to be very alive to the time of day where money's concerned.'

When she left after having placed a very much more demanding order, she had given Abigail much to ponder. So the rich Lucy

Ludwell-Paradise had come at his lordship's suggestion, had she? Abigail felt a twinge of resentment that her first customer had not come purely out of admiration of her handiwork, but common-sense told her that pride was irrelevant. The important thing was customers, no matter how they came. She must remember to thank him.

The opportunity to do so came more quickly than she had anticipated. So much business arrived in Mrs Ludwell-Paradise's wake that, within a fortnight, Abigail was joined by Sarah, the fourteen-year-old daughter of Nick Camberwell, the Raleigh's ostler. The arrangement was informal but if Sarah's skills seemed likely to match her enthusiasm, Abigail undertook to offer her an apprenticeship. It was early days yet, however; Sarah could be trusted to match thread to fabric but selecting the right ribbons and laces was a matter that required more experienced judgement. Having spent some thirty minutes with Mrs Hunter choosing ribbons that were just right for Mrs Ludwell-Paradise's new gown, Abigail stepped out of the shop and was brought up short by the figure of Lord Jasper emerging from the silversmith's next door. It seemed as if he would do no more than acknowledge her presence with a brief salute, but Abigail impulsively laid a hand on his arm.

'Lord Jasper! I've been hoping to see you,' she began, not noticing the interested gaze of some passers-by. 'I've been most anxious to thank you.'

Lord Jasper looked from her hand to her face in a manner that caused her to flush and immediately withdraw the former. 'You've nothing for which to thank me, madam,' he said, stiffly formal, and began to move towards his waiting horse.

Abigail was not to be deflected. 'That's not so, my lord. My understanding is that Mrs Ludwell-Paradise came to me on your explicit recommendation. She has placed a further order and already I have sufficient bookings to take on an assistant. You've most certainly earned my thanks.'

Abigail wondered momentarily whether it was relief that flitted across his face. The coldness of his voice was undiminished, however. 'Then you have misunderstood the situation. Mrs Ludwell-Paradise, knowing – as everyone in Williamsburg must – that you were once in my service, asked me about your work. I told her you excelled in sewing. I forebore to mention that I had precious little satisfaction from you in any other role.'

The inference was unmistakable and characteristic of him. It was also insulting. Abigail coloured. 'There was never any question of my assuming any other role,' she said indignantly.

'You think not? I assure you, it's generally assumed to be the

197

situation when a slave, bond or freehold, is particularly well endowed with Nature's charms.'

'You know perfectly well that in your household I was a seamstress and nothing else, my lord.'

'Forgive my correcting you, Mrs Vatsetter. You were also a female footman, albeit only briefly. At best a role which is somewhat *outré*, don't you think?'

'I had no choice,' Abigail reminded him.

'Just as you would have had no choice had I decided to push you into the role everyone believes you to have filled.'

'I'm sure you're mistaken. Not everyone believes the worst.'

'I bow to your superior knowledge of the world. I'm sure you're right.' The irony of his tone made it perfectly clear both statements were the precise opposite of his beliefs and Abigail, stung, knew he was probably right.

'At least believe me when I say I'm determined to carve out a respectable career for myself now that I'm free,' she declared.

'Respectable?' Lord Jasper had gathered up his reins and now swung himself into the saddle. He looked down at Abigail, his cold eyes expressionless. 'If that's your goal, a little more reserve when you greet your former master in the street might not come amiss.'

Abigail was far too busy in the next few weeks to give so much as a second thought to Lord Jasper's influence on her success or his parting shot. If it had been his suggestion that had sent Mrs Ludwell-Paradise to her, it was the garments she made for that lady that brought the ladies of Williamsburg to her door. She had as much work as she could handle.

There was no doubt that the forthcoming Newington wedding was responsible for much of the massive demand and Abigail could only be grateful that it had coincided so conveniently with her own scheme. She had few quiet moments in which to ponder her situation — which was probably just as well, but in those quiet moments she sometimes came close to despair. She had loved Lance Haworth with every fibre she possessed and despite her resolution to forget him, she still loved him. He had treated her abominably but she knew that, if he came through the door with news of Blanche's death, he would need only to open his arms for Abigail to fly into them. She despised herself for that realisation and tried to tell herself it was for the sake of the child she carried, but she knew it was more than that. She hungered for his warmth, his caresses, his body, and was the more desolate because they were denied her.

As she expected, business tailed off in the immediate aftermath of the wedding but before Abigail had time to worry seriously, it began to pick up again. Her relief was tempered by the fact that, once the Newington wedding was no longer in the forefront of local gossip, Lance's marriage took its place.

Blanche had made no secret to her friends of her impatience to 'get her hands' on the Haworth house and bring it into fashion and, since her husband seemed perfectly willing to accommodate her in this, the talk was all of what Blanche Haworth had done, was going to do, and ought – in the opinion of the speaker – to do, coupled with speculation as to how much of the refurbishment would find its way into local tradesmen's hands. All this Abigail was obliged to listen to. Had anyone else been involved, she would have been amused; as it was, she said 'yes' and 'no' and 'really?' in the appropriate places and prayed that the subject would soon be changed.

Her business was such that she now bought cloth by the bolt from Mrs Hunter instead of simply keeping swatches and ordering by the ell as she needed it. These bolts were stored on shelves which she had had erected at the end of the room, not far from the roughly made table whose clumsily excessive length had proved a boon when it came to laying out and cutting the great expanses of cloth which current fashion called for. The bolts were heavy and usually these days Abigail had Sarah get them down for her, but she kept a stool handy, for Sarah was sometimes busy elsewhere and Abigail found the lifting less strain if she started with the additional height the stool gave her.

She was due to give Mrs Bracken-Carter a first fitting later that day but the material had only come in from Norfolk the previous evening and from Mrs Hunter that morning. Abigail had no time to waste if she was not to keep the customer waiting. Sarah, with characteristic thoroughness, had stacked the full bolt neatly away on top of the others but now she was out delivering a completed gown. Abigail would have been happier had the girl been there to get it down but was not unduly perturbed by her absence and carefully placed the stool in the position most convenient for reaching up to that particular shelf.

The fabric was slubbed and did not slide easily across the worsted beneath. It would necessitate several sharp tugs before Abigail could get a firm enough grip to lift it down. Accordingly, she tugged, but she was too close to the shelf to exert sufficient leverage from her position below the stack of bales. Foreseeing failure, she was just thinking she should move the stool further out and try again when one last tug proved effective and the bolt tipped into her arms, catching her off-balance.

The stool wavered and tipped, and Abigail fell to the floor, the bolt crashing down on top of her as the legs of the stool slipped away.

She lay there winded for several seconds and when she managed to push the bolt away, she found she was shaking as if with an ague. Instinctively, she put her hands to her belly. It seemed no different. She forced herself to take several deep breaths before trying to move and found herself considerably calmer as a result. When she stood up, however, her legs were still trembling and she made herself rest for a few minutes before deciding how best to tackle the formidable task of lifting the bolt up from the floor.

She was still in her chair when Sarah bounced in, stopping on the threshold when she saw the overtoppled stool, the bolt of material and the unusual sight of her employer sitting down.

'Whatever have you done?' the girl said brightly and, without waiting for an answer, bent down and lifted the heavy bolt with some difficulty on to the table. 'Why they don't make these things lighter defeats me,' she rattled on, pausing only to right the stool. 'Are you all right, ma'am? You looks a bit shaken.'

'Only because it was unexpected,' Abigail reassured her. 'Thank you for picking it up. Come – give me a hand. We've time to make up and it's high time you learnt to cut out.'

With Sarah's help, Abigail made sufficient progress on Mrs Bracken-Carter's gown to feel that the fitting would not be wasted. She still felt a little shaken, which she supposed was not surprising, and rather wished the walk across town could be postponed or delegated. It could not, of course, and by late afternoon she was on her way to Francis Street.

The fitting was a success. Mrs Bracken-Carter was delighted with the soft crimson that suited her to admiration. The only preference she expressed that conflicted with Abigail's was for back-lacing.

'I'm so glad I left the choice of fabric to you, my dear. Your taste is always impeccable.'

Abigail murmured her thanks and mastered her face with an effort. Such a sharp pain! Could the child not pick its time to kick with some discretion?

She wrapped the freshly pinned gown with care and took her leave. Crossing Francis Street in the deepening dusk, she was making her way down the lane that connected it with Duke of Gloucester Street when she was forced to stop and catch her breath, so strong was the sudden spasm that gripped her belly. She had only gone a few yards further on when another spasm shot through her, making her crouch over as if with cramp. By the time she came to the end of the road, she knew that these excruciating pains were not diminishing. She paused on the corner, resting for a few moments against the bole of a large willow while she tried to collect her thoughts.

200

Was it possible her time had come early? She should have a month — maybe more — still to go. Yet surely this was more than the kicking of an exceptionally lusty child? Another excruciating pain racked her body and Abigail could no longer deceive herself. No matter what the calendar said, her child was coming.

Panic overwhelmed her. Could she get home? She needed to cross Duke of Gloucester Street and make her way down one of the roads that led to the parallel Nicholson Street. Then there was the longer stretch to her cabin opposite the gaol. It was not a particularly short walk at the best of times. Now she wondered if it was even possible.

She crossed the road and made her way past the printer's shop. Another pain brought her to a halt and she knew she was likely to need help before she got home. This, then, was not the best route because there were no more buildings at which help might be obtained until its end. She retraced her steps the few yards to the main thoroughfare but by the time she had reached the end of the block she knew she could go no further. The Haworth house was on the opposite corner. Was there a more fitting place to seek help? It was almost with relief she hammered on the door. Lance may have wanted her out of the way but he could not be so callous as to refuse her the assistance she now so desperately needed.

When Noah opened it, she was almost fainting. She managed to support herself against the door-jamb.

'Mr Haworth,' she gasped. 'Please, I need him. Fetch him urgently.'

Noah hesitated. The girl had been sent packing in peculiar circumstances and he risked a beating at best if he let her in. On the other hand, her distress was genuine. As he hesitated, a door opened behind him. Blanche Haworth appeared.

'What on earth is going on, Noah? Why are you standing there letting a draught run through the house? Who is at the door?'

Noah stood aside without a word and Blanche was faced with the woman who had formed part of her husband's household until he got rid of her. The woman had been generally regarded as a beauty, though that was an opinion Blanche had never shared. Nor would anyone else who saw her at this moment, she thought. What did she want here? Lance had called her a trouble-maker and dismissed her, though Blanche had sometimes wondered whether there had been more to it than that. Catching sight of Noah's greedily curious eyes, Blanche dismissed him quickly.

'What do you want?' she asked coldly when Noah had gone.

'Help me,' Abigail whispered. 'Fetch Mr Haworth, I beg you. I think my time has come.'

Blanche stared at her, the colour draining from her cheeks to be replaced by white-hot anger. 'Oh, no,' she said, her voice soft with menace. 'No child of yours will see the light of day within these walls. Get back to the hovel I believe you call home. Get help from among your own kind.'

'I can't,' Abigail protested weakly. 'I'll not get that far. Fetch your husband – let him decide.'

'He's not here and, if he were, would be of the same mind. Be gone, and if you don't reach home, so be it. There are ditches enough at the roadside.'

She pushed Abigail roughly away from the door-jamb and slammed the door.

Abigail clutched at the railings and then, as she started to right herself, cried out in alarm as she felt her waters burst. Panic-stricken, she began to run, heedless of direction. But she stumbled and fell within a few yards, vaguely aware in the dim light that a carriage had pulled to a sudden halt close by.

'What in damnation . . . ?' a voice exclaimed.

Then someone was leaning over her. 'What in the name of all that's holy . . . ?' and then, as he realised her skirts were sodden, 'Dear God!'

She felt herself lifted up and placed on the carriage's narrow seat. The coachman, exhorted to 'push them,' raised his whip, dropped his hand and the carriage rattled and swayed along the rutted streets until the gates of the Cuddesdon house dictated a more cautious pace and the carriage pulled up almost sedately in front of the house.

Lord Jasper was out of the carriage before it had stopped and Jabez opened the front door in time to see him lift a body from the vehicle and give his instructions to the coachman.

'Get you to Dr Wheatley and bring him back with you. I don't care what he's doing, get him. Drag him bodily if you must.'

'But the horses, my lord – they're about done.'

'You'll be about done if you don't do as I say, Sam. They're replaceable. So are you. Go!'

Sam whipped up the team and went.

Jabez opened the door to its fullest extent, his carefully schooled features betraying no recognition of the woman in his master's arms.

'Where to?' he asked laconically.

'The Northeast Chamber, I think. I believe Jubilation keeps the bed made up in there.'

'For unexpected visitors,' Jabez confirmed with unconscious irony. He ran upstairs ahead of Lord Jasper and flung the door open, then strode over and threw back the bed-clothes.

Lord Jasper laid Abigail gently down on the huge bed and flinched as her body contorted with pain. 'Tell Jublation we need her here. Then go and fetch the midwife. Wheatley's on his way, I hope, but he'll want someone else.'

'I'll send the boy right away.'

'You'll do no such thing. You'll go yourself. I'll risk no mistakes.'

Jabez went and Jubilation was at the door in seconds. One look told her all she needed to know. She leant over the banisters and bawled down for hot water and clean sheets and then returned to the room and stood, hands on hips, looking down at Abigail for a few moments before glancing at Lord Jasper.

'Yours?' she asked bluntly.

'No.'

'Then you'll not know how far gone she is.'

'No.'

Jubilation sniffed. 'Not far enough, is my guess. Whoever's it is, I don't give much for its chances.'

'What can I do to help? I've sent for the doctor and the midwife but there must be something else.'

'Get down to the kitchen and hurry those girls up. Then keep out of the way.'

Dr Wheatley and the midwife arrived on the doorstep simultaneously and Lord Jasper, telling Jabez to take Beulah straight up to Jubilation, led the doctor into the library.

'We have a situation of some delicacy here,' he began.

'I rather thought we might,' the doctor said. 'I assure you, I'm the soul of discretion.'

'Be under no misapprehensions, Wheatley, the child isn't mine. Mrs Vatsetter left my service some time ago. I presume the child is her late husband's, a fact which suggests it must be seriously premature. It's birth in this house will give rise to precisely the gossip I'm anxious to avoid,' Lord Jasper concluded harshly.

'I imagine you would be − very understandable,' the physician agreed.

'For Mrs Vatsetter's reputation, you fool. I don't give a damn for my own. For her sake, I'd prefer no word of where the child was born to leak out.'

'Your servants will know − and the midwife,' Dr Wheatley pointed out.

'The servants will do as I say and I don't think Beulah will risk offending me. She'll get a more than generous price for her silence.'

'I believe you, Lord Jasper, but a baby is not something easily concealed and I would wish you to be under no illusion: I'll not stand by and let the child die.'

'I'm not suggesting you should but, if the child is as premature as it must be, I don't think the situation will arise. Of course, you're the better judge of that. Come.'

He led the way upstairs and checked on the threshold at the scene before him. Beulah had freed the bedclothes at the foot of the bed, the more easily to do her work. The room seemed in disarray and Abigail, her fair hair glued to her brow by the sweat that streamed down, was panting for breath in one of the brief interludes between the searing pains.

Beulah looked up as they came in. 'It'll not be long,' she said, 'and there's two.' Dr Wheatley strode across to the bed and his quick, experienced examination endorsed the midwife's opinion.

Without considering that he had no place there, Lord Jasper went over to the bed and took Abigail's hand. A resurgent pain made her clasp his involuntarily and she smiled weakly; a shadow crossed her face.

'What is it, Abby?' Lord Jasper said gently. 'You're in the best hands Williamsburg can provide.'

'The dress!' Her agitation increased. 'Mrs Bracken-Carter's dress! Where is it? What happened to it?'

'To perdition with Mrs Bracken-Carter – and her dress! They're the least of your problems,' and then, seeing that such a response had hardly served to calm her unease, he added, 'If it's something you were carrying, then it's in the carriage. It will be kept safe.'

'My lord, this is no place for you. You shouldn't be here,' the doctor reminded him. Lord Jasper hesitated briefly and looked down at Abigail, still clutching his hand.

'He's right, you know,' he told her gently as he disengaged it. 'I'll be back later.'

He withdrew to his library and several brandies later the piercing scream he had been dreading rang through the house. It was followed by a silence so profound as to be unnerving and then, a long time after, the sound of a baby's crying. Draining his glass, Lord Jasper was about to make his way upstairs to see what was happening when he was pre-empted by the appearance of Dr Wheatley, closely followed by Jubilation.

'There was a boy,' the doctor said.

'Was?'

The doctor nodded. 'One of each. The boy died. The girl is sickly but with care she may survive. They're by no means as premature as we had assumed. At best it would appear that Mrs Vatsetter anticipated her wedding.'

Lord Jasper ignored the inference. 'And how is she?'

'She will recover, God willing.' Dr Wheatley paused. 'Vatsetter had red hair, if I remember aright. His wife's is fair, yet both children are dark. Are you sure they're not yours, my lord?'

'Quite sure.'

Dr Wheatley looked at him without comment. It was impossible to tell whether he believed him or not. 'Do you wish me to take care of the funeral arrangements?' he asked.

Lord Jasper thought quickly. 'Best not,' he said. 'If the child is so far advanced, Mrs Vatsetter's reputation could be ruined indeed. Better if she disappears for a week or two. A mystery over the one surviving birth is probably better than the truth.'

The doctor sniffed. 'In view of the remaining child's colouring, one must consider whether the reputation you're so anxious she should avoid is not the one she deserves.'

'Mrs Vatsetter's no whore, Wheatley, but if this gets out she'll have no other way of earning her keep.'

Jubilation coughed discreetly and both men looked at her. 'I've already told Dr Wheatley as how Abigail's my sister's child, my lord. I told you about my sister, though doubtless you've forgotten. She was taken by her master which is how come Abigail's so fair – and Beulah will testify to that, being midwife when she was born. No wonder the babes are dark, though I doubt Ezra Vatsetter knew his wife's pedigree. What's more, that poor dead scrap upstairs was conceived in slavery, as no one can deny, and the laws of burial don't apply to slaves.'

A slow smile spread across Lord Jasper's face. 'She's right, you know, Wheatley.'

'That woman upstairs never had a black mother!'

'And I've never known Jubilation to lie, so why should she start now? Besides, stranger things have happened than the occasional throw-back. If the children were conceived before the marriage to Vatsetter, then it may well have happened when she belonged to me and the chances are we'll never know the truth of it. Let it go, Wheatley. Who'll be hurt by bending the law – if that's what we're doing – in this?'

The doctor shook his head. 'No one, I suppose, but it's wrong and you know it, my lord.'

'Doesn't common humanity enter into it? Will you be satisfied if I promise you that Mrs Vatsetter will have the choice? If she wants a Christian burial, no one will stand in the way.'

'I think in that situation – and, as you say, my lord, taking common humanity into account – I'm prepared to leave it to you to do what seems best.'

When Lord Jasper had seen him out, he ran upstairs. Jubilation had already returned to the room where the midwife was making ready to leave.

'Don't go just yet,' he told her. 'Jubilation will have seen to it there's refreshment for you and I would see you before you go. Jubilation, take everyone down, please – and thank you.'

As the door closed quietly behind them, he went over to the bed, now freshly made with sweet-smelling sheets, and stood looking down at Abigail's face, pale and tired but no longer tight with pain. Her eyes were closed but she was not asleep and when he sat down on the edge of the bed, her eyelids fluttered open. It was a moment or two before she recognised him.

He took her hand and enclosed it in both of his. 'How do you feel?' he asked.

'He's dead,' Abigail whispered.

'He came too soon. He couldn't have been saved but you still have a daughter,' he told her gently.

Tears filled Abigail's eyes and her gaze moved from Lord Jasper's face to the day-bed a few yards away where lay a covered and swaddled bundle. 'He was a lovely child,' she said.

Lord Jasper followed her gaze. 'You saw him?'

Abigail nodded. 'Beulah said it was best but, oh, my lord, I would have been so proud of him.'

'Then that is what you must remember, but in remembering that, don't forget to be proud of the girl, too – she's as much deserving of pride as a son.' Gently he smoothed her hair back from her forehead as if to postpone the one question to which he most wanted an answer.

'Did you want his child so much?' he asked at last.

'I loved him,' she said simply. 'Of course I wanted it – them,' she amended hastily. Abigail's eyes searched his face. 'You knew, didn't you?'

'I had guessed – and I blame myself.'

'Why? You weren't their father.'

'That's not what I meant. If I'd not taken you as bond-slave in that dreadful game, you would never have met Lance Haworth and none of this would have happened.'

'Then my father is to blame to staking me in the first place.'

'Perhaps. I can take little comfort in the thought, however.' He hesitated. 'There is one other thing. I'd prefer not to have to mention it but I gave Dr Wheatley my word and it can't wait. We must consider the question of burial. As a still-born child, a full-scale funeral isn't necessary but even a simpler ceremony will expose you to comment I'd wish to avoid. Dr Wheatley has conceded that, since the children were at least conceived in slavery, the rules for slaves might be applied.'

Abigail looked puzzled. 'How do they differ?'

'Let me just say that it would be perfectly possible to bury him quietly in the garden with Jabez to say a few words — he is a preacher, of sorts. Naturally not in holy orders, but much respected. A marker will make sure the place is never forgotten.'

'And only friends from this house will be there?'

Lord Jasper nodded. Abigail looked across at the small bundle that represented so much of the tangible evidence of her love for Lance Haworth. Lord Jasper felt her hand tremble and knew that the tears so necessary to assuage her grief were not far off. Abigail held them in check, however, and pulled her gaze away from the magnet that was her child. 'I should like that, my lord.'

A knock heralded Jubilation's return. 'You've been here long enough, my lord. Abigail needs to rest. All settled?'

He rose and smiled. 'It is — I'll tell Jabez. I hope I never drive you to perjure yourself again, Jubilation.'

'I needed no driving, though I don't doubt I'll burn in Hell for it. Still, which were the greater sin?'

'To let Williamsburg know all the details. You'll not burn in Hell for kindness — just a week or two in Purgatory for lying.'

Jubilation laughed. 'With you for a character reference, my lord, I'd not bet on it!'

Abigail expressed a wish to be present at the burial and so, since she was so weak, Lord Jasper carried her down to the grove of peach trees where the tiny grave had been prepared, and set her in a chair brought out for the purpose.

'Did you want a name for the child?' Jabez asked gently.

'Oh, yes. He must have a name otherwise it would be as if he had no identity. "Chance", I think. It may not be a Christian name but it is most fitting since, but for chance, he might well have been born in one of Blanche Haworth's recommended ditches and then perhaps I'd have had neither of my children.'

Lord Jasper looked at her sharply. He did not know exactly what she was referring to but he could make an informed guess. Abigail had, after all, been only a few yards from the Haworth house when he had found her. It gave him another score to settle but he made no comment.

Jabez, Bible in hand, improvised as was the custom among slaves.

'Dear Lord,' he began. 'Take this child, Chance, conceived in innocence, that never lived to do anyone ill, and make up to him in Heaven what he never had on earth, for Your love is infinite. Amen.'

Lord Jasper Cuddesdon, cynic, was surprised to feel tears pricking his eyes. Jabez' prayer might be simple but it contained the very essence of the case distilled through a humanity rarely found in the more formal expressions of orthodoxy.

Abigail said simply, 'Thank you, Jabez,' but as the soil was returned whence it came, she appealed silently to Lord Jasper to take her away. He carried her back to her room and laid her gently on the bed but when he turned to leave her, Abigail's hand restrained him.

'I've not yet thanked you for all you've done,' she said. 'I'm only just beginning to realise what might have been my fate, had you not been passing.'

He placed a finger on her lips, cutting off the rest of her words. 'To tell you truth, my dear, I did nothing for you I'd not have done for a whelping bitch.'

'To be sure,' Abigail replied with something like her old spirit, 'but that would not have risked attracting public opprobrium. You may make light of it, but I do not.'

Quite without warning, she burst into tears, burying her face in the well-cut shoulder of his coat. He enfolded her in his arms and held her there, his cheek resting on her hair, raising it only to shake his head at Jubilation who made as if to relieve him of his burden. He stayed with Abigail while the sobs wrenched themselves from the depths of her being to tear at her body as a storm tears at the landscape.

Her sobs eased eventually and with that easing came an inevitable lessening of her physical torment. At last Lord Jasper felt she had less need of his protective hold and he laid her gently back upon her pillows. Jubilation came quietly over and stood beside him, the surviving baby in her arms.

'She'll be all right now, my lord.'

'I know, but see she's not left.'

Chapter Eleven

When her immediate grief had subsided from torment into a permanently gnawing ache, Abigail began to feel guilty that she had neglected the living daughter for the dead son and immersed herself into caring for Rebecca with almost as much intensity as she had mourned her twin.

'It's unhealthy,' Jubilation told her master, 'and it's my belief the sooner she's back earning her own living, the sooner that child'll get a bit of healthy neglect, if you know what I mean.'

Lord Jasper did and was inclined to agree with his housekeeper. He sent for Sarah Camberwell and paid her her wages, telling her that Mrs Vatsetter would be back soon and encouraging her to do what she could to keep the newly established business ticking over. He did not convey to her his feeling that Abigail's obsession with her daughter might lead to her neglecting that business totally, but because that was his fear, he began deliberately to distance himself from her, expressing a purely superficial interest in her well-being and none at all in that of her daughter.

As Abigail's strength increased, so did her determination to return home. It was allied to a feeling akin to embarrassment. In this house she had been seen at her most vulnerable and everyone here knew the extent of her weakness. She felt a deep need to distance herself and, by plunging back into business, to prove herself no longer either weak or vulnerable.

She saw little of Lord Jasper during the rest of her stay and the relationship between them was a strange one. Because he had seen her through the worst experience of her life, Abigail knew that she would always thereafter be able to speak to him frankly; she knew, too, that despite her dislike of him, Lord Jasper was the only one she could safely trust. Yet there was a constraint. He had seen her physically and emotionally stripped of delicacy and respectability and now he seemed to avoid her, perhaps because his fastidiousness was revolted by the memory of what he had seen. Conscious of what she took to be his feelings, Abigail indefinably withdrew on his rare visits which consequently became even more infrequent and the converse between them more constrained. She could trust him but she still could not let herself like him.

Lord Jasper, too, was conscious of the constraint between them and knew that it was at least partly of his own deliberate making. He guessed that it also stemmed from the embarrassment natural to any young woman who had been obliged to accept the sort of help that only a husband had the right to offer. Abigail had never liked him, he knew, and he was honest enough to admit – if only to himself – that he had only himself to blame for that. But in the hours of her ordeal he had learnt the great unpalatable truth: Abigail loved Lance Haworth with a greater love than any man had a right to expect and she mourned the loss of the child because, with Lance married, it had represented her union with him. Those hours when his arms had provided the protection her vulnerability needed, Lord Jasper had hoped – assumed, even – would lead to a thawing of the ice barrier that circumstances and temperament had built between them. Instead, he felt her withdraw infinitesimally from him each time he visited her. He was not Lance Haworth and she wanted no one else. Without him, she devoted her entire attention to his child. Lord Jasper hated the way the distance between them increased whenever they met yet he suspected that too much sympathy would hinder her return to her normal mood and behaviour. So his visits became less frequent and much shorter until he did no more than bid her good morning or good night. It was almost a relief when, three weeks after Chance's funeral, Abigail sought him out to tell him she was leaving.

'Are you sure it's not too soon?' he asked.

'Dr Wheatley says not and we have encroached upon your hospitality too long.'

'You needn't feel that. You're welcome to remain as long as it takes to make you completely well.'

'I know that, my lord, and I'm most grateful, but if I stay much longer in such inactivity, I shall start to mope. It will do me good to get back to work – if any work remains, that is,' she added, a hint of fearful pessimism in her voice.

'I think it will: Mrs Bracken-Carter's dress was returned to Sarah who has been minding the shop as they say here. Her father was finally convinced that Tagus was protection enough, though what protection that great, galumphing puppy can offer is beyond me.'

'You gave him to me with that in mind,' Abigail reminded him.

'I was considering what he would grow into, not what he is! At all events, Sarah has been there while you've been recovering.'

'Was Sarah given a reason why I should choose to do so at your house, my lord?'

'Naturally — one would not wish to encourage gossip. She knows that Rebecca came early and Jabez found you. Knowing that you had belonged to me at one time and unable to think of a better place to bring you, he brought you here, somewhat to my displeasure. The child was premature and you were both sickly, so here you have stayed.'

Abigail looked doubtful. 'A less than entirely convincing story,' she suggested.

'On its own, I agree. Fortunately we have Dr Wheatley's visits and you've the appearance of someone who has been very ill. Corroborative detail that will stifle curiosity. No mention has been made to anyone of a second child, nor to how advanced in development they both were, a fact which, if there were known to be two of them, would lead everyone to speculate on the date of their conception. One child, a little more advanced than expected will give rise only to the occasional nudge, or so Dr Wheatley suggests — a view which Jubilation endorses.'

So Abigail returned to her cabin and found that Sarah had had the sense to do one important thing on her own initiative. She had personally visited all those clients with outstanding orders and apologised on Abigail's behalf for the slight delay.

The customers found it annoying but they had known their dressmaker's condition and had no hesitation in attributing the delay to that and, of course, Abigail's work was sufficiently superior to be worth the wait ... for a time, at least.

Abigail found Sarah's care of her and her child very touching. The girl would let her do nothing that involved standing for any length of time. 'I've seen women in your position before. They think they're fine and next thing you know they're weak at the knees and trembling like a blancmange. You may feel better, but you stay sat down, ma'am, less'n you've *got* to move. You'll be fit all the sooner if you do.'

It was advice Abigail knew was sound and she followed it, tolerating the girl's almost suffocating care.

Such was the backlog of orders that Abigail had only limited time to devote to Rebecca but, with Sarah's help, that backlog was soon cleared and Abigail began to work on the steady stream that now came in. There were more orders than one seamstress and one apprentice could handle and Abigail looked despairingly round the little room one morning.

'If I knew where to put her, Sarah, I'd take another apprentice,' she declared.

'We'd cut each other's ears off by mistake if we'd a third one wielding shears in here, that's for sure,' Sarah laughed.

Some days after that exchange they had an unexpected visitor. Lord Jasper knocked and entered. A flustered Sarah bobbed curtsy after curtsy and Tagus bounded happily about, raking his claws down the visitor's gleaming boots.

'I begin to feel that hound was a mistake, Mrs Vatsetter,' he said.

'Not an unalloyed delight, I grant you,' Abigail agreed, 'but he's good-natured enough and will grow out of his worst excesses.'

'I hope you're right, if only for the sake of my boots. I thought it was time I came to see how you did.' He looked her over critically. 'You look a great deal better than you did when you left us.'

'Thanks to Sarah. She's been a tower of strength. My old nurse couldn't have looked after me better.'

'Good. And Rebecca?'

'She thrives.' Abigail rocked the cradle she had had made. 'She doesn't get the attention I'd like to give her, but it doesn't seem to do her much harm.'

'Children are resilient animals,' Lord Jasper commented without enthusiasm. 'And business?'

'As you see ...' Abigail indicated the gowns in various stages of completion. 'As much as I can handle.'

'Then expand.'

'Where would I put another hand? We're on top of each other already.'

'Is there enough work to support another woman?'

'Undoubtedly − and more. It isn't the work, my lord, but the space.'

'Then for goodness' sake, woman, move!'

'It's all very well for you to state the obvious, my lord, but it isn't that simple. Quite apart from the problem of finding suitable premises, there is the little matter of paying for them.'

He stared at her. 'Are you telling me you're not making money?' And then, before she could answer, he turned to Sarah. 'Take the pail and go and draw some water − and don't hurry back. I'm giving your mistress business advice and it's not for your young ears.'

Sarah bobbed a frightened curtsy and scuttled out of the cabin, pail in hand. Lord Jasper had a nasty, cutting edge to his voice on occasion and she wouldn't put it past him to follow his instructions with a blow.

'You frightened the life out of the poor girl,' Abigail protested.

212

'It will do her no harm,' he said shortly. 'Are you doing no more than breaking even?'

'Not at all, but look at all the fabric here — the profits go to extend the range.'

'There's a house standing empty opposite Bruton Church. Would that suit?'

'I know it — from the outside, at least. It's far too big a jump, my lord. If I could afford it — which I beg leave to doubt — I couldn't furnish it.'

'You know,' he said in the tone of one dispassionately considering a hypothesis, 'you have one besetting sin, Mrs Vatsetter, and unless you can rid yourself of it, at least in business, it will be the ruin of you.'

'Indeed?' Abigail said frostily. 'Am I to be told what this besetting sin is?'

'Caution. A reluctance to take risks.'

'Caution is a sin?' Abigail exclaimed. 'The reverse is unpleasantly close to gambling and I've told you before I'm no gambler.'

'You say yourself you've work for at least one more hand. Use those profits to pay for a house which is big enough to allow you to expand still further when trade warrants it.'

Abigail considered. It made sense and, despite her deep-seated dislike of anything risky, she had never yet been given bad business advice by Lord Jasper. 'I couldn't buy it,' she said at last. 'Would the owner let it, do you think?'

'I can guarantee it — and at a very moderate rate. You've only to say the word and my secretary will draw up the papers.'

'Your secretary? Did you come here intending to offer me the house?' Abigail asked suspiciously.

'My only problem was how to work round to it without your realising what I was doing,' he said apologetically. 'I've noticed how stubborn you can be but property deteriorates very quickly in this climate if it isn't occupied and I was beginning to despair. You will be doing me a favour if you take it.'

Abigail looked at him suspiciously but his face was as bland as his tone and told her nothing.

She left Tagus to watch the cabin and took Sarah with her when she went to look over the house Lord Jasper had offered. He heart sank deeper with every door they opened. It was far larger even than it looked from the outside. How was she ever to furnish all these rooms? And how could she dressmake and keep house at the same time? Business might justify a new apprentice but it did not yet run to servants, and a slave she refused to have.

Sarah had no qualms abouts its suitability. 'It's perfect, ma'am!' she enthused. 'What does furniture matter? We can do that bit by bit as we go and if we're not using rooms, they don't need cleaning and dusting, do they? Just think, ma'am: this room for storing fabrics, the front parlour – that *does* need to be well furnished, I admit – for sitting the customers down and showing them pattern books and swatches. Then that little room behind there for fittings: if business really thrives only your special customers will be able to expect you to go to them. There's another room to keep the dummies in and the unfinished dresses, where no one will be able to see what anyone's ordered before they choose to wear it. Later there will be a bedroom for little Rebecca but all we need to live in is the kitchen with a couple of mattresses on the floor. Oh, ma'am, can't you see the possibilities?'

Abigail could, though her mind had not been leaping so far into the future. The girl was right – and so was Lord Jasper. She was too cautious. She smiled at the girl's enthusiasm.

'You're a very ambitious child, Sarah. I hadn't realised it before.'

'I'm an ostler's daughter,' Sarah replied, 'and I'm not ending up an ostler's wife. There's plenty of women in the colony runs businesses. More, they say, than back in England, and I aim to be one of them.'

Abigail took the house. She let it be known that no new orders would be accepted for a week and she and Sarah, together with Sarah's younger sister, Lizzie, scrubbed and polished and sewed. The front parlour soon boasted amply draped curtains inside the shutters, an elegance that left Sarah gasping in admiration.

The cabinet-maker was happy to be relieved of two chairs in the English style which had been left on his hands by a bankrupt merchant who could not pay for what he had ordered. A carpet was out of the question but Sarah and Lizzie spread polish on the boards, tied thick rags to their feet and skated happily over the floor for two days, their hilarity as it became increasingly hazardous echoing through the almost empty house. When they had finished, the parlour floor boasted a sheen that many a housekeeper would have given her eye-teeth to achieve by more conventional means.

Business prospered. Sarah was promoted to first hand and two new apprentices were taken on. Gradually the rooms acquired some furniture and Lizzie came to look after it. Abigail began to feel the lack of a manservant but they were a commodity in limited supply within the colony, except as slaves, and she lacked the time and disliked the element of chance involved in advertising in England for one. She was also far too busy to be able to spare much time for her private grief, though often, when she was alone, her thoughts turned to Lance. He and his wife had left Williamsburg for their plantation the day after Abigail's appeal to Blanche and had not so far returned. This caused some comment for, not only was their departure both sudden and unplanned but it came in the middle of Blanche's much-vaunted refurbishment of the Haworth house. But William Beauregard Quenington tapped the side of his nose and told people the two love-birds had decided they needed more time to themselves than Williamsburg's hectic social life permitted.

Abigail was not sorry to see the Haworth house shut up. It meant she could begin to come to terms with her loss and the treatment she had received, for she was convinced that Chance need not have died had Blanche given her the help she sought, without the rsk of constant reminders in the shape of the Haworths. Now that she lived in so central a part of the town, she could not have failed to catch sight of one or other of them from time to time.

There were times when a corroding bitterness led her to dream of taking revenge on Lance. He had seduced her with, she was now quite sure, no intention beyond his own immediate gratification. He had obtained ownership of her not, as she had imagined, because he loved her, but to get back at Lord Jasper, though for what reason she remained unclear. He had rejected her utterly when he had learned of her plight. Finally, she had been turned away from his house when she had most needed his help. Was it surprising she should feel bitter and contemplate some vague, unspecified revenge? How could she do other than hate a man who had led her to suffer such ineffable misery? She chose to ignore the close relationship between hatred and love.

Then she met him. She was returning from Mrs Hunter's. On her way there she had noticed, with a slight shock, that the Haworth house was no longer shuttered, but so important had her discussions with the milliner been, that she had forgotten all about it. She was still thinking about business and therefore oblivious to her surroundings when she turned out of the milliner's gate and stepped onto the footpath to be brought up short by the all too familiar figure of Lance Haworth. It would be difficult to say which of the two was the more disconcerted but Lance made the quicker recovery.

'Mrs Vatsetter! A successful business woman, I hear?'

Abigail could only nod. She had dreaded their inevitable meeting but she had not realised the turmoil it would create. Faced so suddenly with this, the man who had meant so much to her, she had no time to anticipate and therefore control her emotions. The sheer animal attraction of the man was undiminished. She hated him. She despised him. Yet she knew with awful clarity that if he beckoned, she

215

would follow — and she despised herself for it.

Abigail might despise herself for what was in her heart but she had too much pride to let it be seen. She forced a smile.

'Had you not given me the opportunity to buy my freedom, I should now be living a very different life.'

Lance frowned. 'I'm not at all sure you didn't chouse me out of my dues.'

'My recollection is that it was you who tried to get the better of me — or can't you bear to think you failed?'

He shrugged. 'It's past history, though I'd dearly love to know how you raised the money.'

'All you need to know relevant to our agreement is that Lord Jasper didn't stake me.'

'So it would appear, though I'm by no means convinced.' His voice softened. 'How are you, Abby? I've often worried.'

'So much so that you left town,' she said tartly. 'There's nothing wrong with me, sir. I'm fully recovered from . . . from the indisposition that brought me to your door.'

'You had a child, I believe. A boy or a girl?'

'I don't believe it need concern you, sir,' Abigail said, a determination in her voice that was far removed from her inner feeling. 'Doubtless if you ask around, someone will enlighten you.'

'I have a right to know.' His eyes suddenly hardened and Abigail saw again the harsh ruthlessness that characterised him when matters were not to his liking.

'You forewent any right in that respect when you married me to your overseer. Good day, Mr Haworth.'

For a moment Abigail thought he was going to stop her. He certainly seemed angry enough to disregard the attention any ensuing scene might attract, but he thought better of it and stepped aside to allow her to proceed.

She did so with business far from her thoughts. That sudden change of expression had come in the very nick of time. His customary charm and apparent concern had almost erased her memories of how unpleasant Lance could be when he set his mind to it. He had not changed. If charm could not get him what he wanted, then threats would follow. She must never forget the two contrasting sides to his character, nor the speed with which he could change. That was what she must not forget.

What she could not forget was the joy she had once felt in his arms. It was something she was, in any case, loath to forget: never again would Lance Haworth seduce her but with her recent experience so fresh in her mind, it was unlikely she would ever trust another man to approach so closely, physcially or emotionally.

Some days after the encounter with Lance, Lord Jasper hailed her across Francis Street. 'I hear you've taken Lizzie Camberwell into service,' he said.

Abigail confirmed the rumour. 'Why do you mention it, Lord Jasper? Do you disapprove?'

He shrugged. 'Not at all, they're a hard-working family. A slave would be cheaper: no wages to find.'

'I'll have no slaves in my house,' replied Abigail in a voice that brooked no argument. 'I've been owned. I've no desire to own others.'

She made her views equally clear to those who expressed similar sentiments, as her clients frequently did. It was not a view calculated to win popularity but, whereas someone else who expressed it would have been ostracised both financially and socially, Abigail's history explained it sufficiently for her to be regarded merely as somewhat eccentric, though people never failed to remind themselves that Lance Haworth, who had come to Virginia in circumstances not too dissimilar to Abigail's, had no such qualms.

Despite her determination to have nothing to do with the institution of slavery, Abigail nevertheless invariably cast her eye over the posters relating to the regular slave auctions held in the town. Sometimes these were huge affairs disposing of whole boatloads of slaves fresh from Africa, though these were as often sold in Norfolk as in Williamsburg. More frequently they were smaller, representing the disposal of surplus stock and on these occasions the announcements would list a few named slaves whose identity might be expected to lure buyers and high prices. When she saw 'Mr Haworth's Iago' listed on one such poster, the forthcoming sale achieved a stomach-churning immediacy the others had lacked. Iago was a big, strong, healthy man, not the sort of slave owners willingly parted with, in general. Why, then, was Lance selling him? And why at public auction? Iago was the sort of slave who, if he was sold at all, would be the subject of a very private deal. She went home deep in thought.

Iago had proved himself a good friend to her. Indeed, if she were absolutely honest about it, if it hadn't been for him she would probably have been hanged months ago for Ezra's murder. One's life must be the biggest debt it was possible to owe anyone and, if Iago was being sold at auction like this, it looked as if the time might have come for her to repay that debt. It behoved her to buy him and then give him his freedom, if that could be done without placing him in danger of being rounded up and re-enslaved. She rather suspected that that could only be achieved by keeping his freedom secret and employing him in the same way she employed Lizzie. There was no doubt she could use a manservant: this was a big house and she frequently handled quite a lot of money, to say nothing of the valuable bolts of silks and velvets, brocades and taffetas in the store room. Tagus was of limited value as a guard-dog: he was perfectly willing to give tongue but anyone who had met him knew him to be a great, soft, affectionate lump and no one who had met him once would ever fear him. A manservant of the right type – and Iago would make a formidable adversary – could well be a useful precautionary investment.

Of course, in view of her frequently expressed opinions, she would look at best a fool and at worst a hypocrite, but that could not be helped and was unlikely to be more than a nine-day wonder. She had had enough experience of wagging tongues and nudging elbows to be impervious to them. Her problem lay elsewhere. There was no reason why a woman should not buy a slave, but it was unthinkable that a woman should attend a public auction in order to do so. The opprobrium that would follow such an action did not worry Abigail unduly but the loss of business that would ensue as outraged ladies returned their dressmaking demands to their maids was another matter. Furthermore, she had no idea how much a slave such as Iago would cost. Quite a lot, she suspected. She toyed with the idea of speaking to the auctioneer about it but dismissed it. If he knew she was interested and the sort of price she was expecting to pay, he would have an incentive to push the bidding up to at least that price and possibly higher whereas, if he had no idea and there was some good reason why Lance was selling Iago, then she might well get him much cheaper. The only person who could give her sound advice was Lord Jasper. She slept on the scheme for two nights and then, being still of the same mind, took herself up Palace Green to the Cuddesdon house.

If Abigail had expected Lord Jasper to make some cutting remark about her apparent change of mind, she was disappointed. He seemed merely politely surprised.

'You know this slave, I presume?'

'Yes, my lord. He's a good man.'

'I doubt if Haworth would agree with you. Do you know why he's up for sale?'

'No. I confess I was a little surprised – he's not that sort that owners are usually prepared to part with.'

'Precisely. Haworth has said nothing, of course, but the word is this man's a trouble-maker and Haworth will be glad to see the back of him.'

'That must be to my advantage, surely? It can only bring the price down,' Abigail said.

'It would suggest he's a totally unsuitable acquisition for a lady's household.'

Abigail hesitated. 'In what way is he a trouble-maker?'

'I've no idea. I only repeat the rumour.'

'Then in that case, I'll take the risk. How much will he cost?'

Lord Jasper permitted himself the hint of a smile. 'Mrs Vatsetter taking a risk? We'll make a gamester out of you yet! As to the price, it's difficult to say. It depends on the extent to which the bids are affected by the rumour. In normal circumstances, he would be very expensive indeed.'

'In normal circumstances he wouldn't be up for sale at all,' Abigail pointed out.

'Even so, you won't be the only one prepared to take a chance. If he can be brought to heel, he'll make a good stud as well as being a good worker. He could fetch as much as five hundred guineas. Half that is a reasonable expectation.'

Abigail visibly blenched. 'So much!' Then she remembered the hangman's noose. Even five hundred guineas was not an excessive amount to pay for one's life. 'Would you be willing to bid for me, my lord?'

'No, but I'll get my agent to,' he said, looking at her through narrowed eyes. 'To what limit does he go?'

Abigail considered. 'As low as he can but as high as he must, I suppose,' she said.

'I repeat my warning, Mrs Vatsetter: I don't think this slave is suitable for a lady's household. Won't you let me advise my man to find a more appropriate one?'

'I appreciate your concern, Lord Jasper,' Abigail said politely, 'but, no. I want Iago.'

His hooded lids came down over his eyes and rose again, leaving Abigail with the oddest impression that in the process they had somehow veiled any expression. 'Very well, Mrs Vatsetter. I'll convey your instructions to my agent.'

Three days later Iago was delivered to Abigail's door, sullen and resentful and bearing on his back the marks of a recent whipping. He glowered still further when he saw who was mistress of this house. Lord Jasper's agent got Abigail to sign the various documents involved and handed over the bill of sale. He glanced doubtfully at Iago before he left.

'Are you sure you're happy about this, Mis' Vatsetter?' he asked.

'Perfectly,' Abigail told him, though Iago's changed appearance had raised some doubts.

When the door had closed behind the agent, she told Iago to sit down, but he refused.

'No, ma'am. It ain't fittin'.'

'As you wish. They tell me you're a trouble-maker.'

'I daresay they do.'

'Are you?'

'I've stopped acting dumb and saying, "Yes sah, no sah" and a couple of times I've done said what I think. If that's making trouble, then, yes, ma'am, I'm a trouble-maker.'

'Mr Haworth wouldn't have liked that,' Abigail agreed.

He grinned. 'He didn't.'

'I owe you a lot, Iago, Your quick action saved me from a hanging. Buying you gives me the chance to repay you.'

'You reckon?' His voice was bitter. 'How so?'

'There are no slaves in this house and I've always vowed I'd never own another human being. I've broken that vow but only so that I can give you your freedom.'

'And what would I do with my freedom?'

In so far as Abigail had thought about his possible reaction, she had assumed that surprise, even gratitude, might be the predominating emotions. She had not anticipated suspicion or cynicism.

'It means you work for wages − and I'll be happy if you work for me, but you don't have to. Once you're free, you can work for anyone who offers you a job and live anywhere in the colonies you like.'

'No, ma'am. That's what being free means to a white man. You've been here long enough to know it don't mean that to a black man. In the first place, there ain't no white man in Virginia goin' to offer work to a free black. It would be only a matter of time before I was rounded up as a renegade and shipped off to another colony and sold, and since I wouldn't belong to you no more, there wouldn't be one thing you could do about it. That's what freedom means.'

'Are you telling me you don't want your freedom?'

'Course I want it. What I'm asking is, what use is it to me? You tell me a way I can take it and keep it, and I'll take it fast enough.'

'I suppose the only way we can arrange that is not to let anyone know you're free,' Abigail told him. 'If we do that, you'd live here and work for me, but everyone else − including the apprentices − would have to believe you were still a slave. There'd be little satisfaction in that arrangement, I think.'

'Little satisfaction, maybe,' he said, 'but a lot more safety. Is that a serious offer?'

'I'd hardly make it as a jest.'

'You'd be surprised what white folks can do. You mean it, then?'

'I mean it.'

'And if I don't want it?'

'Then you remain a slave, and I've gone back on my vows.'

'Under your scheme, everyone'll think you have, anyway.'

'True, but I shall know otherwise, and so will you. We're the only ones who count.'

Iago looked at her long and hard. 'Virginia's toughened you up. Not but what you didn't need it. I'll go along with that scheme.'

Abigail held out her hand. 'I'll draw up the paper tonight and let you have it. You'd better find a safe place to keep it. There's a room you can have over the porch. I'll tell Lizzie to show you to it and then we'll have to get you some decent clothes.'

He looked at her outstretched hand and hesitated. Then he took it in a firm grip and they shook. 'I sure hope you don't live to regret this, Mis' Vatsetter,' Iago said.

Abigail smiled ruefully. 'So do I, Iago. So do I.'

Chapter Twelve

With Abigail's expanding business came the problem at which Lucy Ludwell-Paradise had hinted: bad debts. Abigail had taken that lady's advice and offered discounts for prompt payment. These had been very effective in the early days when she had desperately needed to have funds coming in, and she still had a core of customers – mostly themselves the wives of tradesmen – who preferred discount to credit. As time went on, however, many clients considered that the extent of the patronage they bestowed upon Abigail entitled them to delay paying her bills until their next quarter's allowance had arrived. That had been an inconvenience but when one or two ladies, having presumably received their long-awaited allowances, then made only token payments, Abigail was uncertain what to do. She needed their custom but this sort of custom could lead to bankruptcy. Had Lord Jasper been in Williamsburg, she would have sought his advice but he was up-river on his plantation and his secretary did not know when he would return. It remained therefore a source of some anxiety hovering at the back of her mind over the next few weeks.

Abigail's clients frequently, in the privacy of the fitting-room, revealed the most intimate secrets to her. She did not make the mistake of assuming that this put her on anything like a level footing with them. She had not yet reached the level of business success which would permit her to be treated socially as their near-equal. That would not happen until she had sufficient skilled hands to allow her to play a purely supervisory role in her business. Even then it was probable that recollections of her bond-slave origins would further hinder her social advancement even though her recent acquisition, despite her earlier protestations, of a slave of her own had to some extent redeemed her in the opinion of many. She was therefore both surprised and delighted to receive an invitation to the Governor's Concert.

This event had been much looked forward to in Williamsburg, the musicians having been brought from England. Abigail had heard about it from her ladies who, naturally, required special toilettes for the occasion. She had pangs of home-sickness for the first time as she listened to their chatter, the more so since it appeared that the programme was to include the music of that brilliant young Italian Domenico Scarlatti. Abigail had first heard his work in the year she came out. It had been at the Cutteslowe House concert, so perhaps that was why she had felt such an affection for the music. Whatever the reason, an invitation to listen again to that briliant harpischord music — not to mention the Handel and Bach that were also to be heard — was one for which she felt a surge of gratitude.

Yet to whom should this gratitude be directed? Certainly not to the Governor who had probably never heard of her, and certainly not to any of her clients who, affable as they might be, would not suggest their dressmaker should be a guest at the Palace. There was Lord Jasper, of course, but he had been out of town for weeks and so could hardly have arranged for the invitation to be sent, even if so touching a gesture had occurred to him.

Then she remembered: Lance Haworth. In those days of bliss on the voyage over when she had, in the intimacy of their embrace, talked without restraint of what was in her heart, she had told him of the little things, unimportant in themselves, that meant so much to her. She had described the naive wonder with which she had first heard professional musicians and of how she would never forget the music of those recitals so much enjoyed in London. At the time she had thought him to be taking little notice of what she said, being more intent on kissing and caressing her on to the heights of joy she was so eager to attain. Now it seemed she had been mistaken, since there was no one else who would have thought to have the invitation sent.

She was unsure what its arrival might mean. Was she to infer that Lance regretted his treatment of her? That seemed most unlikely though there was the possibility that, for the sake of his daughter, he might wish to heal the breach he had created. It was widely rumoured that both he and Blanche were unhappy at the latter's failure to conceive but it was, Abigail decided dispassionately, far too early in their marriage for that to affect his attitude to his daughter. It was far more probable that this gesture was an acknowledgement of the fact that, since they could not fail to encounter one another from time to time, they should endeavour to do so on a basis devoid of animosity. This was not quite the reasoning she would normally have associated with Lance Haworth but, whatever his motives, it was an invitation she would accept with very real pleasure.

The forthcoming concert was the first occasion to draw attention to the deficiencies of Abigail's wardrobe. She toyed, but only very briefly, with the idea of wearing her Court dress. She rejected it because it was far too grand to be suitable for a dressmaker moving in exalted circles for the first time. She needed to dress in a way that, while it indicated that she knew her place, also demonstrated the standard of her skill. She would be as much a walking advertisement for her business as any of the clients for whom she was already making suitable toilettes, but it would never do to outshine them.

She settled on a pale amber figured brocade which she wore in the currently fashionable shepherdess style over the wide bell of a hooped petticoat. Three tiers of lace covered the arm to just below the elbow and were echoed by two layers edging the deep décolletage. An overskirt was not worn with this style; instead, a generously gathered apron edged with a very deep border of lace accentuated the tiny waist. Sarah helped Abigail to dress her hair which they left un-powdered, one golden ringlet falling nonchalantly over her shoulder. Two items completed the toilette: a small lace cap held in place by a yellow rose and, since Abigail owned no jewellery, a band of dark amber velvet round her neck.

When Abigail studied herself in the glass she felt justifiably pleased with what she saw and knew she could face the evening ahead with a confidence that would be unshaken by any surprise at her presence expressed by the other guests.

Iago, who had gradually taken upon himself the role of major domo and acquitted himself in that capacity to admiration, was as appreciative as any woman could wish.

'You'll put them all in the shade, Mis' Vatsetter, for all they've the jewels you lack,' he said.

Abigail laughed. 'I've no desire to do any such thing,' she told him. 'They're my customers. They must be the more richly dressed.'

'They will be, but rich ain't necessarily elegant, now is it?' he replied and Sarah, who had been helping Abigail with her hair was, not for the first time, more than a little surprised that Mrs Vatsetter let the slave speak to her with such freedom. It wasn't even as if he had been attached to the family for years. In Sarah's opinion, if Mrs Vatsetter wasn't careful, Iago would get out of hand.

Another of her concerns was that her mistress should hire a carriage for the evening and thus arrive in style, but Abigail shook her head at the suggestion.

'The Palace is but a short walk,' she reminded her. 'A carriage would be an unjustifiable extravagance. With Iago as escort, I shall do very well.'

So, with a hooded wrap over her head, pattens over her amber satin slippers and Iago two obedient steps behind her, she walked briskly up past Palace Green and the gates of the Cuddesdon house to the turnaround in front of the disproportionately narrow Palace gateway set in a high brick wall. The gateposts were surmounted by a lion and a unicorn, and a wrought-iron coat of arms bridged the space between. Two soldiers stood guard outside the massive gates and it was said that that was all the Palace needed to prevent attack from that direction. Abigail had been told this several times but had never been quite sure who might be expected to assault the Palace. The French, perhaps? Or the Indians who were a byword for savagery but none of whom was ever seen in the capital?

Once inside, she handed her cloak and pattens to Iago and looked about her. The rooms were already quite crowded so her arrival had attracted no notice. Or so she thought until a hand under her elbow made her start.

'One might almost imagine we had conferred in order to appear together to our mutual advantage.' Lord Jasper's silken voice was unmistakable and when Abigail turned, she saw at once what he meant. His velvet coat and breeches were of a deep, rich brown which could have been expressly chosen to complement her own amber. Any dullness in the colour was spectacularly off-set by the ornate gold thread embroided on cuffs, pockets and facings; a silk damask waistcoat precisely matched the velvet and, alone among the men present, Lord Jasper wore his own hair, unpowdered but caught back in the current fashion and secured with a broad ribbon.

'Indeed, they might, my lord,' Abigail laughed. 'Do we remain together and set them talking or move to opposite ends of the room and hope no one notices?'

Lord Jasper bowed. 'Whichever you prefer, Mrs Vatsetter.'

'Such unaccustomed gallantry, my lord! I'm overwhelmed! Have you been back in Williamsburg long? I was told you were visting your plantation with no expectation of an early return.'

'I returned this morning. Can it be that I've been missed?'

'I'm sure your many friends must have longed for your return.'

'Unlikely, I imagine, and not what I meant. Have you missed me?'

His tone was perfectly serious but Abigail knew that was just to discompose her so she answered lightly, 'Very much, my lord. I've been most anxious to ask your advice on a matter of business.'

For a moment she almost thought she had succeeded in disconcerting him but the impression was a fleeting one and his saturnine face quickly reverted to its customary inscrutable expression.

225

'I shall naturally be happy to advise you. Would it be convenient for me to call tomorrow?'

Abigail hesitated. 'I'd prefer to visit you, my lord, if it would not be inconvenient.'

He raised one sardonic eyebrow and bowed. 'As you wish, Mrs Vatsetter. Shall we say eleven o'clock?'

He turned then to acknowledge a greeting from another guest and, since Abigail could not impose herself upon the conversation, she moved away and was soon separated from Lord Jasper by the crowd moving towards the ballroom.

Although her presence was acknowledged – with thinly veiled surprise – by several of her clients, she felt very alone. Never before had she been to this sort of event without an escort, and to do so now was attended not only by a feeling of awkwardness but also by a sense of loss that there was no one with whom to exchange even the most trivial observation.

She took her place on one of the gilded chairs and after admiring as well as she could from this distance the portraits of King Charles II and his queen, Catherine of Braganza, she was left with only the backs of the people in front to amuse her. Most of the guests were already seated when Lance and Blanche Haworth arrived. They moved down the central aisle to seats at the front so Abigail had a very good view of them as they passed, unconscious of her presence.

Even though she had convinced herself that her invitation must have been procured only as a peace-offering, and told herself she must read nothing more into it, she could not quite repress the sudden leap in her heart when she saw Lance's broad shoulders towering above the rest of the audience. Once the concert started, however, she found herself immersed in the music and when the interval came, she was sorry to be brought back to the present.

The guests made their way slowly to an adjoining room where refreshments of a modest sort were available and Abigail went with the gently flowing tide, conscious once more of her unescorted condition.

'I trust you found the music to your taste, Mrs Vatsetter.' The soft familiar voice made her look up with a smile.

'Very much so, Lord Jasper,' she said. 'I'm so glad to have been invited. I learnt to enjoy music in London and this programme, in particular, brings back memories.'

'Then it's fortunate indeed that the Governor sought my opinion on the matter.'

'You decided what should be played?' Abigail could not disguise her surprise.

'Hardly, but the Governor felt the original programme lacked a certain balance and I suggested the music of Sr Scarlatti.'

'Then it is the most happy coincidence,' Abigail said warmly, 'for it is the Scarlatti I particularly like.'

'Perhaps you will express your gratitude by allowing me to procure you some refreshment,' Lord Jasper replied as they finally reached the doorway. 'The choice is orgeat or lemonade, I believe.'

'Lemonade, my lord, if you please,' Abigail told him, reflecting how pleasant it was to have a *cavaliere servente,* if only for a short while.

She was sipping the cool, refreshing drink when she saw Lance Haworth within arm's reach, apparently separated from his wife by the crush. Aware of her suddenly heightened colour, she nevertheless desired more than anything to let him know that she considered the breach healed. She must thank him for arranging her invitation.

'Excuse me, my lord – I must have a brief word with Mr Haworth,' she said, and without pausing to consider Lord Jasper's reaction, she touched Lance's brocaded sleeve.

He turned and his smile faded when he saw who it was. Oblivious to what she did not wish to see, Abigail's own smile was radiant.

'Forgive me, Mr Haworth, but I must be allowed to thank you for persuading the Governor to invite me. It was a kind thought that has been greatly appreciated.' The warmth of Abigail's voice turned many interested heads.

Lance stared at her for a few seconds as if not entirely sure it was she who had spoken. Then he looked her insolently up and down.

'You are mistaken, Mrs ... Vatsetter.' The pause subtly suggested he had had some difficulty in remembering who she was. 'The Governor's Palace is hardly the place for a dressmaker or a bond-slave. Neither my wife nor I would suggest such a solecism.'

Abigail flushed with embarrassment and felt suddenly both giddy and faint, so unexpected was the unkindness of his reply. Lord Jasper's hand was under her arm with a vice-like grip that forced her to remain standing while his acid tongue bit into the audience.

'A fitting remark from one former indentured servant to another,' he said. 'Fortunately the Governor, unlike you, Haworth, is a gentleman and gives no consideration to such petty distinctions.'

Colour surged into Lance's cheeks. 'If there were no ladies present, Cuddesdon, I'd make you eat those words.'

Lord Jasper smiled unpleasantly. 'I very much doubt it. Whether with swords or pistols, I fancy I have you at a disadvantage. However, I shall be happy to oblige you if you are serious. I can only regret that fisticuffs are not acceptable under the Code of Honour, for I'm sure you would then excel.'

Lance's flush deepened at the insult but, since skill with neither sword nor pistol had ever been part of his youthful training, he knew that to pursue the challenge was to invite defeat. Instead, he took refuge once more behind the presence of ladies.

'Were there no ladies here, my lord, it would be a different matter. I've no desire to offend their sensibilities – but don't allow that to mislead you into thinking the matter done with.' He bowed exaggeratedly and made his way back through the crowd to rejoin his wife.

'Mrs Vatsetter needs air,' Lord Jasper told the bystanders still crowded round and they stood helpfully aside so that he could lead her into the cool, uncrowded vestibule.

A footman brought a chair on to which Abigail subsided gratefully, and another, at a sign from Lord Jasper, brought her a glass of water.

When she had had time to compose herself, Lord Jasper bent over her. 'I know you've been enjoying the music, but wouldn't you prefer to go home now?' he asked.

Abigail stood up. 'I'm sorry to have been the cause of such a spectacle, however unwittingly,' she said, 'but I am most certainly *not* going home. If I cry craven now, I shall never be able to lift my head again.' She paused and looked at him hesitantly. 'I own I would find it a great deal easier if you would accompany me back in,' she added.

Lord Jasper laughed. 'Good girl! I thought for a few moments there you were going to dissolve into missish vapours. I'm delighted to see you can still muster spirit when the occasion demands. 'Now?'

'Now,' Abigail agreed.

She paused in the doorway of the ballroom, her hand on his arm, and Lord Jasper heard her take a deep breath before proceeding into the room, her head held high. Inevitably the cynosure of all eyes, it took no little courage to walk past so interested an audience, and Abigail suspected that if she had been on her own she might well have turned tail and run.

In the event, it was Lance Haworth and his wife who did that. It did not for one moment cross Lance's mind that Abigail might return to the concert after his insult and although his behaviour would bring its own condemnation, he felt that the victor might well, in the eyes of the onlookers, be the one who stayed in the field. In any case, his position in society was not as fragile as Abigail's; he could afford the gamble. Had he not made himself forget that unflattering incident with the brandy decanter, he might have been less complacent, but he had succeeded in putting it out of his mind and so he did not remember that Abigail had a distressing propensity for behaving in a way most unbecoming in a well brought-up young woman.

When he heard the rustle of people turning round, he himself turned to see what had attracted their attention. Observing Abigail, entirely self-possessed, progressing down the room on Lord Jasper's arm, Lance paled and the titters that rippled through the audience as the recent protagonists drew level with one another were as much as he could bear. He looked away and became deeply interested in removing a speck of dust from his sleeve, but when the titters were replaced by whispers that were hardly *sotto voce,* his nerve failed. A word in Blanche's ear was followed by her sudden need to press a dainty handkerchief to her brow and immediately her compassionate husband escorted her from the room.

The audience was delighted. Who would have imagined that the Governor's dry concert would turn out to be so very entertaining? 'Entertaining' would not have been Abigail's word for it, however, and she had considerable difficulty concentrating on the music once more. She studied the musicians with outwardly rapt attention, blissfully unaware that those of the audience who were in a position to do so studiously kept one eye on her. In discussions afterwards to which Abigail was naturally not privy, opinion was divided between those who admired her courage and those who declared her a 'hard case'. Whichever view they held, none thought any the worse of her, though several speculated upon the nature of the game Lord Jasper was playing.

Several people spoke very affably to her when the concert finally ended and they made their way out, a fact which enabled Abigail to relax slightly. It would not have surprised her if they had cut her dead. Had the incident occurred in London, that was undoubtedly what would have happened.

'What time did you tell your carriage to return?' Lord Jasper asked as he placed her cloak round her shoulders.

Abigail laughed a little shakily. 'You know I have no carriage! I walked here and shall walk back. Iago escorted me, so I was safe enough.'

'He'll not accompany you home, however. My carriage will be here shortly and you will return in it. Send Iago off.'

Abigail stared at him, unsure whether to be amused or shocked. 'You've ordered your carriage? But, my lord, your house is scarce two minutes' walk from the Palace!'

'Three, to be precise, if one includes both drives. The distance is irrelevant. You surely do not expect a man of fashion to walk? Who know what footpads might lurk along the way!'

'Between here and the Cuddesdon house? Why do you act the fop, my lord, when we both know you are nothing of the sort?'

'Others are less perspicacious. Besides, it amuses me. Will you allow me to put my carriage at your disposal tonight?'

Abigail sighed. 'As a matter of fact, I should welcome it – but how will you manage?'

Lord Jasper smiled blandly. 'I shall walk – what else?'

Punctually at eleven o'clock the next day, Abigail was shown into Lord Jasper's library. He rose as she entered and moved to a side table.

'Madeira?'

'Thank you, yes, my lord.'

He poured some into a glass and handed it to her. 'Congratulations, Mrs Vatsetter.'

'On what?'

'On appearing to have lost no sleep over last night's unpleasantness.'

Abigail laughed ruefully. 'Then appearances are false for I tossed and turned interminably. I daresay tomorrow I shall look quite hagged.'

'Impossible,' he said gallantly. 'You handled yourself well, you know. There is one thing that I confess arouses my curiosity.'

'My lord?'

'Why did you think that it was Lance Haworth who procured an invitation for you?'

Abigail coloured. 'It was the programme. When we were on the *Alice Nancy,* I told him how much pleasure a particular concert had given me in London. It was the one at Cutteslowe House – perhaps you recall it: you were in England at the time.'

'Being rejected, as I recall, by an extremely arrogant young woman enjoying her first Season.'

'What did you expect, with the reputation you enjoyed?' Abigail retorted, unabashed.

'I confess, I'd not looked at it from that angle,' Lord Jasper commented. 'I'm sure your decision was a wise one, but we digress – you had told Haworth about the concert (and yes, Mrs Vatsetter, I was there myself) – so you thought ...?'

'I thought he'd remembered and persuaded the Governor – or more probably the Governor's secretary – to send me an invitation.'

'Forgive me for being obtuse, but why on earth – bearing in mind the way Haworth has treated you in the past – should he do such a thing?'

'We're obliged to live in the same town,' Abigail explained. 'Occasional encounters are inevitable and it must be preferable for us to be able to meet without too much constraint. I assumed the invitation was an indication that we might do so.'

'You amaze me. Doesn't it occur to you that, had your acquaintance with Mr Haworth been attended by rather *more* constraint, you would have been spared a great deal of suffering?'

Abigail flushed. 'I laid myself open to that and you know very well it's not what I meant.'

'You lay yourself a great deal too open, it seems to me, both to Lance Haworth and my sarcasm. Dare I inquire how you interpret his unpardonable behaviour?'

'I shouldn't have attempted to thank him in so public a place. I see that now. A note would have sufficed.'

'But you don't doubt he was responsible for your invitation?'

'Of course not! Who else could have guessed the pleasure it would give me?'

'Who, indeed?' Lord Jasper seemed more interested in the clarity of his Madeira than in the topic under discussion, for he held his glass up to the light and turned it, concentrating his entire attention on it for several minutes.

'You obviously think me very foolish,' Abigail said defensively, moving over to the window.

'I think you very young,' he replied. 'In many respects you're far from foolish.'

'But not where Lance Haworth is concerned?'

He moved towards her than and stood slightly behind her, observing the view across the terrace and over the lawns towards the peach grove.

'Do you love him so much, Abby?' he asked gently.

Abigail looked up at him startled, not by the question, but by the tone – and by the use of the almost forgotten diminutive.

'No!' she exclaimed and then hesitated. 'Sometimes it seems ... I don't know.'

'If you can't answer unequivocally "yes", then the answer must be "no".'

Abigail considered the matter. 'I suppose so,' she admitted reluctantly, 'but when he's near ...'

'You still feel drawn to him.'

Abigail nodded.

'It will fade. Without love, it always fades. Love can't grow unless it's nurtured on both sides, you know, and Haworth has done precious little nurturing.'

'When I'm being honest with myself, I realise that he probably never did love me,' Abigail admitted. 'It isn't much consolation

231

because it simply underlines my foolishness.'

'It would have taken a far more experienced woman than you were – or are – to resist a man of Lance Haworth's attraction in the circumstances into which you were plunged. That he took advantage of those circumstances only underlines what a blackguard he can be. But you can't go on carrying a torch for him indefinitely. You are young and beautiful – and clever. You'll never entirely forget Haworth but you should leave the way open for other admirers.'

That made Abigail laugh. 'They're not precisely beating a path to my door,' she said, and then the cloud of uncertainty descended once more. 'In any case, it's not as simple as that, is it?'

'What do you mean?'

'I could never marry another man without telling him the truth about Rebecca, and what man, knowing that, would still wish to marry me?'

'None would rejoice in the news but you will find a man eventually who will love you in spite of it.'

'Are you sure?' Abigail said doubtfully, wondering as she spoke how such a suitor would greet the details of his predecessor's death.

'I was never more sure of anything in my life.' Lord Jasper's tone changed abruptly. 'But this was not what you came to hear. You needed advice, you said. Sit down. What is the problem?'

Abigail explained briefly. When she had finished, Lord Jasper shook his head and pursed his lips.

'Inevitable,' he said at last. 'I take it you can't afford to tell them to take their custom elsewhere?'

'At the moment there's nowhere else to take it but if I start doing that, it's only a matter of time before someone sets up in competition so, no, I can't.'

'You already offer a discount for prompt payment, I believe?' Abigail nodded. 'Very well. Extend it so that the discount is greater the sooner they pay.'

'That's no help when a woman has already overspent her allowance.'

'Let it be known that payment after a certain time – say three months – will attract interest. They won't like it, and some of them will only pay off the interest, but that doesn't matter – every subsequent order they place will also earn interest. If I know the world, you'll soon recoup the costs of each garment but they will have to go on paying the interest on an ever-increasing debt.'

Abigail screwed up her nose in distaste. 'I don't like it, my lord.'

'I didn't think you would. You'll like bankruptcy even less.' He paused and looked at her as if uncertain whether to say what he was clearly minded to say.

'You look as if you've further advice,' Abigail remarked.

'I have, but I fancy it will be even less to your taste. I take it you now have some capital behind you?'

Abigail nodded. 'I've been very successful but too afraid of being penniless to spend more than I must.'

'Very wise, but make that money work. I'm sure these ladies who overspend on their allowances would be happy to receive a small advance – at interest, of course – to tide them over. You might never get the capital back but so long as the interest comes in, what have you to worry about?'

'In short, my lord, you're suggesting I set myself up as a money-lender?'

'Precisely.'

'You were right. I like it even less. It's hardly a very ladylike occupation.'

'Neither is being a bond-slave.'

Abigail laughed. 'I grant you that and, since I seem to have put my old life so far behind me, what difference will a little more distance make?'

Lord Jasper lifted the decanter. 'Shall we drink to it, Mrs Vatsetter?'

Abigail was happy to do so and they raised their glasses. As she caught his eye over the rim, Abigail suddenly realised that she no longer disliked this man. She had trusted him without reserve since that frightening night when her children had been born and he had given her the only practical help she had needed. She had initially felt some awkwardness in his presence afterwards but it had been smoothed away by his very matter-of-fact manner. Her loathing of him had diminished from that time. Now, even the dislike was gone, though there was still something about him which she found both frightening and distancing. She rather thought it was the fact that he always had himself fully under control so that it was impossible to gauge exactly what he was thinking or what he was feeling.

'Deep in thought, Mrs Vatsetter?'

'Yes, indeed. I was thinking how very grateful I am for your advice – on all matters,' she added.

He took the empty glass from her and raised her hand to his lips. 'I'm gratified you think so. May I express the hope that you will continue to seek it?' Once again there was that disconcerting irony in his voice.

Abigail decided to ignore it. 'You may depend upon it, Lord Jasper – at least until it leads me astray.'

Although she had disliked Lord Jasper's suggestion, Abigail could not deny it made sound business sense. What she had not anticipated was the alacrity with which her new venture was taken up by her clients.

It was all very discreet, of course. Customers were always complaining of the inadequacy of their allowances. What could be more natural than that their dressmaker should offer to help them over their temporary difficulties? Abigail's problem lay not in finding people who needed to borrow money but in ensuring that she did not extend herself too far.

She achieved this initially by asking the first few customers who availed themselves of the service not to mention it to anyone else. The reason she gave — with absolute truth — was her fear of the embarrassment which would be caused if she came to the limits of what she called her 'little nest-egg'.

The customers promised faithfully but sooner or later there would be one very dear friend who would be told — in the strictest confidence — of Mrs Vatsetter's extremely helpful service and inevitably that friend imparted the information to a very dear friend of her own. It was particularly appreciated that Mrs Vatsetter did not seem unduly worried about the repayment of the initial loan. Ladies who had been more than a little afraid that, if they could pay only the interest, their husbands might receive a letter (or worse, a visit) from the dressmaker, were soon reassured. In short, Mrs Vatsetter behaved in such an extremely tactful and ladylike way that it was a pleasure to do business with her.

Lord Jasper observed her success with an ironic eye and advice which, for once, Abigail rejected.

'You need another house,' he told her. 'Keep this one for the dressmaking side of your business, but you can afford to live in more style now and it would be better to conduct the purely financial business from a separate establishment.'

Abigail shook her head. 'I think not, Lord Jasper. For one thing, it would cause resentment if I were seen to live too high on the hog, as Lizzie puts it, on the interest they pay me. At the moment, because I am seen to live modestly, my ladies still regard me as that prettily-behaved Mrs Vatsetter who is so obliging. For another, any woman can visit a dressmaker without attracting comment. That would not be the case if she had to visit a separate house in order to borrow money.'

'I bow to your superior knowledge of your own sex but aren't you forgetting their husbands? It isn't only women who need money — and men tend to need much more. Will men visit the dressmaker?'

Abigail looked at him in surprise. 'Of course they will. What could be more natural than that a husband should collect his wife or

234

daughter after a fitting? And naturally, were he to arrive a little early, a dish of tea in the adjoining parlour would probably be very acceptable.'

'Not all men have wives or daughters,' he pointed out. 'What excuse would a man in my position have to visit a dressmaker?'

'Do you expect me to believe that you've never provided one of the more accommodating ladies of your acquaintance with a gown? Or with more intimate articles of apparel?'

'You display a lamentable lack of delicacy, Mrs Vatsetter,' he said severely. 'Besides, all I was ever required to do was to pay the bill.'

'How very unromantic!' Abigail exclaimed. 'I'm sure a satin undress-gown with lace-trimmed sleeves and ... and embroidered with rosebuds – something you had ordered as a surprise – would have been much more appreciated than a cold cash transaction.'

'Do you indeed? You very much mistake the case if you think romance enters into these little *affaires*. It's much more probable that the lady would be decidedly put out by her inability to claim a higher price than the dressmaker was asking.'

'You are a cynic, my lord,' said Abigail, laughing.

'Not at all. Merely a realist. However, since men in my position are very much in the minority in Williamsburg, I'll not press you on the matter.'

The possibility of the facility she offered the wives being extended to the husbands was one which Abigail had foreseen and it was not long after her exchange with Lord Jasper that one of her customers arrived accompanied by her husband. The gentleman expressed his readiness to wait for his wife and was very happy to be served tea and cakes in the prettily appointed private parlour. He broached the subject with some diffidence and was relieved that Mrs Vatsetter seemed not the least surprised and was perfectly happy to accommodate him. He was a little taken aback to have a properly drawn up formal contract placed before him for his perusal while Mrs Vatsetter and his wife looked at pattern-books: he had not thought one so young – and a woman – would be so well prepared. But the terms were very reasonable and he was rather short of ready cash, so he signed it before the dressmaker returned.

In quite a remarkably short space of time, Abigail's dressmaking was of secondary financial importance. It still flourished but it catered for a finite market. There seemed no such limits to the extent to which people were willing to borrow money. She took care to remain modest and unpretentious and she soon realised the importance of keeping her ear to the ground. She needed to know how her clients' businesses were progressing and what they planned. It was wiser to advise a man to move cautiously than to allow him to overreach himself and then be obliged to foreclose.

Businessmen did not relish such advice from a girl but so often she seemed to have an uncanny instinct for their affairs, and her advice was always reasonable, that eventually they even sought her opinion. Abigail developed a very real talent for the sort of business she was now engaged in but there was nothing uncanny about her instincts: she employed an agent in Norfolk and another in Yorktown and was at least as familiar as their owners with every ship that sailed and every cargo carried.

The continued presence of Iago was a distinct advantage in this new phase of her business. The fact of Abigail's door being opened to callers by a very large manservant in the prime of life upon whom she could reasonably be expected to call if a visitor got out of hand, was a guarantee that no such situation would arise. At no time did either of them refer to the death of Ezra Vatsetter yet both tacitly accepted that it was a bond between them that subtly changed their relationship from that of servant and mistress to that of colleagues, though Abigail suspected that the outside world would be more likely to use the word 'conspirators'. There was a trust between them that owed nothing to the fact that the life of each depended upon the silence of the other, and Iago identified himself whole-heartedly with Abigail's interests. He was helped in this by the fact that it crossed no one's mind he was anything other than a slave. People spoke freely in front of him on the assumption that he was either deaf or stupid, just as they spoke freely in front of their own slaves who, under the same illusion as their masters, were perfectly willing to gossip to another of their own kind.

So it was from Iago that Abigail learnt of the speculation concerning Rebecca's paternity. As the child grew from infant to toddler, her resemblance to her father became more striking, particularly her colouring. Her dark tumbling curls were in such dramatic contrast to her mother's fairness that comment was inevitable. When people remembered the grizzled red hair and sun-sensitive skin of the unpleasant and unlamented Ezra Vatsetter, they tapped their noses significantly at one another. Hadn't Lance Haworth won her at the extraordinary party where she had been dressed as a footman? And then she was whisked off to Kingswood and the next anyone knew she'd been married off to that dreadful overseer -- and look what resulted!

'They've drawn their own conclusions.' Iago told her, 'and they're asking themselves if Vatsetter ever knew and, if he didn't, what he'd have done once the child was born.'

'He knew. He didn't like it, but he knew before he married me, though I don't suppose anyone would believe that.'

'They surely won't so it's just as well they ain't goin' to be told. When the rumour gets back to Mr Haworth, he ain't goin' to be none too pleased, and Mis' Haworth'll be purely angry.'

Abigail sighed. 'I don't suppose there's any means of preventing her hearing it?'

'A juicy titbit like that? Not even a whisper of a chance. In fact, seein' as how she's so put out at not having a child of her own yet — and hasn't made no secret of it, neither — I'll bet a pound to a shilling that some kind soul makes sure she knows.'

The accuracy of Iago's prediction was brought home to Abigail a very few weeks later. With a rare couple of hours to spare, she took Rebecca up to the Palace Green, a pleasant, tree-shaded sward where children frequently went to play with tops and hoops. Rebecca was too young for such pleasures but she enjoyed watching the older children and Abigail enjoyed the rare pleasure of strolling with neither purpose nor direction, able to indulge herself with the pleasure of studying her daughter. She felt a pang, as she always did, that there was no proud father with whom to exchange exclamations of parental pride. There was a deeper pang, too, that Rebecca must play alone.

Abigail glanced across the Green to the Cuddesdon house and let her mind's eye conjure up the peach grove where lay her still-born son. She was welcome to visit his grave whenever she wanted to but she preferred not to avail herself of that freedom. She could never forget but it was better if others did so and, on those occasions when she needed Lord Jasper's advice, she invariably visited him, unorthodox as it might be, because there was always a good chance they would talk in the room from which she could see that grove of peach trees. She brought her attention back to her daughter and her heart skipped a beat at the child's resemblance to her father. Lord Jasper had told her it wasn't love she felt for Lance. Perhaps he was right but, if so, what was it that she felt? She called Rebecca to her and gave her an unexpected hug and Rebecca, thinking this was a new game, gave an excited squeal and stumbled off, hoping her mother would repeat the exercise.

They turned a corner into Duke of Gloucester Street on the way home and came face to face with Blanche Haworth. It was not the sort of encounter one slides gracefully past with murmured apologies but an outright confrontation of the sort that normally calls forth a more positive acceptance of blame by both parties.

Blanche's eyes took in Abigail who, despite the understated quality of her apparel, no longer bore any resemblance to a bond-slave, and then flew to the child at her side. The colour faded from her magnolia-cream complexion and Abigail deduced that the gossip must have reached her ears. She stared at Rebecca, unable to drag her eyes away.

'Mrs Vatsetter,' she acknowledged at last.

'Mrs Haworth,' Abigail replied.

Blanche's gaze returned to Rebecca. 'Is this your daughter?'

'This is Rebecca,' Abigail agreed.

Blanche was fast recovering her sang-froid. 'Such a pity your husband died so suddenly and in such tragic circumstances,' she said. 'He would have been proud of her, I'm sure.'

'He was looking forward to her birth,' Abigail said with perfect truth, though the reasons were not those Blanche was likely to assume. 'I'm hardly impartial, of course, but I think any father would be proud of her. Don't you?'

She had the satisfaction of knowing she had flustered the other woman. Blanche offered a polite, if somewhat incoherent, agreement and went on her way with noticeable haste.

When Abigail reached home, she handed Rebecca over to Lizzie and, as she fumbled with the cords at the neck of her cloak so that Iago could take it, realised that she was trembling. Iago noticed it, too.

'You're upset, Mis' Vatsetter. What's happened?'

'Nothing – well, nothing of any importance,' she amended. 'On our way home we bumped – quite literally, I'm afraid – into Mrs Haworth. Iago, I think you're right. I'm sure she's heard the gossip about Becky.'

He shrugged. 'It would be strange if she hadn't. Did she comment on it?'

'Not in so many words; she could hardly take her eyes off the child and – oh, Iago, I know this sounds fanciful, but there was such a strange look in her eyes: very intense and yet somehow distant. Do you know what I mean?'

He steered her gently towards the private parlour. 'I know what you want,' he said and when she was sitting down he poured her a glass of the Madeira that was always offered to waiting husbands. He watched her drink it. 'Unless the Haworths take to livin' at Kingswood all the time, you're goin' to have to accustom yourself to meeting them about the place, just as they'll have to get used to seein' little Becky around.'

'I know that, it's just that Mrs Haworth seemed so strange. Oh, Iago, if only things had turned out differently!'

'You needs to forget that man Haworth and find one who'll treat you right,' Iago said dispassionately.

Abigail rose and moved over to the window overlooking the walled garden. She sighed. 'It's not just the loss of the man I love,' she said. 'It's more than that. It's having no one with whom to share. I mean, to share everything, from the funny incident that happened in the fitting-room to the big decisions. Oh, I know when it comes to business I can seek Lord Jasper's advice, but the final decision has to be entirely mine and sometimes – just sometimes – I wish it wasn't so.'

Iago came over and stood behind her. 'I know. They call it isolation and it's a lonely existence. Like being black, but free, in a place like Virginia.'

Abigail looked at him over her shoulder. 'I suppose it must be. I'd not thought of that. It would seem I did you no favours by freeing you.'

'You couldn't hardly have done me a bigger one but there's no denyin' it increased my isolation.'

'Increased it?' she echoed. 'How were you isolated before? After all, you were part of a cohesive community.'

'I lived in it. I'm not sure I was ever part of it. It didn't never seem right, somehow and then, after – well, after certain events, I reckoned I'd nailed my colours to the mast, as they say, even if you were the only one as knew about it. I couldn't go back to yes sah, no sah, three bags full, sah, not without doin' somethin' else to counter-balance it.'

'What did you do?' Abigail's interest was genuine. Iago was revealing facets of whose existence she had been quite ignorant.

'You'd left Kingswood by then, so you don't need to know and it's best you don't. Some things are better not shared.'

'They told me before I bought you that you had a reputation as a trouble-maker,' Abigail said. 'I thought it probably meant you'd argued with Mr Haworth. It sounds as if there was more to it than that.'

Iago permitted himself a grim smile. 'I never argued with Mas' Haworth – that would only lead to beatings and he'd stick to his orginal intention, anyway. No, I took darn' good care he couldn't never nail me for anything specific. But he's no fool. He knew I was up to something, so he got rid of me. Pity, really, Kingswood was handy.'

'In what way?'

'You find yourself a map and work it out,' he said evasively. 'But why did you buy me if I was a trouble-maker?'

239

'I was warned against it but I felt that, even if it was true, it was the least I could do. Your silence saved my life.'

It was the first time either of them had referred explicitly to the events surrounding Ezra's death and with the reference came a subtle, intangible change in their relationship from colleagues to friends.

'Weren't you afraid I'd take the opportunity to blackmail you? It would be easy enough,' he said.

'It never crossed my mind,' Abigail told him truthfully.

He accepted her statement without comment, referring instead to her earlier unease. 'Do you feel calmer now, ma'am?'

'Calmer — and happier, too, I think. In an odd way, the fact that there's someone else in the house who also feels isolated by definition makes me feel less so. And now I must get back to the workroom. Sarah is anxious to show me some new pattern-books.'

As she passed him on her way to the door, Abigail glanced up at his face and was surprised to see an unexpected warmth in his eyes. Warmth, she thought suddenly, was something she no more associated with Iago than with Lord Jasper. It registered as an oddity. She gave no thought to its meaning.

Chapter Thirteen

One consequence of her business which Abigail had not foreseen was that she gradually became acceptable in Williamsburg society, despite the adverse effect any gossip might have been expected to have. It surprised her because she knew it could never have happened in London. Despite the experiences she had had herself – experiences which most assuredly would not have happened to a girl of her sort in London – she still could not accurately predict the colonial reaction to any given set of circumstances, the more so because everyone prided themselves on being so English. The reasons were simple: her debtors were anxious that she should think well of them; foreclosure did not seem to be one of Mrs Vatsetter's weapons but it was a good idea to do what one could to keep in her good books. Then there was the undeniable fact that, no matter what her origins as a bond-slave might have been and no matter where she was invited, no one would have to blush for Mrs Vatsetter's manners.

From the time she had started lending money, she had extended her interest in the colony far beyond Williamsburg and its environs. If she were to make shrewd judgments, she needed as extensive a range of background information as she could obtain and Iago was a very useful source. She had wondered for some time if Lance Haworth's affairs were beginning to decline – it was nothing she could put her finger on but an almost superstitious 'feeling' she had. Confirmation that all was not entirely well came from Iago. He poured her wine at lunch one day, saying as he did so, 'Do Haworths owe you any money?'

'None at all. I'm about the last person they'd come to. why?'

He shrugged. 'Maybe when they're desperate, they'll come. Old man Quenington's cut off their funds.'

'Lance Haworth should be rich enough in his own right not to need his father-in-law's assistance.'

'Maybe. I'm just tellin' you what the word is. Wouldn't do any harm to find out for sure, would it?'

Abigail put her ear a little closer to the ground. Wherever Iago had obtained his gossip, no word concerning William Quenington filtered back to Mrs Vatsetter but it seemed that Blanche, never a good payer, was being more tardy than ever, to the inconvenience and impotent annoyance of many a local trader. So much of the colony's prosperity depended upon trade with England that knowledge of ships and their cargoes was of prime importance to her business and she often knew the outcome of voyages before the ship-owners concerned. Abigail was one of the first to learn that Lance lost two successive ships laden with tobacco and indigo in Atlantic storms and, from Iago, that an attempt to extend his plantation into the wilderness that bounded it had failed when Indians in the pay of the French wiped out all vestiges of colonial life beyond the previous boundaries.

'You and I must count ourselves lucky to have got away from Kingswood,' Abigail commented. 'We might well have been among those working the virgin land.'

'He'd sunk a lot of money into the scheme,' Iago told her. 'They say he's turned to cards and dice to retrieve his fortune.'

Abigail turned the information over in her mind when Iago had returned to his more usual duties. Lance must be getting desperate, she thought. With all his short-comings, he was generally considered no more than a purely social gamester though there was no denying he took risks enough in business.

It was natural she should take an interest in Haworth affairs, and not only on the off-chance she was asked to intercede in them yet she found that she did so with no strong personal feelings. She certainly did not weep to see his business failing, but neither did she vengefully rejoice. She could almost feel sorry for him. He had built up a fortune from nothing, just as she was doing, and she knew how she would feel if hers was sinking so inexorably. There was, however, one aspect of his affairs in which she took a particularly keen interest − and would have done so, no matter who had been the owner. Lance's one remaining major asset was his plantation and the plantations were very literally the root source of the colony's wealth. The activities in the hinterland of the French and their Indian allies were making it as impossible to carve out new plantations as to extend the existing ones, and a plantation was something Abigail would be very happy to acquire. If Kingswood should come on the market, she would go to considerable lengths to buy it. She knew she was likely to be outbid. Lance's father-in-law would surely come to his aid, if only to add it to the already huge Beauregard plantation. Lord Jasper, another near

242

neighbour, might well be interested, and both these men could pay much more than Abigail. No, if it came to a straight sale, she was unlikely to be successful but there were more ways than one of skinning a cat and if some other means of acquiring Kingswood should present itself, Abigail would take advantage of them.

When Iago announced in a voice devoid of expression that a Mrs Haworth was in the front parlour and would like the courtesy of a few words with Mrs Vatsetter, Abigail was not as surprised as she might otherwise have been. She wasted no time assuming that Blanche might have come to order a toilette.

Blanche rose as Abigail entered but stepped back involuntarily at the sight of Tagus beside her.

'A dog in the house!' she exclaimed, wrinkling her nose fastidiously.

'My protection,' Abigail replied. 'I see no one without him. Pray be seated, Mrs Haworth. You're safe enough but, if you prefer, I can have him removed and ask Iago to attend us.'

Blanche shuddered. 'Thank you, but I prefer the dog. I'm only amazed that you haven't been murdered in your bed with that slave in the house.'

Blanche Haworth noticeably lacked the opulent bloom that had been among Blanche Quenington's attractions. Abigail was surprised to see that a veritable maquillage covered the once-perfect complexion but her keen dressmaker's eye soon spotted the hint of an inadequately disguised bruise around one eye which perhaps accounted for such a lavish application of powder and paint. So Lance had had to force her to come, had he?

Abigail sat opposite her visitor, one hand idly playing with Tagus' long ears. 'Well, Mrs Haworth?' This was the woman who had turned her away when she had most needed help. Abigail saw no reason to make Blanche Haworth's mission any the easier.

'My husband . . . that is to say, I have come to plead with you on his behalf,' she began.

'Your husband sent you?'

'No, no, not at all. It was entirely my own idea!' Blanche laughed nervously. 'I declare, I think he'd kill me if he knew where I was!'

'It looks as if he's already tried to do so,' Abigail commented dispassionately.

Blanche's hand flew to her face, unconsciously confirming Abigail's guess. 'An accident, Mrs Vatsetter. The door of a cupboard in the kitchen — you know how it is.'

'I'm happy to say my experience does not yet run to being hit by a cupboard and any husband who did so would live to regret it,' she

said, resisting the temptation to add, 'but not for long.' ' "To plead",
you said. For what?'

'Money – a loan. My husband finds himself temporarily embarrassed. It's not to any very great extent, you understand, but there are
one or two little matters he would like to settle rather quickly and he
worries quite unnecessarily about them, you know. I thought I would
come and see you. Your discretion in such matters is highly spoken
of.'

'Why don't you make application to your father?' asked Abigail,
who found the picture of Lance worrying unnecessarily over anything
a difficult one to believe.

'Papa and Lance do not ... no longer see eye to eye on such
things.'

'You mean he has franked your husband long enough and will
throw no more good money after bad?'

'I have to admit, Papa does see it in those terms. He's quite wrong,
of course,' Blanche hastened to assure her. 'Lance knows exactly
what he's doing.'

'I'm sure he does,' Abigail said smoothly. 'Tell me, just how
"little" are these one or two matters he's anxious to settle quickly?'

'He says ... I mean, I fancy five thousand guineas would see him
clear – and I know you have lent more than that.'

Now there's a coincidence, Abigail thought. 'A nice round sum,'
she said aloud.

Blanche agreed brightly that it was, wasn't it? 'So you will lend it?'
she asked hopefully.

'Tell me, Mrs Haworth, in view of the way I've been treated by
both you and your husband, why on earth should I help him?'

Blanche looked as if she had been slapped. It was plainly a
consideration which had never crossed her mind – which didn't,
Abigail thought, say much for her imagination or her husband's,
since he seemed to be behind this application. The wife recovered
herself with an effort.

'We both regret that, I assure you. You can have no idea how often
we've both felt we behaved badly towards you and have wished to put
matters right.'

'Really? You've both hidden your remorse remarkably well! I
confess to being a shade puzzled as to how borrowing money from me
can be regarded as an expiation.'

'I know how much you meant to Lance – he has spoken of it so
often I've been quite jealous,' Blanche spoke as if the words might
choke her. 'And you, Mrs Vatsetter, have been far from indifferent to
him. I don't pretend to know the whole story but anyone who sees,

... who has seen ... your daughter must be able to guess at something of the truth. Surely you'd not let a man with whom you shared so much risk everying he has worked for, for the sake of so paltry a sum.'

Abigail, sickened by Blanche's sycophantic hypocrisy, was sorely tempted to show her the door but reminded herself that it would be foolish indeed to throw away the possible opportunities her visit offered.

'So now the "one or two little matters" have blossomed into "all he has worked for",' she commented. 'From what I've heard, it would take a great deal more than five thousand guineas to tow your husband out of the River Tick, even if I regarded that figure as a paltry sum − which, I assure you, Mrs Howarth, I do not. Nor, I suspect, would you had you ever been a bond-slave.'

'You won't help us?'

'Not on your pleading. When Lance Haworth comes himself to beg, then perhaps − and only perhaps − I may do so.'

'You can't expect so proud a man to come begging to his former slave!' Blanche protested.

'No? Then you can hardly expect me to help.'

'You're a hard woman, Mrs Vatsetter.'

'I may have become so. If I have, you have only yourself and your husband to blame. We are shaped by our experiences.'

Abigail found herself more shaken by the encounter than she cared to admit. She betrayed no hint of it while Blanche Haworth was with her, but when she had gone, Abigail felt the need for something a little stronger than tea to calm her sufficiently to weigh up both the visit and its possible consequences.

She had barely had time to pour herself a glass of Madeira when the door opened and Iago came in.

'You just made a mistake,' he said. 'You don't want to have Lance Haworth in this house nor nowhere near it.'

Abigail stared at him in some annoyance. 'Does that opinion mean you were listening at the keyhole?'

'Ear jammed so close I could feel the draught,' he agreed cheerfully. 'Of course I was listening! I've as much interest as what happens to that man as you have, and my advice is to have no truck with him.'

'You run this household admirably, Iago, and I've never regretted employing you, but on this matter you're out of line. You know nothing of business. If I need advice in that field, it will not be to you I turn.'

'Fair enough,' he said, 'but I'm not offering you business advice

245

right now. I'm telling you to steer clear of Lance Haworth. He's been no friend to either of us and you've even less cause to help him than I have. You can bet your last penny he'll do you down if he can.'

'It's true I've no reason to trust him but we both know he has need of capital just now and my business is lending it — against adequate security, naturally. If he can provide the security, why should I not do business with him?'

'Because it's my belief you're more than half in love with him still and that'll cloud your judgment. I'd guess he's only coming to you at all because no one else will touch him — and that's no great recommendation. You'll make up your own mind, I don't doubt. All I say is, plug up the loop-holes because, if you don't, he'll sure as hell find one to wriggle through when the time comes to settle up.'

Abigail opened her mouth to call him to task for his impudence but sent him about his business instead. Her innate honesty obliged her to admit that, unwelcome as his frank opinion might be, there was more than a grain of shrewd truth in what he said. Perhaps she needed someone like Iago to concentrate her mind on what really mattered.

She had no idea whether Lance would come. It might well be the last indignity to which he would not be prepared to sink. He might be willing to let his wife come — to send her, even — and negotiate on his behalf, but draw the line at pleading with his erstwhile bond-slave and mistress himself . . . ? Abigail would think the better of him if that proved to be the case. She did not even know if she wanted him to come. There would be a sort of vicious satisfaction in seeing him reduced to an approximation of the state to which he had reduced her, but Iago had been right. Abigail still held in her mind the picture of the Lance she had known on the boat: not just piratically handsome, but confident, strong and determined. In spite of all that had happened since, that was the picture she wished to retain. She had loved Lance and maybe part of her still did. Nothing could alter that and the memory was the more dear because it seemed unlikely she would ever love again. Love involved absolute trust and, if one man could betray her trust as brutally as Lance had done, how could she be sure another would not do the same?

If she was destined not to love again, it was all the more important that the memory of that one great passion should be undiminished. Lance had treated her appallingly but never — except when she had faced him with a broken decanter in her hand, and that was rather different — had she seen him without the confidence, strength and determination that she remembered and that had drawn her to him in the first place. The image had faded a little during the confrontation with Lord Jasper at the concert but she had been too upset herself for it to have had much impact. On balance, she decided, she would rather he didn't come.

He came. It was not in Lance Haworth's nature to fawn obsequiously in order to ingratiate himself. Clearly resentful of the need to come, his manner was sullen but he kept his tongue in check. He needed Abigail now in the only way that really mattered to him and he was not losing her for the want of a careful word.

When Abigail entered the room and saw him there, even though she was prepared for him, her heart gave a sickening lurch that betokened the expectation of a possibly unpleasant interview. It did not normally precede such interviews but then, Abigail had never before done business with the man who had fathered her children.

Lance rose as she came in. 'My wife said you insisted on seeing me personally.'

Abigail indicated that he should resume his seat and sat down herself at the elegant walnut bureau she had had shipped out from England. 'Naturally. I imagine Mrs Haworth is not fully cognisant of all aspects of your affairs.'

'She knows all she needs to know.'

'Very likely. I, however, need to know rather more than she.'

'Things stand very badly with me, Abigail.' There was a pleading note in his voice.

'That much I knew long before you sent your wife to plead your case.'

'So she told you I sent her? I suspected as much.' His voice was bitter.

'She didn't need to tell me: you should have let the bruise fade before you made her come. I own, I didn't think you'd be one to beat your wife.'

'Unlike the man you married, I suppose? She's as much the cause of my present state as any failed business venture. She imagines money flows down from the Alleghenies with the melting snow! Blanche's idea of economy is to send one bonnet back to the milliner and order a more expensive one in its place.'

'Are you surprised? You knew when you married her that her father indulged her every whim,' Abigail pointed out. 'If you didn't, you must have been the only person in Williamsburg in ignorance of it.'

'I was happy enough to follow his example at first,' Lance admitted. 'she had a free hand − and a free purse − to refurnish both the town and the plantation houses as she thought fit, and on top of that were clothes and jewels, but her appetite for spending seemed to grow with feeding and I had expected it to become sated eventually.'

'So you want five thousand guineas?'

Lance hesitated. 'That would hold the bailiffs off for a while. It wouldn't enable me to get back on my feet.'

'What assets have you?'

'The plantation – and the Williamsburg house.'

'Your wife's dowry?'

'Gone.'

Abigail looked at him thoughtfully. 'You have indeed sunk low,' she said. 'Mortgages?'

'On both properties – but they represent less than a third of their value,' he added hastily.

'Who holds them?'

'My father-in-law.'

'If your immediate debts were settled, what investment would you need to put you back on your feet?'

'A ship and a crew. Better still, two of them.'

Abigail knew he was right. Lance's misfortune had been the combination of the loss of two uninsured ships and their cargo, the predictable failure of his venture into the wilderness, and his wife's extravagance. Ships were always a risk but they usually paid off generously in the long run; nothing could be salvaged from the wilderness venture; it remained to be seen whether Lance could now control his wife's excesses. Abigail was inclined to think he could – and would, if only to preserve his only interests.

She forced herself to put out of her mind all considerations of what he had once been to her or of what he had subsequently done. Lance had built up a fortune from nothing at least once and could certainly do so again. If she staked him and he succeeded, she would profit substantially. If she staked him and he failed, she would, provided she held the mortgages to the plantation and the town house, get the plantation she wanted. Either way, it represented the biggest investment she had ever made. That fact made her a little nervous but, even so, she could not see that she had anything to lose.

'If I back you, what return do you offer?' she asked at last.

Lance's face brightened perceptibly. 'You come in with me as partner,' he said. 'An equal share in everything.'

Abigail shook her head. 'No. If you fail, everything I own could go to pay the partnership's debts. I'll not invest on those terms.'

'On what terms, then?' Lance's voice was apprehensive.

'I shall redeem the mortgages. Against the security of the plantation and the town house – against the *full* security, I'm interested in no thirds or halves – I'll advance you what is needed to pay the most pressing creditors, many of whom will become much less pressing when they know I'm behind you. I'll finance the purchase of one ship, the charter of another and, if you can negotiate cargo no other way, the purchase of a cargo for each. You will undertake to insure both the ships and their cargoes. I expect no return for four months. After that, interest becomes due and failure to pay the full interest due in any one month will mean I take possession of everything. In addition, I expect the capital back within the year.'

'That's impossible!' Lance protested.

'Did you think I'd given the matter no prior thought? Don't take me for a fool, Lance. I know how much can be made in one year with two ships, and so do you. It's how you made your fortune the first time around.'

'And the interest?'

'A flat ten per cent on the outstanding capital each month.'

'Good God, Abigail, that's usury!'

'I prefer to call it an incentive. If you don't like it, you're free to go elsewhere.'

'Damn you, I suspect you know I can't.'

Abigail was sharpening a quill as he spoke and when he had finished, she looked up, pulling towards her a paper which was already covered with writing. 'Well?' she said.

'I've no choice. Draw up the papers and I'll sign.'

'It's already drawn up. Perhaps you'd like to read it through.' She handed him the document.

Lance looked at her as if he were seeing her for the first time. 'You were sure of yourself,' he commented.

'Not at all. I'm a business woman – I've merely done my homework.'

When the document was duly signed, Abigail folded it and sealed it. Then she pushed it neatly into one of the little cubby-holes at the back of the bureau, closed the lid and dropped the little key into the reticule that hung at her waist.

'If you will but wait here, I'll fetch the gold you need. Tagus will keep you company. He's a good-natured dog, but I always advise people to keep quite still until I return.'

At the sound of his name, the hound thumped his tail on the floor and licked his lips, revealing large white teeth as he did so. Lance, who had thought perhaps Abigail had been a little naive to let him see where she had put the agreement and then leave the room, decided that perhaps she was not, and decided to follow her advice.

She returned a few minutes later and dropped the pouch of guineas into his hand, remembering the very different circumstances in which she had once before done the same thing. When Lance had gone, she sent a note to Mr Quenington informing him that she held the mortgages on the remaining two-thirds of the Haworth properties and was redeeming his third. Father-in-law or not, William Quenington was not a man who would wish to retain the other third when the balance was encumbered.

Abigail was not altogether surprised when Iago, having seen Lance safely on his way, returned to the parlour and closed the door behind himself.

'Is that arrangement safe enough?' he asked.

'Listening again, I take it,' she commented and went on without waiting for a reply. 'It should be. Nothing is completely fool-proof but I don't think I could have done much better.'

'You can't lose everything?'

'I don't see how.' She paused. 'You're very concerned,' she remarked.

'Pure selfishness,' he told her. 'I'm a free black man in a slave colony. I don't give much for my chances of staying free if you can't pay my wages no more – and a free man's got to eat, same as a slave.'

Abigail smiled, rather perfunctorily. 'If the worst comes to the worst, we can always share a roof,' she said. 'If they think you're a slave, they won't think it odd.'

'You reckon?' he said enigmatically and turned to the dog. 'Come on, Tagus, there's a hambone in the kitchen for you.'

It was not until the next day – the very early hours of the next day, as it happened – that the full enormity of what she had done dawned on Abigail. One moment she was asleep. The next she was sitting bolt upright, suddenly drained of warmth. So unusual was her action that it alerted Tagus, curled up on the foot of the bed. He, too, sat bolt upright but he quickly grasped the fact that there was nothing untoward going on, so he returned to his former position and was soon sound asleep again.

Once Abigail had assured herself that it was not strange noises that had woken her, it did not take long before she realised what had: she had committed so much of her capital to Lance's affairs that only one little thing needed to go wrong for her to face possible ruin. She had covered the risks where Lance was concerned as thoroughly as possible but what if one of her other clients let her down? It was true she stood to gain substantially from the Haworth deal. Lance had called her terms unsurious. They were, but he had been asking for more than a few guineas to tide him over. By the time the ships had been acquired and equipped, she would be left with very little room for financial manoeuvre until the interest – or the property – fell

250

due. She shivered at the thought, then snuggled down beneath the blankets but there was no more sleep that night. How could she have allowed herself to calculate her backing for Lance in isolation from the rest of her business? She had always prided herself on her business caution. It had certainly deserted her this time. Iago's forebodings seemed suddenly all too well founded.

When Lizzie, long since promoted from maid-of-all-work to something undefined but closely approaching housekeeper, brought her her morning chocolate, a task she refused to relinquish, Abigail was still awake but heavy-eyed and uncharacteristically irritable. By the time she was dressed she knew that she needed either to be reassured that she had acted sensibly or to be told that she was a fool – and then advised how to cover the risk she had taken. There being only one person with whom she could discuss business with complete frankness, Abigail sent a note to the Cuddesdon house requesting permission to call upon his lordship later that day.

Instead of the expected reply, a note was returned suggesting that, since Lord Jasper did not intend to be at home that day, Mrs Vatsetter might do him the honour of driving with him within the hour. Abigail was not entirely delighted with the suggestion. Knowing how much of her own information came from the gossip of slaves and servants, she had no wish to discuss business within earshot of groom or coachman but, when Lord Japser drew rein outside her house, those reservations vanished. He was alone.

She looked critically at the carriage. 'An extraordinary vehicle, my lord,' she said. 'What is it?'

'I haven't yet decided what to call it,' he replied. 'It's something between a calèche and a chaise. More comfortable than the one and faster than the other. I hope it will prove more suitable than either on the tracks that pass for roads in this colony, but you may be the judge of that.'

Abigail gathered up her skirts and climbed up beside him. 'From which I take it this is your new toy,' she said as she arranged herself comfortably.

'How well you know me! I hope to set a fashion.'

'I wish you more luck than you encountered when you sought to make female footmen all the rage.'

'This is much less provocative,' he assured her. 'Whether the good burgesses of Williamsburg will altogether approve of your driving with me unchaperoned, is another matter.'

'The good burgesses of Williamsburg may go hang,' Abigail told him affably.

'Dear me, such violence of sentiment in one so young, not to mention such disregard for the proprieties. One confesses to some curiosity as to what brought this about.'

'Then one will have to possess one's soul in patience, I'm afraid. Is it wise to drive in tandem without a groom?' Abigail added as they negotiated the crowded street.

'Afraid you'll be overturned, Mrs Vatsetter? I'm generally held to be a tolerably competent whip. The trails through our forests are too narrow for a pair to be driven with any semblance of speed. I learn from the esquimaux.'

If he had intended Abigail to be startled, he succeeded.

'I'm almost afraid to ask precisely what you learn from them,' she said.

'Did you know that on forest trails they harness their dogs in single file, like this, while on open snowfields they hitch them in a broad fan?'

'No, my lord, I did not. The customs of the esquimaux play little part in the education of English girls.' She looked at him curiously. 'Do you know any esquimaux?' she asked.

'None, so far as I'm aware.'

'Then how ...?'

'I read a lot, Mrs Vatsetter. It's a pastime I recommend.'

Once clear of Williamsburg, Lord Jasper headed north and dropped his hands. For some time he was obliged to give his entire attention to his horses and to the handling of the new carriage, but it proved to be all he had hoped for and before long they were threading their way through the forests that lay behind the town. He eventually slowed down to a walk and finally drew rein altogether in a clearing just off the trail where the grass led down to a pool not quite large enough to be a lake. Tall oaks surrounded it, the sunlight filtering through the dark leaves on to grass cropped short by white-tailed deer.

Lord Jasper jumped down and tethered his leader to the iron weight which was kept in the carriage for the purpose, and then reached up to help Abigail alight.

She brushed her skirt smooth and then looked about her. 'I'd no idea such beauty existed within so short a distance,' she remarked.

'I like it − it reminds me a little of home.'

'Do you miss England?' she asked curiously.

'Only when I'm maudlin. Do you?'

Abigail thought about that as they strolled down to the poolside. 'No, I don't think I do,' she said at last.

They stopped where a tall, straight oak stood sentinel away from its peers, very close to the pool's edge. It was curiously relaxing here,

Abigail thought, and she leant back against the bole and closed her eyes.

'Tired, Mrs Vatsetter?'

The dry tone opened her eyes and she found her escort was leaning over her, one arm outstretched for support against the tree. She laughed a little ruefully.

'I suppose I must be,' she said. 'I think I did a very foolish thing yesterday.'

'Was that why you wanted to see me?'

'Yes. I need advice.'

'I seem to recall that the last time I offered you advice, you ignored it and were proved right,' he reminded her.

'This is different.' As briefly as possible, Abigail related the gist of her meetings with Lance Haworth and his wife. As the tale progressed, Lord Jasper grew very still.

He remained silent for some time after she had finished and when he spoke, his voice was tight and harsh. 'Are you still besotted with the man?'

'Besotted? No!' Abigail shook her head indignantly.

'Then what induced you to help him? Let him sink!'

'If he hadn't come to me, I'd not have lifted a finger to help him out of the difficulty I knew he was in.'

'Ah, I see! You wanted the satisfaction of seeing him crawl.'

'It wasn't even that. I loved him once − you know that better than anyone. I don't think I love him any more, though Iago says I do, but I can't forget what we once had. I don't even think I want to. I thought I'd calculated this business matter very carefully. I want his plantation, you see. If he just sank, I should have had to bid against others. If I hold his mortgages when he sinks, Kingswood become mine.'

'That I understand. Why, then, do more than hold the mortgages? You're making it possible for him to rebuild his fortune.'

'If I hold only the mortgages and he succeeds, I stand to regain my capital and some interest but it would be a long time coming in. This way, if he succeeds, I also make a fortune − and quickly.'

'But at the risk that you've not left yourself enough capital with which to work − especially if someone else defaults.'

'That's why I had a restless night.'

'You deserve it,' Lord Jasper said curtly. 'You're a fool − and, as such, a gambler of the worst kind. I thought you'd learnt better than to let your feelings influence your business.'

'My feelings for Lance Haworth − whatever they may be − don't enter into it. They didn't influence me. I know that, my lord.'

'You obviously believe that but I think you're mistaken.Didn't it cross your mind that here was a man who, like you, had begun with nothing and do you not feel that to be a bond of a kind?'

Abigail considered. 'I suppose it has crossed my mind at various times but that is only to be expected. I don't think it influenced me in this respect.'

'Perhaps not. I think you were influenced at least in part by what had been between you. Perhaps you weren't altogether aware of it but nonetheless it clouded your judgment.'

'It's something that can never be entirely forgotten, my lord.'

'So I'm beginning to realise. There are time when you must disregard it.' He looked at her thoughtfully. 'Why do you want his plantation? Because you think you, and not Blanche Quenington, should have been its mistress?'

'Good gracious, no! How obsessed you think me! That never even nudged at the corner of my mind. No, I've a theory I'd like to put into practice.'

'Theories are rarely good business,' Lord Jasper warned.

'This might be. Plantations − sensibly managed plantations,' she amended, 'rarely fail. I should like to see whether it isn't possible to run a plantation successfully without slaves.'

'You surely don't intend to do all the work yourself?'

'Don't be facetious, my lord. Of course not. All the people I employ are free. They work for wages and they work well. Why should the same principle not hold good on a plantation?'

'You would need an immensely greater workforce than you currently employ. That brings its own difficulties.'

'And the manager would have to be carefully chosen. What do you think?'

'The profits would be smaller without slaves.'

'Not necessarily. The plantation feeds its slaves. People earning wages provide their own food. A plantation store would take care of that. I doubt if there would be much difference.'

It seemed to Abigail that he was watching her very keenly, though she could think of no reason why he should. 'To whom have you been talking?' he asked at last.

'To no one,' Abigail told him, surprised. 'You're the first to whom I've mentioned it.'

'Keep it that way,' he advised her. 'This colony is built on slavery. That sort of idea is enough to have you tarred and feathered' He paused and Abigail had the feeling he was choosing his next words with care. 'You said all the people you employ were free. Does that extend to the slave you bought from Haworth?'

Abigail hesitated. Her instinct was to assure him that she acted on her ideals but there was Iago's safety to consider and she could tell no one without his consent. 'Why?' she asked defensively.

'His presence in your household has caused comment in the town. Hasn't your network of information gatherers reported the general drift to you?'

She shook her head. 'I don't see why there should be any comment. Plenty of women have a male house-slave among their others.'

'True, but not when the woman is a young widow and the slave is both young and handsome, and has what some would describe as a proprietorial manner towards his ... mistress. If he were to prove to be free, I'd not give much for his chances. Would you?'

Abigail shook her head.

Lord Jasper took her arm and turned her so that she was obliged to face him. 'Tell me the truth, Abby. Is there any foundation to the rumours?'

She shook her head again, more vehemently. 'No, my lord. None at all.'

A long silence ensued and Abigail, glancing sideways at Lord Jasper, saw that he was sunk deep in thoughts from which he seemed to glean little satisfaction. She hesitated to intrude upon them but the converse had digressed from finding a possible solution to her dilemma. She laid a hand gently on his sleeve. 'My lord?' she said.

Her words jolted him out of his reverie. He started, smiled unexpectedly and put his hand over hers, then lifted it gently and kissed the tips of her fingers. Abigail's startled eyes flew to his face and saw there an expression of tenderness that set her heart beating in an entirely unexpected way. With desperate clarity she suddenly saw through the confusing mists of past love and past loathing. That loathing had gradually faded into trust and now was transformed into something else. The memory of the older love would always remain but now she knew that the love itself had faded, too, and was no more.

She saw all this with a clarity that was desperate because it came too late. Her history since she arrived in Virginia saw to that.

Flustered and unsure, she withdrew her hand. Lord Jasper's unnecessary gallantry was suddenly distressing. He made no attempt to retain it and when she glanced up at him again, having regained something of composure, the expression she had been so sure she had seen was gone and he presented his normal sardonic face to the world.

'Yes, Mrs Vatsetter?'

He was right. She was a fool. It was a lowering thought. Better not to dwell on the impossible. With a forced brightness she said aloud,

'We digressed, my lord. I asked to see you, not to discuss what I would do with a plantation but how best to minimise the risk I've taken.'

'Of course. How foolish of me. Business must take precedence, must it not? Dare I assume you persuaded Haworth to sign a contract?'

'I know you believe me infatuated, my lord, but please credit me with common-sense. Of course I did!'

'Then permit me to congratulate you. Lance Haworth has persuaded many a more experienced businessman than you to enter a gentleman's agreement.'

'I prefer to assume there are no gentlemen in business.'

'Very wise, if a trifle harsh. I think you must also assume the worst will happen and that, for whatever reason, you lose everything.'

Abigail shuddered. 'That's surely unduly pessimistic.'

'Let's hope so. It always pays to anticipate the worst, however. In anticipation of that, therefore, you need a sum of money – your stake, as it were – put somewhere where no creditors can get hold of it, so that it will enable you to start again.'

'Go on.'

'I know you will be loath to lessen still further your remaining working capital, but I think you must. Lodge with me a sum sufficient to enable you to begin again. Should you need it, it will appear to your creditors as if I'm franking you. That will have two effects: they'll not be able to lay claim to any money which they believe to be mine, and they will be less likely to press for immediate payment if they think I have sufficient confidence to back you. There's just one small snag I feel I should draw your attention to – particularly in view of something you've just said.'

Abigail sighed. 'A snag is inevitable. It seemed an otherwise ideal solution. What is it?'

'I very much regret that you would have to trust me: if there's any firm evidence – such as a signed agreement – that the money is really yours, your creditors could take it.'

Abigail laughed, but with little mirth. 'The ultimate irony, in fact. It seems the only way out of my quandary and I know of no one else I could trust, so thus be it.'

'Your confidence overwhelms me,' Lord Jasper remarked wryly. 'May I enquire how much you feel disposed to entrust to my dissolute hands?'

'As little as possible, I should think,' Abigail retorted and as soon as the words were uttered, clapped her hand to her mouth in remorse. 'I didn't mean that precisely as it sounded,' she assured him. 'Truly

256

I didn't! I meant that it must be the barest minimum.'

'You started last time with a hundred guineas,' he reminded her.

'I'd prefer not to do so again,' Abigail declared. 'Five thousand has been a symbolic figure but it's excessive in the circumstances. Let's say five hundred. Will you look after five hundred guineas for me, my lord?'

'It will be my pleasure.' He took her hand again and his voice grew serious. 'Are you sure you trust me, Abigail?'

'You've been most truly my friend,' she said warmly. 'I learnt to trust you a long time ago.'

'When I consider that I'm to blame for your being here in the first place, I find that very consoling.'

'Do you?' Abigail asked sceptically. 'You've never seemed a man who stood in much need of consolation.'

'Then you much mistake the matter.'

'My Lord, you have everything to which most people aspire: wealth, standing, respect. Your opinions are valued, your advice sought, your example copied – except in the matter of female footmen, of course. To need consolation one must first be aware of a lack. What can you possibly lack?'

'The love of a good woman?' It was more question than statement.

Abigail shot him a startled look but his face was as uncommunicative as ever. She laughed uncertainly. 'I'm sure you have little difficulty in finding consolation of that sort, my lord. There must be women in plenty to offer it.'

'Indeed, there are – if temporary consolation is what one needs. I was thinking more in terms of a permanent rectification of my position.'

'You're unduly modest, my lord. I'm sure both England and Virginia are full of young women who would be very happy to become Lady Jasper Cuddesdon. You have only to put out lures in earnest.'

'Oh, I do, Mrs Vatsetter. I do. My tragedy is that they are largely disregarded – if, indeed, they're even noticed. Shall we return? I fancy the horses are sufficiently rested.'

His tone indicated that he had become bored with the subject and Abigail, her own feelings in some turmoil, agreed with this suggestion.

He handed her back into the carriage and turned the horses before taking his place beside her. The journey back to Williamsburg was made in silence, both being lost in their own thoughts. Abigail glanced at her companion from time to time but gleaned no comfort from what she saw: his mouth was set and his eyes looked only at the trail.

She had learned to trust Lord Jasper and under the influence of that trust, her loathing for him had diminished to mere dislike and then the dislike itself had vanished like morning mist: one is not aware it is going, only that it has gone. Today he had spoken with some warmth and had kissed her fingers and in that brief moment she had known she loved him. It was illogical, irrational, and had little to do with mere physical desire.

No sooner had she recognised how she felt than she had also recognised the hopelessness of her situation. Nothing she knew or had ever heard about Lord Jasper suggested that he was tolerant of other people's weaknesses even though she knew he could be unexpectedly kind in helping them to cope with the consequences. He was certainly aware of hers – except, she thought guiltily, the true circumstances of Ezra's death.

He had told her once that she would one day find a man who would love her in spite of her past. Her heart, her mind, her soul, now ached for him to be that man – and she knew he could not. In Virginia Lord Jasper was not much liked but he was respected, and not only for his title. Abigail suspected he enjoyed that respect and would be loath to lose it by an alliance with a woman whose career in the colony had begun in bondage, progressed to trade and usury, and who had had a child which, while technically legitimate, was so obviously Lance Haworth's that few citizens could be in much doubt about it. Lord Jasper's reputation in England might be that of a dissolute younger son who was both feared and disliked, but he was still the son of a highly respected Duke and, as such, would always be received – unless he allied himself with such as she. It was all very well for Lord Jasper Cuddesdon to have been prepared to marry Miss Abigail Broughton. Mrs Vatsetter was another kettle of fish altogether.

Every so often – usually when he was annoyed with her – he dropped the cold formality of 'Mrs Vatsetter' and used instead her first name. Even when she had been his bond-slave he had addressed her as 'Miss Broughton'. She had assumed it was an ironic quirk, designed to emphasise her changed situation. Now she suspected it indicated nothing more than a desire to maintain the correct distance between them. It was almost worth exasperating him in order to be able to cherish the small crumb of familiarity her name provoked.

When they drew rein outside her house and Abigail made ready to alight, Lord Jasper laid a lightly restraining hand on her arm.

'You can trust me, you know,' he said, a hint of uncertainty in his voice.

'I do.' Abigail was surprised that he felt the need to reassure her. 'Why should you think otherwise?'

'I thought perhaps . . . there seemed to be a . . . a distance between us. I wondered if that were the cause.'

'Not on my part,' Abigail assured him lightly. 'It must be your imagination, my lord.'

'I'm not generally considered to have one,' he said drily. 'Can I expect you to deposit . . . certain items . . . with me in the near future?'

'Tomorrow, if that will be convenient. There seems little point in delay.'

'Delay might well prove inadvisable,' he agreed. 'Till tomorrow then. Good day, Mrs Vatsetter, and thank you for your company.'

'Not at all, Lord Jasper, I enjoyed the drive. I think *this* fashion may well catch on.'

He laughed and guided her down into the waiting hands of Iago, who had, like any dutiful servant, opened the door on his mistress' return. If Lord Jasper subjected the black man to a rather closer scrutiny than was ordinarily accorded to another person's slave, neither Iago nor Abigail was conscious of it.

Chapter Fourteen

During the ensuing weeks, Lance Haworth acquired two ships and drummed up full holds for both, backed by Abigail's money. That would represent the last of her financial outlay for the time being. She took care to check personally that they were adequately insured and Lloyd's agent in Norfolk congratulated her on having succeeded where others had signally failed.

'Mr Haworth has never before agreed to such a thing,' he told her. 'He prefers to gamble.'

'He had never before been playing with my money,' Abigail reminded him sharply.

The ships sailed and Abigail had nothing to do but cross her fingers and wait.

Then Rebecca disappeared.

The news was brought back by a distraught nursemaid who had already spent well over an hour scouring the streets of Williamsburg for her charge. Dora had taken the child to the market. Rebecca was a bright, lively toddler who enjoyed the bustle, colour and noise of the market square and the promise of an outing there was always a guarantee of good behaviour in the meantime. She like to be lifted up in Dora's arms so that she could see everything that was going on from a particularly good vantage point, but she was a heavy child and carrying her to the market place was no easy undertaking, yet she was still too small to be asked to walk that far. Consequently, the maid was always glad of a brief respite when they arrived, and invariably put little Becky down with strict instructions to hold on to Dora's skirt.

'And she's always been as good as gold, ma'am, and even if we do stroll round a bit, she always holds either my hand or my apron strings,' a tearful nursemaid explained to her only slightly less tearful mistress.

'Clearly something went wrong on this occasion,' Abigail said, controlling both her apprehension and her anger only because she knew she would get no sense out of the girl if she herself lost her temper. 'How did you get separated? You must have some idea. Cast your mind, back, Dora. Try to retrace events after you got there.'

'Haven't I been trying to do just that ever since I realised she was gone? I stopped and put her down while I got my breath and I told her most particular — like I always do — not to let go and I'd pick her up again in a minute. Then Mrs Widley happened along. You know her, ma'am — she the woman as had all that bother when the Jameson's cow got into her cabbage patch. A dreadful business, that was, and the Jamesons not the least bit apologetic.'

'Yes, yes,' Abigail interrupted her flow impatiently, 'but this has nothing to do with Becky's disappearance. Get on with it, do.'

'But it does, ma'am. You see, Mrs Widley was telling me about the letter her husband wrote to Mr Jameson — and a good, strong letter it seems to have been — and I was so engrossed that ... well, I think more time must have passed than I realised and when I looked down, little Becky wasn't there.'

Abigail heaved a sigh of exasperation but held her tongue except to say, 'And then?'

'Well, you can imagine, ma'am — I was panic-struck! I thought at first she'd be round about and we both looked, Mrs Widley and I. Looked and called, but there wasn't no answer. Mrs Widley couldn't stop, she had her marketing to do so it's understandable, I suppose, though I'd have been grateful of her help. Still that wasn't to be, so I scoured the market place for her, and that's a fact. No one seems to have noticed her, not shopkeepers nor stallholders nor slaves nor housewives. It's like she vanished off the face of the earth. 'Course I didn't leave it at that, Mis' Vatsetter. I went round all the streets close by. Heavens, ma'am, she's only three! She can't have wandered far! All the same, not hide nor hair of her could I find, not to mention no one who'd seen a trace of her, neither.'

Abigail turned to Iago who together with the rest of the household had anxiously congregated in the hallway. 'What do I do, Iago?' she implored, panic not far from her voice. 'How can we find her?'

'First we goes into the parlour and we sits you down and you has a tot of rum. That'll calm your nerves, ma'am. Then we looks at this thing logically and acts accordingly.' He shepherded her into the front parlour as he spoke and made no attempt to dissuade the rest of the household from following. Their help was going to be essential. They might as well be party to any discussion. He made sure Abigail had taken a few sips of the liquor she so disliked before he continued.

'There's only one thing to be done, so far as I can see. 'First of all, we shuts up shop here, with Mis' Vatsetter's permission, and everyone goes out to search. Mis' Vatsetter stays here, of course, and I reckon Miss Sarah'd better stay to keep her company.'

'No!' Abigail interrupted. 'I want to get out there, too. I want to find my baby!'

'Sure — don't we all know that? And what if someone else altogether finds little Becky and brings her back? Don't you think she'll be scared and want her mother right away? No, ma'am, with respect, you ought to stay here — and Miss Sarah with you to keep your spirits up.'

'He's right, Mrs Vatsetter,' Sarah Camberwell assured her. 'It doesn't do to be alone at a time like this and we've known each other a long time now. I'm the one to stay with you.'

'We'll divide this town up street by street,' Iago went on, 'one on each side. And we'll call at every house and we'll ask them to look in their outhouses and sheds and if they find her to bring her home. Then, when we've got to the other end, we'll divide up in the same way and tackle the cross-streets. It'll take the rest of the day if we have to do them all. Let's hope we don't. It's my guess that more than likely some kind soul has already found her wandering and is feeding her milk and cookies before bringing her home.'

Everyone nodded agreement that this was the most likely eventuality and, since Iago's plan could scarcely be bettered, they set about implementing it.

Abigail stayed in the front parlour, in a chair by the window, anxiously watching the street beyond her picket fence. Sarah tried in vain to persuade her to move to a more comfortable room or to do a little sewing — anything to occupy her mind — but Abigail just shook her head. All too frequently, in Sarah's opinion, she leapt to her feet, positive she had heard someone at the door, even though no one could have come up the short path without being observed from her vantage point, and the inevitable disillusionment plunged her deeper and deeper in despair.

As time wore on and no one returned with Becky, Sarah found it more and more difficult to sound optimistic. It was inconceivable that, in a town as small as Williamsburg, a child could disappear so completely, but the more time that passed, the more likely it seemed that the inconceivable seemed to have happened. When finally the well-organised search party returned empty-handed — and not only empty-handed but with no hint of a sighting of the missing child — Abigail was truly distraught.

Iago took it upon himself to send for Dr Wheatley who took one

262

look at Abigail and prescribed a sleeping-draught. He heard what steps the household had so far taken and nodded his head. 'There's nothing more to be done till morning. Everyone in Williamsburg must now be on the alert for a crying child. I'll drop in at Chownings Tavern on the way home and have a word there. In the morning we'll organise a search-party into the wilderness. I'll get the landlord to set it in motion. You've proved yourself a good man, Iago, but it's no good asking you to take charge of a search-party, though I've no doubt you could do it. The citizens will take no instructions from a slave.'

'We did,' Lizzie pointed out.

'You're females.' The doctor disposed of that argument. 'In the meantime, keep Mrs Vatsetter asleep. There's nothing she can do except worry, and that will do no one any good.'

When he had gone and Abigail had been persuaded to drink the opiate he had left, Iago, Sarah and Lizzie conferred with each other away from the lesser mortals of the household.

'It's my belief we ought to send for Lord Jasper,' Sarah said. 'It seems to me, he's the one she always turns to for advice – leastways, that's what I reckon she sees him for, for I'm sure she doesn't like him above half – and there's no denying, he has the reputation of knowing everything that goes on in the colony.'

'I don't reckon he concerns himself much with lost children,' Iago said. 'The doctor's got the right idea. If she's not in the town itself, she must have wandered further. Though how a mite of that age managed it, I'll not hazard a guess.'

Lizzie shivered. 'If that's the case, we'll be lucky if they find more than a few bones,' she said. 'We'd better not tell Mis' Vatsetter about that search. Let's just hope she's wandered into someone's woodshed.'

'All the same,' Sarah insisted, 'I don't think it would do any harm to have a word with his lordship.'

The messenger sent first thing in the morning to the Cuddesdon house returned with the information that Lord Jasper was in Yorktown and not expected to return for several days. Between them, Sarah and Lizzie managed to keep Abigail more or less sedated throughout that first night and the following day and night as well, but on the second morning heavy-eyed despite her enforced sleep, she refused to co-operate any further.

'What sort of an unnatural mother do you think I am?' she demanded. 'Do you fondly imagine I *want* to sleep while my child is wandering goodness knows where, or, worse, is starving in some outhouse?'

263

'Of course we don't. No one thinks that,' Sarah assured her. 'As for outhouses, that's just what Iago's been doing all day yesterday and today, too. Not making himself very popular, either, since he's saying in effect that people haven't looked thoroughly on their own account. Still, they let him get on with it. He tells them it's better to be safe than sure, and they can't argue with that, though he's taken some abuse over it – and not all of it verbal, by the look of him.'

'Has anyone thought to send for Lord Jasper?' Abigail persisted. 'He's the one who'll know what to do.'

'Yes, ma'am, we have. We sent a messenger yesterday morning, first thing, because we know you value his advice. He's in Yorktown and not expected back for some time. His secretary knows the situation and as soon as his lordship gets back, he'll be informed, but don't you worry, we'll have little Becky back safe and well long before that.'

Iago returned in the late afternoon, sunk in thought, and not, if his face were anything to go by, pleasant thought.

'You've heard something, haven't you?' Lizzie said accusingly.

'Not about Becky, not directly, no,' he replied. 'No connection at all, I shouldn't wonder. Still . . .'

'What is it? What have you heard? Tell us – we'll say if we think there's a connection,' Lizzie insisted.

He shook his head. 'No. It's not that sort of thing. Guess I'd better have a word with Mis' Vatsetter.'

Abigail jumped to her feet when he came into the room and went towards him, her hands outstretched. 'You have news?' she asked. 'You've heard something?'

He took her hands and clasped them in his own and led her away from the window to the elegant sofa. 'Not really – not exactly,' he began. 'Sit down. I've heard nothing directly about Becky but I did hear of a strange coincidence.'

Abigail sat down and he sat beside her, still clasping her hands as if some of his own strength would pass to her for, if what he had heard had the significance he suspected, Abigail was going to need all the strength she could muster.

'What is it?' Abigail asked.

'I've been out hunting in sheds and outhouses, whether people like it or no, and mostly it's no, but I've also been gossiping in kitchens. I don't have to tell you how valuable that can be: masters always think their slaves are fools, and say things they'd never say if they knew they weren't. Not that this is what's been heard in the dining-room. Mis' Vatsetter, it seems Mis' Haworth went missing at about the same time as your Rebecca.'

Abigail stared at him. 'Iago, what are you saying?'

'It seems there was words this morning between her and her man and she done left the house in a temper and ain't been back since. No one ain't seen hide nor hair of her. Mas' Haworth's sent to her friends, but she ain't been there. One person did see her walking towards the market-place and only noticed her because she weren't wearing a cloak which struck her as odd, and someone else *thought* they saw her in the market, but can't be sure — "Not enough to swear on" was what they said.'

'It's pure coincidence,' Abigail insisted as if afraid to face any other possibility.

'That may well be. There's a bit more.' He hesitated, choosing his words with care. 'They do say — and this is kitchen gossip that's not just of today, only I've never thought it needful to bring it up before — they do say as Mis' Haworth feels it badly, not having fallen for a baby in so long. They say she's not altogether normal about it. Most women'd be disappointed but if that's the Lord's will, they learn to live with it. Not Mis' Haworth. They reckon she's always been given everything she's wanted, from a humming-top to Lance Haworth, and that she don't see no reason why she shouldn't have a child, as well. Seeing your Becky, and how like she is to her father for all she's supposed to be Vatsetter's, don't ease matters none, and neither does the gossip that resemblance has caused. She's a bitter woman, Mis' Vatsetter. Bitter and jealous.'

Abigail gazed at him blankly, in silence, for a moment and then covered her face with her hands. Then she glanced fearfully up at him again. 'Bitter and jealous enough to do away with her?' she asked.

Iago put his arm round her shoulder, a comforting gesture that Abigail barely noticed save to appreciate its intent. 'I don't reckon so,' he said. 'If she's that dead-set on a baby, she'll want to keep her, especially since she's her husband's child. If she's as much off-balance about it as they say, I don't doubt she'll have convinced herself it's her own child before too long.'

Abigail shuddered. 'That's terrible!'

'Not half as terrible as wandering off into the wilderness and being eaten by wolves or bears — or savages. If I'm right, at least Mis' Haworth'll keep her safe.'

'*If* you're right — and if not? Iago, if you *are* right, where can she have taken the child? I can'tbelieve she's hidden her in Williamsburg. If she had, some word would have leaked out by now.'

'Kingswood is my guess. She'd have to get to Jamestown and that's a long, hot walk, especially with a heavy child to carry, but it ain't impossible. Blanche Haworth's tougher than she looks and she was born and bred here — she don't notice the heat the way you do. Once she's there, a boat is all she needs and Blanche Quenington Haworth won't have any difficulty getting taken on board, that's for sure.'

'What do we do?' Abigail asked despairingly.

Iago's clasp tightened as he faced the facts. 'That's the problem. Even if my guess is accurate, it's still a guess and there ain't much in the way of evidence to support it. We can't do nothin' until we knows for sure Mis' Haworth's got her — and got her there. It'll be hard, Mis' Vatsetter, but you're just going to have to sit and wait until my snoopin' gives us something more. Maybe I'll go snoop in Jamestown and maybe take a trip up-river myself.'

'Do whatever you think best,' Abigail told him. 'Let me know what you need in the way of money — hire a horse, boat — whatever you need.'

He smiled grimly. 'I'll tell you what I need, ma'am. A letter from you saying I'm about your business. I don't have no great craving to be strung up from a tree as a runaway.'

Abigail assured him it would be forthcoming but his plan to set out for Jamestown at first light was put back when, on coming out of the Raleigh Tavern's stables with a hired hack, he saw Lance Haworth walking in a direction which could, conceivably, lead him to Abigail's house. It could be coincidence, of course, though Iago had little faith in coincidences. That is to say, he accepted that they occurred but suspected that they did so far less frequently than was generally assumed. He hastily led his horse back into the stable on the pretext of having forgotten something, and set out in the wake of his former owner. By the time Lance turned into Abigail's gate, Iago was close behind him so that Lizzie opened the door to them both.

'I'll see your mistress,' Lance declared, removing his hat and his gloves as he spoke as if there were no question of his being received.

'Well, I don't know . . .' Lizzie began doubtfully, glancing beyond him in appeal at Iago.

'I'll ask Mis' Vatsetter if she's seeing anyone,' he said, nodding dismissal at Lizzie, who was only too happy to go.

He went into the parlour where Abigail still insisted on sitting. She had, of course, observed Lance's arrival and sprang up when Iago entered. 'What does he want?' she asked anxiously.

Iago shook his head. 'I don't know, but be careful, ma'am. He looks like the cat that's just had the cream. D'you want me to stay?'

She nodded. 'I think it might be best.'

When Lance was shown into the room, she realised how apt Iago's description of him had been. He looked remarkably pleased with himself and was not quite able to conceal a smug half-smile which deepened infinitesimally when he observed how careworn Abigail looked.

'Your daughter's missing, I gather.'

Abigail held out her hands imploringly. 'You seem pleased, Lance. Do you have news of her?'

'I know where she is, if that's what you mean.'

'Of course it is! Where is she? Is it far? Why haven't you brought her with you? Is she all right?'

'One thing at a time,' Lance said, removing her hand from his sleeve which she had clutched involuntarily. He flicked the broad cloth as if removing a speck of dirt. It was a gesture the overwrought Abigail scarcely noticed but Iago did and his misgivings deepened. 'She's in good health,' Lance went on, 'and she's being well cared for.' He paused.

'Thank God!' Abigail exlaimed. 'but where is she? Why isn't she with you? You must have realised how worried I've been?'

'I thought there was a good chance you'd be upset,' he agreed. 'Naturally, my instinct was to return the child to her mother and thereby witness a touching scene, no doubt, but I never like to let pleasure interfere with business and that's why I'm here — without her.'

Abigail felt a cold chill creep over her. 'What do you mean?' she asked suspiciously.

'It's really very simple: I have the power to return your daughter to you and, by the same token, you have the power to return my I.O.U. to me.'

'Your I.O.U.?' she echoed. 'do you mean the financial agreement you signed?'

'What else? We've not been dicing together, have we?'

Abigail had no need to ponder the consequences of his suggestion. One word summed them up: ruin. Far too much of her capital was tied up in Lance's ventures, one way or another, but at least it was secured on his property. If she wrote off his debt as he suggested, he would regain his freeholds and all the money she had advanced would become, in effect, a gift. Ruin was not too strong a word for it. Against that consideration was Rebecca, and Abigail knew there was no contest. She could — would have to — start again but Becky was irreplaceable, both in her own right and for what she represented.

Both men, watching her face, knew there was no question which she would choose. Iago stepped in before she could give her inevitable decision.

'Wait on, Mis' Vatsetter,' he said. 'what Mas' Haworth says is all very well, but we don't have no proof he's either got little Becky or

267

knows where she is. You don't want to be fool enough to fall for an old trick like that.'

Lance's face darkened with fury and only the fact that Iago was no longer his property prevented him from striking him.

'Is that how you let your slaves talk to you?' he said. 'No wonder there's gossip!'

'He's right, though,' Abigail said. 'You've produced no proof. I'd be a fool indeed if I returned your contract without more evidence than your word.'

Instead of replying, Lance felt in his pocket and brought out a ruby velvet ribbon. It was a colour that particularly suited Rebecca's dark hair and the velvet was crushed exactly as if it had been tied in a bow. Abigail had no doubt it was the one her daughter had been wearing when she disappeared, but once again Iago stepped in before she could speak.

'It could be hers,' he conceded, 'but then again, maybe not. She always wore that colour — well, 'most always. It'd be a good guess. where did you get Miss Becky's ribbons, ma'am? Mis' Hunter's?'

Abigail was too distressed to follow his drift. 'You know I do. Where else would I buy them?'

'That's right — and where else would anyone else get them? And where else could they get the self-same ribbons, anyway? A ruby velvet ribbon from Mis' Hunter's is going to be a pretty safe bet.'

'But this has been tied in a bow,' Abigail explained.

Iago took it from her and tied it into a loose bow, in roughly the same place as it had been previously tied. 'Any fool can tie a ribbon into a bow.'

Abigail was completely bewildered. She now had Iago's drift — or thought she had — but where did that leave her? If there was a chance of getting her child back, that chance had to be taken. All Iago had done was to emphasise the extent of her gamble, for a gamble it undoubtedly was.

'What do I do? Iago, I have to take the chance.'

'No, you don't, not yet, at all events. You've had assurance the child's well and cared for. Mas' Haworth ain't going to let that situation change, not if he wants his debt cleared. I reckon he ought to bring something that he can't fake — something you know she was wearing that he won't be able to get copied — not at short notice, at any rate.'

Abigail hated the thought of the delay Iago's suggestion must entail, but it made sense. If Lance knew where Rebecca was — or even had her himself — he would be able to prove it. If he didn't, then demanding further proof could not make the situation worse.

'You're right,' she said. 'Bring me her dress: I made it myself and shall certainly recognise my own handiwork. I'll give you another that she may wear meanwhile. Iago, ask Lizzie or Sarah to run upstairs and fetch one of Becky's dresses.'

Lance scowled as the man left the room. 'That nigger takes a sight too much on his shoulders,' he said. 'You give him too much freedom.'

'Iago has proved a very sound investment,' Abigail told him. 'I don't listen to his advice on business matters but he's a good judge of character and I don't lightly disregard his evaluation of people.'

Iago returned just then with a printed calico dress, a smaller version of something Abigail herself might have worn. He handed it over to Lance. 'You've no excuse not to bring the other one,' he said. 'Mis' Vatsetter will give you two days. If you're not back by then, she'll know it was a trick. Meantime, we'll not stop looking.'

'You even speak for your mistress now, do you?' The words were almost a snarl but both he and his listeners knew the intended insult was provoked by the frustration of a plan which, but for the presence of his erstwhile slave, would have been speedily and satisfactorily executed. Lance did not like delays. Things could all too easily go wrong during them. 'I may need longer than two days,' he added, knowing that this delay would also sharpen Abigail's anxiety and make her less likely to listen to anything beyond her motherly concern.

Iago guessed what was in Lance's mind but, if Rebecca was, as he suspected, at Kingswood, two days would be cutting it very fine. 'Three,' he said, 'and if you don't return with the dress by then, Mis' Vatsetter'll lay charges against you. I don't reckon even a white man can try to weasel out of a debt this way.'

This time Lance did raise his hand but Abigail stepped hastily between the two men.

'You strike the man I bought,' she said, 'and you *will* answer for it in the courts.'

When Lance finally left the house, there was no sign of the smug half-smile that had accompanied his entrance.

Abigail turned to her manservant. 'At worst you've stopped him cheating me and at best you've simply delayed my ruin by three days,' she said. 'I'm not even sure I can bear another three days of waiting. Why, Iago? Was it worth the effort?'

He smiled grimly. 'It gives us what we need — time. Mis' Vatsetter, I reckon Becky's at Kingswood. It's my guess that's where Mis' Haworth done took her. I don't reckon Mas' Haworth had anything to do with it — not then. But if he went to the plantation in search of his wife – and he left town as soon as it became obvious she wasn't coming back – and found what she'd done, he'd soon enough think of a way to turn it to his advantage. By winning time, I've given us room to move. If I'm right, I should be able to get there and back with her before they know she's gone.'

'But Lance Haworth has a head start,' Abigail pointed out. 'the last thing you want is for him to see you on the river: he'll know at once what you're doing.'

Iago tapped the side of his nose. 'That's right, ma'am, but, like they say, there's more ways than one of skinning a cat. Leave it with me. I don't promise nothing, but I'll sure as hell try.'

A knock at the front door which they scarcely noticed was followed by the appearance of a flustered Lizzie. 'It's Lord Jasper to see you, ma'am. He seems a touch impatient.'

This opinion was given added weight by that nobleman's appearance at her shoulder, demonstrating his unwillingness to wait for permission to come in.

'Excuse my dirt, Mrs Vatsetter,' he said, coming into the room past Lizzie who beat a hasty retreat. 'I'm just returned from Yorktown and was greeted by your sad news. I know how distraught you must be. Is there any word of the child? Anything I can do?'

'Thank you, my lord. We do have word of her – of a sort – but there's nothing you can do. Iago has a plan which we hope will result in her return.'

Lord Jasper raised one eyebrow. 'Indeed? May I be party to the situation?'

Abigail glanced at Iago, who shrugged his assent. There was no suspicion that his lordship was implicated in the disappearance and he could be a useful ally. Briefly, Abigail explained what had happened and outlined Iago's scheme.

Lord Jasper looked at him with deceptively lazy eyes under hooded lids. 'Alone?' he queried.

Iago stiffened. 'It's man's work,' he said. 'The rest of this household is female.'

'I couldn't agree more. That is not, however, quite what I asked. Never mind. Let it ride. I would suggest that you might get upstream more quickly and occasion less comment if you appear to be accompanying me to Copenore. Perhaps we can devise some stratagem that will answer the case. That is, if you're prepared to trust a white man as your partner.' There was an almost imperceptible emphasis on the word 'white' which passed Abigail by but Iago noticed it and stiffened.

'If you're just back from Yorktown, my lord, you'll not be wanting to trail up to Copenore right away,' he said.

'I'd certainly prefer to stay at home for a day or two,' Lord Jasper agreed, 'but this seems to be a situation calling for a certain degree of self-denial, don't you think? If you think I'll wilt on you like some delicate blossom, you'll be agreeably surprised. I don't think you'll find me wanting.'

Iago grinned. 'No, my lord. I ain't never taken you for a milk-sop.'

'Good. Then it's agreed. Mrs Vatsetter, will you be all right in the care of the Camberwell girls?'

'Certainly,' Abigail assured him. 'The knowledge that something positive is being done at last should ease my mind a little, if only for a short while. I'll try to find some work that will occupy my mind.'

'Do you have a sleeping-draught in the house?'

'Dr Wheatley prescribed some and I know there's some left – I refused to take any after a while. I preferred to be conscious.'

'Take it tonight – and tomorrow night as well if we're not back by then. Tossing and turning all night, listening for a knock at the door, will do you no good at all – and from the look of you that's exactly what you've been doing. I promise that if by chance we return at night, you will be woken up.'

Abigail smiled a little wanly. 'It's sound advice, my lord, as yours always is. Be sure I shall follow it.'

'Good. Iago – come up to the Cuddesdon house and I'll see you've a good horse under you. We need to make all speed to Jamestown for we'll have little control over our speed upriver.'

'I've a horse ready saddled at the Raleigh,' Iago told him.

'Leave it there. Mine will be faster. Join me as soon as may be.'

He left without further ceremony. Iago looked rather doubtful. 'You can trust him,' Abigail said. 'He's one of the few people I am prepared to trust completely.'

'You're white,' he told her shortly and without enlarging upon the statement.

Abigail was not at all sure what he meant by the comment but there were far more pressing matters than the need for an explanation so she ignored it. Instead, she caught his arm. 'Come back as quickly as you can, Iago,' she begged him. 'Even if you don't find her, I need to know. You will, won't you?'

He put his hand over hers and patted it gently. 'Of course we will. You'll not find us kicking our heels, I promise you.'

It was an assurance with which Abigail must needs be content.

When Iago dropped into the Raleigh's stables to say he no longer had need of the horse, he was interested to learn that Lance Haworth's visit to the capital was likely to be a brief one.

'His groom says he's no respect for his horses,' Ned Camberwell confided. Iago might be a slave, but he had good reports of him from Sarah and Lizzie. They had said there was nothing in the tales going about and their father was inclined to believe them. 'He's rid that animal back from Jamestown and now he's stopping for nothing more than a luncheon and then he's off again. That animal needs more than a couple of hours rest. Serve him right if it collapses under him.'

'He works everything too hard,' Iago told him. 'Slaves as well as livestock.'

'Yes, well, you'd know about that, of course,' Ned said, slightly embarrassed at having to be reminded it was a slave he was talking to: this one expressed opinions so much like a thinking man that it was easy to forget.

Iago knew exactly the effect his remark would have on the ostler. It would stop him speculating upon whether Iago had been unduly interested in his former owner – and if he did, would give an apparent reason for any interest. The fact that he *had* been Iago's owner would be enough to account for it. Iago hurried to the Cuddesdon house with the news that Lance was still in Williamsburg and, given God-speed, they might well get to Kingswood before him.

Lord Jasper slapped him on the back. 'Well done,' he said. 'How well do you ride?'

'I stick on.'

'I guessed that might be the case. I've had them saddle a big brute for you. You've probably seen him – Jabez usually rides him when he needs a mount. He's up to your weight and he'll go forever but he'll play you up to start with. Just hang on and he'll give up. If he throws you at the beginning, you'll never ride him.'

Iago knew the horse by sight: a big, rangy chestnut with an unkind eye. The beast seemed in a more generous mood on this occasion, contenting himself with a few experimental bucks in the stable yard before settling down to the task in hand.

They rode sedately through the streets of Williamsburg, Iago keeping the requisite number of discreet paces behind Lord Jasper. The latter gave no appearance of haste, pausing once or twice to pass the time of day with one burgess or another, and once to compliment a lady on her toilette, a courtesy which, Iago noted ironically, was received with a nauseating amount of fluttering eyelashes and simpering disclaimers.

Once they were clear of the town, it was a different story. 'That's satisfied all the gossips from whom Haworth might learn of our departure,' Lord Jasper said. 'The one thing that will emerge is that we were in no hurry. Now we can go.' he clapped his spurs into his horse's sides and took off on the dusty road to Jamestown with Iago hard on his heels.

Shortly before they were within sight of the remains of Jamestown, Lord Jasper drew rein.

'How well known are you in this place?' he asked.

Iago shrugged. 'I ain't — leastways, I was brought through here when Mas' Haworth decided to sell me in Williamsburg. If anyone recalls me, they'll recall I was going to be sold. If they see me with you, they'll reckon it was you as bought me.'

Lord Jasper nodded and they covered the remaining mile to the old capital at an unhurried trot, thus enabling their mounts to cool down gradually to lessen the chances of their catching a chill in the possibly careless hands of the ostler at Jamestown, and giving a chance for the sweat to dry so that the speed with which they had travelled was not too apparent. There was a livery stable of sorts which held horses for short periods until either a groom came out to fetch them or their owners returned to Jamestown. To the ostler here, Lord Jasper gave very explicit and detailed instructions, knowing that the awe in which he was held would ensure their execution. He looked at the empty wharf and frowned.

'No sign of the *Sparrowhawk,* I see?'

'No, my lord,' the ostler said, surprised. 'Mr Haworth sent it on down to Norfolk yesterday. Said a cargo was more important than his convenience and if he needed to go back to Kingswood, he'd just have to hire a skiff.'

'Pity. I was hoping we could beg a ride up to Copenore in it,' Lord Jasper commented, relieved to have learnt that its absence was in no way due to Lance's having somehow reached here ahead of them. 'It would appear to be us who must hire a skiff. Thank God I brought a good, strong man with me.'

The ostler grinned. 'Aye, it's a tidy row, is that.'

There was no difficulty in hiring a skiff and, while Iago sat amidships and manned the oars, Lord Jasper took such ease as was possible on a hard seat in the stern, which was exactly what any onlooker would have expected from a man of his rank. Once out of sight of the last wooden shack, however, he reached down for the second pair of oars and joined Iago in the long, hard haul against the current.

It was evening when they finally shipped oars upstream of the open stretch surrounding Kingswood's landing-stage and well concealed

273

under the over-hanging trees. They had needed considerable determination to cover the last stretch of water: it would have been so much more tempting to pull in under the trees that lined the downstream banks of the plantation. They dared not do so, however, for fear that Lance Haworth, whom they presumed would find his way upstream in their wake, might catch a glimpse of the skiff and investigate the after all legitimate purpose of it being tied up at the landing-stage. The rowers remained in the skiff, resting from the arduous journey and glad that nightfall, when they might more safely move, was half an hour or more away. They exchanged no words, made no plans. They listened to the chirping of the crickets and the whistling song of the chickadees, knowing that the alien sound of the human voice would travel a long way, even through the dense forests. Only when the call of the chickadees was replaced by the first low hoots of a distant Great Horned Owl, did they know the time was right to make their move.

First checking that the skiff was securely tied, they slipped ashore and made their way stealthily through the thick forest in the direction of the house. Both men wore dark clothes and Lord Jasper noted that Iago moved through the undergrowth with the skill and silence of an Indian − a talent unexpected in a slave. Iago's familiarity with the plantation gave him precedence over his companion and Lord Jasper followed as nearly as possible in his footsteps, emulating as well as he could the black man's almost professional stealth.

They paused when they came to the edge of the forest. Here they had no choice but to cross an open field of tobacco, a crop which offered little cover to a man, even if he crouched as he ran. With gestures, Iago indicated that they would head directly down the rows of tobacco as fast as they could until they reached the bulk of a drying shed which loomed at the other side of the field. Lord Jasper nodded his understanding and they set off at a crouching run. It was an uncomfortable posture to maintain, and once again Lord Jasper observed that Iago seemed to execute it with the speed and ease of long practice. They both knew there was a good chance that everyone in the slave quarters would be too busy preparing and eating their evening meal to be looking out across the field, and that the lights in the still unshuttered rooms of the house would make it impossible to see anything dark moving outside unless it came directly into the patch of light cast on the ground from the windows.

When they reached the drying shed, they paused. The wooden planks of its walls had gaps between to allow the circulation of air. It meant that the shed was not sound-proof. They waited for a long time, their ears alert for the slightest sound among the hanging bunches of tobacco but there was none, not even the faint rustling of drying leaves in what little breeze there was. Once Iago was satisfied they were quite alone, he tapped Lord Jasper's sleeve and beckoned him away from the immediate wall of the shed and far enough out into its shadow to be able to see the house, some two or three hundred yards away. Lights blazed in most rooms on the ground floor but in only two on the floor above. A balcony ran the length of the of the front and back of the house at first-floor level, but did not continue round the sides, each of which accommodated a massive brick chimney. Under the balcony was a white-painted porch, and additional shade was afforded those who chose to sit out on it by a vine which climbed the pillars and stretched along the bottom of the balcony.

'The bedchamber on the right will be Mis' Haworth's,' Iago whispered. 'The one at the far end on the left is a small room. I'd guess that's where Becky is.'

'Will the vine hold our weight?' Lord Jasper asked doubtfully. There was no other apparent way of reaching the balcony.

Iago shook his head. 'A boy's, maybe, but not us. Against the far wall, there's an old magnolia − they say it's been there for fifty years. That'll take one of us, I reckon, and it reaches over to the balcony. I don't reckon it'll be too difficult. Our troubles start if the window's fastened.'

Lord Jasper considered that highly probable, if only to prevent a small child falling off the balcony, nor was that likely to be the least of their problems. 'Won't there be a nursemaid in there with her?' he asked.

'I don't reckon so. My guess is she'll be down in the kitchen having her supper. And if she's not, well, maybe we take them both.'

Lord Jasper stared at him. 'You're mad,' he said without emphasis.

Iago chuckled. 'Any nursemaid'll recognise me and let me take the child but if she stays, they'll get it out of her and she'll be blamed − and punished. If she comes with us, she gets away. She won't turn that offer down.'

'And risk being hanged for a runaway?' Lord Jasper asked.

'That won't happen,' Iago said positively.

Lord Jasper made no immediate reply, seeming to ponder his companion's words. Then he said, 'That makes it even more essential for you to go in for the child. In any case, she knows you best and that will ease any fear she has. I'll be ready to take her from you.'

'Let's go.'

They made their way cautiously and unobserved across the intervening space and then sped across the lawn out of range of the lighted windows, taking full advantage of the shrubs at one end of the garden. They paused for breath once they were under the deeper shadow of the magnolia. Its flowers were finished and the lush green of its profusion of leaves was excellent cover. Lord Jasper reached into its depths and felt the trunk. It was as gnarled and solid as he had hoped it would be. Iago certainly knew what he was about.

There was a certain amount of rustling in the leaves as Iago climbed speedily up to the balcony and stepped soundlessly on to it. He edged cautiously along to the full-length sash window that gave on to the balcony and peered gingerly round the frame so that he had a good chance of seeing someone inside the room before they saw him. His first glance having revealed nothing untoward, he edged further forward, gradually increasing his range of vision until he could see the whole room. No one was awake there — no servant bustling about, no nursemaid rocking by the fire, no one sitting up in bed. In short, no one whom surprise would induce to utter a warning cry. Beside the empty bed was a cot. Iago had seen it before: it had been stored in one of the outhouses when Lance had taken over the plantation. His wife must have rescued it in the early, more hopeful, days of their marriage and had it polished and refurbished for the baby she had never had. It was a little confined for a three-year-old but that was all to the present good: a baby would have been lost in its wooden-sided depths but a prominent hump told him it wasn't empty. One glance at the catch on the window told him it was fastened.

He sighed. It was a nuisance, but not unexpected. He took a gleaming, slim-bladed knife from a sheath at his belt. His recollection was that the windows at Kingswood were not too well-fitting and he prayed that one of Blanche's reforms had not been to replace them. He doubted it: Mis' Haworth was far more concerned with the superiority of her furniture than with structural shortcomings her visitors would hardly notice. It took a little pushing, but the blade was forced between the two halves of the window without too much difficulty. It took rather longer to push the catch back but — happily — someone had greased it, so its resistance was less.

The catch safely eased, Iago paused before sliding up the bottom half of the full-length window. He had not been able to work in total silence and had no intention of proceeding until he was sure he had not so far been overheard. Then he slid the window up and stepped quietly into the room. He glanced into the little boat-shaped hanging cot to make sure it was Rebecca who occupied it and then stepped quickly over to the door. A careless nursemaid had not thought to lock it when she left, even though the key was on the outside. As speedily as silence allowed, he opened the door, removed the key and locked the door from the inside. If anyone came, he would have a short warning. Only then did he return to the cot.

Becky was his biggest risk. Any child awoken suddenly could be expected to cry out. His hope was that, if he could prevent that initial frightened exclamation, the sight of a familiar face would reassure the child. He leant over the cot and put one hand firmly over Becky's mouth.

She woke instantly and he felt her mouth open under his hand. Her eyes, grey and clear like her father's, opened wide in terror.

'Shh,' he whispered. 'It's me – Iago. I've come to take you home to your mamma but you'll have to be very, very quiet.' He put his finger to his lips to illustrate his meaning as he gradually lifted his other hand from her mouth. To his relief, she seemed to understand and made no attempt to call out. When he reached down to lift her out of the cot, she flung her arms round his neck and hugged him tightly. Iago viewed her white night-shift and cap with dismay. They had still to get away unseen and that garment would make them easily visible. He glanced round the room, but neither cot nor bed had dark blankets. He stood Becky on the floor, detaching her clinging arms with difficulty and removed his jacket. Fortunately his shirt was dark brown homespun, so wrapping her in his jacket and removing her tell-tale lace cap which he stuffed into the pocket – the fewer clues as to what any pursuers were looking for, the better – he carried her over to the window and lifted her across the sill. He put her down again then so that he could slide the window back into place and then, picking her up once more, made his way quickly to the edge of the balcony.

Iago knew he had not made the ascent in total silence. The descent was bound to be noisier.

'We're going to play an exciting game, Miss Becky,' he told her. 'I'm going to put you down and then I'll crouch down, too, and I want you to climb on my back and cling on to me round my neck like a little monkey. Will you do that?'

Rebecca, her eyes fixed to his face, nodded vigorously.

'Then we're going to climb down that tree,' he went on, his hushed voice conveying more to the child of the adventure of it all than the words. 'I'm going to need both hands, so you've got to hang on really hard. Lord Jasper's down there and he'll take you as soon as you're within reach.'

She nodded again and, with a little help from Iago, clambered onto his back. This was one part of the enterprise where the jacket had to be discarded and thrown down first: if Rebecca put her arms in the sleeves, she would not be able to cling to her rescuer and it certainly would not stay in place by any other means.

Iago knew that Becky's strength would not be sufficient to allow her to cling on for very long without his supporting hand beneath her. It behoved him to climb down the magnolia as quickly as possible and risk the inevitable increase in noise. He sat astride the balcony and made sure his charge was firmly settled and confident before reaching over with one leg to locate his first foothold.

The protruberance on his back made it even more difficult to descend swiftly than he had anticipated and Iago could feel Becky's grip slackening every time a branch knocked against her. Fortunately Lord Jasper was just as conscious of the danger and was able, by dint of reaching up as far as he could, to catch her just as her little arms could cling on no longer. He hurriedly wrapped her in the jacket again as Iago made the last few feet to the ground and they were about to retrace their steps across the garden when the window of the room immediately adjacent to them on the porch went up.

Lord Jasper clapped his hand over Rebecca's mouth and whispered 'Shh,' in her ear, and both he and Iago stepped hastily back into the deeper shadows cast by the magnolia. A man's distorted shadow was thrown on to the porch and the grass beyond. There was silence for several seconds.

'They ain't no one there, Mis' Haworth,' Noah's voice said. 'I reckon it's just the wind getting up.' The shadow held a hand out to the fresh air. 'There's a breeze alright. I reckon maybe we're in for a stormy night.'

The shadow withdrew and the window slid down. The listeners, their ears stretched to infinity, heard the slight click of the catch being fastened and then, to their surprised delight, the wooden internal shutters were unfolded across that window and its companion. No light now streamed out of that room to illuminate part of the garden.

Nevertheless, they kept well away from the house as they had done before, making what use they could of the shade of shrubs and trees until they reached the drying shed once more. Here they had an unexpected stroke of luck. As they paused for breath before tackling the exposed field of tobacco, they heard footsteps on the drive that led down to the landing-stage. From their position, they could just make out the tall, broad-shouldered form of Lance Haworth as he hastened up the drive and then cut across the garden towards the lighted windows of the house. At least there was now no danger of passing him on their way downstream.

Only when he had disappeared did the two men and their burden slip out of the shadows and run as fast as they could between the rows of tobacco. Iago carried Rebecca now and that made it impossible to crouch over to any useful effect. Speed was of the essence and they prayed silently that no one should see them. Iago led the way unerringly back to the skiff and the two men guided the light boat into mid-stream and sculled easily down the current. They were half way to Jamestown before either of them spoke.

'Where do you put them ashore?' Lord Jasper asked suddenly.

Iago did not answer at once. When he did, he sounded mystified. 'My lord?'

'You heard me. Where do you put runaways ashore?'

Iago shook his head and his face and voice took on the appearance and sound of complete stupidity. 'Sorry, sah. You done lost me.'

'I'm no more a fool than you are and you can drop the "Yes sah, No sah" act, I've heard you speak English almost as well as any white colonist – and better than many. Haworth got rid of you as a trouble-maker. He thought that would lower the price less than revealing that all too often he couldn't find you. He thought you got drunk somewhere and had found a place to sleep it off. You're not the only one who picks up kitchen gossip – my Jabez is pretty adept at it, too. Does Mrs Vatsetter have difficulty finding you?'

'I ain't never given Mis' Vatsetter cause for worry,' Iago said in a plaintive tone that, from someone else, might have been convincing.

'I don't suppose you have. You've only to come back with some useful titbit of business information and she doesn't think to ask where you've been, does she?'

Iago shrugged. 'No reason why she should.'

'She hasn't my suspicious mind,' Lord Jasper told him. 'You seem to forget that I've watched you in action tonight. You move through woodland with the stealth of much practice, as if your life depended on it.'

'Is you saying' it didn't tonight?' Iago asked, apparently bewildered.

'Of course not, but I suspect mine was just as much at risk as yours, and it didn't result in my being suddenly proficient in the skill. Then there was the nursemaid.'

'They wasn't no nursemaid there,' Iago said.

'No, but there might have been. What was it you said? That if she came with us she'd get away; that she wouldn't turn the offer down; and that she wouldn't hang for being a runaway. You were very positive about that. I've been pondering why on and off ever since – whenever I had a moment to think, that is.'

Iago shook his head. 'You're way ahead of me, sah,' he said.

'Am I? Somehow I doubt it. Have a care, Iago. You'll be lynched if anyone else finds out – and Mrs Vatsetter wouldn't want to lose a good ... slave.' There was an infinitesimal pause before the last word and its significance did not pass Iago by. He made no answer and Lord Jasper chose not to pursue the matter. The journey continued in silence.

Lord Jasper judged that it mattered not at all who in Jamestown saw them with Rebecca: Iago was known to be Abigail's and they were too far ahead of Lance Haworth to be in any danger of being overtaken by him now. It was therefore a simple matter for Lord Jasper to take Rebecca up in front of him and ride out of the old capital quite openly. She expressed a clear preference for riding in front of Iago, but Lord Jasper pointed out to her somewhat brusquely that, since her safety was his first consideration, she would ride with the better horseman. It was doubtful whether she understood his words but she recognised the authority in his tone – to say nothing of his extremely unrelenting grasp – and finally succumbed to a superior power.

Abigail had refused to take a sleeping-draught. She was sure the two men would return that night and was determined to be up to greet them when they did. She preferred not to consider what she would do if they came empty-handed. So, when the horses were tied to the painted iron jockey placed at the gate for that purpose and their riders came up the path, it was Abigail, not Lizzie, who opened the door.

Joy flooded her face and transformed features that had fast become haggard since Rebecca's disappearnace. She held out her arms to take Rebecca from Lord Jasper's arms and hugged the child to her, overcome with emotion and bereft of words. Finally she looked up at them through her tears.

'Thank you,' she said. 'Oh, thank you so much. What can I say? I though I'd lost her, too. That would have been more than I could bear.'

Lord Jasper interrupted her effusions. 'You both need sleep,' he said. 'Your thanks can wait till tomorrow or the next day or whenever you've recovered from your ordeal. I think you'll find your daughter is more resilient than you – one good night's sleep and she'll be tormenting your household as if nothing had happened. Iago will tell you about it when you're more yourself. I'll take my leave. Good night, Mrs Vatsetter.'

He left the room and the servants clustered outside the door parted before him. He paused.'Little Rebecca is unharmed,' he said. 'the best thing you people can do is to go to bed and let this house run like clockwork tomorrow so that Mrs Vatsetter may sleep.'

A kitchen-boy scurried to open the front door for him and when it had closed behind him, Sarah endorsed his opinion.

'The last thing Mrs Vatsetter wants right now is all of us pestering her with questions that, like as not, she hasn't got the answers to yet. Do you all get off and when I've had a word with Iago, I'll follow you.'

They drifted reluctantly away and, as they did so, Abigail emerged with Rebecca in her arms and Iago in her wake. She smiled vaguely at her household and carried the child upstairs. Rebecca was almost asleep when Abigail laid her down and removed the jacket that still enveloped her. She frowned when she saw the strange nightshift her daughter was wearing, knowing it must have been provided by Blanche. She handed Iago his jacket, her eyes still on the child as if she might disappear if Abigail looked away.

'You'll find a clean night-shift in the top drawer of that chest, Iago,' she said. 'Would you hand it to me, please? This isn't one of ours. It must come off.'

Instead of obeying her, Iago leant over and covered Rebecca up. 'She's asleep, ma'am, and that's the best thing for her. You can change it in the morning. His lordship's right. Sleep's the best thing for you, too. I'll fetch you some chocolate.'

Abigail knew he was right about the night-shift but she hated to see her child lying there in a garment provided by the woman who had stolen her. Still, it wasn't quite so painful now that she couldn't see it, and little Becky needed her sleep. She tucked the coverlet up under her daughter's chin and then pulled a chair up to the bed and sat beside it, her eyes still on the child's soundly sleeping face.

This was where Iago found her a few minutes later when he returned with a tray of hot chocolate. He pulled up the nursemaid's worktable and set the tray down upon it.

'Your chocolate, ma'am,' he said and hesitated. 'You will go to bed when you've finished it, won't you?'

Abigail glanced up at him and smiled vaguely. 'Yes, of course. As soon as I've finished.'

He left her and made his way to his own room over the porch but then stopped with his hand on the door-knob, frowning. Then he went downstairs and into the kitchen. He left the door open so that he could hear any movement on the floor above and sat in the cook's chair by the embers of the fire, deep in his own thoughts and with only the striking of the long-case clock in the hall to remind him of the passing of time.

When an hour and a half had passed with no sound of Abigail returning to her own room, he made his way upstairs and quietly opened Rebecca's door. Abigail was still sitting beside the bed but she seemed less rigid, less tense than she had been. She heard the knob turn and glanced up, and smiled when she saw who it was.

'Can't you sleep, either?' she whispered.

'I haven't tried,' he said. 'You're the one that needs to sleep. Becky's safe enough: the window's fastened and so are the shutters. Leave Tagus in here to wake the household if anything happens and go to bed.' He bent down and took hold of her arm. 'Come on, ma'am. You know it's good advice.'

It was, and Abigail allowed herself to be led out of the room and Tagus let in. Iago guided her the short distance along the landing to her own bedchamber and opened the door before stepping in to light the bedside candle from the tinder-box beside it. 'There you are,' he said. 'I promise you Becky will be safe enough.'

Abigail was overcome with a mixture of emotions among which gratitude and relief mingled prominently, together with an uncontrollable desire to weep. Iago was the pillar of strength who had done so much and who now, alone among her acquaintance, remained to care what became of her. Instinctively, she turned to him, clung to him like a child, and burst into tears.

Iago was initially taken aback. Had Abigail been black, he would have known what to do but she wasn't and the fact that he was a free man made no difference to that fact. Still, comfort was what she needed, black or white, and after a momentary hesitation, he folded her in his arms and let her cry.

The tears were tears of relief and for the second time in her life, Abigail experienced the ineffable comfort that a man's arms can afford the troubled spirit. She wept for a long time and when the tears had eased the tension that even Becky's return had not entirely lifted, they became less. She lifted her tear-stained face and her fingers stroked Iago's cheek.

'You're a kind man, Iago,' she whispered.

Suddenly he who had become so accustomed to being a man sufficient entirely to himself, felt a surge of something more than sympathy and understanding to one whom circumstances had forced into the same lonely existence. Without thought to the possible consequences, his lips met hers, gently, understandingly at first and then with the increasing passion of loneliness. He felt that passion returned with something not far from the frenzy of physical desire and reached out to push the door gently closed.

'Are you sure?' he whispered, conscious now that this was something he had unknowingly wanted for a long time. 'Quite sure?' he emphasised.

'Quite sure,' she told him.

There was no sleep that night as the hunger that had gnawed at her body and soul since Lance's rejection, and which she had thought only he could satisfy, was eased by Iago whose own hunger found gratification in his mistress' eager, welcoming body.

He left her before the household was astir and then she slept, a smile of child-like innocence on her lips which led Lizzie, when she came to see if Mrs Vatsetter was ready for her morning chocolate, to tiptoe out again and report to the kitchen that Becky's return had done wonders for Mrs V., and no mistake, an observation which surprised no one.

Neither Abigail nor Iago referred to the previous night, nor did they need to. They both knew that Abigail's three years of sleeping alone were over. All the same, neither of them was under any illusion about the consequences if their relationship became known, and Iago always retired to his own room and was always there when the household awoke.

Chapter Fifteen

Lance might not have seen who took Rebecca from Kingswood but it took only limited questioning in the right quarters to find out. The townspeople might attribute little significance to Iago's attendance on Lord Jasper, but Lance Haworth had good reason to draw his own conclusions and the information that they had hired a skiff would have left him in no doubt, even if an ostler at Jamestown had not noticed the little girl they carried on their return.

He knew he had lost his trump card. That alone was enough to make him very angry indeed, the more so because there was nothing he could directly do about it. Since it was inevitable that Abigail would have been told where her child had been, he must deal warily with her and he wisely concluded that, for the present, at least, he had better avoid her altogether. He intended to get his I.O.U. back somehow, but it would have to wait a little longer. Nor could he immediately see any way of getting revenge on Lord Jasper: the latter's wealth and influence, to say nothing of the mixture of fear and respect in which he was generally held – and not least by Lance Haworth himself – rendered him unassailable. The man must have an Achilles' heel, but Lance Haworth had never discovered it.

Iago was a different matter. He was a slave. The inference that he must therefore have been working entirely under orders was not something which in any way mitigated Lance's desire to hit back at someone for frustrating his plans. There was already gossip that Abigail might be his mistress in more ways than one, even though the occasional sly question put to other members of Abigail's household produced nothing but obviously genuine surprise.

Lance knew that any campaign would have to be subtly waged. He had no wish for its origins to be traced back to himself: if that happened, someone might find it incumbent upon themselves to reveal Lance's part in Rebecca's disapparance. In Abigail's shoes,

Lance would already have done so, but for some reason nothing beyond the fact of the child's recovery had been made public, quite possibly to prevent any further gossip on the subject of Rebecca's likeness to her mother's former owner. Whatever the reason, Lance was glad of it. He had no desire to see himself and his wife completely ostracised. A hint here, an innuendo there, a hastily retracted assumption somewhere else – all these built on the foundations gossip had previously laid and sharpened people's observations. They noticed that Mrs Vatsetter trusted her slave with the quite considerable sums of money needed to settle various household bills and that, in addition, he seemed to have money of his own to spend. Furthermore, he made decisions concerning the running of the household without consulting her. It was true, his decisions were of no greater magnitude than those of any free butler but Iago was a slave.

Or was he?

Once the idea had been mooted, it took hold because, if it was accepted, many things fell into place which had previously been unaccountable. If Abigail Vatsetter had taken her slave as her lover, that was certainly scandalous and enough to put her beyond the association of decent people, but it wouldn't be the first time it had happened. If, however, the slave was a free man, then that put, as one wit expressed it, quite a different complexion on the matter. It was one thing for a black slave to become free the moment he set foot in England, but in Virginia being black was synonymous with being a slave. To be black, free and take a white mistress was an incomprehensible breach of all the laws of civilised living.

The speculation inevitably reached Lord Jasper's ears when it was still in its infancy and he recalled his conversation with Abigail on the same subject. He recalled, too, her assurances and wondered whether anything had changed since Rebecca's rescue. That was many weeks ago now. He rarely encountered her although he quite often saw Iago about the town and, although it was perfectly possible for a resourceful man to find an excuse to visit a money lender, Lord Jasper had no desire to give a visit a particularity that would lead Abigail merely to think that he had not believed her in the first place. So it was Iago he tackled.

Lord Jasper happened to emerge from Chownings Tavern one morning at precisely the time Iago was returning from one of his information gathering forays and their encounter bore all the hallmarks of an accidental meeting.

'Has Rebecca made a complete recovery from her ordeal?' he asked.

285

'She seems none the worse for it,' Iago told him. 'For a while she'd not let her mother out of her sight, but that's understandable, I suppose, and she's certainly got over that now. Mis' Vatsetter dismissed the nursemaid, of course.'

'So I heard. No one will think the worse of her for that.' He paused. 'Other things are not so easily accepted.'

Iago's face went blank, like a suddenly shuttered window. 'What do you mean?'

'Let's stroll, it occasions less remark,' Lord Jasper replied, suiting the action to the words. Iago fell in beside him. 'You're no fool,' Lord Jasper went on. 'You must have heard the gossip even if it hasn't reached Mrs Vatsetter. It's dangerous stuff, Iago, whether or not it's true.'

'Do you believe it?' Iago asked.

Lord Jasper shrugged. 'It's of no importance what I believe. It's what the other good citizens believe that should give you cause for concern.'

'They'll find no proof.'

'Once they've convinced themselves, they'll need none. You must realise that. Does Mrs Vatsetter know the extent of the talk?'

Iago hesitated. 'I don't think so. She's never referred to it and I've not mentioned it. Seemed no point in worrying her unnecessarily.'

'Then I suggest you do. To leave her in ignorance is a misguided kindness. There's been talk ever since she bought you but it's only risen to its present level since Rebecca's return. I suspect there's just one person behind it but there's nothing I can do about that. Warn her, Iago. You owe her that, at least.'

That night, as Abigail lay in the comfort of Iago's arms, he did as Lord Jasper had advised. Abigail snuggled closer to him, the drowsy warmth of fulfilment smothering anxiety.

'They've been saying that for a long time – long before it was true.'

'They didn't suspect I was free,' he pointed out.

'I don't see why they should do so now. You and I are the only people who know for sure and they're not likely to ask us.'

'All the same, we should be careful. A crowd can become a mob in a mighty short time.'

Abigail looked up at him. 'I don't see that we could be more circumspect than we are, do you?'

Iago said nothing. Her comment was true enough but, even so, he took even greater care that the rest of the household was asleep before leaving his room for hers and equal caution in his return before dawn. He also kept his ears very much on the alert for any indication of a hardening of the rumour but there seemed to be none and, as the weeks continued to go by, his watchfulness declined into routine.

It was Jabez who picked up the first stirrings of something more than gossip. He returned to the Cuddesdon house very late one night and went straight to the drawing-room where Lord Jasper sat over a book.

'They're movin', my lord,' he announced dramatically.

Lord Jasper raised his eyes over the volume and gazed expressionlessly at Jabez for a few moments. 'Explain yourself,' he said at last. He glanced at the clock on the mantel. 'One o'clock in the morning is not a time when one reckons to be interrupted,' he said.

'No my lord. Nor you wouldn't want me to leave this till later.' Jabez was unmoved by the reprimand. 'It's Mis' Vatsetter's Iago — they reckon tonight's the night. They've convinced themselves they're closer than they ought to be. They don't reckon he's a slave no longer — and they've got it into their heads that it's Iago as helps runaways.'

He had the satisfaction of knowing he had Lord Jasper's undivided attention. 'Where did you get this?' he asked.

'Happened to be chatting with Ludwell-Paradise's Bessie,' Jabez told him. 'One of their men heard it discussed in the card-room after dinner. The ladies don't know about it. Once they're asleep the men'll go fetch him. Don't know what they plan to do with Mis' Vatsetter,' he added apologetically.

Lord Jasper threw down the book. 'How long ago was this?'

'An hour since. I couldn't get away before without Bessie demanding why, but they was still playing when I left.'

'Get down to the stables and saddle me a horse,' Lord Jasper ordered, snatching up his coat.

'Done, my lord. Leastways, it is by now — I got one of the boys out of bed before coming over here.'

'Good man. Now fetch me the spare set of keys to the Vatsetter house. Top left-hand drawer of my desk.'

Jabez permitted himself the hint of a smile and dropped them on to the table beside his master's chair.

Lord Jasper snatched them up and smiled grimly. 'Before me on all counts. Let's hope for Iago's sake I can get there before the others.'

The street was deserted when Lord Jasper leapt from his horse, ran up the short path and let himself in after the minimum amount of fumbling with the keys. He took the stairs in twos and threes. He had no idea which room was Iago's but Abigail's could only be the main bedchamber and this was no time for the niceties of social custom.

He threw open the door. 'Abby, wake up,' he said, reaching out for the tinderbox that stood beside every bed, and lighting the bedside candle. Its small flame illuminated Abigail's face and he shook her. 'Abby, wake up. Where does Ia –' He caught sight of Iago's face only barely within the little pool of light and the name remained incomplete. Lord Jasper stood very still for several seconds while the implications of the scene before him sank in and it was the stirrings of the figures in the bed in response to the light and his voice that brought him back to his purpose. He shook Iago. 'Wake up, man! For God's sake, wake up!'

They awoke simultaneously. Lord Jasper was looking round the room. 'Where are your clothes? Where's your own room? Get dressed – but don't light a candle. Don't let them know you're up. There's a horse at the front. It's mine. Take it and get as far away as you can. If anyone knows how to get out of the colony, it's you. Don't delay – Jabez says they're coming for you.'

Iago was fully awake now and Abigail only slightly less so. Iago leapt out of bed and paused only to say, 'If I make it, I'll get someone to write to you and let you know.' Then he was gone.

Abigail expected Lord Jasper to follow him but her alarm for Iago changed to alarm for herself when the uninvited guest himself began to disrobe and slid into the empty space beside her. She shrank away from him. Was that what he thought of her? She supposed it was what most of the men of Virginia would think, but she had never categorised Lord Jasper with them and did not welcome the revelation that he was no different.

'Don't be a fool, woman,' he snapped as they both heard the sound of rapidly retreating hooves. 'If they're going to burst in here, they've got to find you in bed with someone to account for the clear evidence that two people have been sleeping in this bed. My presence may give rise to gossip we'd neither of us welcome, but it won't get you run out of town.'

He reached over her and with his finger and thumb snuffed the candle. They lay in silence, listening to the sound of the night and then gradually became aware that those sounds were being augmented, quietly at first and then, increasingly clearly, by the sound of a number of people – the murmur of voices, the shuffle of feet – approaching the house.

Abigail stiffened and threw Lord Jasper a frightened glance.

'Ssh,' he whispered, sensing her tension. 'Relax. We're lovers, remember? That's what they've got to find. If you're as rigid as a plank, even those idiots won't be fooled.' He pulled the coverlet well up as he spoke and turned on his side beside her, one arm across her

288

body over the quilt. 'Close your eyes,' he commanded, 'and when you wake up, seem sleepy.'

Sleep was the furthest thing from her mind at this precise moment but the advice was sound and Abigail was quietly grateful that at least her companion was unaware of the irony of the situation whereby, in order to save Iago, she was welcoming to her bed the very man whose presence there she had once dreaded.

There was an insistent hammering at the front door and Abigail stirred as if to get up and answer it but Lord Jasper's restraining arm held her still. 'Let them wake the servants,' he said. 'If there were no one with you, you'd not answer the door in the middle of the night, would you? Besides, the more people who see us together, the better Iago's chances.'

They heard someone go downstairs and then Lizzie's voice exclaiming, 'You can't burst in like this! You can't go upstairs − Mrs Vatsetter's asleep!'

A man's voice said, 'Which room is that slave's?' and then, Lizzie having presumably pointed to it, the sound of a door being flung open. There was a pause and then the same voice said, 'It's empty. Not been slept in.' This information was greeted by some unpleasant chuckles and the voice − which by now both listeners had privately identified as belonging to the potman from the King's Arms − went on, 'Where's your mistress's room, then?'

Seconds later, the door of that burst open, too, and a lantern was held aloft.

Two figures, one of them dark-haired, were clearly discernible under the coverlet and, with a trimphant 'Aha!' the potman whipped the covers from the dark-haired figure. 'Out, boy!' he said. We'll teach you to have ideas about white women!'

The fact that his victim was not black, and his precise identity, struck the man simultaneously as Lord Jasper turned over in response to this rude awakening, sat up, reclaimed the covers, stared from one to the other of the intruders and demanded, 'What, in the name of ...?' And then, in an icy voice, 'Perhaps you would be kind enough to explain this intrusion into a lady's bedchamber?'

The intruders fell back, but not without a certain amount of nudging and sniggering. The potman stood as firm as he dared. 'Hardly a lady, my lord,' he said.

'If you repeat that remark outside these four walls, I'll see you hang on one pretext or another,' Lord Jasper told him and the potman had no doubt he would.

'We're looking for Mis' Vatsetter's Iago,' another man said, coming to the potman's rescue.

'In Mrs Vatsetter's bed?' Lord Jasper inquired incredulously. 'Surely his own room would be a more likely place to find him?'

'Except that he ain't there,' someone said with satisfaction.

'Doubtless he is pursuing his own interests,' Lord Jasper suggested. 'I don't envy you the task of searching the bed of every female slave in the colony, though.'

There was a pause while they thought about that, then one, brighter than the others, asked, 'And how did you get here, my lord?'

Lord Jasper remembered the horse he had told Iago to take. 'I walked.'

'In boots? Must have been very uncomfortable, my lord. We thought it was one of your horses we saw heading down Francis Street, just before we got here. Didn't think nothing of it at the time, of course, except that it was late to be out. You sure that nigger ain't took it and run? Wouldn't put it past him. Still, don't you worry none. We'll get him back — the horse and the nigger.'

Abigail felt it was time she played some part in this. 'Iago has my permission to come and go as he chooses,' she said. 'He's a good hand and doesn't abuse such privileges.'

'With respect, ma'am, if you believe that, you're a bigger fool than anyone's ever took you for. Privileges is for white men. Niggers gets fed and housed and clothed just as long as they works well, and when they don't, you sells them. You ask his lordship if that ain't so.' And he looked to Lord Jasper for endorsement.

'I have to admit that seems to be the prevailing attitude,' Lord Jasper confirmed.

The potman, who had been silent during this exchange, felt his control of the situation slipping and decided it was his turn to butt in. 'Runaways is what we don't hold with,' he declared. 'There's been a sight too many in recent years, and that's a fact. Getting clean away, too, most of 'em. We'll get this one back for you, ma'am, make no mistake.'

'There's no need to put yourselves out,' Abigail insisted. 'I'm quite sure Iago will be back and that the horse you saw had nothing to do with him.'

'All the same, we'll get the dogs out and follow,' the potman said. 'Even you wouldn't want a runaway who's also a horse-thief, now would you? If we're wrong, there's no harm done. If we're right — well, it's high time an example was set.' He bowed sheepishly towards Lord Jasper. 'Sorry to have burst in on you like this, my lord, but all in a good cause. No offence, I hope?'

'On the contrary, very considerable offence — and not least to Mrs Vatsetter who does not appear to be a recipient of your apologies.'

The man flushed. 'Sorry, Mis' Vatsetter. Couldn't be helped — not in the circumstances. Hope you understand.'

'I think you may assume we both understand — perfectly,' Lord Jasper said in icy tones that made the intruders back hastily out of the room, glad that they could not be held responsible for what had occurred.

Neither Abigail nor Lord Jasper spoke until they heard the front door close and then Lizzie's steps up to her own room on the floor above.

'Will they pursue him?' she asked at last.

'Almost certainly, I should think, if only to compensate for having been made to look fools. We've bought him some time, though — and a little more still to come while they get themselves mounted and some dogs collected.'

'Will they catch him?'

'I don't know. I hope not. If anyone can get away, it should be Iago. He knows the route well enough.'

'The route? What route? What are you talking about?'

'Hadn't you realised? He's been systematically helping slaves to escape for years. I think it started before he left Kingswood.'

'Is that why you warned me he was a trouble-maker?'

Lord Jasper shook his head. 'No, that was the story Haworth put about. My guess is that he had an idea what Iago was up to but had no wish to see an otherwise valuable slave hang so he decided to sell him for what he could get — that way he didn't lose completely.'

Abigail digested this in silence. 'If you've known this for so long, my lord, why haven't you done anything about it?'

'I don't "know" it at all — I merely make an educated assumption based on a number of observations, particularly certain aspects connected with our retrieval of your daughter. As to why I haven't done anything — why should I? It doesn't affect me in any way.'

'And what do we do now, my lord?' Abigail asked.

'We wait — and we pray. We pray that we neither see nor hear of Iago again — unless he does get someone to write to you on his behalf. Apart from that, we get on with our lives as if nothing has happened, though I'm afraid you're going to be the butt of a great deal of unjustified gossip.'

Abigail sighed. 'It won't be the first time and it certainly won't be the last.'

Lord Jasper frowned. 'You seem very sure of that.'

Abigail shrugged. 'It seems to be my destiny, don't you think?' she said lightly.

Three days later Lord Jasper knocked on her door and demanded to see Mrs Vatsetter. He took her by the elbow and guided her to the little sitting-room at the back of the house where they could be sure of no business interruptions. He closed the door behind them and told Abigail to sit down.

Ignoring the instruction, she steadied herself against the small work-table. 'You've heard something,' she said intuitively.

He nodded. 'They've caught Iago. He should have kept the horse and put as much distance between himself and civilization as he could but he turned it loose, guessing it would find its way home, I imagine. The dogs tracked him down and they caught him as he swam the Pamunkey.' He hesitated. 'They hanged him, Abby.'

She stared at him in horror. 'How could they? My lord – he was a free man.'

He nodded. 'I thought he might be, but they weren't to know that, were they? And even if they had, it would have made no difference.' He looked at her stricken face. 'I'm sorry, Abby, but it was always a doomed alliance. You must have known that or you wouldn't have bothered to deny the relationship when I asked you.'

'I didn't lie, my lord. There was nothing between us at that time. It was after Becky's return. I don't really know how it came about. I don't think either of us did. It was just . . . we were both so *lonely.* He was a good man. He was kind and gentle and . . . and all the things . . . .' Her voice tailed off.

'. . . other men aren't,' he finished for her, his voice harsh. 'I suppose your somewhat limited experience will have led you to believe Iago was in some way unique. Perhaps he was. You'll wish to grieve alone, I don't doubt.' He bowed formally and left her, closing the door quietly behind him and advising Lizzie that Mrs Vatsetter would rather not be disturbed for the time being.

Abigail sank into a chair with her face in her hands, overwhelmed by a mixture of grief and guilt. The guilt was simple to explain. If, having bought Iago, he had remained a slave with a slave's proper distance, none of the gossip, none of these calamitous events, would have happened. Her motives had been of the best: Iago had helped her when she had most been in need of help. It was true he had had his own reasons for wanting to see Ezra dead, but there had been no need for him to have shielded her from the consequences of her actions. Yet he had done so, even though it exposed him to risk. His freedom – even a freedom he dared not acknowledge – had seemed a small enough recompense, yet it was that very freedom which had created the seeds of a self-confidence not expected of slaves which had in its turn aroused the first suspicions that things were not as they should have been. And now he was dead.

The grief was more complex. There was the grief anyone must feel for a life unnecessarily curtailed. There was the grief at the loss of a very dear friend, for Abigail, no matter how close she and Iago had been to each other, still thought of him more as a friend than a lover and suspected that his feelings for her had been similar. She had summed it up precisely when she had told Lord Jasper that they had both been lonely. They were both isolated from the community in which they lived, though in different ways: he by virtue of his colour and believed status, she by the nature of the money-lending part of her business as well as Becky's paternity. They shared the bond of Ezra's murder. Each found a comfort in the other's arms that was available to them from no one else. Iago would not now feel the lack of that comfort, but Abigail would. Then there was the deeper grief which was not for Iago at all, but for herself. Lord Jasper had acted as he did to save Iago, though it had not yet occureed to Abigail to ask herself why he should wish to, and in doing so had caught them in a situation which left no room for misunderstanding and would very effectively put paid to any faint hope Abigail might have had — and she was honest enough to acknowledge that any such hope had always been very faint indeed — that Lord Jasper might at some future date come to return the love she had discovered herself to hold for him. It was a bitterly cruel irony that Williamsburg should now believe her to be the one thing she could never be: she would have forced herself to be content with being Lord Jasper's mistress but she knew the Cuddesdon family to be notoriously proud and, while there had been just a very slim chance that he would set up a mistress who had already borne Lance Haworth a child — two children, she reminded herself, thinking of the sad little grave in the peach grove — he would not take in any capacity a woman who had taken a black lover.

There was another complication in her life, but this was one she could remedy. She had placed her financial backing on the quick-sands of Lance Haworth's business and she must do something soon to retrieve her own position. In this colony only those with money behind them had true freedom and she had put hers at risk. Revenge against Lance no longer seemed so important; Kingswood became a bonus. She had more urgent need of her interest, her capital — and the first payment must soon be due.

She soon realised how crucial Iago had become to her business enterprises. In his absence, the supply of critically useful information dried up and she felt as if she were functioning blindfold. In particular, she had not the slightest idea how Lance's affairs were prospering. She still had her agents in Norfolk, of course, and knew they would let her know as soon as Lance's ships berthed. It was a matter of some concern that there seemed to be no sign of them at all, but such were the vagaries of weather and the availability of cargo that she took comfort in the fact that at least she had not heard of any great disaster overtaking them. She sent Lance a note reminding him that payment would soon be due. She considered suggesting that an indication of how things stood would be welcomed but she forbore, rightly judging that he would interpret such a request as a sign of incipient panic and she wanted to give him no hint that he might have the upper hand in any of their dealings. Her note received no reply.

Two weeks later, she was burgled. Tagus had slept in her bed-chamber ever since Iago's death and on the night in question, Abigail was awakened by a growl from the foot of her bed. Instantly awake, she hissed, 'Shh!' and listened. Tagus' growl decreased to a low rumbling and he came round to the side of the bed and licked her hand.

Abigail strained her ears. She almost thought she could hear something but, had Tagus not been so certain, she would have discounted it. She threw back the bedclothes and sat up cautiously, listening. Then she swung her legs over the side and stepped on to the rug, one hand on the tall bed-post to ease her up with the minimum of noise. She tiptoed to the door and turned the knob carefully so that no click would alert any intruder. She peered out. There was nothing to be seen but she thought she could hear faint rustlings.

Keeping one hand on Tagus' head to prevent his charging precipitately down the stairs, Abigail crept over to the banisters and, crouching down, peered through. Tagus was right. A faintly flickering light shone under the door of the parlour in which she conducted business. A candle. Someone was in there. Her immediate feeling was one of panic because there was no Iago to send down, only a houshold of women. She discounted any possibility that it might be one of them in the parlour — if it had been, Tagus would not have growled. What was she to do? If she raised the alarm, the intruder would be gone but if she went down herself she would be easily overpowered and, in any case, she was in no state to tackle an intruder.

Then common-sense prevailed over panic. Whoever it was would be disappointed: no gold — indeed, no valuables of any kind — were kept in that room. Frighten him away and then have the blacksmith put bars over the windows. Yes, that was the solution.

She released her restraining hand and Tagus shot down the stairs, baying. He stopped outside the parlour, dug ferociously and impotently at the heavy door and went on baying. The light disappeared.

Tagus' noise brought the servants running, armed with pokers, fire-irons, anything they could lay their hands on. They paused when they saw Abigail at the head of the stairs.

'I think he's gone, whoever he was,' she told them, 'but let's make sure, shall we? I don't think any burglar will tackle all of us. Come on.'

They flung open the parlour door and no one was sorry to find the room empty, the billowing curtains indicating clearly enough the burglar's route into and out of the house. Sarah immediately lowered the sash and locked the window while Abigail lit a candle.

'The lock on the shutter's been broken, ma'am,' Sarah said.

'No matter. I'll have it barred tomorrow. Let's see what's gone.'

The bureau had been forced open and papers lay scattered on the lowered flap while many more had been blown on to the floor.

'These can wait till morning,' Abigail decided. 'There's nothing here of use to anyone. If our visitor expected to find money in the bureau, I'm afraid he was sorely disappointed. I don't suppose he will return but we'll leave Tagus down here for the rest of the night, just in case.'

Since everyone was a little shaken, Abigail recommended a tot of rum all round and when she returned to her room with hers, she was quite surprised how calm she felt. She sank onto the bed and made the uncomfortable effort now necessary to get her legs up on the mattress, too. Her mind was still racing and she sipped the rum because she knew it would help her to sleep, but her chief feeling now that the burglar had been routed was amusement that whoever it was had had so wasted a night. She slept without a qualm and woke with only a feeling of annoyance that all those papers littering the parlour must be sorted out – an unnecessary waste of a morning, but a job that only she could do.

It was as tedious as she had anticipated and when she had finished, she leant back in her chair, stretching her aching back. She was puzzled and a great deal less sanguine than she had been the night before. Two things were missing: the agreement signed by Lance Haworth and the mortgages redeemed from William Quenington.

She cast her mind back. Lance had seen where she put the document, and the other documents peeping out of the pigeon-holes at the back of the bureau must have indicated that this was where such things were kept permanently. Without that document she had no proof the agreement had ever existed. Of course, Lance had a copy of his own, but if hers had been taken it was likely that he would very soon see to it that both were destroyed. Abigail did not imagine that Lance himself had broken in: he would have made sure he was somewhere else altogether and, even if he had not taken so simple a precaution, he was of too distinctive a build to go unrecognised even on a dark night. However, he would have had no difficulty finding someone else to do it — for a price.

Whoever had actually carried out the burglary, there could be little doubt who had been behind it and Abigail's anger mounted. She did not believe Lance had been behind Becky's disappearance — that was undoubtedly Blanche's deranged work — but he hadn't hesitated to turn even that to his own advantage. That scheme to wriggle out of his debt had been thwarted. Now, with his debt due to be called in, he had removed the evidence that it had ever existed.

Anger was joined by panic. The money she had lent Lance was crucial to her life in the colony. Even more important, it was crucial to her child's future. Money was going to be the only thing that would enable her to build some sort of stable life here. What's more, a respectable reserve would not be enough. She needed the sort of fortune she stood to gain whether or not Lance's ships came home and now it looked as if she had lost her means of claiming against him.

Her next instinct was to seek out Lord Jasper and ask his advice. He had always advised her well in the past and there was no reason why he should not do so again, but she hesitated. She had seen little of him since he brought the news of Iago's death, and that little consisted entirely of brief encounters and exchanged 'Good days'. Doubtless Lord Jasper would give her advice, though she could imagine all too clearly how coldly distant his manner would be. No, this was something she must tackle on her own. She might as well get into the habit: it wouldn't be very long before she would have to be entirely self-reliant.

The date fell due when Lance should either start paying the interest on her capital or lose Kingswood. There was no word from the Haworth house. This was not in itself alarming: Abigail had already learned that very few debtors voluntarily paid their dues on time. It was only worrying because the burglary gave an added dimension to this particular tardiness. Abigail thought it might be unwise to force the issue at this stage. A letter demanding payment forthwith was unlikely to be productive. If, on the other hand, she played for time, perhaps something would come up — an idea, an opportunity. It was equally important that Lance should not be under the illusion she had retired from the battle-ground. So she sent him a note reminding him that the date was well past but suggesting that, since she knew his ships had still not returned to Virginia, she was prepared to hold back on her demands for settlement until they knew whether the voyages had been successful. She was not altogether surprised to receive neither acknowledgment nor answer.

The ships had still not returned several weeks later.

Chapter Sixteen

Much had been forgiven Abigail Vatsetter. She could hardly be held to blame for having been a bond-slave, she had made a great success of her two business ventures and it was hardly surprising that so beautiful a woman would have had a somewhat irregular association with one of her owners – indeed, those who knew her rather better than others had often expressed the opinion that she probably hadn't had much choice in the matter. Many of the women found it harder to forgive her apparent relationship with Lord Jasper. These things happened, of course, but it was expected they would be handled with discretion. No one chose to consider that it was only the uninvited intrusion of the townsmen that brought the situation to public attention, and somehow the fact that both Mrs Vatsetter and Lord Jasper were unencumbered by spouses seemed to make the illicit union appear all the more shocking.

'The thing is, what are we going to do about it?' Mrs Bracken-Carter asked. 'We can hardly continue to receive Mrs Vatsetter.'

There was general agreement on this point, its being tacitly understood that it would never do to expose possibly susceptible husbands to a woman of so little principle.

There was the added problem that no one who owed Mrs Vatsetter money – and some ladies had quite considerable debts outstanding – could afford to cut their association with her completely though several resolved to get out of her debt as soon as they could so that they need not be seen to associate with such a woman. This was not something they were prepared to discuss openly with one another since one could never depend one hundred per cent upon the discretion of one's friends. Mrs Vatsetter's dressmaking business was another matter altogether.

Mrs Brush-Everard was adamant. 'I shall order no more garments from Mrs Vatsetter,' she said. 'I shall go back to having my maid dress me, though if Sarah Camberwell should choose to set up on her own account after this, I shall be perfectly ready to take my custom to her.'

Mrs Wythe and Mrs Bracken-Carter nodded their full agreement but Mrs Ludwell-Paradise demurred. 'As you choose, ladies, but my money will go where the skill is. Sarah Camberwell's a good dressmaker — and so she should be, for she's been well-taught — but she hasn't the discerning eye, the infallible taste, of Mrs Vatsetter, and you know it. I haven't the slightest intention of returning to provincial standards of dress and I fancy my standing in the community is sufficient to carry me through a continued professional acquaintance with Mrs Vatsetter.'

Since Lucy Ludwell-Paradise's own reputation was not entirely devoid of intriguing question-marks, this declaration induced some pursed lips and a somewhat self-conscious silence which was broken by Mrs Wythe.

'Personally, I see nothing reprehensible in provincial elegance,' she said.

Mrs Ludwell-Paradise smiled her sweetest smile. 'You don't find the words mutually exclusive?' she asked and paused briefly before adding, 'No, I don't suppose you do.'

That seemed to kill further discussion rather effectively and the conversation became more general, if less interesting.

Abigail did not therefore find herself totally shunned. Social invitation ceased forthwith and fewer people seemed in need of loans — which, she reminded herself, was not necessarily a bad thing, since she was seriously overstretched to Lance Haworth. Calls on the dressmaking business eased off, too, but not to the extent she had expected though Sarah gave her a hint of how the wind lay when she reported a comment she had received.

'It's been suggested I set up on my own,' she said as they sat over supper one evning.

'Why not? You could do worse,' Abigail replied.

Sarah shook her head. 'I'm a good enough craftswoman,' she said. 'I haven't got your eye, though. I've never mingled in the top rank and I suspect you have, though you never talk about your past. But it shows in the clothes you make, the clothes you wear, your general taste. It's not only that, either: Lord Jasper treats you as an equal and, for all he's perfectly gentlemanly, even to people he must hate, there's not many he regards as an equal.'

Abigail told her it was a nonsensical notion and changed the subject. She had seen nothing of Lord Jasper since he had brought the news of Iago's death. There was no reason why he should have called, of course. All the same, she felt the loss of his support very keenly, the more so because her feelings towards him had changed. She supposed it was probably all to the good that he had distanced himself from her — it certainly made the impossibility of anything closer between them easier to bear. As for Sarah's revelation, Abigail was not surprised that it had been made and could only be grateful for Sarah's loyalty. The girl was right: she lacked Abigail's elusive flair, but that would not have prevented most girls from setting up on their own, even if they had recognised their shortcoming.

She did, in fact, toy briefly with the idea of selling out to her assistant and making a new start somewhere else. It was a superficially appealing idea, but common-sense reminded her that, no matter where she went, her story would eventually follow her and she might be better advised to stay in a town where the facts were known. It seemed as if her business would remain ticking over. The social ostracism hurt but it was something she could brazen out. She discovered very quickly that, while people would quite literally pass by on the other side if they saw her coming, very, very few had the nerve to ignore a smiling, apparently self-confident 'Good morning' — Abigail reasoned that, if she could keep that little peephole of civility open, there was a chance it might later be pushed further without anyone's realising the fact before it was too late to close it up completely.

There was still no sign of Lance's ships. Abigail watched the calendar with increasing anxiety, her only consolation being that there was no message of disaster from Lloyd's. For the first time she found herself seriously considering the possibility of living in Norfolk so that she would be able to check every day for herself. The agent had promised to send her any news, good or bad, but the waiting was nerve-racking.

At last the messenger came. He carried a brief note several days old. The two ships had returned, fully laden, and with them two others, chartered in England — and uninsured — also with full cargoes. The news of the two ships chartered in England was something of a surprise: the outward-going cargoes must have sold very well there to warrant taking on new vessels and the captains must have been confident of a highly profitable return cargo. It was unlikely Lance would make enough to pay off his whole debt (assuming he intended to pay off any at all) but he would certainly be able to pay off the initial two or even three repayments. Unless he renegued.

That afternoon Lord Jasper called. He beckoned a child over, tossed him a penny and told him to walk his steaming horse up and down until he came out again. Then he hammered imperiously on the door and was shown into the same parlour from which the Haworth papers had disappeared.

When Abigail came in, very conscious of a restraint between them, he was pacing up and down the small room.

'Forgive my dirt, Mrs Vatsetter: I come straight from the wharf at Jamestown.' He threw a pouch onto the table. It fell heavily and the contents jingled.

'What's this?' Abigail asked.

'Your five hundred guineas. You're safe now. Haworth's cargo has made a fortune for both of you.'

'You seem very sure,' Abigail said doubtfully.

'I am. I watched the sale. He gambled, of course, but it paid off.' He paused and looked at her as if a little puzzled and more than a little displeased. 'I own I was surprised you agreed to such a deal. From the way you've always spoken, I should have though it repugnant to you.'

'Why? What do you mean?'

He shrugged. 'I'd not have thought you'd approve that particular cargo. But perhaps the fortune involved placated your principles.'

'The return cargo should be innocuous enough. He was bringing back such items from the manufactories around Liverpool as would fetch high prices here. Their precise nature was left to the captains' discretion – as is customary.'

'You don't know, then!' Lord Jasper exclaimed. 'they've been sailing the Golden Triangle, my dear. Haworth's captains have brought back four shiploads of prime slaves.'

Abigail paled. 'Surely he would not!'

'Does he know your views?'

'No. Why should he? It was never discussed.'

'So you did not forbid him to bring slaves?'

'I gave him quite specific instructions as to the nature of the return cargo and it was to be brought direct from England. No wonder they've been so long getting back here! How could he do such a thing when he knows what it's like not to be free!'

'He keeps slaves at Kingswood,' Lord Jasper pointed out.

'I know, and I wish he didn't, but that's not quite the same thing as bringing them over, is it?'

'A fine distinction. You must salve your conscience with the knowledge that at least you run no risk of suffering the same plight.'

'I don't suppose you can be expected to see the matter as I do,' Abigail said, rather sadly. 'After all, you've never been in a similar situation and you've made your own fortune from the labour of your slaves.'

Lord Jasper did not speak for a long time. He gazed, frowning, out of the window, apparently deep in thought and Abigail wondered what she had said to cause such apparent displeasure. Finally he turned and looked down at her.

'I keep no slaves,' he said. 'Nor ever have — save one.'

Abigail stared at him. 'But Jabez — Jubilation — all of them!'

'Free. As free as ever you made Iago.'

'I don't believe it.'

'As you choose. Nevertheless, it is so.'

'But I heard not the slightest hint of it — and I lived in your house for weeks! I worked with them! And more recently, when I told you of my plans for a plantation, you said I'd be tarred and feathered if people knew what I wanted to do. If what you say is true, the thought of such treatment doesn't seem to have deterred you.'

'I have one great advantage over a mere Mrs Vatsetter,' he told her. 'My father is the Duke of Cutteslowe. He may not live in the colonies but he has the ear of those with influence here. No one would risk incurring his displeasure. You see — I can't even claim bravery! The consequences would be borne by my workers, not by me. You kept Iago's freedom secret, didn't you? I imagine it was because freed slaves are all too often rounded up by unscrupulous traders and taken back into captivity, to be sold in a different colony where there is little chance of their plight reaching the ears of whoever freed them. That's why none of my people breathes a word and I am guided by their wishes in the matter.'

'They might almost as well not be free,' Abigail commented.

'It must seem like that to them sometimes,' he agreed. 'Iago was an intelligent man. I'm sure he felt the same.'

'He did, and one would have expected that to lead to some bitterness, but he seemed to feel none. How long has this been your philosophy?' she added, curious.

'It brought me here. My father disagreed as much with my ideas as with my dissolute life. He packed me off here and told me to put my ideas into practice and not to come back until I had either made a fortune or was prepared to admit my error and reform my ways. I chose to make a fortune.'

'You told me once it was because you seduced a clergyman's daughter,' Abigail reminded him.

'There was that as well, of course,' he agreed blandly.

Abigail eyed him suspiciously but thought it a topic better not pursued. 'If those are your views, why did you take me as a bond-slave?'

'That's another matter altogether,' he said shortly, 'and one I don't propose to discuss.'

Abigail scrutinised his face but it told her nothing. She held up the pouch of gold. 'Take this, my lord. I may have need of it yet.'

'You intend to refuse Haworth's profits? That would be foolish beyond reasons! The cargo has been landed and sold. I regret it as much as you but to refuse the money would be a Pyrrhic gesture — and the utmost folly!'

'I'm unlikely to have the chance,' Abigail said bitterly and told him about the burglary.

'Why did you say nothing to me at the time?' Lord Jasper asked when she had finished.

Abigail hesitated, unwilling to refer to the constraints she had felt must attach to any intercourse between them at that time. 'I did think about doing so,' she told him, 'but what would have been the point? I could think of nothing you could have done, especially since it seemed sensible to assume the documents would have been destroyed.'

'What do you propose doing now? I can assure you Haworth can afford to repay it all. He may well wish to retain some to finance his next cargo, of course, but if you chose to insist, it wouldn't cause him any great hardship.'

'I'll wait and see whether he comes to redeem any of it at all. His next cargo is the least of my problems at the moment. He may be intending to pay back the capital and chouse me only out of the interest.'

'You have a touching faith in Lance Haworth,' Lord Jasper said bitterly.

'On the contrary, I have none at all. I'm clutching at straws, I know that. But he has scarcely had time to contact me yet. I've no wish to face ruin, my lord. I'll give the Devil himself the benefit of the doubt before I have to accept defeat and with my other businesses both barely holding their own, it behoves me to play such cards as I have left with very great care.'

'Cutting you, are they?' he said without either rancour or sympathy.

'You must know they are, my lord,' she said stiffly.

'What else did you expect?

Lord Jasper picked up the pouch of gold and accepted his *congé*. He paused as he passed her in the doorway and his finger flicked against her cheek. 'You've never lacked courage, Abby, though where you inherited it from is beyond me. I've a feeling it will see you through socially, but business is another matter. You're as big a gambler as your father ever was with the added disadvantage that you don't think you are, and you're as bad a judge of character as your mother. Emotion has no part in business decisions, Abby. If you pull yourself through this one, try to remember that.'

Abigail knew that there must be some very sharp set-down in answer to this but, since it entirely escaped her, she was obliged to see him go without his ears having received the benefit of it. It was a failure that rankled for the rest of the day.

For three days Abigail waited in growing despair for a message from Lance. There was none, though she several times heard comments as to his fortune in pulling himself back so spectacularly from the brink of bankruptcy.

She sent him a note.

Mrs Vatsetter congratulates Mr Haworth on his recent good fortune and requests the pleasure of a visit from him at his earliest convenience to discuss the conclusion of their business.

Sarah delivered it and came back empty-handed.

Again Abigail waited. It seemed Mr Haworth's earliest convenience was likely to be verylate indeed.

Abigail now knew without any shadow of doubt that if she was to retrieve anything at all of what was due her from Lance's successful voyages, she was going to have to fight for it. If Lance had no intention of coming to her, she must go to him. It was not an encounter she would look forward to but neither was it one she would back away from.

Having made up her mind – and having spent another sleepless night during which no other alternative occurred to her – Abigail made her way down Duke of Gloucester Street to the Haworth house. All too clearly she recalled the last time she came here and the reception she was given. She took a deep breath, mounted the short flight of steps and knocked on the door.

She was kept waiting for so long that at first she wondered whether it would be opened at all but at last she heard a bolt drawn back, a key turned, and Noah peered out. 'Yes?' he said.

'You know me, Noah,' Abigail said, forcing a confidence into her tone that she was far from feeling. 'Tell Mr Haworth I'm here to see him.'

The door closed in her face, to the intrigued interest of some passers-by, who paused to speculate upon the purpose of this clearly uninvited visit. The key turned once more and she heard Noah's footsteps fading away. He hadn't shot the bolt home so presumably he expected to be back. She waited, very conscious of the curious stares of passers-by. Noah reappeared.

'Go 'way,' he said. 'Mas' Haworth'll not see you – not now, not ever,' and he began to close the door.

Quickly Abigail put her foot in the narrowing gap between door and jamb. 'Tell Mr Haworth I shall remain on his doorstep until he does,' she said, and to emphasise her point, she sat down on the top step, smoothing her skirts over her knees as if in preparation for a long stay.

Again the door was closed and the key turned. Again Noah's footsteps faded away. This time, however, Abigail's wait was much shorter. Presumably Lance did not relish the idea of a former mistress encamped on his doorstep. Noah held the door wide. 'Come in,' he said grudgingly.

Blanche Haworth had spent a small fortune turning the comfortably provincial house into an extravagantly modish one, Abigail thought, comparing the hall she had known with the one she now entered. If the same expense had been lavished elsewhere in the house, it was no wonder Lance had found himself in difficulties.

Noah threw open the door of Lance's office. Blanche's extravagant taste had not been allowed to penetrate here, Abigail noticed. Lance was alone in the room. He offered no greeting, no smile.

'What do you want, Abigail?'

Very well, if he wanted to come straight to the point, Abigail had no objection. 'My money,' she said.

He did smile then, slowly and unpleasantly, a smile that not quite reached his eyes. 'What money would that be?' he asked.

'Don't play games, Lance. You know perfectly well what money it is. I backed your recent venture and you made a fortune. Some of that fortune is mine.'

'I owe you nothing.'

'You owe me – at the very least – several months' interest. My information is that you've made enough to repay me in full with interest but since that might leave you with insufficient to finance your next venture, I'll settle for half now, the rest when your boats next come in.'

'You'll settle for nothing. I owe you nothing and you can't prove otherwise. Everyone in Williamsburg knows how careful you are to get agreements down in black and white. Where is an agreement signed by me? Produce it and I'll pay.'

'You know you signed one and that you had a copy,' Abigail said. 'Why do you assume I can't produce my copy of it?'

'Because you were burgled and it was one of two items stolen. You can no more produce those documents than you can prove I ever admitted their existence.'

The door opened then and Blanche came in. 'Is the woman still here?' she asked coldly.

'She has some cock-and-bull story about being owed money,' Lance answered. 'I think I've just succeeded in convincing her she's wrong.'

Abigail turned to Blanche. 'I think you recall visiting me, Mrs Haworth, and pleading with me to help your husband.'

'I've no such recollection, Mrs Vatsetter, I assure you.'

'Indeed? I'm reasonably confident that my assistant, Sarah Camberwell, will remember admitting you.'

Abigail had the momentary satisfaction of having shaken them both, but it was short-lived.

'You must mean the occasion when I came to order a gown,' Blanche replied after a brief pause during which she appeared to be searching her memory.

'How strange, if that was the purpose of your visit, that my books have no records of the transaction,' Abigail said.

'Not at all. If you recollect, I saw nothing to my taste and therefore placed no order after all.'

'Penniless again, Abigail?' Lance taunted, advancing towards her. 'I heard you'd overstretched yourself.' He was very close to her now, so close that she was obliged to back against the wall. Still he advanced until he could pin her against the panelling between his outstretched arms.

'I'll gladly take you back into service again,' he said softly but not so softly that his wife could not hear. 'Under the old terms, of course. I should never have let you go − I've regretted it many a time.' His eyes raked her body insolently. 'I'll tell you this, Abigail Vatsetter: I had more satisfaction from you than I've ever had from my wife. You'll not be neglected in my service, I promise you.' He lowered his head to kiss her but she twisted swiftly away and ducked under his arm.

'I don't deny I've made mistakes,' she said, 'but I'm not so stupid that I'll repeat them. Overstretched I may be, but I'm not penniless − not yet.'

'Nor need you be,' Blanche interjected. Her face was drained of colour and her dark eyes glittered with impotent anger. Abigail could almost feel it in her to pity the other woman. No husband could have uttered a heavier insult than Lance had just done. 'You have my husband's daughter. Bring her to me and he will repay you every penny − capital and interest. She'll have a better home here than any you can offer her. I'll love her as if she were my own.' Her voice was rising to a pitch that was almost frenzied and Abigail could see that

Lance was as shaken by his wife's suggestion as Abigail was herself. There was little doubt that he would prefer the money to the child.

She kept her own voice carefully calm. 'No, Mrs Haworth. Becky is not for sale. I'd rather be penniless than lose my child.' And she turned to go.

Blanche caught her arm. 'Rebecca would be with her father. That's important. We could give her both parents. You'll never be able to do that.' Desperate appeal filled her voice.

'Perhaps not, but I'll do the best I can.' Abigail replied. 'Mrs Haworth, I sympathise with you in your plight but I'm not prepared even to consider so outrageous a suggestion. First you steal Becky, then you try to buy her. Those are not the acts of a reasonable woman.'

She managed to pull away from Blanche's clutching hand and hastened from the room. Lance's mocking laughter followed her, though whether it was directed at her or at his wife, she neither knew nor cared. She was oblivious to the white fury on Blanche Haworth's face.

Abigail did some rapid thinking on the way back to her house. There was no point in pursuing Lance's debt. He had got the better of her and there was nothing to be done about it — nothing she could see at the moment, anyhow. She must cut her losses and retrench. She had several financial irons in the fire,all of them small but none of them speculative. They would not be ready yet awhile. She still had her dressmaking business, even though trade had fallen off, and she had five hundred guineas. Since she was not bankrupt and, with care, should be able to avoid that unhappy fate, she could take possession of the money Lord Jasper was holding with no fear of creditors pouncing on it. She would not lend for the time being and fortunately had never herself been in the habit of borrowing. Perhaps it would be better to move to smaller premises, especially since most of her staff had left. A pity — business success depends so much on confidence. It would inspire little if she were seen to be retrenching to such an extent, but that could not be helped.

As soon as she reached home, Abigail sat down and wrote a note to Lord Jasper requesting an interview at his earliest convenience. The messenger returned with the answer that his lordship was engaged for the rest of the day but would be happy to see her on the morrow. This gave her the remainder of that day to indulge in the futile exercise of berating herself for her stupidity — which she did, and from which she gleaned no satisfaction whatever. She knew it was quite useless to contemplate any sort of action to establish her rightful claim to Lance's new fortune: he had closed every conceivable avenue. She could pass the word around and hope to sow some doubt in people's minds, but that was not nearly enough and might easily rebound on her.

Lance clearly thought her finished. Abigail was quite sure he would not otherwise have made his suggestion that she should once more be bound to him. If anything had been needed to reassure her that his old hold on her was done with, it was that action and its accompanying words. Abigail shuddered. The only feeling it had aroused was revulsion, a revulsion intensified by the fact that his actions and his remarks were deliberately calculated to wound his wife. Abigail had neither liking nor respect for Blanche Haworth but she was Lance's wife and, whatever might pass between them in private, he should not hold her up to the ridicule of others. If there was one thing Lance's behaviour had reinforced, it was Abigail's determination to prove that she was still a financial force to be reckoned with. The first step towards that goal would be her visit to Lord Jasper.

He looked up curiously as Jabez showed her into his office. He observed the set to her mouth and the tilt to her chin that betokened trouble for someone.

A familiar leather pouch lay on the desk before Lord Jasper and Abigail nodded towards it as she sat down. 'Mine?' she asked.

He pushed it across the table towards her. 'I thought this might be what you were coming for. Did you have any success with Haworth yesterday?'

'None at all.' Abigail frowned. Could she do nothing without Lord Jasper's being informed of it? 'It was as I feared – he denies all knowledge of our arrangement, and has so successfully blocked all possible avenues by which I might have proved my claim that there's nothing I can do.'

'You don't seem particularly downcast by the discovery.'

'It wasn't entirely unexpected, was it? No, "downcast" isn't the word. Just angry. I don't like being cheated, nor do I like his assumption that he has succeeded in ruining me. He even suggested I should return to his service!'

Lord Jasper observed his long-fingered, well-manicured hands minutely. 'Did you avail yourself of the offer?' he asked evenly, not looking at her.

Abigail's sigh was one of sheer exasperation and it brought his head up very quickly, ensuring his full attention. 'I do *wish* you'd rid yourself of the notion that I'm still mooning over Lance Haworth like some love-sick calf. No, of course I didn't – and, before you ask, I shouldn't have done so even had I been as destitute as he thought.'

'You relieve me, Mrs Vatsetter,' Lord Jasper murmured. 'You've no idea how much you relieve me.'

'Nor was I prepared to let them have Becky in return for the capital and interest that are rightfully mine.'

Lord Jasper stared at her. 'Was that seriously proposed?'

'By Blanche, yes. I think it came as a great surprise to her husband.'

'I imagine it might. He would infinitely prefer the money.'

'He believes me finished. I suspect he thinks I shall creep out of Williamsburg with my tail between my legs. Well, I shan't. I'm absolutely determined to prove him wrong. I shall need this money, of course, and I'm going to be obliged to retrench, which is why I've come to see you.'

'What have I to do with your retrenchment?'

'You're my landlord. I shall have to move into more modest accommodation for the time being and therefore I'm giving notice that I shall vacate the house as soon as I can find somewhere else.'

'You've nowhere else in mind?'

'How could I have?' Abigail asked reasonably. 'I didn't know it would be necessary until I'd seen the Haworths.'

'Then do me the favour of remaining where you are. The house needs to be lived in and it will do your financial enterprises no good if you're seen to move to smaller premises.'

'I realise that, my lord, but I really have no choice. I must pare my expenses where I can and that's the most obvious place.'

'But a false economy, none the less. If I reduce the rent by half, on the understanding that you will let me know when you're once more in a position to pay the full amount, will you agree to remain?'

Abigail hesitated. She had not been prepared for so generous an offer, particularly when she considered the way in which Lord Jasper had distanced himself from her affairs recently. Besides, she had no wish to be beholden to anyone and although Lord Jasper had always been generous with his advice, never before had his generosity extended to his own pocket. There was no denying he was right, however – she had already recognised that such a move would undermine confidence in her business.

'Are you sure?' she asked doubtfully.

'If I weren't, I should not have been so foolish as to offer,' he pointed out.

'Then I shall be very happy to continue on those terms.' Abigail picked up the pouch of gold and squeezed it into her reticule.

Lord Jasper stood up and preceded her to the door. There he paused. 'Tell me, Mrs Vatsetter, does your standing in Williamsburg bring you an invitation to Mrs Ludwell-Paradise's little party?'

'Of course not. You know perfectly well I'm no longer received, though Sarah and I are making one or two gowns for it.'

309

'Only one or two? Hmm. Still, you surprise me – Lucy Ludwell-Paradise has never been one to adhere too strictly to convention.'

'One of the gowns is for her. She has been as generous as anyone could expect,' Abigail said, and then hesitated as if that were not all she wished to say.

'There's something else?'

Abigail looked up at him shyly and a shade wistfully. 'You've reverted to the formal "Mrs Vatsetter",' she said. 'I much preferred "Abby".'

His eyes widened suddenly under their hooded lids and something flickered there that Abigail did not understand. His voice, however, told her nothing. 'I shall endeavour to remember that.' He took her hand and raised it to his lips. 'Good day, Abby.'

It was a gesture that raised her spirits out of all proportion to its significance.

She smiled. 'Good day, my lord.'

Chapter Seventeen

Lucy Ludwell-Paradise might be a widow but she saw no reason why that should preclude her enjoying herself, particularly when her considerable fortune made it so easy. Her frequent evening parties were informal affairs but invitations to them were much sought after, the ladies of Williamsburg vying with one another to hit precisely the right note of informality while, at the same time, leaving no one in any doubt that they could display their husband's wealth had it been appropriate. Abigail had always been very busy before a Ludwell-Paradise party.

There was less work on this occasion and Abigail sent up a silent prayer of thanks for what there was – and made quite sure that the workroom excelled itself. A couple more orders trickled in and she and Sarah worked night and day to ensure that they were completed on time and to perfection. Those who had remained loyal would have no cause to regret it.

The widow herself always took precedence. She had been Abigail's first customer and had remained one of her best. Other clients, no matter how exalted, might occasionally have had to accept being fitted by Sarah Camberwell. Not Mrs Ludwell-Paradise. Mrs Vatsetter alone attended to her, and when her other ladies made the occasional disgruntled comment, Abigail smiled her sweetest smile and reminded them that it was Mrs Ludwell-Paradise who gave her her start. A lesser artist might have lost their custom, but Mrs Vatsetter's attention some of the time was better than the guaranteed attention of any other dressmaker in the colony, so the customers sighed but remained. Abigail made her way the short distance to the Ludwell-Paradise house with her patroness' latest gown, well covered from scrutiny, over her arm. The order had been placed some time before and this was to be its final fitting. The heavily embroidered satin was of a subtle shade of crushed strawberry which became the widow well, as she was the first to acknowledge.

'I've never regretted following Lord Jasper's advice and coming to you, you know, Mrs Vatsetter. I own I was very disinclined to do so at the time, but he persuaded me and it was one of the most sensible things I've ever done.'

Abigail tried to remember the conversation she had had on the subject with Lord Jasper all those years ago. Surely he had denied passing any but a fleeting comment on her work? 'Lord Jasper's advice, ma'am?' she said, her tone indicating a readiness to hear more.

Mrs Ludwell-Paradise hesitated. 'I was supposed not to mention it, but that was a long time ago. It can do no harm now. He came one evening and urged me to patronise you. Of course, I was careful to scrutinise the gown Mrs Hunter was displaying for you before I finally took the risk but I've been the best dressed woman in Williamsburg ever since.' She paused, turning in front of the cheval-glass and craning her neck to look at the back of the gown. 'Lovely. Absolutely lovely. You realise, of course, that it caused no little speculation, Lord Jasper helping a former slave to set up in business – and a beautiful one at that! Not that it came to anything, of course. He's always been such a misogynist – well, no, not that, exactly,' she hastened to correct herself. 'There have been plenty of the other sort, real high-fliers, some of them. That was before you came. But until the rumours that he had offered for Blanche Quenington, he had never shown the slightest inclination to make any of the connections permanent. And between you and me, Mrs Vatsetter, I've never entirely believed he *did* offer for Blanche. Lance Haworth is very handsome, of course, but quite frankly, even if you discount the title, what woman would choose him if she could have Jasper Cuddesdon? If I were ten years younger, now ... but I'm not and there's no use speculating on what might have been, but nevertheless ...!

Mrs Ludwell-Paradise rattled on, while Abigail made some small but crucial adjustments here and there, knowing that she was under no obligation to reply. This was probably just as well because she had been given plenty to think about.

At last the fitting was over and a highly satisfied customer stepped carefully out of the gown. She watched Abigail fold it and put it inside its protective linen sheath for the short journey back to the workroom.

'Mrs Vatsetter, may I be frank?' she said suddenly.

'Of course, ma'am. What is it?'

'There's a rumour going round that one of your business ventures has been less than entirely successful.'

'Oh?' Abigail kept her voice non-committal.

'It's said that you are over-extended and in difficulties.'

Abigail chose her words with care. 'There's a grain of truth in the story, ma'am, but only a grain. I'm certainly not in difficulties, although I shall be curtailing some of my activities for a while and concentrating on the dressmaking. There are no debts on my part outstanding — as you're doubtless aware, I've always made a point of settling bills immediately in return for a discount such as I offer my customers.'

Mrs Ludwell-Paradise nodded. 'You mean you won't be lending money for the time being?'

'I should rather say I shall only advance smaller sums for shorter periods but I anticipate a return to normal before long.'

'You've been here long enough to have learnt that in this colony only success matters. Then there is the question of your daughter. You did say I might be frank?'

'I did, ma'am.'

'You made a mistake, Mrs Vatsetter. A liaison of the sort with which you are credited is best kept very, very quiet. Quite unjust, of course: the men in this colony are hardly noted for contenting themselves with their wives but so long as they confine themselves to their slaves, no one thinks anything of it. The same freedom has never extended to us. You've stepped over the bounds of propriety — once, probably with little choice, but on the other occasions? You were no longer bonded then.'

'I know that, ma'am, but I'm not ashamed of Becky, nor of her association with her father for which I seek no excuses. I loved him.'

'With respect, Mrs Vatsetter, that is totally irrelevant.'

'With respect, Mrs Ludwell-Paradise, that is the only thing that really matters.'

Mrs Ludwell-Paradise compressed her lips and for a few moments Abigail thought she had lost her most steadfast patroness. Then Mrs Ludwell-Paradise laughed. 'No one can deny you have the courage of your convictions — even if those convictions are misguided. Very well, Mrs Vatsetter. I've been setting the colony by its ears for years and I can only admire your courage in doing so far more drastically than I ever dreamed of. Your continued success depends upon two things: dispelling the rumours of your financial situation and overcoming the more recent prejudice against you. The former will be the easier task, but you don't need me to tell you that. I shall continue to receive you and we'll see what good that does. It follows that I hope you will attend this forthcoming little gathering. You won't find it easy. Are you game?'

'Never more so, ma'am. I couldn't have a more generous offer. I'm under no illusions as to how difficult it will be − but others will attach importance to your receiving me, and that will be a help. I've been fortunate all along in having your support, ma'am. I can only thank you for its continuance.'

'Not at all − I shall extract my pound of flesh when your business is once more flourishing. You shall make me a gown by way of thanks.'

Abigail laughed. 'It will be a pleasure, ma'am.'

Mrs Ludwell-Paradise patted her cheek almost affectionately. 'Don't worry, Mrs Vatsetter. Social acceptance here is directly related to financial standing and present success is never hindered by past failures in that sphere. Scandal, of course, is another matter.'

Abigail had been given a great deal to think about. Lucy Ludwell-Paradise might cultivate the image of a social butterfly but Abigail knew her to be shrewd and discerning. If word had already begun to circulate that her affairs were in poor order, it was imperative she appear as much as possible and be seen to display complete confidence. It was not difficult to guess the source of these rumours, and almost before Mrs Ludwell-Paradise had finished uttering her invitation, Abigail had mentally reviewed her wardrobe and decided to wear something previously seen. Upon more mature reflection, she changed her mind. It would be difficult, given the time at her disposal, but something new − an overt indication that financial considerations were not paramount − was called for.

More thought-provoking were Mrs Ludwell-Paradise's revelations concerning Lord Jasper. A long time ago, Abigail had guessed that he lay behind Mrs Ludwell-Paradise's patronage to a greater extent than either had admitted. Now it seemed that he had not merely suggested the idea but had also gone to some lengths to persuade the wealthy widow it was a good one.

Why should Lord Jasper have put himself to so much trouble? It might quite possibly have sprung from a feeling of responsibility towards one who had been brought here against her own volition. Had he not subsequently expressed such a sense of responsibility?

Mrs Ludwell-Paradise had said that Lord Jasper had taken many mistresses but none since Abigail had arrived in Virginia. Abigail did not doubt the former statement: there was nothing equivocal about his reputation in England. When he had asked her father for her hand, Abigail had rejected him outright, and among her reasons had been this reputation as a libertine and a gamester. It was true that since she had been here, she had heard no whisper of any mistress and, in the small, self-obsessed world of Williamsburg it would have escaped neither notice nor comment. Until now, it was not a matter to which she had given any thought.

How tempting it would be to imagine that his changed habits might be due to her presence, and how foolish in her present circumstances to indulge such flights of fancy!

She turned instead to the question of Blanche Quenington. Abigail had no way of knowing whether Lord Jasper had proposed marriage to her directly, or — since it was the way he had offered for Abigail — through Blanche's father. The Cuddesdon servants certainly thought he had, and Abigail, when she heard of it, had thought them well-suited. She no longer thought that and, in any case, Blanche's marriage to Lance made it irrelevant, but she now knew Lord Jasper well enough to realise that he would never have risked a proposal if he did not expect — or desire — to be accepted.

Then why had he offered for her, a girl scarcely out of the schoolroom, whom he had seen perhaps twice and with whom he had had no converse save the social trivia obligatory at large functions? It certainly hadn't been for her dowry. But Abigail could not delude herself it had been for love, either: there had never been anything in his manner to suggest he had any feelings towards her at all. Perhaps, as her father thought, he merely wanted a well brought up wife of good family to wisk back to the colonies. Why he should then have taken her as a bond-slave was a further mystery, though she more than half suspected it was in a fit of pique at having his offer of the previous year so adamantly rejected. The idea that he might be suffering from unrequited love was an appealing one but quite out of character with what she thought she knew of Lord Jasper. At no time had he made any attempt to woo her and, in any case, events subsequent to her arrival in Virginia must soon have extinguished any inclination to pursue that course.

The press of people had already reached uncomfortable proportions when Abigail entered the Ludwell-Paradise house, having taken good care not to be among the first to arrive. She smiled and bowed to her aquaintance and tried to ignore the fact that most of them seemed not to be aware of her presence.

Never one to ignore a challenge, Mrs Ludwell-Paradise bore down upon her and made quite sure her voice carried to every corner of the charmingly elegant rooms.

'Mrs Vatsetter! See, the gown becomes me admirably! How gratifying it must be to look around at such a crush and to know that at least the female half of those present owes much of its elegance, if not its beauty, to your skill!'

315

Abigail smiled at her gratefully. 'Gratifying, indeed, ma'am. I'm already plotting how to excel myself next time.'

This sally produced a ripple of reluctantly appreciative laughter which eased the tension and when her hostess moved away, Abigail found her place had been taken by Lord Jasper.

'I fancy you struck precisely the right note there, Mrs Vatsetter,' he said. He lowered his voice and added with mock earnestness, 'You will forgive the formal address in public, I trust?'

She smiled but ignored the question. 'I have our hostess to thank for giving me such a lead. I confess I'd not otherwise have dared so vulgar a remark.'

'I shouldn't worry about that: it might have led to your banishment from the court of King George, but sensibilities are less finely honed here. This is not England, you know, for all its citizens' efforts.'

'I had noticed that, strangely enough,' Abigail observed. 'Quite apart from anything else, I wouldn't be here. No dressmaker would be invited to an assembly such as this in England, not even one of impeccable morals.'

'In England you'd not have been a dressmaker.' His voice was no longer light and Abigail almost believed she caught a hint of regret.

'In England I should by now have been married off to some ruddy faced, corpulent squire who was willing to exchange my breeding for a few thousand guineas,' she said briskly.

Lord Jasper seemed taken aback. 'Is that how you saw your future?' he asked.

'If my father was prepared to use me as a gambling stake, he would hardly have drawn back from anything so respectable as marriage,' Abigail pointed out reasonably.

'He didn't compel you to marry me,' Lord Jasper reminded her.

'Only because he wasn't sufficiently desperate to face the scene that would have ensued had he tried. Courage in the face of adversity was never one of his strong points.'

'As bad as that, was I?'

Abigail looked at him aghast, uncertain how offended he might be. 'My lord, I must apologise – I forgot to whom I was talking. It's unforgivable when I think how kind you've been.'

'Not at all,' he said politely. 'You were not to know I had these . . . er . . . hidden depths when we met in London, were you?'

'That's true enough. In fact, on our very brief acquaintance I wasn't aware that you had any depths at all, hidden or otherwise.'

'Perhaps I should have ingratiated myself in to your good opinion before offering for you.'

'I shouldn't think a man who "ingratiates" himself would be likely to arouse any sentiment beyond disgust,' Abigail told him roundly. 'If you mean it might have been a good idea to let me know you better, then you're probably right. It really was an act of incredible folly to offer for a seventeen-year-old girl who scarcely knew you, and to do so through the medium of her father.'

'It is the generally accepted way of going about things,' he protested.

'Rakes and libertines, however, are supposed to be more passionate, less conventional,' she told him.

Lord Jasper looked at her curiously. 'Are you telling me, Mrs Vatsetter, that if I had swept you off your feet – physically, if I understand you correctly – and had then proposed, you'd have accepted me?'

'I shouldn't think so for a moment! I imagine I should have been more likely to scream for help and had you thrown out. You have the reputation of a very wicked man, you know.'

'Am I permitted to observe that your reasoning seems to be remarkably inconsistent?'

'We are talking of a girl of only seventeen,' Abigail reminded him.

'Quite so. I was forgetting.' It looked for a moment as if he were about to say something else when a slight bustle drew attention to the door through which Lance Haworth and his wife were entering. Abigail stiffened and was aware of Lord Jasper's hand under her arm. 'Unconcerned should be your watchword for the time being,' he murmured.

Among the welcoming comments, Abigail found it particularly galling to catch the odd remark congratulating Lance on the recent change in his fortunes and she steeled herself for the necessity of having to bid him at least good evening. It proved entirely unnecessary, however, for when the Haworths' progress through the crush brought them near enough to speak, both looked straight through her, though they smiled and nodded at Lord Jasper before moving on.

'How disconcerting it must be to find oneself invisible.' Lord Jasper's amused voice dispersed any annoyance she might have felt, and she laughed.

'I shall recover from the shock, I dare say,' she told him.

She moved to the saloon where refreshments had been laid out with a lavish hand and was gratefully conscious of Lord Jasper's continued presence at her elbow.

'Where will you begin, Mrs Vatsetter?' he asked. 'You should be able to find enough here to sustain you for another twenty-four hours – quite an economy for one who is retrenching.'

'One of which I don't propose taking advantage, however,' Abigail retorted. 'I'd be extremely unwell if I attempted to eat even a quarter of a day's supply. Spun sugar and syllabubs may be delicious. They're hardly sustaining.'

She stepped back as she spoke and was immediately aware of treading on someone's foot and of a far from muffled exclamation from its owner. Turning at once to apologise, she found herself face to face with Blanche Haworth. There were few people to whom she had less desire to apologise but it was plainly Blanche's foot she had stepped on so there was nothing for it but to do so.

'Please forgive my carelessness, Mrs Haworth,' she said. 'I hadn't realised there was someone so close behind me.'

Blanche laughed. It was a humourless bark that attracted far more attention than Abigail would have wished. 'Don't distress yourself, Mrs Vatsetter. One doesn't expect the manners of a lady from a whore.'

The remark was guaranteed to secure the interest already aroused by the humourless and intemperate laugh.

Abigail maintained her temper and the outward appearance of calm. 'I have said I'm sorry, Mrs Haworth. I fail to see what else I can do in the circumstances.'

'You can remove yourself from the company,' Blanche told her insolently. 'If you had one spark of decency you wouldn't have had the gall to present yourself at such an assembly.'

Abigail was vividly conscious of the avid audience Blanche had attracted. She kept her voice deliberately restrained, refusing to allow Blanche or the onlookers the satisfaction of seeing her provoked.

'I'm a dressmaker, Mrs Haworth, a fact of which everyone here is aware. I can see no lack of decency in that to preclude my presence.'

'Dressmaking may be respectable enough,' Blanche retorted. 'Some might claim the same for money-lending, though I'm not among their number. But you are not simply a dressmaker and a usurer, are you, Mrs Vatsetter? Everyone here also knows you to be a whore. They may not be aware that you're a murderess, too.'

There was a delighted gasp from the bystanders and a horrified Lucy Ludwell-Paradise gave up her attempt to reach the protagonists. The confrontation had gone too far to be defused.

The colour drained from Abigail's face and her stomach gave a sickening lurch but she stood her ground, drawing herself up with a dignity she was far from feeling. 'You are offensive, Mrs Haworth,' she said. 'I've no wish to exchange abuse with you, and to continue this unpleasantness is insulting to our hostess.'

'It's your presence that's insulting. You've wormed your way into Williamsburg society by cunningly disguising the truth. No one would have accepted you or patronised you had they known your secret. I, who knew, have never been a customer.'

There were knowing nods. It was true that Blanche Haworth, alone among Williamsburg's wealthy wives, had never been dressed by Mrs Vatsetter.

Lord Jasper intervened. 'Haworth, the resolution of this impasse is in our hands, I think. We can do nothing about the speculation your wife has provoked but I suggest you and she withdraw and I undertake to persuade Mrs Vatsetter to do the same. We can then but hope Mrs Ludwell-Paradise and her guests will forgive this unfortunate incident.'

His hostess threw him a look of gratitude. Abigail, too, was grateful for his attempt but knew it had come too late. Even if he was able to stop Blanche's revelations it could only be a temporary measure: curiosity had been thoroughly whetted now and there could be few present who would rest until they had the whole story – or Blanche's version of it, though Abigail was mystified as to what she could know of Ezra's death. Still, Mrs Haworth was unlikely to be reticent on a subject she had chosen to introduce. It might be better to brazen it out. She would be ruined anyway and at least she would have the opportunity of rebutting any of Blanche's wilder excesses of fantasy and try to explain that events had not been quite as they might be made to sound. There was also an element of revenge in her mind. Abigail's future in Virginia was probably doomed. She would do what she could to bring the Haworths down with her.

'You're very kind, Lord Jasper,' Abigail said before Lance had time to respond. 'I think perhaps Mrs Haworth should have the opportunity to explain herself.'

Any fear the onlookers might have had that Blanche would now retract was soon dispelled.

'We all know about your child, and most people will have drawn their own conclusions as to how you managed to convince my husband's overseer that your daughter was his. You certainly never pretended to love him, did you? Such a brief marriage, too, and such a tragic end! He disappears and then, a few days later, what's left of him turns up in the hog-swill. How drunk was he, Mrs Vatsetter? Did you run away after you'd pushed him in and busy yourself elsewhere, or did you watch him drown? Did you go back each day until he was found, to see how much of him was left? You weren't precisely grief-stricken, as I understand it.'

Abigail heaved a sigh of relief. Blanche knew nothing. She was stabbing in the dark. Intelligent guesses, but nothing more. Above all, no evidence.

'No, Mrs Haworth, I wasn't grief-stricken. I married Ezra Vatsetter at your husband's command. I was his slave, remember. He wanted to disguise the fact that I carried his child because, if you had known that, you might have cried off and he needed the fortune you brought to the marriage. Ezra knew who the father was. There was no duplicity. As it turned out – and as your husband must have known – he was a violent man, but once we were married there was nothing I could do about that: I was his wife and wives have to bear whatever their husbands mete out. You should know that as well as anyone. I wasn't sorry he died, I'd be lying if I said he was, but I didn't push him into the trough. They say he was drunk and fell in. He was certainly very drunk.'

'I doubt if anyone here believes that version of events,' Blanche sneered. 'My husband's slaves might tell a different story.'

Lord Jasper took hold of Abigail's arm. 'Come, Mrs Vatsetter,' he said gently. 'You don't have to stay and listen to this. Let me drive you home.'

She shook him off, though she gained unexpected strength from his continued presence and evident support. 'No, my lord. We're not finished yet. Very well, Mrs Haworth. You cast doubt on my word. Do you imagine people will be happier to accept yours? You are, after all, the woman who stole the child I had by your husband and who, only a few days ago, tried to buy her from me.'

The audience gasped. They remembered Rebecca's disappearance and the women knew of Blanche's desperation at her childless plight but they had not connected the two until now, Mrs Vatsetter having been remarkably reticent about the circumstances of her daughter's return.

'I had two children,' Abigail went on. She turned to Lance. 'Becky had a brother. You didn't know that, did you? You might have had an heir if you'd not turned me off. As it was, your wife turned me from the house when I went into labour too soon and the boy was born dead, though Becky survived. I love both my children dearly, both the dead and the living for their own sakes and for the love I once bore their father. If having loved the father of my children makes me a whore in your estimation, so be it. Perhaps it's time to let the good citizens of Williamsburg know the rest of the story. Mrs Haworth stole Becky for reasons we can only pity, but when you found out what she had done, you offered to exchange her for the contract under which you owed me money, didn't you? And when that plan was frustrated by Lord Jasper and Iago, you had my house burgled and the contract stolen. Then, when I came to you for the money I was owed, your wife offered, in your presence, to repay me in full in return for my daughter. Frankly, Mr Haworth, I'd rather be an honest whore.' Abigail turned to her hostess. 'Mrs Ludwell-Paradise,' she said, 'I can only beg your forgiveness for this altercation which was none of my seeking. I'm sure you're wishing me elsewhere so I'll embarrass you no further. Lord Jasper, if I might avail myself of your earlier offer, I should be most grateful.'

He bowed. 'My carriage is at your disposal, Mrs Vatsetter.' He escorted her from the room and sent a page to have that vehicle brought round. When Sam drew rein in front of the house, Lord Jasper handed Abigail up into the carriage himself, raised the step and closed the door.

Her eyes widened with disappointment. She had assumed he would come with her. Clearly he had no such intention.

Reading her mind as clearly as if she had spoken, he said, 'No, Abby. You go home alone. It's more important that I remain to see whether anything can be salvaged from this fracas, though I confess it seems improbable. Get someone to make you a sleeping-draught. Tomorrow is soon enough for you to consider what you should do.'

Abigail rested her head against the squabs and tears rolled silently down her cheeks. His words were kind enough but kind words were not what she stood in need of just now. She did not doubt that if he could do anything to mitigate the effects of the evening's events, he would do so. But neither did she doubt that, in returning to the party as soon as she was safely on her way home, he was distancing himself from any part in her affairs. She could hardly blame him, but that was no consolation.

She had told the Camberwells and Billy not to wait up for her, so the house was silent and in almost total darkness save for a lamp on the table inside the door. Abigail picked it up to light the way upstairs, but then she paused with her foot on the bottom step. Lord Jasper had recommended a sleeping draught and nothing short of that would prevent her tossing and turning all night, going over and over the events in which she had just participated. She made her way to the kitchen and mulled a posset well laced with rum to which she added a few drops of laudanum, and this she took up to her bedchamber. She certainly slept, but woke heavy-eyed and burdened almost immediately with recollections of the night before. When Lizzie brought her chocolate and was about to fling the curtains wide as usual, Abigail told her sharply to leave them; light enough came through as it was.

She sipped her chocolate and tried to come to terms with the fact that, sooner or later, she would have to face the world – or, at least, that part of it resident in Williamsburg. She shuddered. There were some things of which she could be quite sure: any fragile re-acceptance she had begun to establish was broken because Blanche had raised a question over Ezra's death which would never quite go away. It remained to be seen whether the Haworths would suffer similar opprobrium.

Abigail thought she could live with social ostracism simply by ignoring it. Financial failure was another matter and it was most unlikely that the ladies of Williamsburg would continue to patronise her, no matter how clever her gowns. She had intended to depend upon dressmaking to provide once more the capital needed to extend her money-lending activities again. Not only was that source likely to dry up, but the good citizens of Williamsburg would now go elsewhere for their finance − and Abigail had little doubt that others would soon fill the gap she left. All she could do was to call in any outstanding loans, sell her dressmaking stock for what she could get, and leave. Where she could go was another matter altogether. Her reputation would follow her sooner or later to any of the other American colonies, and the prospect of returning to England was scarcely more enticing.

Besides, to leave would mean abandoning two things she held dear. Little Chance was buried in Williamsburg and, although the child had never lived and Abigail was but rarely able to visit his grave, it was a bond that she was loath to let distance break. Nor did she wish to place herself where Jasper Cuddesdon would be but a memory. If she had previously had a faint hope that he might have any regard for her despite his knowledge of her history, the hope must fade entirely away now that it was general knowledge and had in addition attracted further and more damning speculation. It might have been true, as he had once said, that she would one day find a man who loved her in spite of her past. She would not find one prepared to love her when that past included a question over her husband's death.

Her despair in the days following that disastrous party was only deepened by the fact that Lord Jasper neither visited her nor wrote. She had no idea what might have transpired at the Ludwell-Paradise house after she had left. She had no idea what she should do for the best. So she did nothing.

Orders were cancelled and Abigail began to wonder if she could even afford to keep on the Camberwell sisters. Several cautious burgesses repaid their loans to obviate the necessity of calling at her house and this, while it ensured her solvency, meant she had no income. In the space of three days, Abigail had sunk from being an astute businesswoman with every expectation of rebuilding a flourishing concern to being an astute business woman with no business to rebuild and no prospect of any.

At last, Lord Jasper called. Abigail's heart leapt when Sarah told her he was waiting and when he entered the room where she had been sitting, she rose and ran to him, her hands outstretched, pent-up tears stinging her eyes. A glance at his face, as sardonic as ever but now with a stern inflexibility she could not remember having seen before, caused her to falter and her hands fell uncertainly to her sides.

'My lord? This is indeed a surprise.'

'How are you, Abigail? You've had an unpleasant few days, I imagine,' he said. The words were kind, the tone unbending.

Abigail almost smiled, so great was the understatement, but her voice trembled. 'Unpleasant is one way of putting it, sir. My business is almost totally finished and I'd welcome advice on how to proceed.'

'You've only yourself to blame,' he told her harshly. 'Whatever induced you to get embroiled in an argument with Blanche Haworth?'

'That's unfair, my lord!' Abigail protessted, goaded momentarily out of a state that had been close to self-pity. 'You were there. You know it was Mrs Haworth who instigated it.'

'If you had but swallowed her initial insult and moved away, the only person who would have appeared in an unfavourable light was Blanche Haworth. But no, you had to stand on your dignity and offer her one opportunity after another.'

'Am I to stand and accept insults, then? Would you have done so?' Abigail blazed.

'Why shouldn't you? Her charges were true enough. You *are* a dressmaker and a usurer and, while I concede that "whore" is overstating the case, you surely won't deny that you can hardly claim moral probity. As to what I would have done, that is quite irrelevant.'

Abigail could not dispute any of these arguments, least of all his entirely accurate conclusion that she should have accepted the first insult and moved away. She found no consolation in the fact that her instincts had been so mistaken.

'In any event, it's done now and nothing of it can be undone. Where do I proceed from here? What do I do now?'

Lord Jasper shrugged. 'Tuck your tail between your legs like a whipped cur and scuttle off somewhere else, I suppose.'

'Do you imagine I haven't thought about that?' she demanded. 'Where do I go? The Carolinas? Pennsylvania? Massachusetts Bay? How long before news of my past follows me, do you think? Do I then scuttle off yet again? No, my lord, there's no future that way.'

'Then return to England.'

Abigail shook her head and spoke more calmly. 'Nor that, either, my lord. Sooner or later word would follow me. My family would be tarnished by my notoriety.'

'Your father has hardly left it immaculate,' Lord Jasper pointed out.

'If no more is heard of me, that will soon fade. I've younger brothers to consider. A reprobate sister is not what they need.'

'That seems effectively to dispose of all your possible lines of action, so far as I can judge. What will you do? Jump in the James?'

Suddenly Abigail knew there was only one thing she could do. She set her mouth firmly and lifted her chin in a defiant gesture he had seen before and feared he might never see again.

'I'll stay here, my lord. I've nothing more to lose and, while my notoriety will doubtless remain, there'll be other scandals to replace this one as a conversation-piece. In the meantime, I'm not destitute. I shall contrive. If the worst comes to the worst, I can always open a bawdy-house,' she added, a challenging gleam in her eye. 'At least the worthy citizens would consider it entirely in character.'

'I trust you will do me the small favour of not opening it in any house you rent from me,' Lord Jasper said with sardonic courtesy. 'I'd also be obliged if you'd not open one anywhere else in the immediate future.'

'As you wish, my lord. I shall let things simmer down for a month or two before making up my mind, in any case.'

'Very magnanimous.' He flicked her cheek carelessly and Abigail fancied she glimpsed an approving and not altogether unsympathetic smile at variance with the irony of his words. 'When I came in I thought you had the look of one sunk deep into a melancholia. It seems I was much mistaken. Melancholia doesn't suit you. This house is yours — as my guest, not my tenant — for as long as you wish. Provided you don't turn it into a bawdy-house, of course,' he added.

Abigail thanked him and then glanced up at him, feeling suddenly shy. 'Shall I see you again, my lord?' she asked doubtfully.

'If you are to remain in Williamsburg, I rather imagine it's inevitable, don't you? Good day, Mrs Vatsetter.'

Chapter Eighteen

It did not go unnoticed in Williamsburg that, while Mrs Vatsetter was seldom seen abroad in the days immediately following the Ludwell-Paradise fiasco, the reverse was true of the Haworths. Neither Lance nor his wife was widely liked but, as more than one burgess was heard to remark, 'You've got to admire their gall.' The admiration was considerably helped by the fact that Lance had succeeded, in just one venture, in restoring his fortunes to a very respectable level if not, perhaps, to what they had been before his marriage. That fact of his success was in part due to his having behaved extremely reprehensibly towards the woman who backed him was, by some citizens at least, held to be proof of his business cunning. Others felt that it placed him beyond the pale.

Abigail, by contrast, had been generally liked and many people regretted that any association with her, however slight, must now be curtailed. The ladies, in particular, mourned the loss of the best dressmaker they had ever known. It was unavoidable, of course. There were now too many unanswered questions for Mrs Vatsetter ever to be acceptable again.

There was much speculation as to what she would do now. The general consensus was that she would leave the colony. The question was, where would she choose to settle? The idea that, since the Carolinas and Maryland were too close, she might head for Pennsylvania caused much merriment: the Quakers might be dissenting heretics and unnecessarily tolerant of many things, but they would hardly welcome a woman of such notoriety in their midst!

Speculation about Abigail's future soon withered for lack of nourishment, its subject appearing to be oblivious to ostracism and to have sufficient funds to maintain a restricted, but perfectly reasonable, houshold. It was replaced by a more fruitful topic. There had been a whisper prior to the Ludwell-Paradise affair that the

Haworths intended to hold a party to celebrate the restoration of their fortunes. No one was surprised that the whispers had died down in the aftermath of that extraordinary evening, but now they revived, to be confirmed by the arrival of cards of invitation. Kitchen gossip, to which no one ever admitted listening although they somehow managed to hear it just the same, said it was to be an exceptionally lavish affair. The guest list was said to be comprehensive and to extend beyond Williamsburg to all the plantation owners on the tidewater and even as far as Norfolk and Yorktown. Every tavern and ordinary in the town was booked to capacity. Some said that even the Governor hoped to attend. Others felt that this was unlikely. Already one or two high sticklers were known to have declined the invitation, feeling that whatever opprobrium might, quite rightly, attach to Mrs Vatsetter, Lance and Blanche Haworth were not exactly beyond reproach. These people were in a minority and likely to remain so, especially once it became known that Lord Jasper had accepted. Curiosity ensured that most of Williamsburg would be there.

Lord Jasper had no intention of missing it. He had examined the gilt-edged invitation with his customary sardonic smile. There had never been any love lost between Lance Haworth and him, but Lance had not dared to exclude the richest man in the colony and one who could, if he chose, exert sufficient influence in London to break anyone who lacked equal patronage.

Never careless of his appearance, Lord Jasper dressed with particular meticulousness on this occasion. To his valet's surprise, he selected a suit that was at least three years old, though he had never before worn it in Virginia. Of a singularly delicate shade of lilac, embellished to the point of encrustation with silver thread, it would have looked merely foppish on a lesser man. But Lord Jasper, though no giant, was tall and lean with shoulders that set off a well-cut coat to perfection. His valet reflected that it was strange how this particular colour made his master look almost sinister, an impression enhanced by wearing his hair *poudré,* something his lordship rarely permitted away from London. Diamonds glittered on his shoe-buckles, flashed from the hilt of his dress-sword, and a particularly fine stone reflected fire in the folds of his cravat.

As Lord Jasper stood before the glass, flicking the last ruffle over his wrists, his valet stepped back with a justifiably satisfied smile.

'I fancy we have excelled ourselves, my lord,' he said.

'Let us hope our ability doesn't stop here,' his master replied cryptically.

Lord Jasper made sure he was the last to arrive and his entrance caused something of a stir. There was not a guest present who had not felt convinced that, in this occasion at least, he himself would outshine everyone else. When Lord Jasper appeared there was not a guest present who did not privately acknowledge failure. He was affability itself to his host and bowed so low over his hostess' hand that Mrs Ludwell-Paradise, with the familiarity of an old friend, chided him.

'Trying to fix your interest with the wife, Jasper? Not your style at all!'

'Do you refer to this particular wife, or to "fixing my interest" with wives in general?'

'Both.' She took his arm and led him into the room. 'To tell you the truth, I've always though Mrs Vatsetter was more your style, but that's out of the question now, of course. Pity.'

'Match-making, Lucy?' he quizzed her.

'Not at all. Haven't I just said it was out of the question? Still, it goes against the grain to see a man like you in want of a wife.'

'Your concern is flattering but unnecessary. Don't meddle in my affairs, Lucy.'

She opened her eyes wide and fluttered her fan. 'As if I should dream of it! I just don't want to see you die a bachelor, Jasper. That's all.'

'Then you may rest assured. I've no such intention.'

The Haworths had spared no expense to reinstate themselves in Williamsburg's regard. A small orchestra had been engaged and was persuaded, without much difficulty, to play some country dances so that an impromptu ball could be held, to the delight of the younger people present. It was noticed that Lord Jasper chose not to dance but he was heard to compliment Mrs Haworth on the sumptuous refreshments laid out in one of the adjoining saloons, though he partook of very little.

The evening was well advanced before word circulated that card-tables had been set out in one of the smaller rooms at the back of the house. Several of the guests who found bezique and whist more to their taste than dancing, repaired there and settled down to enjoy the rest of the night while the more adventurous played piquet for stakes that inevitably increased as the night wore on. Lord Jasper watched the play with the slightly bored air of one who seeks greater excitement.

'Is piquet not to your taste, my lord?' Lance Haworth's voice at his elbow drew his attention from the table.

'It passes an hour or so, Mr Haworth, but I confess it lacks the excitement I desire.'

Lance smiled knowingly. 'Of course – you prefer games of pure chance. Dice as I recall.'

Lord Jasper bowed. 'My preference is biased: it is the one game above all others in which I find Fortune tends to smile on me.'

'Not the last time we played together,' Lance reminded him. 'I was the recipient of Fortune's favours that night.'

'So you were!' Lord Jasper sounded as if he had forgotten all about that evening until Lance had reminded him. He looked around the room. 'Fortune is certainly smiling on you at the moment. Do you care to put her to the test?'

Lance's eyes narrowed suspiciously. If he could have thought of anything he had that Lord Jasper might particularly desire – such as a bond-slave – he would have suspected his guest of trying to set him up for fleecing. He could think of nothing and Lord Jasper's love of dice was well known, so he smiled.

'Why not? A return game is long overdue.'

Another table was brought and an unbroken set of dice produced. After their initial interest, many onlookers moved away: a game of dice's interest lay less in the skill involved than in the amount staked on any given throw and this game started modestly enough, with the luck fairly evenly balanced. If anything, Lance Haworth was slightly ahead and consequently was happy to agree to a raising of the stakes – and to a limit on the game.

'Let us continue until the clock strikes three,' Lord Jasper suggested.

Lance glanced at the ornate timepiece whose face peered out between ormolu cupids. One o'clock. Two hours. He calculated quickly. At their present rate that was too short a time for him to be bankrupted, especially since the luck was running his way. Nevertheless, it could be sailing close to the wind.

'Very well,' he said.

'Naturally, the game finishes before that if one of us is ruined,' Lord Jasper said blandly.

'Naturally.' It went without saying, yet the fact that it had been said left Lance with a faint feeling of unease.

News that an incentive had been added to the game's excitement soon circulated and in a very short time the two players had an audience of some size.

The pattern of the game remained unchanged at first: some throws Lord Jasper won, others were taken by his host, with the latter remaining slightly ahead. Then, imperceptibly at first, the balance of play began to change. Lord Jasper began to creep ahead. It was nothing to worry about, Lance told himself. It was just one of the inevitabilities of the game. But he was worried none the less, and sought to redress the balance quickly by increasing the stake, a suggestion to which Lord Jasper was perfectly willing to accede, though a raised eyebrow implied that he was faintly surprised it had been made.

Far from redressing the balance, this move served only to accelerate the decline in Lance's fortunes until he had no more gold and was obliged to ask his opponent to accept his note of hand. Lance was uncomfortably aware that the last time this situation had arisen, when their positions were reversed, he had refused to accept Lord Jasper's I.O.U.s and wondered whether his guest would serve him the same way. Many of those watching had the same thought. Lord Jasper, however, declared himself perfectly willing to accept his host's scrips. Paper, ink, quill and sand were sent for and the contest proceeded.

The luck now seemed set firmly in Lord Jasper's favour and the pile of paper mounted. Lance won the occasional throw and every time that happened, he felt sure his luck had changed at last and he had only to continue playing to regain what he had lost.

When word filtered through to Blanche that her husband was playing deep, she made such haste to the card-room as was possible without revealing her concern to her guests. She could not quite control a gasp when she saw the amount of paper held by Lord Jasper, and took small comfort in the fact that neither man appeared to be drinking.

It was true a brandy-glass stood by each and Lord Jasper's eyes glittered dangerously in the candle-light, but neither reached for his glass and Blanche knew her husband well enough to recognise that he was sober. She longed to break into his concentration and bring him to his senses; to tell him to stop before they lost everything they had so recently regained, but she dared not. Neither Lance nor any of the assembled guests would condone such an action.

Lance kept glancing nervously at the clock, uncertain whether to hope for the final hour to strike before he lost everything or to hope for its delay until his luck changed. Lord Jasper seemed oblivious to the passing time. The clock ticked inexorably on and the dice fell inexorably in Lord Jasper's favour.

At three minutes to three, Lord Jasper swept the mortgage to the Haworth house on to his pile. Lance was pale and shaking.

'I concede defeat, my lord. You have ruined me,' he said.

'Not at all — the clock has not yet struck three and you've not yet staked your plantation,' Lord Jasper replied softly.

No one spoke. The tension was tangible. The ivory sticks of Blanche's fan were heard to snap, so hard was she gripping them.

Lance reached for the paper, glancing again at that creeping gold hand. He dared not write so slowly that the bystanders would realise he was hoping to delay until it was too late. He wrote, and pushed the paper into the middle of the table.

Lord Jasper threw. Four and three.

Lance picked up the dice, glanced at the clock, shook and threw. Five and two.

Gasps escaped the onlookers so simultaneously that it sounded like the gasp of one body.

Lord Jasper threw again. Two and one.

Lance smiled. It looked as if his luck had turned at last. He glanced at the clock again, hoping this time that it would delay until he had thrown. He would be unfortunate indeed to lose now. He shook.

The clock struck one.

He threw.

The clock struck twice.

The dice rolled and settled.

The clock struck for the third time.

He had thrown two ones.

The night sky had acquired the faint grey tinge that presages the rising sun when Lord Jasper dismissed his carriage outside Abigail's house and made his way round to the back. A startled Lizzie Camberwell was laying the kitchen fire when he entered. He put a finger to his lips.

'Is Mrs Vatsetter in bed?'

'Of course she is, my lord! Heavens above, where else should she be at this ungodly hour? It can't be much more than four o'clock!'

'Half past, to be precise. I need to see her.'

'Well, you'll just have to wait. She won't be about for hours yet.'

'I'll go up. She'll see me, all right. Does she still have the same room?'

'Yes, my lord, but you can't go up there. It's ... it's not seemly.'

Lord Jasper took two golden guineas out of his pocket and placed them on the scrubbed table. 'In a minute Tagus will be down. Do you and he keep company here until you're sent for.'

'I've better things to do than to sit around the kitchen with a dog,' Lizzie told him indignantly, 'especially when Mrs Vatsetter has given Billy, whose job this is, the day off. I've the house to clean before she gets up and then there's her breakfast to see to, to say nothing of the child's.'

'Leave it. Have a good, lazy morning at my expense. I'll take the blame.'

Lizzie sniffed and eyed the coins. 'Well, I could do the marketing real early, I suppose. Shall I leave a note for Sarah when she comes?

She's been at home for a couple of nights while mother's been sick.'

'Do. Tell her to get Becky up and take her home with her. She'll not be needed today.'

Lizzie looked at him suspiciously. 'I hope I'm doing the right thing,' she said doubtfully.

'You are,' he promised, and Lizzie decided there was little point in trying to decipher what lay behind the almost private smile that accompanied these words.

Lord Jasper ran lightly up the stairs and opened the bedroom door gently. Tagus' low growl told him he had the right room.

'Here, boy. Here,' he whispered.

Tagus thumped his tail once, poured himself off the end of the bed and padded over to the door, his long tail gently waving.

'Out!' Lord Jasper whispered imperiously, and out Tagus went. He could hear the faint sounds of Lizzie's activity below and that meant a titbit if he were clever. Lord Jasper closed the door behind him and stood a moment until his eyes had grown accustomed to the dim light. Then he stepped over to the huge bed and smiled down at the figure curled up and sound asleep beneath the covers. He recalled another occasion when he had disturbed her in bed and felt a surge of relief that on this occasion she was at least alone. He had not really expected anything else, of course, yet at the back of his mind there had always been the unwelcome possibility ... A tinderbox stood beside the candle on a small table near the bed. He struck the flint as the flickering light penetrated her closed lids, Abigail stirred and woke up.

She stared at the candle, puzzled, and then became dimly aware that she was not alone. Here eyes flew open, fear banishing puzzlement until she recognised the man standing there. Then uncertainty returned.

'Lord Jasper? What are you doing here?' Her eyes turned to the curtained window. 'It's still dark! My lord, you shouldn't be here!' And she sat up in bed clutching the bedclothes to her chin.

Instead of offering an immediate explanation, her visitor extracted a heavy pouch from his pocket and dropped it on the bed. 'Your debts,' he said. Then he took a rolled-up paper from inside his embroidered waistcoat and dropped it beside the pouch. 'Your plantation.'

Abigail stared from Lord Jasper to the things he had dropped on the bed. 'What on earth do you mean?' she demanded.

'Lance Haworth has seen fit to return to you all he owes – and more besides.'

'Voluntarily?' her tone was suspicious.

331

'Entirely. I merely had to mention that I found dice more exciting than piquet and he was happy to accommodate me, especially when he recalled that the last time we played, the luck was with him.'

Abigail pushed the pouch and the scroll towards him. 'Then those are yours, not mine.' She paused while the implications of his story sank in. 'Have you ruined him?'

'Not at all,' he told her blandly. 'I gave him a hundred guineas to enable him to start again.'

'Magnanimous,' she remarked.

'I thought so. It was certainly more than he deserved. May I sit down?'

There was a pointed inflection to the question which drew Abigail's attention to her shortcomings as a hostess and flustered her.

'Yes of course. How rude of me − please do.' She hoped he would not remark upon the inadequacy of her reply and was then still more flustered when, instead of drawing up a chair as she had expected, he sat on the edge of the bed. 'My lord, I really don't think ... I mean ....' her voice tailed away.

He took her hand in both of his and raised it to his lips with an intensity so unexpected that Abigail suspected herself of reading into it more of her own feelings than his, and, as he did so, the candlelight caught the embroidery which gleamed richly in the lambent flame.

'Such magnificence!' she exclaimed involuntarily. 'Of course, the Haworth's reception. I'd forgotten. Was it very grand?'

'Every attempt was made to make it so. I fancy the ladies are feeling the lack of their dressmaker.'

Abigail frowned and traced the silver thread on his cuff with her finger. 'Isn't this the coat you wore when you diced with my father?' she asked.

'I should have guessed you'd recognise it. It brought me the good fortune to win you once. I hoped it would act as a talisman this time, too.' There was a warmth in his voice that Abigail knew was not imagined but she was almost afraid to acknowledge it.

'Except that I was not there to be won,' she pointed out.

'Very true, I overlooked that. And now that we're discussing my apparel, I must say I find it confoundedly uncomfortable.'

He took off the coat made heavy by the weight of silver thread and threw it on the end of the bed, closely followed by the almost equally heavy long-fronted waistcoat. 'That's a great deal more comfortable, I assure you,' he said, a disturbing glint in his eye.

'My lord, this is really not at all the thing,' Abigail protested. 'Goodness knows what time it is. You shouldn't be here at all.'

'I expect if we were to draw the curtains, we'd find the sun colouring the horizon, if ignorance of the time is important to you. I infinitely prefer them closed.' He took her hand again and his voice lost its mocking tone. 'Abigail, do you still dislike me?'

She shook her head. 'No, my lord,' she whispered, 'nor have I done so for a long time.'

He kissed the hand he held and then his lips sought the pulse throbbing in her wrist. His eyes lingered on her face as if he would read there what was in her heart. His finger gently traced the line of her cheek and Abigail's head turned towards it as a cat rubs against the stroking hand. Then he took her gently in his arms and kissed her with unimagined tenderness and, as her arms reached up to draw him closer, they sank against the pillows, each oblivious to everything except the other.

'I feared this moment would never come,' he said at last. 'I knew I had won your trust but I thought I must learn to be content with that.'

Abigail smiled softly. 'And weren't you willing to be content with that?' she whispered.

'Only if there was hope of nothing more. Abby, my love, I have made so many mistakes. Time and again I've done the very thing calculated to set you against me when all I sought to do was to demonstrate my feelings for you.' He paused and gently pushed one golden curl back from her brow. 'Are you sure you no longer feel as I know you once did?' he asked doubtfully.

'It's the only thing I am sure about. Oh, my lord, I thought it was too late!' And she clung to him like a child.

He crushed her to him then with all the force of a passion held in check until the time was right. Abigail gasped at the strength and unexpectedness of his embrace and her body arched within his arms as if it reached out for his. He loosed the ribbons that tied her nightgown and pushed it gently from her shoulders but this time he sought no bruises. His lips caressed her neck and the thrusting, sensuous curve of her breasts. Abigail's hands sunk deep into the muscles of his shoulders, drawing him ever closer, but he pulled away from her then and threw the bedclothes back. He tore the nightgown from her unresisting body and paused then, looking down at the beauty before him. Abigail lifted her hands to his cravat.

'Come, my lord,' she whispered. 'It is not fitting that only I should lie here naked.'

They lay together naked in each other's arms in gentle mutual caress until the desire they had each held back for so long flared with renewed vigour and both knew there would be no more restraint. With the delight of anticipation, Abigail felt him enter her and she gave herself to him with all the force at her command. Together they moved as one body in a crescendo of desire until the world exploded in an ecstasy of pain.

And when that ecstasy had dissolved into the bliss of fulfilment and they lay, drowsy with contentment in each other's arms, Abigail knew that now, at last, she had known happiness beyond compare and would treasure the memory forever, no matter what the future might hold.

As the burgeoning day filtered through the curtains, Lord Jasper reached out and snuffed the candle between his fingers. Abigail stirred as the acrid smoke wafted across the bed.

'My lord, you should be gone. Lizzie will be here with breakfast soon and then Becky will be up.'

'There'll be no breakfast and no Lizzie,' he told her. 'For the princely sum of two guineas, she decided to go marketing instead. She may even have taken Tagus with her. Sarah will have taken Becky when she arrives so we need not be disturbed until we wish to be.'

'How extremely arbitrary, my lord!' Abigail said with mock indignation.

He kissed her, effectively stifling even mock-protest. 'Abby, my love, don't you feel we've progressed to an intimacy that could, with propriety, abandon "my lord"?'

Abigail chuckled. 'I fancy "propriety" would not be the word most people would use in connection with our ... intimacy.'

'I think neither of us feels a need to consider the opinion of most people. Tell me, Abby: do you have a taste to become Lady Jasper?'

Abigail hesitated a moment and then nestled into his arms so that he could not easily detect the hurt in her face. She kept her voice deliberately light. 'don't tease me, Jasper, Not now.'

He sat bolt upright at that. 'Tease! Do you think I'm so foolish as to offer marriage to someone I hope will not accept?'

Abigail shook her head. 'Whatever others may say, I know you to be an honourable man. You don't have to marry me just because we've made love. After all,' she added bitterly, 'you weren't the first.'

He took her in his arms and held her close, cradling her to him as if he sought to protect her from the world outside. 'I told you once that you would find a man who loved you in spite of the past. I was that man then and I am still. I'd be lying if I said I didn't care that I'm not the first — and you would not be deceived. But the past is past. Abby, I've loved you from the moment I first set eyes on you and nothing has happened since to alter that. Will you marry me?'

She put her hand over his lips. 'Don't say that. Not yet.' She hesitated, the temptation to remain silent on one particular subject almost overwhelming. 'There's one thing you don't know. Blanche Haworth accused me of killing Ezra. She was guessing but she was horribly close to the truth. It didn't happen as she imagined, but it happened.' As briefly as she could, she recounted the events in the barn and Iago's part in them.

Lord Jasper heard her in a silence that was terrifying for Abigail and his face told her nothing. His reaction when it came was totally unexpected. 'So that was the bond between you and Iago,' he said. 'I knew there was something but I thought perhaps he had . . . consoled you in other ways. As to Ezra Vatsetter: the man's reputation was notorious. Sooner or later someone – probably another Iago – would have killed him. I'd be happier if it hadn't been you and now, of course, having told me all this, you've no choice but to marry me.'

Abigail was startled. 'How so?'

He smiled. 'How else can you ensure I don't lay evidence against you?'

She looked at him doubtfully. 'Doesn't it bother you that I've killed one husband? Doesn't it make you hesitate to be the second?'

'Not at all.' He kissed her briefly. 'I shall simply ban the use of pitchforks in my stables, thus removing temptation.'

Abigail reached up to draw his lips once more close to hers and kissed him. 'Have you considered what Williamsburg will say?' she whispered.

He drew away from her then. 'You're right, my dear. I've given it no thought at all. It will place everyone in an impossible position – you are not to be received while I, on the other hand, must be humoured at all costs. Whatever will they do?'

Abigail giggled. 'I dare say they'll find some compromise solution.' Then she grew serious. 'Have you considered that you would acquire an immediate family?'

'I have. Believe me, I'd rather find myself with your daughter on my hands than your father and brothers, as would have been the case had you accepted me in the first place. Come, Abby, you've not given me an answer yet. I'm forced to derive what comfort I can from the fact that at least this time you haven't turned me down out of hand.'

'It will cause such gossip!'

'Once they've got over the shock, they'll tell each other we're really very well suited.'

'Are you really sure?' Abigail asked doubtfully.

'Lucy Ludwell-Paradise said as much to me not so long ago.'

'I don't mean that. Are you sure you want to marry me?'

'I've never been more sure of anything.'

Abigail reached up and clasped her hands around his neck. 'Then

– yes, Jasper, I have a taste to be a lady.'

It was a long time before either of them felt any further need to talk and it was Abigail who finally drew back a little from her lover's embrace. 'Why did you take me as a bond-slave, Jasper, if you loved me as you say?'

'I thought if I could bring you here, away from your family and friends, you'd come to love me. I didn't bargain for ... for your meeting someone else.'

'And when I did, you proposed to Blanche Quenington?'

'I most certainly did not,' he declared emphatically. 'Whatever put that idea into your head?'

'It was generally believed she had received an offer from you,' Abigail told him.

He shook his head. 'I had several hints both from the lady herself and from her father that an offer would be favourably received, but I took good care not to make one. I fancy the title was the main attraction.'

'Undoubtedly.' Abigail laughed and her mind went back over what had happened since she set foot in Virginia. One by one, events began to slip into place. 'Was it you who arranged for me to be invited to the concert?' she asked.

'Of course. I'd seen you at an almost identical recital and watched the undisguised delight with which you listened to the music. I had hoped the connection would be as obvious to you as it was to me,' he added with a hint of sadness in his voice. 'I thought we might have the same music at our wedding-breakfast. Would you like that?'

Abigail laughed. 'Above anything! is all your planning so well advanced?'

'Not at all – I've not dared obtain a licence yet. As a gamester it seemed like tempting Fate, but now I need hesitate no longer. We've waited so long, Abby, yet there must be still further delays. Do you mind?'

'Terribly,' she assured him with a kiss. 'Oh, Jasper, give me time to make my bride-clothes.'

'Never! Get Sarah to make them.' He sat up suddenly and reached down the bed for his coat. 'You put me in mind of something I had nearly forgotten.'

He reached into the deep pocket and held up the heavy necklace of diamonds and sapphires that Abigail had never thought to see again.

'It will please me if you will wear this at our wedding,' he said.

Abigail stared at it. 'Where did you get it?' she began and then the truth dawned. 'You didn't sell it, did you? The money that bought my freedom and set me up in business was yours all along.'

He nodded. 'Of course. What else in all honour — to say nothing of love — could I do? I had brought the woman I loved to this place and as a direct consequence I had lost her — or so it seemed then — and she was in considerable difficulties. Abby, I longed to take you in my arms and beg you to let me deal with Lance Haworth, yet I knew you would not be disposed to accept my help and I could hardly blame you in the circumstances. What else could I do but advance you the money you needed in a way that I knew you would find acceptable? It was a deceit but it was well-meant, a small restitution for the harm I had unintentionally done you. Do you mind?'

Her answer was to draw him to her and then words became superfluous.

It was to be a long, long time that day before the sun was allowed to stream into Abigail Vatsetter's bedchamber.